Only the Scars Remain

by

Dara Morris

Cypress Bayou Series
Book One

Only the Scars Remain

Cover Art by *Kim Mendoza*

The Wild Rose Press, Inc.
PO Box 708
Adams Basin, NY 14410-0708
Visit us at www.thewildrosepress.com

Publishing History
First Edition, 2021
Trade Paperback ISBN 978-1-5092-3660-2
Digital ISBN 978-1-5092-3661-9

Cypress Bayou Series
Published in the United States of America

"Four, please," she said to the tall form that'd gone in front of her. Glancing over to make sure the correct floor was pressed; she froze. That long, uneven scar that stretched across his agile, big hand... She'd recognize it half blind; she'd caressed it so often.

Ryan.

She didn't even have to see his face to know, that scar from so long ago was like a brand that had been forced upon him to forever remind them of that night. Her eyes slowly traveled up his lean torso and broad shoulders till finally, she raised her head. Their gazes collided as she registered the grim surprise in his clear, blue penetrating stare. His devastatingly good looks had matured into a rugged handsomeness that literally took her breath away, she felt light-headed as she studied his set expression, her heart pounding madly in her chest. Gone was the rakish black hair she'd glided her fingers gently through as he'd slept. Now his soft, dark as night waves were cropped close to his head and emphasized the masculine planes of his lean face. Confidence radiated from all six foot plus of him, clad in jeans and a light blue button down shirt.

Praise for Only the Scars Remain

BEST BOOK OF THE YEAR FOR ME!!!

"Dara Morris has a fantastic, convincing way with words. She makes you feel as if you are transported to little Louisiana town & you have known these characters forever! A true, sweet, gritty, heartwrenching, beautiful, magical modern day romance that will totally pull your heart strings in ALL directions. An extremely riveting tale that played with all of my emotions. There were moments that I wanted to scream with anger, was giggly with excitement, sobbed like a big baby, & felt pure joy for my new found (fictional) friends. So hard to put down it will make you late for work, speed through your housework, & go to sleep in the wee hours of the morning. Lol!!! You'd be a fool not to read this AMAZING book. Thanks Dara Morris!"

~ Customer Review, Dalalas03

Dedication

This novel is dedicated to my big brother, Kelsey Lee Bridges. After only twenty eight years in this walk of life, your passing stunned me and left a broken bond that aches still. You are immortalized in the cherished memories of the people who loved you. I hope you're catching lots of fish in heaven, free from the torture that refused to leave you. I love you and not a day goes past that I don't miss you.

PROLOGUE

AUGUST 2005

Alyssa pressed the gas pedal, but her tires only spun and sunk even deeper in the wide ruts of the red dirt road. She slammed her hand against the steering wheel. "Dammit. I knew I shouldn't have come out this way," she muttered, and opened the door of her small four door hatchback. Mud oozed up the sides of her favorite sandals as she picked her way over to the grass. "Ooh, this just gets better and better."

"What?" Alyssa picked up her cell phone in disbelief. "No signal?" She dropped it back in her purse and gazed down the desolate road where her sister lived for a long minute. An endless sea of deep green cotton fields stretched on the opposite side of her, and behind her lay the slow moving waters of the Red River.

Uncertainty haunted her, but with a deep, indrawn breath, she moved forward. Alyssa raised her eyes to study the heavy gray clouds in the gloomy sky. "Don't rain on me too."

She could smell the water, that loamy, faintly fishy scent as she made her way closer to the river's edge. A gust of wind blew and Alyssa lifted her face, savoring the rush of cool air against her hot skin. She pushed her long hair out of her eyes as dread churned her stomach into knots. She was almost there. .

She hated coming down this road and Fran knew it. But they were as close as only sisters could be, siblings who had endured things no child should. Fran was flighty and prone to drinking like their parents had been. Alyssa worried about her and for good reason, usually she felt like she was the older sister, not the younger. But Fran was engaged now, and Lucas brought a happiness to her Alyssa had never seen.

Her heart thumped a wild dance against her chest as she stepped upon the lush grass of the perfect little clearing. A circle of lofty trees thickened here, forming a crown of thick, swaying branches that hung to the ground in some places. Like an arrow to a bull's eye, she found it.

Their tree.

The letters were larger, spread out from years of growth, but still plainly etched into the rough bark surrounded by a crude sketch of a heart.

RS + AM

Alyssa stopped before the stately oak tree and traced their timeworn initials with trembling fingers, remembering Ryan, always *Ryan.* A vivid image of a blood-streaked blade falling to the ground right where she stood flitted through her mind, along with the terror she had felt. Fueled by cheap liquor and the recklessness only youth can bring, Alyssa had once believed that magical night was their beginning, not the beginning to an end. It had caused so many changes, so much heartache.

Well, heartbreak for me, changes for both of us, though.

Ryan was gone, he hadn't returned home since that summer ten years past. Alyssa wrapped her arms around her waist, anguish filling her soul for all that had been, and all that was lost. As she stared painfully upon their initials forever inscribed, she shivered as she was catapulted back to when their friendship had led to a fierce, sweet hell of an extraordinary love.

CHAPTER 1

JULY 1993

"Fran, Alyssa!" their mother hollered from the front porch. "I need y'all to go to the store!"

"In this heat? I can't wait to buy me a car," Alyssa muttered to her sister.

"Me either. It's embarrassing riding a bike!"

"Well, just tell people that's how you stay in shape. That's what I do."

Fran laughed and grabbed the box of nail polish off of the wooden swing where they'd painted their nails. Shaded by towering pine trees and set in the corner of the big yard, it was Alyssa's favorite spot at their house.

"Well, it's about time," Mama snapped as they walked into the kitchen. Alyssa spied the glass of wine in her mother's hand and groaned inwardly. Mama was even meaner when she drank.

"Here's five dollars, we need some bread."

Alyssa took the money from her mother's hand. "Yes ma'am."

Maybe Ryan would be there. She perked up at the thought. He worked at Mack's, the local grocery store that sold everything from chicken feed to milk.

"And I need a lighter too, so don't be dilly dallying." Joyce fixed her hard green eyes on them and frowned. Only thirty-three years old, but she looked

4

forty. Streaks of gray dulled her light brown hair and years of hard living had made its mark on her thin, fine boned face. In her younger days she had been stunning. Alyssa had seen pictures, but sometimes had to force herself to remember this was the same woman standing before her.

The sun shone high in the sky, and warmed Alyssa's bare arms. They rode over the dirt yard onto the shoulder of the gravel road and began pedaling, glad to be away from the oppressive presence of their mother.

"Woo-Hoo, race you down to the stop sign," her sister sang out, light blond hair streaming out from behind her. At seventeen, Fran was the eldest by a year.

Alyssa stood up on the pedals to gain more speed and set off after her. They lived on Sutton Road, out on the outskirts of Cypress Bayou, Louisiana. A mix of small houses and trailers lined one side, and on the other was a waving, green cornfield.

Alyssa parked her bike and entered the air conditioned store with relief. Mr. Mack, the owner, greeted them as they passed by the registers, dark eyes twinkling in his lined face.

"Hot enough for ya'?"

"*Too* hot," Alyssa said with a smile. Since she was a little girl she'd adored him, first for the lollipops he gave all the kids, and then for his kindness. A gentle giant, his heart was as big as him.

"What's your daddy been up to?"

Alyssa twirled a strand of long hair around her finger. "Oh, not much," she said off handedly. She hated it when people asked about her parents; she was always at a loss of what to say. "Well, I'm going to find my sister, Mr. Mack." She took off after Fran, and almost collided with Ryan as she turned down an aisle.

"Whoa, slow down, Alyssa! Trying to knock me over?" he asked with a deep laugh, and steadied her by placing his big hands on her shoulders.

"Now how in the world could I knock *you* over," she grinned up at him. She ran her eyes over his athletic build and gestured dramatically towards him. Tall and broad shouldered, his lean torso made way to long muscled legs. He laughed loudly, a sound that sent shivers of delight coursing through her.

"Knowing you, you'll figure out a way to," Ryan teased. He released his grip from her shoulders, and ran a hand through the midnight black hair tousled casually around his handsome face. "So what are you doing tomorrow?"

"I have to babysit until noon. After that," she shrugged her shoulders, "nothing much."

"Come swimming with me out at the river around two or so. Will you?"

"Yeah, that sounds fun."

Even white teeth gleamed against his tanned skin in a heart stopping grin. "Good. They'll be some other people out there too. Our usual spot. But I better get to back to work; Mr. Mack has got his eye on us." His sapphire blue gaze warmed as he looked down at her. "Don't forget about tomorrow."

She shook her head and smiled back. "I won't."

On the long ride home, Alyssa thought about Ryan. Since they were children, he had been there; no one was more important in her small world other than Fran. They had spent many evenings chasing fireflies, free spirited children running and playing happily in each other's company. He lived about a mile down the road, and Fran and he were in the same grade.

When she was younger, she'd tag along with him and his friends fishing at the river. He'd patiently put the worm on the hook for her and when she'd squealed at the sharp fins on the fish, he'd laughed and helped her take it off.

There had always been a special bond between them, and she knew he felt it too. She'd loved him wholeheartedly from the time she was a little girl, and it hadn't changed in the years that passed, only strengthened.

She remembered a few years ago when, Scotty, one of the neighborhood boys, had rammed his bike into hers and sent her flying into the gravel. Ryan had come running.

"*Are you okay?*" he'd asked.

"*I think I am,*" she'd answered, dazed from the impact.

Ryan then turned on Scotty. *"What's the matter with you,"* he'd grated out furiously, *"picking on girls. If you want to mess with somebody, here I am."*

Scotty had backed off, wanting no part of Ryan Sutherby.

Ryan then gently helped her to her feet, and took her to his house. His grandmother had washed the blood off her skinned knees and palms, clucking worriedly the whole time while bandaging her scraped skin. This was a novelty for Alyssa, Mama would have cared less.

Ryan lived with his grandmother, a sweet woman who didn't have a mean bone in her body. Everybody around simply knew her as Ms. Clare. Alyssa thought it must be heaven to live with the saintly woman, and wondered if he knew how fortunate he was. But Ryan might not feel so lucky; his parents had passed away in a car accident when he was only four.

Stop dreaming about Ryan. She followed her sister into their yard and sighed. *To him, you're just a good friend.*

"Do you want one or two?"

"Two. I'm starving."

Alyssa flipped a grilled cheese sandwich in the skillet and smiled at her sister. "I can tell. Fix us a glass of tea while I do this."

"Okay."

The hair on the nape of her neck prickled as she heard tires crunching on the gravel driveway. She shot Fran a wary glance, *Daddy's home.*

The old truck door slammed shut, and Alyssa stiffened as he stomped into the kitchen. She studied his flushed face with a familiar, sinking dread. He pulled his cap off, the top of his light curly hair a darker shade of blonde. His faded blue jean work shirt strained on his burly arms as he pointed at the stove.

"What in the hell is that? I ain't eating no damn sandwich for supper." Beer can in hand; Daddy strode into the living room right off the kitchen where Mama sat. "What the hell you been doin' all day while I've been workin' my ass off? A man shouldn't have to come home to a goddamn sandwich for supper. No good, sorry excuse for a wife." His menacing face matched the ugly words his mouth spewed.

Mama arose unsteadily. "Stay away from me, you crazy son of a bitch. Go tell Cindy to fix you some damn food! I heard all about you and that whore!"

8

Alyssa drew in a sharp breath as she watched her parents. Rumors had been flying through town for weeks that Billy was cheating on his wife with Cindy, a waitress at the local bar.

Daddy steadily advanced towards Mama and raised his meaty hand. Fran shrank back against her, trembling.

Daddy cuffed Mama hard on the head, and Mama fell to her knees on the threadbare carpet. "Now get your sorry ass up and cook!" He stomped across the kitchen and flung the door open.

Good riddance, don't ever come back. Alyssa glared out the window as the old truck rattled away.

Fran went to help their mother up, but only got her hands shoved away instead.

"Just leave me the hell alone."

Alyssa eyed her mother from across the kitchen, and wondered why she was so cold hearted. Was it because of her husband, or had she always been that way? Why didn't they just get divorced if they were so unhappy together? There were so many things she didn't understand.

What she did know was that her father was a cruel, selfish man; and worse when he was drinking. Every day was a tense mystery, never knowing when he would explode. Oh yes, Billy relished in showing off his brute strength. Strong from working in the lumber yard, he thought nothing of hitting his daughters or his wife with his fist, or whatever else he could lay his hands on. Belts, sticks, even an extension cord…

Alyssa ran her fingers over the scars on her lower back where he had whipped her last winter with the cord for talking back and shuddered, the burning pain

9

still fresh in her mind. She had screamed and cried through it, but he had kept on lashing her viciously, as if possessed by a demon. It had hurt immeasurably more that Mama didn't even try to defend her, but allowed it to go on.

Alyssa's eyes narrowed as she thought about her mother's callous treatment of them, despising her for it.

Fran came and sat beside her on the narrow twin bed as she picked up a library book. "Don't start *reading* now. Talk to me."

"What? I just don't feel like talking."

"Well too bad, I'm not just gonna sit here and watch you read either. Let me try out this new style on your hair that I saw in a magazine at work. You'll love it, I promise."

Alyssa put her book down with great reluctance and sighed. "Aren't you off today?"

Her sister grinned. "Hey, I didn't say I wanted to wash your hair, now did I?" Fran worked at the Cut n Curl, shampooing heads.

"No, I guess not." Alyssa laughed.

"Besides, it's not like we have anything else to do. Jeremy had to work tonight, and there's nothing else going on," Fran added. Jeremy was Fran's boyfriend; they'd been dating for a few months now.

Both girls had long, silky hair, although Alyssa's was a shade darker. The next few hours passed quickly, with them trying out different hairstyles on each other.

Since she was born, Alyssa had worn Fran's hand me downs, but since Fran was fastidious about keeping her clothes neat and clean, it hadn't been too bad. *At least we're not boys.* Alyssa giggled to herself, thinking of the neighborhood boys and the holes they'd made in their clothes. *It could've definitely been worse*, she decided. But they both worked now, and bought their own clothes.

Their parents rarely gave them money, not that there was much. Their father certainly didn't make a windfall working at the local lumberyard. And Mama hadn't worked in years, her last job had been at the local dry cleaners, but they had let her go for calling in too much.

"I love my hair, sis. Thanks."

"You're welcome. I just love those loose ringlets around your face." Fran reached out her hand to fix a sun streaked lock.

Alyssa laughed and dodged out of the way. "You are way too much of a perfectionist. Now come on, I'm dying of thirst."

The mournful sounds of old country music echoed from the living room into the kitchen.

"Hand me the glasses, sis." Alyssa slid the jug of sweet tea she'd made earlier out of the refrigerator, irked to see Mama by the table when she turned around.

"Oh, are y'all too good to talk to me or something?" A vehement light glinted in bloodshot eyes.

"No, Mama, we've just been doing each other's hair," Alyssa said carefully. This was dangerous grounds, she knew.

"Oh, you just think you're *something*, don't you? Little Miss Priss with your hair all curled," she said scornfully and gestured towards her head.

Alyssa bit down on her tongue so she wouldn't smart off; all Mama wanted was somebody to argue

11

with since Daddy wasn't there.

Mama cursed as she pulled out a near empty bottle of wine out of the refrigerator.

Headlights flashed through the window, and they could hear Daddy's door slowly creak open. His steel-toed boots scraped the side porch with heavy steps and Alyssa tensed, her stomach churning with dread.

The kitchen door opened and slammed shut.

"You son of a bitch! Where in the hell have you been?" Mama shouted at Daddy as he staggered across the floor. "You go off and leave me here with these two, who did nothin' all day except play with their damn hair. So did Cindy feed you, or just screw you?"

Daddy's eyes widened, and then narrowed to menacing slits. "Apparently you're not just lazy, you're stupid too. Either that or you just plain don't learn a lesson. But I'll teach ya'." He began to remove his belt and advance towards Mama.

Somewhere in her drunken mind, Mama realized his intent. Alyssa saw it in her eyes and the panicked expression on her face. Fran grasped her arm, and their frightened gazes met. Goosebumps rose on Alyssa's arms. *This is about to get really bad. Please God, please make them stop.*

Mama frantically lifted her arms to protect her face. The belt whistled through the air, and landed with a resounding smack against her forearms.

"Aaaahhhh!" Her pained scream rent through the ominous silence of the house as its leather length snaked around to her back.

Their father laughed and lifted his arm again, brass buckle twinkling deceptively in the kitchen light. "You gonna keep your damn mouth shut? Huh? Huh? I can't *heaarr* you," he shouted cruelly.

He hit her again and Mama screeched, "Fuck you!" With a sudden twist of her torso, she kicked him hard in the groin. Daddy buckled to the floor, howling in pain.

"Oh my God, oh my God, Oh my God." Alyssa bit her lip so hard the metallic taste of blood filled her mouth.

Mama stood over him and kicked him in the leg. "Bastard! Go screw Cindy now!"

With a roar he grabbed her calf, and pulled her down on top of him. "You're gonna pay for that, bitch."

Alyssa's eyes widened in horror as their father rolled over on top of Mama, then slammed her head against the kitchen floor. "Stop it!" Alyssa screamed, and threw herself on top of her father. He shook her off as if she weighed nothing, and she hit the ground with a bone- jarring thud.

Scrambling up, she ran and got the broom. "Get off of her, Daddy! You're going to kill her!" Her hands tingled from the force as she smacked him on his back with the wooden end of the broom.

Before she could take a step, he lunged for her and snatched her up against the wall. Breathing heavily, his pale eyes bored into her as he squeezed her upper arms till she couldn't stop her sob of pain.

"Get the hell out of here," he growled.

Fumes of sour beer mixed with the rancid smell of stale cigarettes made her stomach heave.

"You're just like your mama, a pain in the ass." He let go and she fell to the floor in a stunned heap, fighting for breath.

The only sounds in the kitchen were of Fran, crying hysterically. Daddy lit a cigarette, unconcerned.

Alyssa crawled over to where Mama lay, her heart slamming so hard against her chest she felt lightheaded. "Why did you do that!" she screamed at him.

"Shut your mouth, girl." He leaned down and blew a cloud of smoke in her face, a sadistic look in his eyes. Alyssa's whole body was trembling, not knowing what he was about to do next. Finally he rose up, and ground out the cigarette with the heel of his boot.

Alyssa continued to watch him warily, knowing full well it wasn't over. She had seen him drag Mama by her hair around on the floor, kick her and other horrific attacks. And the things he had done with his gun… Alyssa shook even harder. "Just leave us alone," she said in a fierce whisper.

His foot shot out, and sharp pain exploded through her thigh as the force of his kick knocked her into her sister.

"Alyssa!" Fran screamed.

With a disgusted curse, Daddy turned down the hallway.

I hate him, I hate him, Alyssa cried to herself. She snuggled into Fran's embrace for a moment, and then looked at her. "I'm alright, Fran."

"Are you sure?" Her sister's face was blotchy and swollen from crying.

"Yes, I'm sure."

Pulling herself up on wobbly legs, she went to get a cold rag. "Mama, open your eyes," she pleaded, and laid the cloth across her forehead.

Mama began to stir. "Ohhh, my head hurts. That lowdown bastard. I'm gonna kill him one of these days, I swear I am."

"Shhhh, Mama, we're going to help you to the couch. Fran, help me." The sisters slowly raised their mother to a sitting position, and Joyce moaned, holding her head.

"Get me off this damn floor," she bit out ungraciously.

Alyssa and Fran each took a side while she walked to the couch, and sunk down. "Put the washcloth on my neck." The air filled with the stench of cigarettes as Joyce rested her head on her hands, and blew out clouds of smoke.

In the ensuing silence, Alyssa could hear the loud snores of her father. *Thank you, God,* she thought fervently. Fran and Alyssa exchanged weary looks.

"Mama, do you need anything else?" Alyssa asked finally.

"No," she replied, and waved her hand dismissively.

Alyssa quickly shut their bedroom door behind them. Fran marched to the mirror, and then spun around after examining her swollen eyes. "As soon as I can, I am outta here! And you had better come with me, Alyssa! They're gonna kill each other, and probably us too. You know I'm right! They're crazy, both of them!"

Alyssa lay down on her bed, drained and sore all over. "Fran, if you leave, I'm going, too. There's no way I'd live here without you!" She shook her head emphatically and stared up at the ceiling. "Hell, no." Being alone with her parents would be unimaginably horrible, Alyssa shuddered at the thought. "We'll be out of here soon. You turn eighteen in a couple of months, thank goodness."

She closed her eyes, picturing Ryan's face to give

herself a measure of peace, and fell into a restless sleep.

CHAPTER 2

Ryan shielded his eyes and searched the gray-green waters for Alyssa, but there was no sign of her. The hot sun blazed in the deep blue sky, and sparkled off the surface of the Red River where a group of friends splashed around.

"Bout time, man!" Jeremy waved to him, and he joined the other teenagers in the water.

"I'm here now, so let the fun begin," Ryan grinned. Jeremy wrapped his arms around his chest and tried to dunk him, but he was too strong. "Don't think so buddy," he laughed. Diving away from his friend, he enjoyed the feel of the invigorating water against his hot skin as he swam.

A while later, he saw Alyssa and her sister arrive. They set their bicycles at the top of the narrow trail that descended to the river, and walked down to the sandbar. Fran began chatting with her friend, Candice, and applying sun tanning lotion. He looked over at Alyssa, undressing down to her turquoise bathing suit.

What in the hell had happened to her leg? His jaw clenched, Ryan contemplated the large, purple bruise on her thigh suspiciously. Everyone around knew what a son of a bitch her father was. The thought that she was being abused infuriated him, made him want to choke Billy Martin to death with his bare hands.

His gaze moved up to the beautiful profile of

Alyssa's face, and her long, silky hair hanging almost to her waist. Ryan kept his attention on her as she came slowly further out on the sandy bottom. Her green eyes were clear and bright, her heart shaped face smooth and tan. She appeared to be deep in thought as she watched her sister and Jeremy horse around. Jeremy scooped his arms around Fran and tossed her across the water, while Fran shrieked happily. A small smile broke across Alyssa's face, and the sweet dimples he adored emerged. A thrill shot crazily through him, and he had an overwhelming urge to be near her, right at this instant.

"You scared me, Ryan!" she said in surprise as he surfaced in front of her. He was undeniably gorgeous. Dark hair lay down his nape, and crystal blue eyes gleamed at her, surrounded by wet, spiky lashes. Her perusal traveled down to the water droplets that clung to his muscled, powerful chest... He cleared his throat and she hastily glanced back up to meet his amused gaze.

"What took you so long?"

"We got a late start. We were going to leave earlier but...didn't." Her voice trailed off lamely, thinking of the huge argument her parents had gotten into when Billy had left, presumably to see Cindy.

"Okay," he drawled out, and Alyssa winced at the doubtful expression on his face.

"So how long have you been here?" she asked in an overly bright voice, even to her ears.

"Probably about an hour or so." Ryan wondered at the dark cloud that crossed her transparent eyes, and rubbed his foot against hers.

"Please tell me that's your foot, and not something

swimming around down there." A wry smile curved her full lips.

"Yes, scaredy cat," he teased. He grasped her upper arms to bring her closer, and she let out a low gasp. "What's wrong?" he asked in alarm.

She tried to pull away, but he held her still while he examined her arms. His jaw ticked murderously when he discovered the line of purple bruises marring the underside of her smooth, tanned skin. "What happened to you?" he demanded, although he was positive he already knew the answer.

Her long lashes fluttered shut for a moment before she answered. "It's a long story."

"No...Alyssa, what happened to you?"

"Daddy and Mama were fighting, and I had to help Mama. Don't tell anybody, please, Ryan," she whispered.

He shook his head, enraged. His hands returned to her slim upper arms, and stroked them with gentle motions. "I wanna kill that drunken piece of shit. It's not right, hurting his own daughter," he bit out angrily.

"I know," she said softly, "but Fran will be eighteen soon, and then we're going to move out as soon as we can."

Ryan's eyebrows lowered in a frown. "That's not good enough, Alyssa. A lot can happen between now and then. And what about that bruise on your leg? I know that came from that son of a bitch too." Cursing, he cupped her jaw in his hand, his whole body taut and reverberating with frustration.

"Just stay out of it, Ryan. Please."

He didn't answer, his temper simmered in a steady boil as he caressed her smooth cheek with his thumb.

How dare that drunk lay his rough hands on Alyssa and hurt her. She was too sweet, too pure of heart to deserve this treatment. Compared to Billy Martin, Alyssa was a little thing. Although on the cusp of womanhood, her body blossoming, she was still small and slender. There was no way she was able to stand up against the brutish strength of her father. His other hand drew into a fist as he thought about what he would relish doing to Billy Martin. Beat the crap out of him foremost, and give him a taste of his own medicine.

She was still gazing up at him with an appealing look on her pretty face, and he shook his head hard, not about to be put off. "Alyssa…"

"Ryan!" Jeremy shouted, and they both jumped. "Let's play chicken, me and Fran against you and Alyssa."

Ryan sighed heavily and shook his head again; everybody's eyes were now on them. He looked down at her. "Do you want to?"

"Sure," she shrugged, grateful for the change in conversation, and nervous from Ryan's reaction.

"Give us a minute," Ryan shouted back, and Alyssa bit her lip. She didn't think he'd say anything, but still…she didn't want anybody else knowing her family's business. He knew some of it, but she had only told him the basics, and glossed over the worst.

Her parents had made it clear to her often enough, *don't say anything. Do you want them to put you in a foster home?* No, she didn't; she had heard plenty about the horrors of foster homes, and couldn't bear the thought of possibly being separated from Fran. At least she was able to see Ryan and her other friends now. Cypress Bayou was the only home she knew, and she didn't want to leave it.

Ryan clasped Alyssa's hand in his and squeezed, wishing there was some way to help her. The apprehensive look on her small face made his lungs tighten. *Someday that bastard is gonna get his,* he vowed to himself.

"Are you sure you want to play? Does it hurt...?" He gestured towards her arms and leg, and she shook her head quickly.

"Well, alright," he sighed. "You ready?"

She squealed as he lifted her onto his strong shoulders, and his fingers tickled the bottom of her cute feet. Her laughter echoed out against the sandy bank, and he couldn't keep the grin off his face as they spent the afternoon together. All too soon, it was time to head home.

Ryan glanced over at Alyssa, her face pink and sun kissed, pedaling beside her sister. She turned seventeen in a few months; their birthdays were only two weeks apart in November. She was a true Scorpio, mysterious and deep. He didn't feel like he was able to gauge her feelings, and speculated what she thought about him. Sometimes he thought he caught her gazing at him with a longing glint in her eyes. A lot of girls had looked at him like that, but he wasn't interested in them.

Oh, he'd had a few girlfriends, nothing serious though. His past girlfriends had all assured him he was a great kisser. *That was good to know,* he thought to himself humorously, *wouldn't want to disappoint the ladies.*

After cutting through the cornfield, they emerged onto the gravel road. Alyssa's house soon came into view, and he brooded silently as he considered the shabby house and yard. Her father's truck was in the yard, and he had to resist the urge to storm inside and do bodily harm to the man. Ryan would bet his last dollar the bruise on Alyssa's leg had come from a steel -toed boot. And the ones on her upper arms, those had happened because she had been grabbed, and hard. His right hand drew in a fist as he thought, infuriated.

He wiped the forbidding look off his face and turned to Alyssa.

"I had fun today. The water was perfect."

"Yeah, I had a great time." He stroked her soft cheek with one finger. "You know where I'm at if you need me."

"Yes, okay, thanks Ryan."

Ryan sighed, shaking his head. He knew she was just saying that to appease him. "I mean it, Lyssa." That was his pet name for her; he had called her that since grade school. He stared down at her, silently willing her to look up at him.

And it worked. The air between them crackled with intense awareness as her wide eyed green gaze met his.

"I know you do." She gave him a small, devastating smile and he had an overpowering urge to kiss her, explore her sweet mouth.

Alyssa stepped forward and he wrapped his arms around her sun warmed body, feeling as though he could hold her forever. She leaned back and gave him a soft kiss on the cheek. He felt as though she'd branded him, the whole side of his face sizzled.

"Goodbye, Ryan," she whispered.

"Bye, Alyssa," he said slowly, and smoothed her silky hair off her forehead. She closed her eyes for a moment, and when they opened seconds later, he was surprised to see tears swimming in them.

"Thanks for always being here for me," she said in a low voice, and slipped away from him.

Ryan watched her sunny hair swirl enticingly down her back as she caught up with Fran, and his chest tightened with emotion. He knew several guys were attracted to Alyssa, but she didn't appear to notice. She was gorgeous with her smooth, flawless skin, and glowing eyes. Her slim, straight nose and dark gold brows accentuated her dimpled cheeks and full, generous mouth. He thought she was the prettiest girl around. But it wasn't just that, she had a sweet, innocent spirit that drew him in. She wanted to be a nurse, and he knew she'd be perfect at it with her nurturing spirit. Alyssa had a temper and could be bossy, but he liked that about her too.

Fran depended on Alyssa for emotional support; that much was obvious. Because of their house of horrors, she had laughingly told him once. Ryan hadn't laughed, he recalled, he'd wondered who she leaned on.

He arrived home, and found his grandmother in the back yard tending her rows of various vegetables.

"Have fun at the river today?" she called out to him as he approached.

"Yes ma'am, it was great to get out of this heat."

"I'm getting a mess of purple hull peas together for lunch tomorrow. How's that sound with some smoked sausage and cornbread?"

"Sounds good to me."

Nana chuckled, her blue eyes twinkling. "Everything sounds good to you; you're growing like a weed. You're already taller than your daddy was, and he was six feet! Goodness gracious, you're going to have to duck through doors pretty soon."

"What, you'd rather me be short like you?" He smiled affectionately down at her.

"Now, see here! I'm not as short as all that, just shrunk a little when I got older, that's all." She laughed good-naturedly and swatted his arm.

"Whatever you say, Nana," he said jokingly.

"That's right, and you remember that!"

He revered his grandmother; she was funny and full of energy. Her short frame and plump figure were usually swathed in colorful muumuus she made herself on her old Singer sewing machine, and she kept her long, gray hair twisted up in a bun. She loved to tease him, and frequently reminded him she could run circles around him. He wasn't too sure of that, but went along with her anyways.

After gathering all of the ripened vegetables, they headed inside the small, brightly decorated kitchen. It was a cheery room, painted a lemon yellow with knickknacks and plants everywhere.

He placed the basket beside the sink, and washed his hands while his grandmother prattled on about the church fundraiser they were having next weekend. She was heavily involved in her church, and had ensured he'd had a sound Baptist upbringing.

He was more laid back about religion; he didn't understand all of the injustices of the world. Alyssa, for example, where was her divine intervention? He shook his head, not comprehending how such a sweet girl could have so much heaped on her slight shoulders. She had come to church pretty regularly when she was younger, the church bus would pick her and Fran up.

He remembered her faded dresses, she'd only had a few, but her beauty and gentleness had shown through. He'd hated it when kids had picked on her; it certainly wasn't her fault she didn't have the latest fashions. If her parents didn't blow their money on liquor, she might have had nicer clothes. But it didn't happen around him, he made sure of it. He had always stuck up for her, and didn't intend to stop anytime soon. But, he thought guiltily, he couldn't defend her against the biggest demon of them all. *Damn that bastard.*

He sighed, and considered his rumbling belly. Nana had prepared smothered pork chops, rice, and fresh corn on the cob, still warm on the stove. She was an excellent cook, and he an appreciative audience. He ate hungrily, till he was so full he groaned with satisfaction. "That was great, Nana." He gave her a peck on the cheek as she beamed happily, and went to take a shower.

After dressing, he headed toward his room and surveyed the trophies lined on his bookshelf, given for different athletic accomplishments. *Please, let sports help me out of this one horse town.* As much as he loved his grandmother, he wanted *more*.

But where did that leave him and Alyssa? Would she leave too? Or would there ever be an "us" between them? So many unanswered questions.

He lay down heavily on his plaid bedspread. One thing was for sure, he cared deeply about Alyssa and what happened to her, his brows furrowed deep as he thought. Stretching his long arms out, he flexed his hands into tight fists. He would love to get hold of Billy Martin one of these days, and smash him in his ugly face.

He sighed, troubled, hoping all was well in the Martin household tonight. He felt so helpless, unable to help Alyssa, but wanting to so badly. She'd hate him if he said anything to anybody, and to be honest, he didn't think anything would happen anyway. After all, everyone in town knew how Billy was. Hadn't he heard them all talk about it often enough? Ryan closed his eyes, and sent a prayer up. *Lord if you're listening, help that innocent girl out. She needs you.*

CHAPTER 3

Fran dropped a folded towel in the stack beside Alyssa's elbow. "When is Ryan going to ask you to go out with him?"

Alyssa shook her head in disbelief. "Do I look like a mind reader to you or something? We're just friends."

"Ha!" Fran scoffed, "friends my foot! He can't keep his eyes off of you. Even Jeremy said something about it."

"Y'all are both crazy." Alyssa shook her head ruefully. "Ryan just looks out for me, that's all. He's never said anything about us going steady."

"Not *yet*, but mark my words, he will. And why not, you're pretty and smart. He'd be lucky to have you as his girlfriend."

Alyssa smiled, touched by her sister's loyalty. "Thanks, sis."

Still, she thought Fran was reading too much into her and Ryan's friendship. She knew he cared about her, without a doubt. But caring about someone and being in a relationship were two different things, even she knew that. She'd never had a serious boyfriend; the only guy she'd ever been interested in was Ryan.

Alyssa wrapped a long strand of hair around her finger and recalled the hungry way he eyed her lately, his bright blue eyes catching hers in a white-hot stare. She didn't know quite what to make of it and so kept it to herself, not wanting to give false words to hopes.

****

Alyssa hit her alarm with a groan, and looked over at her sister. "Fran, wake up, it's the first day of school."

"I'm getting up," Fran said sleepily.

Alyssa grabbed her outfit hanging on the back of the door, and headed to the bathroom to take a shower. After getting out, she dressed in a new pair of jeans that emphasized her slender curves, and a green blouse that brought out her eyes. Fran curled her hair for her, letting half of it down to hang in golden waves down her back.

"Wow, look at us!" Fran exclaimed.

The bus arrived, and Ryan winked at her as she passed by his seat. *He is so cute.* Fran slid in beside Jeremy, and she settled beside her friend, April, another junior. After the bus pulled up to the school, Ryan stopped her outside by laying a hand on her shoulder.

"Ryan, can you believe you're a senior? This is your last first day of school here. Wait, did I say that right?"

"Yeah," he grinned. "Hard to believe, but I'm glad. And you're right behind me."

"I know; I can't wait to graduate."

Ryan smiled at her, his expression growing warm and soft. "You look really pretty, Alyssa."

"Thanks," she said shyly, and groaned inwardly when she felt her cheeks grow hot.

"Well, come on; don't want to be late on the first day."

He clasped her hand in his till they reached the front door, and her heart fluttered from his closeness.

She took her hand slowly from his, savoring the feel of his long fingers against hers.

"Bye Ryan."

Ryan stood there for a moment, watching her appealing form rush after April. Honey streaked waves tumbled down to her deliciously rounded backside, and only a friend's loud greeting brought him back to the present.

Alyssa couldn't believe Ryan had held her hand to the front door of the school. *What could that mean?* She would ask Fran, but she already knew what she would say. Fran would swear he was madly in love with her, she thought, and rolled her eyes mentally. Dreams of Ryan asking her out filled her mind, and she half listened to the teacher droning on and on about her expectations for the class this semester.

****

"Whew, it's too damn hot out here," Ryan said to LaDarius. He took off his helmet, and swiped his brow wearily. Coach Anderson pushed his "boys" to the max every day at practice, and the results spoke for themselves: three 2A championships in five years.

"Tell me about it." LaDarius squinted up at the sun. LaDarius was his best friend, and also a wide receiver for the team. "Hey, you coming out to the levy after the game Friday night? There's gonna be a bonfire. And beer." He wagged his brows up and down, and grinned. White teeth shone brightly in his dark face as he added, "And you know what they say about ladies and liquor, don't ya?"

"I don't know, maybe."

"Come on, man, we gotta have our captain."

Ryan watched as Jeremy ran a practice drill. *If*

Fran goes, I bet Alyssa will too. "Count me in."

"Alright! It's gonna be one hell of a party," LaDarius said happily.

****

Fran and Alyssa sung along to rock songs on the radio as they readied themselves for the game. Alyssa dressed in a flattering pair of blue jeans and a red and white striped scoop necked top, the school colors. Gold hoop earrings and the heart shaped necklace Fran had gotten her last Christmas finished off her outfit. *Well, good as it's gonna get.* Hopefully Ryan would take notice, and she shivered in anticipation as she studied her reflection in the mirror.

"Come on, Alyssa," Fran called from the living room.

"I'll be right there." She grabbed her purse off of her bed and walked down the short hallway.

"Megan is picking us up, Mama, and dropping us off too," Fran informed their mother.

Mama nodded, her eyes never leaving the television. "Don't be out late. I'm going to bed pretty soon because I've got one of my headaches coming on."

"We won't."

Daddy wasn't home yet, thankfully. They hadn't told him about the bonfire, just the football game, and were counting on him to be asleep before they made it back. He didn't like for them to go out, convinced they would wind up pregnant young like Mama had. He'd thrown a fit before when Fran had come in late, hitting her with his belt, and calling her degrading names. Alyssa had jumped in to defend her sister, and suffered mightily for it. The welts that had covered her back had made sleep almost impossible till they healed.

30

But Fran still snuck out, especially lately with Jeremy. Alyssa would anxiously wait up; all the while praying Fran didn't get caught. It'd be a disaster if she was, for both of them.

Gravel crunched in the yard as a car pulled up and honked.

"That's Megan, bye Mama." Alyssa opened the front door and headed out.

****

"Come sit with us!" April waved them over to a group of their friends in the fourth row of the football stadium. The players were warming up and Alyssa scanned the field, spotting Ryan's towering six foot three form easily in his number seventeen jersey.

"I see who you're looking at," April teased. "And I don't blame you! If I didn't have a boyfriend already, I'd be checking him out, too. He's sooo hot!" she squealed.

"Um, yeah he is," Alyssa said, unable to tear her eyes away. Ryan glanced up towards her, and their gazes sizzled like heat waves before someone shouted his name from the sidelines.

The crowded stands swelled to capacity, and then the game began. They were playing the Warriors, from nearby Milton. Alyssa kept her eyes on Ryan as he stood steady in the pocket, scanning the field for an open receiver. The ball spiraled accurately through the air and landed in the outstretched arms of number eight, Will Cooper. Excited cheers erupted into a happy roar as he ran the ball in for a touchdown.

Alyssa watched Ryan in amazement; he possessed lightning quick reflexes, and played fearlessly. The precision and agility he showed gave no doubts as to why football scouts were visiting the small town of

Cypress Bayou.

She jumped to her feet when he was tackled by four enormous opponents after running it in for eleven yards. "What are they trying to do, kill him?" Alyssa shrieked to Fran. She pressed both hands to her mouth in horror as he lay still, surrounded by the coaching staff. The large crowd grew hushed as Alyssa prayed urgently that he wasn't hurt. She turned to Fran angrily. "They shouldn't be allowed to do that! I can't believe those referees aren't going to do anything!"

"I agree, that was terrible."

Alyssa's heart leapt with relief as Ryan's tall frame slowly stood up, and the fans went wild. "Thank goodness!" Alyssa hugged Fran happily and waved at him, tingling with excitement when he waved back. The jersey molded tight against his muscular physique, emphasizing his lean abdomen and athletic build. He went back in a while later, scoring two more touchdowns and the game ended, 35-24.

"Yes!" The girls exchanged high fives all around. "Except for when Ryan got hurt, that was awesome!" Alyssa shouted to her sister over the cheers of the crowd.

"That win deserves a celebration! I'm ready to go party," Fran said excitedly. "How about you?"

Alyssa scanned the crowd. She didn't see Ryan, although most of the other players had emerged from the locker room.

Fran tugged her arm with a knowing look. "Come on, Ryan will be there."

"He better be," Alyssa grumbled, and flashed her sister a quick smile. "Seriously though Fran, we can't stay long, and do *not* get drunk," she said sternly as they walked down the stadium steps.

"Quit worrying so much. Everything is going to be fine."

"Hey, I'm just looking out for the both of us."

Her sister sighed. "I know, I know."

Jeremy shouted for them from the parking lot, and Fran grabbed her arm. "Let's go!"

****

Ryan pulled up to the levy, adrenaline pumping through him as he heard the thump of rock music. At least fifty people milled about, drinking beer and a potent red concoction out of plastic cups. It was easy to get liquor in Cypress Bayou if you knew the right people.

"Hey Ryan, great game tonight." Jeremy passed him a cold beer, and thumped him on the shoulder.

Ryan took a long drink. "Thanks, man."

He made his way towards the fire and searched the crowd, hoping to see a slender, exquisite girl-woman with stunning green eyes. He broke through a band of people and spotted her.

Alyssa was talking with Will, and the interest in Will's stare was apparent even from where he stood. The dancing firelight had transformed her long hair into a sheet of shimmering gold that tumbled around her angelic profile. Ryan strode towards them, his long legs eating up the distance quickly.

"Hi Ryan." Alyssa smiled.

"Hey buddy, great way to open the season. Thanks for that bullet in the 4th." Will pretended he was catching a ball, and she laughed melodiously at his antics.

Ryan admired her glowing face and shot his

teammate a glare, wishing he would just go away. "Yeah, we did pretty good tonight," he replied irritably. He motioned with a quick, imperceptible nod of his head for Will to leave.

And he took the hint surprisingly well, Ryan noted with satisfaction as Will pointed to where the cars were parked. "Listen, I was just about to grab anther beer. You want one?"

Ryan held up his half full bottle. "Naw, I'm good, I've gotta drive back home."

"Alright, man. Well, I'll see y'all later." Will squeezed Alyssa's elbow in farewell, and Ryan's eyes narrowed dangerously. "Uh, sorry," Will stammered, and dropped the offending appendage.

Ryan grunted in response, noting the perplexed stare on Alyssa's face. "Come on, walk with me." He caught her small hand in his.

"Ryan, you played terrific tonight. I had a great time at the game."

He had wanted to punch Will for daring to flirt with and touch Alyssa. The thought *she's mine*, floated through his mind. Recalling the jealousy that had flooded through him when he saw her with Will, he studied her intently, wondering how she felt about him. She had woven herself into his brain and heart, and there was no escaping.

Alyssa punched him playfully in the arm. "What's the matter with you, you're so quiet."

"Nothing, just a little tired." He grabbed his arm in mock pain, and winced dramatically.

His laughter joined hers, a sound that warmed her heart thoroughly.

"I was so scared when you were tackled. Are you

in pain?"

He chuckled. "That was nothing; I get hit like that all the time."

Alyssa looked at him in disbelief. "Those guys probably weighed at least a thousand pounds, and that was *nothing*? You could've been hurt really bad."

He looked down at her with a half-smile, appearing so dark and seductively beautiful, she shivered. "But I wasn't." His deep voice vibrated through the humid night air.

Her stomach dipped, and she smiled back. 'I'm glad," she said softly, and held on tighter to his hand.

They walked up the grass covered levy hand in hand, and surveyed the dark, murky river. *I bet there are alligators and snakes all out there, just waiting to get a bite of something.* Unconsciously moving nearer to Ryan, he wrapped his arm around her waist. Shock waves swept through her, and she felt Ryan's assessing gaze on her. Taking a sip of her drink, she made a face at the taste.

"How much alcohol did they put in this? That burned the whole way down."

"That's why I stick with beer. I'm scared of that," he joked.

"I see why," she laughed. Alyssa sat down on the cool grass and Ryan followed, sitting close beside her.

"I haven't had a chance to talk with you much, not with football practice and work. How's everything going?"

"Pretty good, although the kitchen window got knocked out yesterday while I was babysitting. Their mom didn't fire me, surprisingly." The infamous Simmons boys were four, six, and eight; stair steppers, as their mom called them.

"I doubt she would fire you, I mean, who else would watch them? They've gone through almost every babysitter in town," he pointed out humorously.

"They are pretty horrible," she laughed.

"Yeah, I've seen those monsters in action at the store. I think even Mr. Mack hates to see them coming."

She grinned back at him. "That's when you know your kids are bad."

He laughed and nodded his head. "How's it going at your house?" he asked, his tone turning serious.

Alyssa didn't say anything for a moment. Ryan studied her classically beautiful profile, the high cheekbones, generous rosebud lips, and smooth brow. His hand itched to smooth long, silky wind whipped strands back from her face as she looked out at the river

"It's the same, no better, no worse," she said quietly, her flat tone betraying her bitterness.

"That bastard better not have hurt you anymore," he said fiercely.

"He hasn't."

"I meant what I said, Alyssa. If he so much as lays a finger on you, I want you to tell me. We'll figure something out."

Surprised, she studied his determined expression. *He really means it.* Her heart melted, and she cupped his taut jaw. "I'll be alright, I'm tougher than you think," she teased in an attempt to lighten the mood.

Ryan's gaze narrowed over her shoulder before swinging back to hers. "I'm tough enough for both of us. Don't try to deal with him, Alyssa, let me do that."

His hand moved to rest on top of hers. He brought

it gently to his lips, and pressed a kiss in her palm. She gasped, her heart jumping skittishly. To her shocked delight, he bent his dark head and kissed her, his tongue caressing the soft line of her lips. Ryan deepened the kiss, whispering, "Open your mouth." She hesitated and then did as he bid, her arms sliding around his neck instinctively. Strong arms wrapped around her, pulling her full against his hard body. She moaned and his embrace tightened; his tongue swirling against hers with bold possession.

"Lyssa," he whispered against her lips. She couldn't think; she was lost in the intoxicating sensations he had awoken in her. The sounds of the night slipped away, all she could hear was his ragged breathing in her ear.

Ryan felt the hesitant touch of Alyssa's tongue as if it were a hot flame. She tasted sweet, fruity, and the knowledge that she wasn't frightened both relieved and aroused him. His roving hands slid down her enticing curves. He lost focus on all but her, his whole being concentrated on the exquisite softness of her mouth. The sensually drugging kiss went on and on, lasting till they were both shaking with desire. Blood rushed madly through his veins, causing his grip to tighten involuntarily on the curve of her hips. She let out a soft cry and his hands relaxed, soothing her sides softly. "Lyssa, we have to stop. I can't take any more," he rasped, and laid his forehead against hers.

"Oh Ryan," she breathed, her soft breath tickling his lips where they still touched.

With his eyes still closed, he drew his hand up to stroke satin strands of hair away from her face. She pressed a kiss to his mouth and snuggled even closer.

He continued stroking her hair, feeling tenderness well inside of him as he studied her kiss-swollen, rosy lips.

"Ryan, did…did you like it?"

He groaned and pulled her in his lap. "Did I like it? Alyssa, I liked it too much. Did you?"

"Oh yes, it was wonderful. Everything I thought it would be. I've never kissed anybody before, I always dreamed it would be with you," she said reverently, and ran her hands down his back, electrifying every muscle.

"Alyssa, you're so sweet." His lips landed against hers in a blazing kiss, and he swallowed her soft, indrawn breath. Their tongues intertwined as he explored the velvety smoothness of her mouth. She boldly returned the kiss and this time he was the one who gasped against her lips. Shifting suddenly, he lifted her over to sit on his thigh, not wanting to scare her off with the evidence of his desire. Ryan tore his mouth away from hers, whispering, "Lyssa, Lyssa," and trailed soft kisses from her jaw to her ear. She trembled in his arms, leaning into him.

"You're an angel," he murmured. She smelled so good, like honeysuckle. Closing his eyes, he fought mightily to bring his raging hormones under control. He held her body against his, and buried his face in her fragrant mass of hair. They stayed that way for long heaven spent moments as he felt her rapid heart rate slow.

"I love you," she whispered close to his ear.

"And I love you, Alyssa, more than you know."

She hugged him hard, eyes shining. "This is the best night of my life."

"Mine too." He rested his head on top hers and kissed her silky crown. Crickets chirped in the air, and she jumped in his arms when a loud splash vibrated in the dark river. Ryan looked down at the girl he had known and loved forever, and tightened his bond in tender possession around her. As he had grown, his feelings had deepened. This was love, true and strong.

Time slipped away, each savoring the intoxicating newness of being in each other's embrace. Unfortunately, reality came with a stinging reminder.

Alyssa squirmed against him and scratched her ankle. "I wish we could stay up here forever, but these mosquitoes will carry us away soon."

"Bloodsucking little bastards." Ryan slapped the back of his neck. "Let's go back by the fire. We'll be safe there."

"I hope so," she smiled.

Extending his hand, he pulled her up. They kissed; a passionate exchange to brand her as his, to ensure she didn't forget this night, just like he never would. Their hearts beat in a mad dance against one another as the beauty of true love bloomed like moonflowers.

CHAPTER 4

"Damn, look at your sister."

"Is she drunk?" Alyssa asked in slow disbelief.

Ryan nodded his head, brows raised as he looked over at her. "Oh yeah, she's definitely drunk."

Fran called out to them from Jeremy's lap. "Alyssa, y'all come do a shot with me! Hello, this is a party! Loosen up!"

Alyssa took the dangling beer bottle from her sister's hand. "I think you've had enough for both of us. How much have you drank?"

"Not that much, just a few beers and a few shots," she giggled, her eyes glazed.

"Fran, what's the matter with you," she said in a low voice. "What if Daddy is awake?" She turned and gave Ryan a beseeching look. "I've got to get her home. And I don't think Jeremy can drive."

"I drove here in my grandmother's car; I can drop you two off.

"This is going to be fun," Alyssa muttered, furious at her sister. Thanks to her, she and Ryan's special night was cut short. She set her hands on her hips. "Get up Fran, and let's walk to Ryan's car."

"I came with Jeremy, and I'm leaving with Jeremy!"

"He can't drive, Fran! Are you insane?" She looked at Jeremy, who shrugged his shoulders noncommittally.

"I'm not leaving you here, Fran. What am I supposed to tell Mama and Daddy when I show up without you?"

"Screw them; they don't give a shit about us. Don't you know that?"

Alyssa said nothing; it hurt to hear it in words, though it was surely true.

She felt Ryan move closer to her. "Let's go, Fran," he said in a harsh tone.

Her sister unsteadily got up from Jeremy's lap, and a cheer rang out from the rowdy crowd.

Alyssa rolled her eyes. "This is ridiculous."

Fran stumbled and giggled the whole way to the car while she glared at her. Of all nights! Fran's timing was terrible.

Alyssa slipped in the passenger side, and twisted around to keep an eye on her sister in the backseat.

"Tell me if you need to pull over, Fran." Ryan adjusted the rearview mirror as he drove down the curvy, gravel road.

"Okay," she replied grimly.

Alyssa shook her head in disbelief. "Fran, do not throw up in here! This is Ryan's grandma's car!"

Fran groaned; her face a sickly shade of white. "I'm gonna puke. Pull over."

Ryan slammed on the brakes, and threw open Fran's door just as she was promptly sick on the side of the road.

Alyssa scrambled out of the car in total exasperation. "Fran, you had better pray Mama and Daddy are asleep when we get home. Oooh, I just can't believe you!"

"Shut up, Alyssa," Fran moaned.

Alyssa blew out an aggravated breath, and helped

her back in the car. The rest of the ride was uneventful with Fran seemingly passed out in the back. Alyssa shot Ryan a quick glance, and he winked at her with a reassuring smile.

"Everything is going to be fine."

"Yeah," she said in a low voice. "I hope so."

Ryan crept up to the edge of the yard with the headlights off. Fran could barely get out of the car, so Alyssa tugged at her. "Stand up, Fran! Hurry up!" She stood and leaned heavily on her shoulder.

"I don't feel good," she slurred.

Ryan pulled her upright when she stumbled. "Here, let me," he said, speaking quietly out of the shadows.

"Careful, she's like dead weight," she warned.

"I can handle it." His strong arm wrapped around Fran, supporting her easily. Alyssa followed nervously to the dark house, her eyes darting in all directions. A tiny glow shone through the darkness, and then went flying to the ground in a shimmering red arc near the front of the house. Alyssa's heart sank as she realized Daddy was outside smoking a cigarette.

"It's damn well after midnight," he yelled. "And the football game was over three hours ago! Where in the hell have you girls been?"

Alyssa quickly put her arm around Fran, and motioned urgently for Ryan to go.

Too late.

"Who's that?" Billy flicked on a flashlight as he peered at them suspiciously.

"Oh, it's just Ryan, Daddy. Fran got sick from some a hotdog she ate at the game and Megan had to leave early, so Ryan offered to drop us off. We had to wait until the coaches talked with all of the players though, and that took a while. Ryan's the captain of the team, you know." Alyssa crossed her fingers mentally, fervently hoping her guise would work.

Billy threw his empty beer can on the ground and walked closer, bushy eyebrows drawing together as he saw the out of it Fran. "I know drunk when I see it, and she's drunk!" he roared.

Yeah, I bet you're the resident expert on that. "She's not drunk, she's just sick like I told you, Daddy." Alyssa strove for a patient tone.

She tried to shoot Ryan a warning look to leave. But his steely gaze was focused on Billy, naked hatred evident as he listened to the exchange between father and daughter.

"Bullshit!" Billy yelled.

Alyssa winced, and tightened her hold around Fran's shoulders as she started to slip from her grasp.

"Boy, what do ya' mean, bringing my girl home drunk?" Billy shouted, focusing his bleary eyes on Ryan.

"Fran is not drunk," Alyssa insisted. "We're going in now. Ryan, thanks for dropping us off."

"Hold up!" Billy shone the light in Fran's face. "Just like I said, she's wasted. You little sluts have been hanging out with boys and drinking! Next you'll be gettin' knocked up! Girl, don't you ever lie to me again!"

Before she could know what he was about to do, his rough hand slapped her hard across the face. It sounded as loud as a shot in the stillness. Alyssa gasped from the pain that blasted through her head, and held her free hand to her fiery cheek. She collapsed to the ground, Fran going too. Her gaze flew over to Ryan, and she watched his stunned eyes flare ominously with fury.

He threw himself at her father with an inhuman roar. "You sorry son of a bitch!"

The two rolled in the ground, each throwing savage blows at the other. Billy punched Ryan hard in the stomach and he stumbled back, his head falling back to the ground.

"No!" Alyssa cried out.

With a vicious glint in his eyes, her father snickered. "Boy, I got more where that come from so you better run on home to your granny. Gal, you stay out of this! I'll deal with you later."

Alyssa ran to Ryan and kneeled beside him. "Just leave him alone!" she screamed at her father.

Ryan caressed her sore cheek with his thumb. "Are you alright?" she whispered, her heart breaking. She'd never wanted him to be dragged into all this, to be hurt.

"Yeah, just had to catch my breath," he said with a crooked grin. "Are you?" His eyebrows drew together in a dark glower as she nodded shakily.

"No, Ryan, please-"

Only one purpose mattered to him at this moment, she could see it in the dangerous set of his face as he evaded her grasp, and again faced her father. "Don't you ever hurt her again, you piece of shit. I'm gonna kill you if you do," he ground out.

"Mighty big words from a dumb kid," Billy scoffed. "Getting your ass kicked once wasn't enough for you, boy?"

"I'm still standing, aren't I?" Ryan taunted. "Not much of an ass kicking. Why don't you try fighting like a man for a change, instead of hitting on your daughters and wife?"

Billy's eyes widened then narrowed into slits. "Oh, so the little bitch has been running her mouth to you, huh? And what are you, her protector or something?"

"Yeah, something like that," Ryan stated determinedly.

Alyssa's fingernails dug into her palms, every nerve tight with love and fear.

Billy shoved Ryan hard across the shoulders. "Then come on with it, boy, show me what you got!"

Alyssa's breath froze in her chest as they circled each other menacingly. Billy punched Ryan in the stomach again, but this time he jumped out of the way so he received only a glancing hit. Ryan then threw a powerful wallop to Billy's face and slammed him in his jaw. Billy's head snapped violently back, and his whole body wavered. Taking advantage of his momentary dazedness, Ryan hit him again in the face and made square contact with his cheek. The older man landed on his bottom in the dirt.

"Don't you ever fucking touch her again, you worthless bastard," Ryan growled in her father's face. "Or I'm gonna come back and beat you within an inch of your life, I swear I will." Billy slumped lower and collapsed to his back in the dirt with a loud groan.

Fran stirred, squinting at Alyssa in bewilderment. "What's goin' on?"

Alyssa barely heard her; she was staring at Ryan, his chest heaving from exertion while he kept his eyes on Billy. She jumped up and threw her arms around him. "I'm so sorry, I didn't meant for any of this to happen," she sobbed.

"Shhhh, I've wanted to do that for a long time," he

soothed. And indeed he had. Ryan felt great, his whole body hummed with satisfaction. He'd never been so angry in his life as when he saw Alyssa fall to the ground from her father's hard blow.

He tilted her chin up and examined the already darkening bruise in furious despair. "Need to put some ice on this," he whispered, and brushed his lips across her swollen cheek. Ryan thought he could drown in her fathomless gaze, and waves of tenderness washed over him as he smoothed silvery tracks of tears away.

"It's over now."

But was it? Would Billy take out his anger on her? Had he made things even worse? He felt torn all of a sudden, not sure if he had done the right thing. But he hadn't thought before he acted, just snapped out of shock and a consuming urge to avenge the girl he loved.

"Fuck!" he snapped, staring at the dark house over the top of her head.

She jumped in his arms. Alyssa seemed to know what was going through his mind because she laid her hand against his tight jaw, and pressed a sweeping caress of a kiss to his lips. "I'm going to be alright."

Ryan shook his head at her in harsh disbelief, and raked his hand through his hair. "You don't know that, Alyssa. How can you say that? What's going to happen when he wakes up?"

She smiled and then cupped her cheek in her hand with a wince. "Maybe he won't remember," she said hopefully. "After all, you did hit him pretty hard."

Only Alyssa could joke at a time like this. Playing along, he quipped, "I could always hit him again. You know, just to make sure."

She laughed softly, and an ache stretched across his chest. He gently kissed her, his lips tingling from the sensuous feel. "I wish I could take you away from all this. I hate leaving you here."

"I hate being here," she whispered. He sighed, and her arms tightened around him.

After a few minutes, she spoke up. "I'm going to take Fran in, before anybody wakes up."

"Alright," he said in slow resignation, and his arms loosened from around her curvy form. "Put some ice on your cheek." He traced a finger over her soft lips. "And I love you."

"I love you too" she whispered. He watched her walk away, and a bleak darkness crept into his soul.

After making sure the door had closed behind them, he walked over to Billy and nudged him with his sneaker. "Still alive," he muttered half -disappointingly when Billy moved his leg.

On the way home, he mulled over the fight, and hated the awful sense of unease coursing through him. He lay awake for several hours before finally falling into a light sleep. A vivid, cruel nightmare of Alyssa calling his name over and over again haunted him and he bolted upright in bed, sweat pouring from him.

* * * *

Alyssa opened her eyes with a groan the next morning. She got out of bed, and gingerly felt her swollen cheek as she tiptoed to the mirror. "That bastard," she whispered fiercely. "He gave me a black eye." The side of her face throbbed in painful waves, and her head hurt even worse. She wished she could put some ice on it, but didn't dare walk into the kitchen.

Was Daddy still outside?

She peered through a slit in the curtains. No sign of him. He must have come in sometime during the night. Alyssa bit her knuckle nervously, filled with remorse over the fight.

I wish we'd never gone to the bonfire, she thought futilely. No, that wasn't true. Actually, she wished Fran hadn't gotten so wasted. She glared at Fran in her bed, snoring softly. This was all her fault. No, that wasn't true, either. Fran was definitely partly to blame, but so was Daddy. And Ryan too, she thought guiltily. He'd looked as if he thoroughly enjoyed knocking Daddy unconscious, for a moment anyway.

But she had already known how Ryan felt about her father, he hated him. Hated him for how he treated her. Because he cared for her. Alyssa's heart fluttered with happiness.

She smiled as she remembered the passionate kiss they had shared last night and the tender look in Ryan's eyes as he said he loved her. Alyssa hugged the memory tightly to herself, knowing she'd never forget it. It had been like she told Ryan, the best night of her life.

But the way it had ended… "Oh my God," she whispered in dread. "What is going to happen now?"

A couple of hours later, Daddy flung their bedroom door open. Alyssa lay on her side, pretending to be asleep.

"Wake up!" he roared.

Her mouth dropped as she took in her father's mottled purple swollen jaw, and his left eye that was swelled shut to just a crease that stretched eerily downward.

"Get up, girl," he shouted at Fran.

Fran sat up and peeked over at her.

Their father pointed wildly at them, a venomous glint in his pale eyes. "You two are never getting out of this house again, you hear me! Just to school and back, and that's it! And I don't ever want to see you around that Sutherby boy again! If he was grown, I'd kill him! He better be glad he's still a minor, so he can hide behind his granny's skirts."

He stooped down to Alyssa as his rank breath hit her in the face. "Looks like you didn't fare too well yourself, missy," he said with a smirk on his thin lips. "Your little boyfriend sure didn't protect you, did he? And don't be tellin' anybody what happened either! I don't want it getting around town some sniveling ass kid gave me a black eye. This never would have happened if I hadn't been half asleep from waiting up on you two little sluts!"

Alyssa shrank back from her father's psychotic madness.

He grabbed her shoulders and shook her hard. "Do you hear me, gal? Answer me!"

"Yes sir," she whispered, and let out a cry of pain when he shoved her hard against the wooden headboard of the bed.

"Next time you better think real hard before you lie to me again, gal," he sneered. With a loud curse, he picked their radio off the dresser and slung it against the wall. It shattered to the floor in pieces and then the door slammed shut.

"What is going on? Oh my God, your face!" Fran sat on the bed and examined her cheek.

Alyssa drew a deep breath, shaken to her core. "Daddy hit me last night, and then him and Ryan got in

49

a fight." She poured out the whole story, weeping in broken sobs.

Fran started to cry along with her. "I'm sorry, so sorry, sis. I didn't mean to get drunk. I never should've done those shots." she sniffed. "I'll be right back. I've got to get you some ice for your face, it is so swollen." She hugged her tight and left out of the room.

Alyssa barely noticed; she was too upset. Not see Ryan again? She couldn't fathom the thought. Besides Fran, he was the only one she truly cared about. She straightened her shoulders determinedly, it would be impossible to keep them apart. After all, there was school, and…

Alyssa began crying again, unable to deal right now with the hopelessness of it all.

****

Meanwhile down the road, Ryan felt like he was on the verge of losing his mind. He was worried sick about Alyssa. He had to know how she was, if she was okay. Had her father took out his fury on her? Christ, what if he had? A cold sweat broke across his forehead at the thought of Alyssa pitted against Billy Martin. For all her bravery, she stood no chance against that madman.

He strode out in the yard and stared helplessly down the road towards her house, not quite sure what he was expecting to see. His stomach coiled in knots as he deliberated what to do. It was Saturday, and he had to be at work at noon. Dammit. He slammed his hand against the side of the screened in porch.

Nana turned from where she was working in her flower garden and frowned. "Ryan, honey, what's the matter with you? You rattled the whole porch just now."

"Nana, would you do me a favor?" He could send her down there with some fresh vegetables or something, and while she was there, she could check on Alyssa...

Ryan's mouth flattened in a straight line as he shook his head. "Never mind." He couldn't risk sending his grandmother to the Martin's house. There was no telling what the atmosphere was like, and his conscience wouldn't allow him to send his unknowing grandmother somewhere where there was possibly danger.

She regarded his set face in bemusement. "Honey, do you need to talk about something? What's happened?"

"Nothing," he replied abruptly, and strode back into the house with long strides.

Later on at work, he stocked while his brain churned constant thoughts about Alyssa. The anxiety was eating him alive. He spied Candice mopping near the register, and walked over to her.

"Hey, could you call and check on Alyssa and Fran? Fran wasn't feeling good last night, and I want to make sure they're both alright."

She gave him a curious look. "Uh sure, soon as I go on break."

"Thanks."

An hour later, she came over to where he was stocking cereal. "No one answered."

"Alright," he said quietly as his fingers crushed a box in his hand.

The rest of the weekend was spent in agony. He went to the river Sunday just in case Alyssa showed up, not surprised to see she didn't. Undoubtedly, her parents

51

had her on lock down.

Ryan thought long and hard about sneaking over there at night, but what if Billy was up? He probably expected him to do just that. Blame set in, although he didn't regret knocking Billy out. He'd had it coming, and had for a long time. But who was paying the price for such a prize? Surely not the girl he loved; the one who was blameless in all of this.

Ryan's pulse raced as he thought their night on the bank of the levy. Never had he experienced such passion, the warmth of Alyssa's lips set him on fire.

His stomach dropped to the pit as he thought. Had he made it impossible to fulfill the love that burned stronger, hotter, than anything he'd ever experienced before? No, he thought furiously. Destiny had led them to the other, and he'd be damned if he'd ever let her go.

****

Ryan jumped out of bed Monday morning, and bounded up the steps of the bus after it squealed to a stop in front of his house. As it rumbled down the gravel road, he breathed a sigh of relief when he saw the sisters out there waiting.

Fran boarded first, followed by Alyssa.

His breath froze in disbelief when he saw her face. Alyssa's cheek was purplish red and horribly swollen, her left eye practically swelled shut. He whispered her name in agonized horror as she sat down beside him on the seat.

"Are you okay? What's happened?" he said in a low voice, and clenched her hand in his.

She shook her head; long, golden hair forming a curtain from prying eyes. "Daddy said I can't go anywhere except to school, and I can't see you anymore."

"He can't do that," he told her fiercely. "He can't be there all the time, we'll find a way."

"I don't know… they've been watching me like a hawk. I can't even go outside without Mama following me. It's been terrible." Her voice broke and a lone tear streaked down her injured skin.

Ryan wiped it away with a gentle fingertip. "Please don't cry, Alyssa. I can't handle it when you do. Especially when you look like this. Dammit," he breathed in a harsh whisper. He closed his eyes, and blotted out the marred perfection of her face while gulping for air in his tight, overcrowded chest.

She rubbed his hand and drew his attention back to her. "Is that better?" she smiled.

"Yes. That's my girl." He reached out a hand to run it down the shining length of her soft, thick hair. He shook his head as he studied her, he was sure her face hurt like hell. "Have you been putting ice on that?" he demanded.

"You sound like Fran," she said with a small smile, and rubbed her swollen cheek carefully. "It feels better than it did. The first day was the roughest. Oh my goodness, I had the worst headache of my entire life."

Ryan sucked in a sharp breath and gritted his teeth, wishing he'd taken a bat to Billy Martin. "Your dad had better look worse than you do."

"Oh, he does," she assured him with a nod. "His jaw is black and blue, and so is his eye. And if you think my face is swollen, you should see his! I don't know what he's going to tell the guys he works with."

"I doubt the truth," he said dryly.

"Oh no, he told me and Fran we had better not say

who hit him." She shrugged her shoulders jerkily. "I hope he's embarrassed."

Ryan shook his head again. "That sorry bastard should be ashamed. Look at what he did to you." He jerked his free arm furiously toward her face.

"I know," she said in a barely audible voice and his heart broke at her fragility, held together by a mix of determination and pure nerve. A tear splashed down on top of their linked hands.

"He doesn't care that he hurt me. And neither does Mama." Rage flowed like all consuming lava through her veins at her mother's indifference, and the old ache pierced anew.

Ryan made a sound of despair from beside her, and she leaned against his strong shoulder. "I care," he said huskily against her ear.

"I know you do," she whispered, and swallowed tears back.

"Alyssa, I have a job. I can find you and Fran a cheap place-"

"No!" Alyssa lifted her head up so quickly a knifelike pain shot through it. "You don't have to do that, Ryan. That would cost a lot of money, and we don't even have a car or anything."

"I will soon."

"You won't if you get us a place. I swear, if anything else happens, me and Fran are going to figure something out."

Ryan grasped her hand tightly, his jaw rigid. "No, you're going to tell me. And then we'll figure it out, together. Alright?"

"Alright." She pulled her hair forward to frame her face. "I'm just going to tell the teachers I tripped and fell against something if they ask. Do you think that'll work?"

Ryan raised his eyebrows, and tried to keep a neutral face as he studied her battered face. Billy, you worthless piece of shit. "Uh, maybe."

Alyssa squared her small shoulders determinedly. "Well, it just has to. I'll keep my head down most of the time anyway, and I won't put my hair up. I'm not going to miss school, because then I won't see you at all."

"It'll work," he agreed then, not able to consider that possibility. The bus pulled up to the school, and he squeezed her hand. "I love you."

"Love you too," she answered quietly.

CHAPTER 5

When not at work at Mack's, Ryan worked on impressing the scouts with LaDarius out on the practice field. He went through the motions of taking the ball, practicing his drop back, to finding him deep on an outside route. They ran a few of their favorites from the old, blue notebook Coach always carried on the sideline, and each time Ryan hit LaDarius at different depths. The sun hung low in the pink and gray streaked sky of the cool November evening as they finished up.

"Thanks for practicing with me, man." Ryan caught the football and walked towards his friend. "Hey, didn't you say you had to leave before dark?"

"Hell, I'm wore out now." LaDarius flexed his arms out. "And I'm supposed to take Susan to the movies."

"Aw, quit whining. That was the same as a regular practice."

"True. You ain't no tougher than Coach, that's for sure." LaDarius caught his keys in the air and grinned. "Ryan, ole buddy, I'll see you later."

"Y'all have fun." Ryan felt a stab of envy. He would love to take Alyssa to the movies, but he might as well try to fly to the moon, he thought grimly.

For the last couple of months, they'd seen each other only on the bus ride to school. They always sat together and talked, but he could sense a change in

Alyssa. She was withdrawing from him and there was nothing he could do about it. He gripped the football hard, anxious and unsettled from the thought. She barely smiled anymore; he hadn't seen the dimples he loved so much in ages. Her high cheekbones were much more pronounced, and purplish shadows shone translucently from under her striking eyes. He worried about her, about her state of mind.

He felt so damn helpless, unable to change the situation, but wanting to so badly. It was a no win situation. If they were caught together, she would suffer. But by not seeing each other, the same unfair punishment occurred. He raked his hand through his hair in frustration. At least he could still go places, see his friends. Alyssa could do none of those things.

Her birthday was in three days, on the 12th. His chest hurt anew at the thought that he couldn't celebrate it with her. She was turning seventeen; they'd be the same age for two weeks. They'd always laughed about that before, but Alyssa wasn't doing much laughing these days.

It made him so angry every time he thought about how things had turned out. It was a hell of a thing to discover the wonder of love, and then to have it snatched so cruelly away.

"Ryan!" Jeremy jogged his way. "Thought I'd find you here," he grinned. "Dude, you won't believe it, but Fran and Alyssa are waiting for us at the levy."

"What!"

"Yeah, their parents went to some retirement party over at the lumberyard, and they'll be gone for a long time. You know how those guys get." Jeremy nodded knowingly.

"Man, that's the best news I've had in a long time," Ryan smiled.

"Me too. Man, I can't stand Billy's drunk ass. I'll be glad when Fran moves in with my cousin. Alyssa should, too. I can't see her being there without Fran."

Ryan frowned. "No, me either. Listen, I'm gonna run in and change. Be back in a flash."

****

Country music pumped through the night air, and a large bonfire blazed in the midst of the darkness. Ryan stopped and searched through the many people. And then he saw her, long hair shining like an amber waterfall in the firelight as she talked with Fran and some other girls. With long strides, he walked straight towards them.

"Hi, Alyssa."

She spun around and gasped, "Ryan!"

Enfolding her in his arms, he closed his eyes and took deep breaths of her sweet honey scent. "Let's go see the river," he murmured in her ear.

They linked hands, and Alyssa called out goodbyes to the laughing girls. The stars shone above in the cool, clear sky, illuminating the grassy bank of the levy they sat upon.

"Ryan, I am so happy to see you."

He groaned, and reached over to pull her in his lap. Joy exploded in her soul as his muscled arms surrounded her. "Me too, Lyssa, me too. I've missed you. It hasn't been the same." She turned her face into his broad shoulder and inhaled his clean, masculine aroma.

"You smell good," she said with a grin.

"Yeah, I just got out of the shower. I was at the

field practicing with LaDarius when Jeremy came and told me the news. Are you sure they're going to be gone for a long time?"

"Yes, they'll be there forever, trust me. Mama won't be able to drag him away before midnight, not when he's with all his drinking buddies," she assured him.

His furrowed brows relaxed. "Good."

He drew her face up, gently kissing her, and her pulse leaped. Threading her fingers through his thick hair, Alyssa dragged him closer. She wanted more, more of him. Her lips caressed his, nipping invitingly, and he moaned her name. She traced the outline of his sensuous lips before sliding in the hot recesses of his mouth. Their tongues tangled, dancing wetly, and he groaned raggedly against her. Excited chills shot down her back, and she held tighter on to him.

The caressing movements of their tongues he had taught her grew wilder and deeper till she thought she would faint from the pleasure. Reluctantly, she tore her lips from his. Pressing her lips to the sensitive hollow in his throat she licked, tasting the saltiness of his skin, and felt him shudder against her. His heart was pounding against her, and she wondered if he could feel her racing pulse.

"Alyssa," he breathed. "You're killing me."

"Well, at least you'll die happy," she smirked impishly.

"I don't know about that," he half- groaned, half-laughed. Shifting her over in his lap, her rounded eyes met his ones wonderingly.

"Yeah…" he said wryly.

"Oh," she whispered. "I'm sorry, Ryan."

He rubbed the soft contours of her mouth with gentle strokes, admiring her unparalleled perfection. Her hair lay in silken, shiny waves around her face and down her back, framing the pale cameo of her face in the moonlight.

"Not your fault, sweetheart. You can't help what you do to me."

His hands ran up and down her sides, caressing her gentle curves. Kissing the tip of her nose, he smiled, feeling as if a giant burden had been lifted off his chest. There was no other person he'd rather be with in the world. Her lips curved radiantly and he kissed each dimple, so grateful to see a real smile cross her winsome face.

"I love you, you know," he said huskily, looking deep into her glowing eyes.

"I know," she grinned.

"Hey, that's not what you're supposed to say!" He tickled her till she shrieked. "Now say it," he growled playfully in her ear.

"I love you too, you big baby," she laughed. She started tickling him where she knew he was the most ticklish on his ribs. They laughed and rolled around on the cool ground, each trying to get the best of each other.

"Stop Ryan, I can't breathe!" He paused, and she jumped on him again. "Tricked you!"

Their laughter rang out across the riverbank, and even the half-moon high above seemed to smile with mirth at their antics.

"Come on Ryan, let's quit being antisocial." Alyssa stood up and tugged at his hand.

"Hey, I can't help it if I want to keep you all to

myself." He circled his strong fingers around her wrist and instead pulled her back down in his lap, not ready to abandon this private stolen time with her just yet.

"Ryan!" she laughed.

"I'm going to kidnap you, that's what I'm going to do," he said into her fragrant cloud of hair.

"You're crazy!"

"Nope, just crazy about you," he murmured.

"Hmph," she teased, feeling her heart soar. She laid her hand on his bristly jaw and looked in his deep blue eyes, soft with love for her. The question she'd been afraid to ask for weeks popped into her mind. "Ryan…what's going to happen when you go away to college next year?"

He straightened up and rested his chin on top of her head. "What do you mean?"

"Well, I'll be here and you'll be…there." she said hesitantly.

"I'll be home some, when I can."

This was like pulling teeth. "But, I mean, between…us?"

Ryan said nothing for a long moment. "Well, I really haven't thought about it. But don't worry, Alyssa, I'll always be here for you. I don't want anything to happen to you, I worry about you."

She stilled, stunned by his revelation. Those weren't exactly the words she'd expected to hear come out of his mouth. "Is that what I am to you, Ryan, some kind of charity case?" She jumped up out of his lap and dodged his staying hand. "Oh, poor little Alyssa, with her horrible parents," she mocked, her voice rising. He rose above her, a dark frown hardening his handsome features.

"Alyssa, that's not what I meant at all and you know it!" he ground out, amazed at her fury.

"I don't want or need your sympathy or help. I never asked for it! You can just go your way, and I'll go mine," she cried out.

"No, that's not about to happen, Alyssa" he bit out, angry now. A muscle ticked in his jaw as he studied her mutinous expression. Clasping her hand, he pulled her close to him.

"You already said you haven't even thought about us when you go away. Just leave me alone!" She twisted in his embrace.

"What do you want me to say? I don't know what college I'm going to yet, don't even know what damn state I'm going to be in! But I'm not staying in this one horse town. I have big plans, and they're never going to happen here in this godforsaken place!" he replied harshly, and watched her face blanch through narrowed slits.

She jerked free, glaring at him. "I've never asked you to stay, have I? Do you think you're the only one with dreams? I'm going to be a nurse, and I know I'll be a damned good one! Maybe that's not as cool as some hotshot football star, but at least I'll be helping people instead of running up and down a field, throwing some stupid ball. Admit it, Ryan! You feel sorry for me, you do! I can see it in your eyes sometimes, by how you look at me." Alyssa started to cry, humiliated by the realization.

"I…I don't feel sorry for you, not exactly."

"Oh!" she gasped in shock. How dare he *pity* her. "I can take care of myself. As soon as we're able, we're moving in with Jeremy's cousin, Casey. She needs someone to help pay the bills, and we're all going to split it." She hugged herself, feeling chilled to the core.

"That's good." he answered quietly.

"Yes, it's *great*." she stressed. Facing him with a stormy look, she put her hands on her hips. "Then you won't have to worry about me anymore, will you? You can take off to that big city that's going to make you so happy!"

He walked towards her slowly, and placed his hands on her shoulders. "Alyssa, I don't know why you're acting this way. You're blowing this all out of proportion," he said soothingly, as if speaking to a small child.

Blood rushed to her head in a hurricane of emotions. "No, I'm not! How would you feel if the person you were in a relationship with felt *sorry* for you, Ryan? Like I'm some stray dog on the side of the road. You wouldn't like it either! That's what this is all about, isn't it?"

"What are you talking about now?" An annoyed scowl crossed his face.

"Us!" she screamed, wanting to smack him. "I see it all perfectly now! This never would have gotten started if you hadn't pitied me!"

His eyebrows shot up in surprise, and he felt like shaking some damn sense into her. "Alyssa, listen to yourself! Okay, so I do feel sorry for you! That makes me a bad person, or something?" he countered furiously. His jaw hardened as his hands tightened on her.

"No, but we began on the wrong foot, I realize that now. I want to be with someone who cares for me because of who I am, not because they feel the need to save me," she cried out, tears streaming down her flushed cheeks.

"I do! Dammit!"

He spun in the direction of the moonlit river. His hands flexed at his side, he felt like punching something out of pure frustration. Ryan took a deep breath as he tried to think of what to say to her, something that would make her understand the depth of his love for her. And while he was it, point out to Alyssa the sheer absurdness of her reaction. His teeth gritted. The sound of footsteps caught his attention, and he spun around to see her running back down the levy, long hair flowing out behind her.

"Alyssa!" His shout echoed across the dark, but she didn't slow down.

****

"What's wrong?"

"Can we just leave now? Please, Fran."

"Uh, sure. Jeremy, we've gotta go." After pulling away from the levy, Fran twisted around in the front seat. "What happened between you and Ryan?"

Alyssa shook her head silently, staring out the window. *How could I have been so stupid? Why didn't I realize it before?* And how cruel of him to admit he hadn't even thought about their future when he went away to college. Was this was some sort of fling to him, just something to occupy his time until he left?

Once home, she took a soothing hot bath and cried her eyes out privately, her soul torn. Gazing at her red, swollen face in the mirror, she took a deep breath. *Get a grip.* It was time to focus on her life, and stop dreaming about something that could never be. Ryan had no plans to stay or return here, he'd made that clear. She couldn't fathom leaving Fran and her friends; she liked living in Cypress Bayou. She loved the friendliness, the small town feel. She didn't understand why Ryan was so desperate to leave it.

Not that he'd asked her to leave with him, anyway. She'd meant what she told him, she had no desire to be pitied. So her life was hard sometimes, so what? There were people who had it way worse than she did, look at those poor children in Africa. Ryan was just an incredibly lucky person, his grandmother thought he walked on water, and he'd been blessed with extraordinary athletic talent. She'd always thought he had a fey-like handsomeness, with his thick, midnight black hair and startling clear, blue eyes. He had no shortage of friends, heck, half the school idolized him.

It was maddening, really. Of course he was drawn to her; she probably intrigued him with her not-so-perfect life. "Oooh!" she fumed, and banged her hairbrush down on the counter. Alyssa stormed out of the bathroom, furious once more.

****

Ryan stared at the ceiling, unable to sleep. *How in the hell had things gotten so messed up*? One minute, everything was great, and the next, out of control. He'd realized it was a mistake to say he felt sorry for her the second the words were out of his mouth. She had her pride, he knew, and he'd shattered it by admitting that. But dammit, he refused to apologize for his admission. She had overreacted, that was all.

He leaned over to his nightstand drawer, and pulled out a black velvet box. The emerald necklace he'd bought for her birthday twinkled merrily at him while he studied it, his jaw ticking. Hopefully, this would help

Dara Morris

mend things between them. He'd had to dip into his precious savings to buy it. He wondered if she'd appreciate his sacrifice, but remembering her anger earlier, was definitely not going to point it out to her.

The next morning, Fran woke her up by shaking her shoulder. "Guess what?"

Alyssa rolled over and blinked sleepily at her sister. "What?"

"Mama said we could go with Megan to the movies today!"

"Really?" She sat up, wide awake now.

Fran smiled and nodded her head. "Would I kid about something as serious as this?"

"Wow, they're releasing the prisoners? Must be a pardon for good behavior," Alyssa snorted sardonically.

"Yeah, I guess so." Fran laughed. "I'm just glad to be getting out of this house. I'm about to go stir crazy sitting in here! Hey, what happened between you and Ryan last night?"

Alyssa sighed and gathered her tousled hair over her shoulder. "Fran, how would you feel if you found out somebody felt sorry for you, pitied you?"

Fran glanced away for a moment. "I wouldn't like it. That's not very flattering."

"No, it's not." Alyssa swallowed down the hard lump in her throat. "Well, last night I found out that's how Ryan feels about me, and so we got in a big argument. And I don't plan on seeing him anymore. He's leaving soon, so I don't see the point of getting so attached. My heart is just going to be broke in the end." Her voice trailed off and she picked at the covers, tears filling her eyes.

"Oh sis, I'm so sorry."

Alyssa pressed her trembling lips together. "Me too."

They ate a bowl of cereal at the table, Fran chattering happily about finally getting to go somewhere. Daddy wasn't up yet; Alyssa had heard him stumble in around one in the morning.

She rinsed her bowl out and went to her room. Studying herself in the mirror, she looked older, wiser somehow. Was it because she turned seventeen in two days?

Fran came in and regarded her with a serious expression. "Are you feeling any better?"

"I don't know, last night I was so mad at Ryan, but now…I'm going to miss him a lot when he leaves."

Fran patted her hand. "You know, there is such a thing as a long distance relationship!"

"But he's not coming back, Fran, and I don't want to leave. Where does that leave us?" Alyssa's heart clenched as if in a vice.

"Well, I don't know," Fran said with a shake of her head.

Mama hollered from her room and broke their pensive conversation. "Fran, Alyssa, call for the ambulance! Your daddy's not waking up!"

"What?" Alyssa stared at her sister in open-mouthed shock before she ran to the phone and dialed 911 breathlessly.

Fran and Mama were beside him when she rushed into the room. Alyssa felt an awful foreboding grip her as she peeked at her still-as-a-stone father, his skin a sickly shade of gray. She dropped to her knees beside the bed and grasped her sister's hand.

The paramedics rushed in with a stretcher and began checking for a pulse. After a few minutes, one straightened up and looked at Mama. "I'm sorry, ma'am, but he's passed away. Most likely sometime during the night, I would say."

Their mother let out a loud cry and collapsed to her knees. She and Fran went to her as the paramedics loaded their father on a stretcher, and pulled a white sheet over his face. The finality of it hit her as they rolled him out the door. She had never really known her father, couldn't remember any kindness from him. What a terrible legacy to leave behind for your family. Alyssa shivered as an icy finger trailed its way up her spine.

Startled when the phone began to ring, she walked slowly to answer it. It was one of their neighbors wanting to know what was going on. Alyssa told him and no sooner had she put the phone down, it rang again. She ignored it, knowing it was only more people being nosy.

Going to the living room window, she stared unseeingly out at the swing.

****

Ryan heard the loud shrill of sirens, and walked outside. Without another thought, he sprinted down the road, his mind churning frantically as he ran.

What was wrong? Please, not Alyssa.

He pounded up the way for what seemed like miles and stopped when he saw an ambulance leave the Martin yard, no lights flashing.

The front door flung open with a bang and Alyssa ran to him, ponytail streaming out behind her. He hugged her slender body close as a tidal wave of relief swept through him.

He drew back to look down at her pale face. "Why was the ambulance here? What in the hell is going on?"

"Daddy passed away," she whispered unevenly.

Ryan stared at her in surprise; he had just seen the sorry drunk at the store the other day. He'd looked fine to him.

"I don't know what it was, maybe his heart or something. He just didn't wake up. The paramedics said he passed in his sleep. And Mama slept beside him last night." Horrified, wide green eyes flew to his.

Ryan shook his head gravely, not wanting her to see his giddiness. After all, Billy was her father. "I'm sorry, Alyssa."

She dropped her head back against his damp shirt. "Thanks," she replied after a long absence of time. With a sigh, she looked toward the house. "I'm going to head back in. Mama is really upset."

"Okay." Tipping her chin up, he gave her a gentle kiss on the lips. "If you need to talk…if you need anything, I'm here for you. Call me." She gave him a faint smile that squeezed his heart with its sweetness.

"I will," she replied softly.

Somewhat pacified, he let her go and watched as she walked inside, slight shoulders slumped.

Three days later, the small and simple funeral was held. Relatives Alyssa hadn't seen in ages arrived to pay their respects, along with men from the lumberyard and most of their neighbors.

Alyssa studied the somber lines of Ryan's handsome face as he entered the funeral home, wondering what was going through his mind. *Was he relieved*?

As for herself, she just felt numb. Voices drifted around her and she nodded at what she thought was the appropriate place, wishing this day to be over with. She couldn't bear to look at her father lying in the silver casket; it disturbed her to know they'd never had a good relationship, and never would. It just didn't seem right to her somehow. It was finished, but then everything was finished where Billy Martin was concerned. He was no longer able to inflict his own brand of wickedness upon his family. Her feelings swam in a frenzied turmoil.

When the time came to walk by the casket, she focused on the pretty flowers instead. Her gaze flicked over to Ryan and she swallowed hard, struck by the brilliant spark of blue fire in his eyes.

At last, the service was done and the three of them went home in the old truck. Mama walked slowly in the house as Alyssa examined her hollow cheeks in concern. "Mama, I'm going to fix you something to eat. People have been dropping off all kinds of yummy things."

"Just a little," she replied in a low voice.

Alyssa went to the refrigerator and placed several covered dishes to place on the counter. Everybody in town had been so nice, so sympathetic...as if Billy Martin wasn't the town drunk. Alyssa squirmed inwardly, had she missed something that others had seen in him?

"Mmm, cheesy spaghetti." Fran dropped a big scoop on her plate, and broke her grim reverie.

"Mama, here's some chicken with dressing." Mama stared down in silence, and picked up her fork. Alyssa caught Fran's attention at the kitchen table. "I'm going to sit outside on the swing. I need some fresh air."

The brisk wind rejuvenated her, warmed her inside despite the chill. She pulled her knees up to her chest and studied the dim house across the yard, peace flooding her soul. No longer could a monster haunt the rooms with his evil whims, and destroy the tender, green girls who had no choice in their dwellings.

CHAPTER 6

"Ryan, come have a talk with me in my office."
Coach Anderson gestured from the sidelines.

"I'll be back." Ryan threw LaDarius the football.
They were warming up for the night's game that was in
a couple of hours.

Coach Anderson beamed as he walked in. "I've got
great news, son." "You've got an offer from New York
State. I just got off the phone with the AD, and they're
offering you a full scholarship with everything
included, the whole works. I can't tell you what to do,
but I think you should take it. With this being a small
school and all, this is the only offer on the table and it's
a damned good one. What do you think?" he asked
eagerly.

Ryan pumped his fist in the air as an exhilarated
grin broke across his face. "New York! Where do I
sign?"

Coach clapped him on the back. "I'm proud of you,
son. You've worked hard for this, and you're one of the
finest players I've had the pleasure to coach."

Coming from Coach Anderson, that was a huge
compliment and Ryan felt humbled by the praise. "I
couldn't have done it without you, Coach. Everything
you've taught me will stay with me, and carry on to my
college playing years. Thank you," he said sincerely.

Coach gave him a fierce bear hug, and Ryan felt a

touch of sadness that he'd no longer be playing for this wonderful man. He knew everything would be different in college, a whole new ballgame.

On his way home that night, he stopped by Alyssa's. He hadn't seen her all week, except for at the funeral. She'd seemed lost in her own remote world, as if she was just going through the motions. He'd kept his attention fastened on her during the service but she hadn't noticed, except for once. Even there, at that unlikely place, sparks of electricity had flown between them.

How to tell her he was leaving, he wondered, when she never even wanted to talk about it? And to New York, at that. So far away, practically across the country. His heart ached as he thought of the hundreds of miles that would separate them. The necklace lay in his pocket; he'd grabbed the box out of the drawer before he left. Feeling nervous and unsure, he shifted his feet as he stood there in the dark.

Before he'd gathered his resolve, Alyssa opened the door and his mouth went dry. Clad in a flowing white robe with the light shining behind her, she looked the picture of an angel. Golden streaked hair flowed down her back softly, and her luminous green eyes glowed. *All that's missing is the halo.*

He cleared his throat and said hoarsely, "Happy late birthday, Alyssa."

"Thanks. I saw you through the window." She smiled, dimples creasing her flawless cheeks.

Dear God, this is going to be hard. And tell me again why I want to leave? "Uh, can you come outside? I need to talk to you."

She tilted her head curiously and nodded. "Sure,

just let me grab my shoes."

They sat on the swing, and Alyssa tucked her shapely legs underneath her. "How is everything? I've missed you these last few days." He tried to ignore the lust surging through every nerve of his body and looked down at his hands.

"Well, it's been a rough week. Mama is taking it harder than I expected, really. I don't know, maybe that's awful to say, but it's the truth."

"I can certainly understand that," he replied dryly.

"She's talking about selling the house and moving in with her cousin, Janice. We told her we want to move in with Casey, and she was okay with it. I don't want to stay here anymore. Too many bad memories," she said quietly. She rubbed her face wearily and drew a shaky breath. "I can't wait to move. I hate living here, I really do."

He took her icy hand, and rubbed it soothingly between his.

"I'm sorry for being such a jerk the other night." Her voice was so low now he could barely hear her.

Seeing him here, Alyssa suddenly couldn't remember why she was so mad the other night. Her senses screamed to be closer to him, his masculinity was overwhelming her. Her resolve not to see him again disintegrated.

"Shhhh, it's over now. It doesn't matter."

He took her in his strong arms, and his hands slid into the hair at her nape. Leaning against his hard chest, Alyssa closed her eyes. His simple presence brought her so much comfort, she thought gratefully. She'd been so agitated, warring with her emotions towards her parents.

She snuggled against his muscled, hard body, loving the way he felt, and the way he made her feel. It was like she couldn't get close enough to him, and she wished she could stay in the safe haven of his arms forever. Her gloominess floated away like a dandelion in the wind.

He smelled irresistibly good and she inhaled deeply, relishing his musky, spicy scent. It was cool, but Ryan's body heat melded with her own, creating an inferno deep within.

He tipped his head down to speak and unable to resist, she caught his lips in hers, nipping seductively at his delicious bottom lip. The kiss exploded like wildfire, leaping and bounding out of control, destroying all obstacles.

Ryan clasped her to him possessively, slanting his lips over her hungrily. Their tongues met in a passionate dance, over and over again, and Alyssa gasped, raggedly moaning his name. He pressed his lips to the slim column of her throat, raining frantic kisses back to her mouth. She tasted so good, so right, he couldn't get enough. A light flicked on in the house, and he ended their kiss with a sharp sense of loss.

"I'm sorry, I…I know this isn't a good time for this," he said huskily, and straightened safely away from her. What was the matter with him, he reproached himself, her father dead not a week ago, and he was behaving like a randy buck.

"It's okay." She smiled at him and stroked his chest, nuzzling her soft body closer to him. He closed his eyes and fought to control his labored breathing. Her smallest caresses aroused him beyond endurance and he placed his hand over hers, stilling her motions abruptly.

"Stop, Alyssa."

Her golden brows crinkled, and he dragged his eyes away from the sight of her swollen, reddened lips.

"I was just rubbing your chest, good grief," she said impatiently.

"I know, but..." he trailed off. She was too innocent; she had no idea what she did to him.

"Well, there. Is that better?" she demanded, and scooted over to the far side of the swing.

"Get back over here," he growled, and hauled her back to his side. She was torturing him, he thought morosely, every time he touched her, he just wanted more, and more...

Pulling himself from his wayward thoughts, he laid his head back on the swing. The blanket of stars above the tall pine trees cast a soft, lulling glow around them, and Ryan inhaled the sharp aromas deeply in his tight lungs. He kept a firm grip on her as she squirmed against him, until finally glaring down at her. "Would you keep still?"

"Of all the nerve!" she huffed. "I move over because you don't want me touching you, so you manhandle me back over to you, and then have the audacity to tell me to be still! I wish I was a big, strong football player so I could pay you back," she griped playfully at him.

"Well, I'm very glad you're not." he laughed.

She grinned back and poked him in the ribs.

Catching her hand in his, he kissed her palm. "Nope, too soft and little." He ran his hands down her gentle curves and shook his head. "You're too girly. Sorry. You wouldn't make it a day out there." He grinned in her indignant face.

"Hmmm, doesn't look too hard to me, just running and throwing that ole' football," she quipped, an affectionate smile curving her lips.

"Babe, it's harder than it looks. Believe me."

"I was just kidding. I know you work very hard," she agreed, and kissed him lightly on the mouth.

He ran his tongue over his lips, savoring the taste of her.

"So, who won tonight? Wait, let me guess." She held a finger over his mouth and his lips quirked in amusement. "The Pirates!"

He nodded and nibbled at her finger.

"I knew it. The whole town loves you, you know." Her cool hand curled up to his nape.

"What about you?"

"Oh Ryan, I do," she whispered back. "You don't even have to ask."

His gut tightened till it hurt. It was bittersweet, hearing what he knew to be true shining forth from her expressive face. His breath caught as he examined the beauty of her, the goodness and sweetness she possessed. He'd always known she was there, just down the road, how on earth could he bear to leave this cxquisitc girl? Swallowing hard, he framed her delicate face with his hands.

"I love you, Alyssa Kay Martin, and don't you ever forget it," he said huskily, the emotion surging within him making his hands shake. He had a sudden, aching, feeling that when he left, she would change somehow.

His eyes devoured her, committing to memory her guileless face. "I love your eyes, Lyssa. You are so beautiful," he whispered.

She felt the muscles in his forearms grow taut. "Something's wrong, I feel it. What's happened?"

Ryan's hands dropped and he stared straight ahead in the darkness. "I've gotten a scholarship."

"Where?" she breathed.

"New York State. It's in East Stansbury, New York."

Alyssa stayed quiet for a long moment, her heart racing. "Congratulations."

His head whipped towards her. "That's all?"

Alyssa saw red. Glaring at him in furious indignation, she jumped up out of the swing. "What the hell do you want me to say, Ryan? I'm so happy for you? I'm glad you got it so you can leave? Great job? Have fun in New York? What?" she screamed.

"All of the above, except for the glad I'm leaving part." He stood up, noting how small she was compared to him, not that she gave a damn. Her angry glare shot daggers up at him, and she looked as if she could cheerfully decapitate him.

"This is funny to you? You're moving hundreds of miles away, and you have the gall to mock me?" She pushed his chest hard with her hands, ticked off to see he didn't even budge. He just stood there in the darkness, gazing down at her with an unreadable expression on his lean, chiseled face.

She closed her eyes, unable to look at him without breaking down. He didn't understand her, not at all. Her throat hurt from unshed tears as she whispered, "I'm going in now. Good night."

She felt like the whole world was closing in on her, and she just wanted to lie in bed with the covers pulled tightly around her. He might as well be moving to

Australia. New York was so far away, she certainly couldn't drive up there for a weekend and neither could he drive home. A myriad of images ran through her brain, piling one horror onto another.

What will he see in a hick like me once he gets around all those sophisticated girls up North? He's so handsome; they'll be following him around like puppy dogs. And he's a quarterback?

Alyssa swallowed convulsively. Strange, she'd thought she'd resigned herself to the fact he was leaving. But hearing the actual words… She steeled herself and walked quickly past him to the house.

"Alyssa, wait!"

Not bothering to slow down when she heard footsteps behind her, she gasped when his strong grip brought her to a standstill.

"Now wait a damn minute before you storm off! You knew this was coming! I don't know why you're so mad at me." Glacial blue eyes gleamed furiously at her in the moonlight.

"You don't know?" she choked disbelievingly. "Because I care about you, you idiot! And I don't want you to leave; I want you to stay, Ryan."

He raked his hand wildly through his hair in that familiar, irritated gesture, and she flinched in hurt from the annoyed flash of anger that crossed his face.

"Alyssa… don't do this. Not now. Hey, I got you a present for your birthday." She shook her head mutely at him and bit her lip so hard he saw a bright drop of blood appear. *Lips I just cherished with my own.* Ryan gazed deep into her huge, shattered eyes and felt as if he was being torn in two. But he had to go, he had to. Tears splashed onto his hand as he tried to wipe them away.

"Sweetheart, please don't cry," he begged, his voice cracking. Ryan closed his eyes to her pain, her distress driving doubt deep into his soul. *What in the hell am I doing?*

Shaken, he pried open her clenched hand and pressed the velvet box within. "Take it," he commanded roughly. He turned his back to her anguished face and strode to the car.

Alyssa stood still for a minute, then ran to the house and slammed the door. The sound reverberated through his tormented brain and he dropped his head on the steering wheel. "Damn, damn, damn." His chest tight, Ryan felt like he was strangling as he fought to drag a measure of air into his lungs.

Alyssa buried the box in her bottom drawer and sat on the twin bed, knees pulled tight to her chest. Everyone else was asleep, thank goodness. How could it be possible he was moving all the way to New York? Were the fates working against her? Was this some sort of sign or something? She kept seeing his lean, strong face in her mind, crystalline eyes dark with emotion. She knew she wasn't seeing things, she knew Ryan loved her. So why was he so adamant about leaving? Obviously, it wasn't enough for him. He needed more, more than who and what she was. The realization stabbed through her like a double-edged sword.

The phone rang, and she rushed to answer it before anybody woke up.

"Alyssa? Did you like your present?" Ryan's deep, familiar voice sent chills through her.

"I haven't opened it, not yet."

His tone rose in exasperation as he demanded,

"Why not?"

"Because I just haven't, Ryan!" Good lord, he could make her so mad. "I will, though." She forced a gentler response.

"Alyssa, I don't like this anymore than you do. If there had been anyplace closer that would've offered, I'd have taken it in a heartbeat. I'm going to miss you and Nana... hell, I'm going to miss everyone. New York will be so different."

Alyssa gripped the telephone hard. "It will, won't it? Ryan, I-I am happy for you, truly." *There, I said it. But you didn't mean a word of it,* a little voice in her brain nagged. All of a sudden, she felt like a horrible, selfish person. There was no happy medium here; it was more of a matter of just deal with it.

"Thanks. I'm happy about it too, but... I don't want to lose you."

A shiver went through her. She had waited for these words from him earlier and he had walked away. "I don't want my heart to be broken. I don't," she whispered.

A long silence stretched over the line before his deep spoken words broke it. "I know you've been hurt in your life, but I wouldn't do that."

You already have. A sad weight settled in her chest. "Ryan...I'll be fine. You don't have to worry about me anymore. I'm going to be fine." She closed her eyes and repeated her last sentence. *Would it be true?*

"What are you saying? So what, I leave and that's it? Is that what you're fucking telling me, Alyssa?"

She flinched from his snarled, furious words. "You're the one leaving, so don't yell at me! I don't want to do this with you, round and round with no solution. Once you get up there, you'll forget all about me! Believe me, all the girls will be falling all over you, Ryan," Alyssa added caustically, picturing it vividly in her mind. With his jet black wavy hair that tousled lazily over his smooth brow, and clear blue eyes that reminded one of a summer sky, oh yes, they'd most definitely be interested.

He started to speak, but she cut him off quickly. "I don't want to wonder if..." She trailed off, realizing with a lurch she didn't trust him, not with her heart anyway.

"You wanted to leave, and now you've got your ticket to do it. So do it." She hung the phone up and wrapped her arms around her middle. *You did the right thing*, she told herself shakily. Ryan's dream in life was coming true and as long as she worked hard, hers would too.

But first, she had to get a job so could move out and buy a car. Trepidation filled her as she thought of all she had to do, and how much money it was going to take to do it. And Ryan would be gone, that was the worse reality of everything she had faced yet. Catching her trembling bottom lip hard with her teeth, she took a deep breath. *You can do this. You have to.*

****

Ryan couldn't believe what he had just heard. He stared at the phone in his hand and slammed it down. What in the hell was wrong with her? Alyssa acted like this was something new, she'd knew damn well all along that he'd planned on getting a scholarship. She must have thought he really wouldn't get one. His eyes narrowed.

And it could work between them, if she'd quit being so stubborn. He'd be home...some. He thought how far New York was, and realized the improbability of that. Once a year, twice tops. The cost of travel, and how busy football was going to keep him, plus he'd have to get a job, not to mention school...

Whispering a curse, he walked outside and sat on the porch, gazing out at the bare, dreary fields. All of a sudden, he wished it was summer already so he could get the hell out of Cypress Bayou.

.

CHAPTER 7

"Dang, sis, you are looking good!" Fran teased.

Alyssa studied her reflection in the mirror, dressed in a black sweater and matching boots that stretched up to her calves. "I take after my big sister, you know."

"Yeah, lucky for you!" Fran grinned.

She drew nervous breaths, her chest tightening the closer the bus came. But Ryan wasn't there in his regular seat. Her heart dropped.

"Hi, April. Let me in." Alyssa sat with a disappointed sigh.

"Morning. Our Christmas break just flew by, didn't it?"

"It sure did." From her vantage point, she could see the rows of filled seats behind her through the bus rearview mirror. *Where was he?*

"Hey, I saw Ryan last Wednesday at the store. I love his truck, it looks brand new!"

Alyssa made a noncommittal sound and turned towards the window so her friend wouldn't see hated tears filling her eyes. *I'm just a regular crybaby these days.* She could already guess what Ryan would say if he found out. *You already knew I was buying a truck,* he'd remind her with an angry scowl, while privately thinking she was nuts probably. But now she'd hardly see him, almost as if he was already gone.

After second period, she heard his deep laugh.

Ryan stood at his locker with a group of friends, strong and confident in a maroon pullover and khaki slacks. As if by a magnet, their gazes were drawn together in a heart-stopping collision. She didn't feel she could survive his lingering perusal and dropped her eyes.

She walked to her class, inwardly quaking, and wished she could just be alone, with no chattering voices interrupting her thoughts. The teacher began to speak and Alyssa raised her hand. "May I go to the office? I don't feel well."

Once home, she dug around for the black velvet box buried deep in her drawer. She'd tried to block out its presence before, somehow she thought of it as a good bye token, instead of a birthday gift. But she was now shamelessly desperate to see it.

"Oh, how pretty," she whispered as she saw the glimmering emerald necklace lying within and clasped it on with shaky fingers. Hopeless tears fell from her eyes and she cried till she felt literally sick, her throat hurting and her head throbbing. Exhausted, she curled into a tight ball and fell into a deep sleep.

The next day she didn't go to school, or the day after. Fran gave her a strange look when she lied and said she had a stomach bug, but said nothing.

On Wednesday, Daddy's death certificate arrived. He'd died from a brain aneurysm.

Mama skimmed over the papers and passed them back to her. "I always told your daddy he was crazy. That just proves me right." She crossed her thin arms over her chest and nodded.

Alyssa raised her eyebrows. "That's not what it means, Mama. He died because he was bleeding inside of his brain. That's what a brain aneurysm is."

"Well, he was still crazy as all get out and mean as a junk yard dog." Mama narrowed her eyes. "And you know it too."

Alyssa silently regarded her mother; she was waiting on her to answer, daring her to disagree.

As if she would.

"He made my life hell. For as long as I can remember. And you weren't much better yourself," she added, betrayed anger swarming her head and heart. Mama pinched her colorless lips together. "I had a lot on my plate, okay? You girls wouldn't understand."

With a sound of disgust, Alyssa shook her head and absently rubbed the uneven scars on her back with one hand. "Why didn't you ever do anything, Mama?" she asked shakily. She didn't have to say more, her mother knew as well as she did the times Daddy had beat her.

Mama fumbled with her lighter and lit a cigarette. "I should've. I was scared of him too, but I still should've."

"Yes, you should've." Alyssa swallowed the aching lump of resentment from her throat, and left the room.

****

Ryan noticed Alyssa's absence at the end of the first day. He'd seen her that morning, beautiful as a model fresh off the runway. Since the night he'd told her he was leaving for New York she'd steered clear of him, and this time was no different. But he knew her, knew her moods, and there was no mistaking that evasive look in her eyes.

By the third day, there was still no show of her. He didn't like this at all, something was obviously wrong.

He found Fran in the hallway after first period. "Where's Alyssa? Why hasn't she been to school?"

Fran eyed him, noting the taut set of his jaw. "She's been sick," she answered carefully.

Straight, dark brows drew together in concern. "What's the matter with her?"

She softened and shrugged her shoulders. "Stomach bug." It was beyond her why Alyssa and Ryan had split up. They made the perfect couple, childhood sweethearts and all, she thought sadly. Alyssa had a sweet, innocent beauty with her dimples and blond streaked long hair, and he was so tall and darkly handsome. She sighed inwardly... *romantic beyond words.*

Ryan's eyes narrowed on her. "Stomach bug? She's been throwing up a lot?"

"Umm...yeah." Fran nodded hastily, she hadn't expected him to ask *that.*

Ryan considered her for a long moment while she squirmed under his scrutiny. "I'm going to stop by there and show her my truck. She hasn't seen it yet."

Fran was positive Alyssa wouldn't want to see him. "Oh, I don't know if that's a-"

Ryan cut her off with a firm shake of his head. "I'll be by later."

"Well, alright," she said weakly.

CHAPTER 8

Alyssa turned from the closet and stared at her sister in dismay. "What! Why didn't you tell him I was sick, Fran?"

"I did! But Ryan said he was still coming. He said he wants to show you his truck."

"Terrific, can't wait," Alyssa grumbled. She still felt down, especially from the horrid memories that had been dredged up earlier.

"Did he say what time?" She glanced out the window. The rain had finally stopped yesterday, leaving it cold and damp. Grey clouds abounded, allowing few glimpses of the thin winter sun.

"No, he just said later."

Alyssa walked to the mirror and even to herself, she looked pale. She brushed her hair, leaving it loose down her back, and put on some lip gloss. Fran sat on the bed, watching.

"I thought you were supposed to be sick. Ryan's never going to believe you now."

Alyssa studied the necklace in the mirror and contemplated whether or not to keep it on. *It's staying,* she decided. She loved it; it was the most beautiful thing she owned. And Ryan had bought it for her...

"I'm feeling better today. He can think whatever he wants to think. I really don't care."

"If you say so," Fran said in a sing-song voice that

made her want to strangle her.

"Did you bring me my work?"

"Yeah, it's in my binder." Fran tilted her blonde head curiously. "When are you going back to school?"

"Probably tomorrow."

"Alyssa, you have to go back to school or you're going to get into trouble! You can't avoid Ryan forever."

Alyssa glared at her sister. "That's not what I'm doing, I've been sick!

"Yeah, right!"

"Don't you have something else better to do rather than irritate me?" She cocked her eyebrows at Fran and waited impatiently.

"Actually, yes I do. Me and Jeremy are going to hang out at AJ's."

"Well darn, I sure hate to hear that." Alyssa heaved a playful sigh of regret. "And how soon are you leaving?"

"Soon enough!" Fran laughed and headed towards the closet.

Alyssa felt so nervous, so on edge, she almost left too.

But for only a moment. *Ryan was coming to see her.* In no way could she ignore the thrills of nervous elation speeding through her veins.

She padded down the hallway on quiet feet and passed by Mama's bedroom. She hated to go in there; it gave her the creeps honestly. Mama's slight frame was knelt over on the floor of her closet, and Alyssa heard the sounds of boxes being moved.

I have nothing to say to that woman. What a pathetic excuse. She could have done *something.*

Alyssa didn't believe for a second that her mother had been that scared of him. After all, she'd fought back to defend herself, now hadn't she? Alyssa shook off her sadness and replaced it with determination. *I can't wait to move out this damn house. Tomorrow, I'm going to put in applications everywhere I can.*

Shadows danced across the moonlit yard as she walked across to the old swing and lay down. Her mind drifting, she gazed up at the naked branches swaying eerily above in the chilly wind. The crunch of gravel caused a hitch in her pulse.

Ryan.

She inhaled a sharp breath and shrunk back against the swing as Mama opened the front door. He was walking back to his truck when he suddenly stopped, and veered towards her.

"Were you not going to say anything?" The deep timbre of his voice sent chills rocketing through her.

She smoothed her tousled hair down and felt light headed as his tall frame towered above her. "What do you want, Ryan?"

"Oh no, not this old trick. Answer my question first." He paused, his words spoken in a terse tone. "Why, Alyssa?"

"Why what?" she asked, stalling for time, but knowing exactly what he meant. The pain she heard in his one simple question spoke to her mirrored soul, for she felt the same.

He regarded her mysterious form and how the wind whipped her long hair around the glowing cameo of her face. Even in the darkness, he could see her small body shiver, and whispered a curse under his breath before sitting down beside her.

"Why are you avoiding me?" It hurt deep in his gut to say the words; Alyssa had never avoided him, indeed just the opposite. But he was more aware of her than ever. Each time they passed, his whole body sizzled with yearning.

Her eyes glowed catlike as the minutes stretched, and the sound of her rapid, nervous breaths echoed in his ears.

Ryan inhaled deep and shook his head roughly, tortured by his sacrifice. "You know, somehow I always thought that you were the one who was broken and needed me, but it's the other way around. I need you, Alyssa," he confessed, baring his soul.

His eyes gleamed at her through the dimness, startling her with the intensity of his gaze. Alyssa gasped and wrapped her arms around him. "I love you," she whispered in his ear. Her heart felt like it was bursting with joy, and she pushed emotional tears back.

He gave her a gentle kiss, caressing her lips softly between his. "I love you too," he said in a low, husky voice.

Overpowering sensations washed over him, love, possessiveness, and the sense he was right where he was supposed to be. Nothing had ever felt more right; they merged like two halves that'd been pulled asunder. *She belongs with me*. Desire swamped through him, her seductive scent and luscious curves set him on fire. The raging, unrelenting fever he had for her was about to burst out of control he feared, an obsession only she could cure.

Snaring her long hair in his fingers, he took her soft lips in a thirsty kiss. His tongue explored the hot cavern, and sucking on her bottom lip, came back for more. Sweat broke out from the heat raging in him and he longed to strip their shirts off, and feel their naked chests pressed against each other. Wanting more, he jerked her hips against his, and she squeaked against his lips in shock from the feel of the hard ridge against her belly.

Reality returned like a bucket of cold water thrown on him and he slowed, kissing her gently on the lips, the cheek, and caught her earlobe between his teeth playfully.

She giggled, the sound like balm to his soul, and he pressed his lips to the beloved clefts in her cheeks. "We have to stop doing this, Alyssa. I can't stand it."

She stiffened against him. "What do you mean?"

"Not being together, that's what I mean. Don't you think we should enjoy what time we have together? I do. I can't be apart from you, not when you're right here."

She closed her eyes. Should she have the happiness he offered? What was at stake? *Only her heart*. Biting her lip, she looked up at him and met his steady gaze. "I think you're right."

"For once you agree with me. Hallelujah," he drawled with a smile. If she would've turned him away…well, he didn't think he would have been able to bear it. He drew his hands up under the silken mass of her hair, and stopped in surprise when he felt the clasp of a chain at her nape.

She leaned up and whispered against his lips, "I love my necklace, it's beautiful. Thank you."

"Just like you are," he murmured, and kissed her in such a passionate, private erotic dance that it had them both fighting to catch their breath when Alyssa finally pulled back. She buried her head in the hollow of his neck and his arms came around her.

"I'll never take it off," she told him long minutes later. Her eyes glistened with tears as his chest tightened from the pronounced fear he felt of losing her again.

"Promise?"

"Pinky promise." She wrapped her pinky around his and shook it.

"Pinky promise," he agreed, and kissed her little finger. "And sealed with a kiss. I want you to think of me whenever you look at it."

"I do," she replied softly.

"I thought of your eyes as soon as I saw it. Just like emeralds…" His voice stumbled, and then came to a halt. How wise was it to deepen the relationship between them when he was on the verge of leaving? As he gazed upon her lovely face, his brain grasped there was no fairness in their fate. He didn't stand a chance of staying away, no more than a hungry bee could resist a tempting, colorful flower in a desert of stark aloneness. Exhaling a deep breath, he pulled her up by their linked hands. "Come on, I want you to see my truck."

Alyssa glanced over at the silent house. "What did Mama tell you?"

"That she didn't know where you were. She said she guessed you left with Fran."

"Oh," Alyssa replied, not exactly sure what she'd expected to hear.

"I still can't believe you were going to let me leave and not even say anything." He dropped his hand and shot her a furious glare.

Guilt washed over her. "I'm sorry…Ryan, let's not

argue now. Please?"

"For now," he said darkly.

She laughed and ran the rest of the way to the red single cab truck. Ryan stalked towards her with a menacing look that turned into an irresistible smile as he came closer, and enclosed his warm hand over her cold one. Alyssa opened the passenger door and inspected the gray interior. "Wow, this is nice! Where'd you get it?"

From Mr. Wilton, a man that goes to church with Nana. It's in practically new shape; he took great care of it. I gave him a down payment, and will pay the rest of it off monthly."

"That was a good deal."

"Yeah, I think so too. Him and Nana go way back, they went to high school together." He leaned down and a warm glow filled her belly. "Come riding with me."

"Okay, let me go change first."

"I'll wait out here."

She encircled her arms around his neck to kiss him. "And I'll be right back," she smiled, and slipped out of his embrace.

He admired the sway of her hips as she walked inside, and the graceful tilt of her neck.

Alyssa came out shortly, dressed in a green v neck sweater and a silky black scarf she'd tossed casually around her shoulders. Gold hoops glittered through the waving amber of her hair, and the emerald at her throat twinkled. Finishing off the look was form fitting jeans that showed off her curves and black leather boots.

He pulled her close and inhaled her sweet scent. "Did you know you're the best looking girl I've ever seen?"

"Ryan! You are so full of it!" she laughed.

"I'm serious, you are."

She swallowed hard as she studied his somber, warm eyes, touched to her very toes. "Well, since you're the most handsome guy alive, I guess we've met our match."

"Yes, we have," he agreed, and swatted her smartly on her bottom.

"Ow! What was that for?"

"For torturing me for the last two months, that's what for. And it's not going to happen again," he growled in her startled face.

Alyssa had to bite her tongue so she wouldn't say it. *Well, you're about to leave for a whole year, so who's torturing who?* She pulled back and gestured towards the truck. *"Are we going, or are you trying to freeze me to death? Is this another part of my punishment or something?"*

Ryan arched a single black brow. "Really, Alyssa? You seemed just fine chilling out there on the swing when I got here. Literally."

She glowered at him and yanked the passenger door open.

"Better buckle up," he said with a devilish grin as he started the engine.

She snapped her seat belt with a flourish. "I planned on it."

He laughed and reached over to squeeze her knee. "Are you okay? Fran told me you were sick."

She admired his masculine profile and long, straight nose. His raven black hair had grown out some and touched upon his ears and nape in thick waves. Tanned, powerful hands gripped the wheel casually, and his broad shoulders seemed to fill half the seat. The sight of him made her whole body shiver with pulsating love.

"Well actually, I'm a lot better now," she said shyly.

He glanced her way as his bright blue eyes gleamed intuitively. "Come over here," he murmured, and she nestled against his warm body with a relieved sigh. "I'm glad you're feeling better, sweetheart," he said in a low voice near her ear.

Alyssa turned into his side, so overcome with emotion she could hardly speak. He was like a mystical touchstone, the way he steadied her fragile nerves. "Because of you, Ryan…because of you," she said simply. His muscled arm drew her closer and she shut her eyes, happiness ricocheting through her.

****

"This is so good." Alyssa licked her lips as Ryan watched in appreciation.

"That's because this diner has the best cheeseburgers in town."

"Mmmm, you're right."

Fluorescent lights above shone down on her shiny hair framing her face, and he reached across the table to tuck it behind her ears.

"Thanks. My hands are all greasy." She grinned and wiggled her fingers.

"My pleasure." He popped a French fry in his mouth.

"I'm going to see if they're hiring before I leave. I've got to find a job."

Ryan scanned the restaurant. It seemed like a decent place to work. Waitresses in old fashioned blue and white uniforms milled about busily in the crowded dining area, and the atmosphere was family friendly. "Yeah, you should. Too bad Mack's isn't hiring, though."

She stroked his hand across the table and whispered, "I love you." Her touch was like lightning bolts upon him.

Shoving his plate of food out of the way, he reached across and framed her dimpled cheeks. "And I love you." Her full lips parted sweetly, and he had to fight the urge to kiss her senseless. "I'm glad you came with me tonight, Lyssa."

"I am too," she replied, eyes glowing.

"Let's ride out to the bayou when we get done here."

Alyssa took a sip of her soda as her forehead creased in a worried frown. "I've never been out there at night."

He laughed deeply. "You'll be fine, I promise."

****

"I use this spotlight when I go fishing at night. It'll light up this whole bayou." Ryan opened his door to get out, but stopped when she grabbed his arm.

"Leave the headlights on too."

"Alright. I'll even hold your hand." An amused grin crossed his face.

She laughed and nodded. "Oh, you're definitely doing that."

Cypress trees on each side of the pier cast looming outlines over the moonlit water as they walked across the weathered boards.

Alyssa heard the rustle of night creatures and shivered. "It's spooky out here," she said in a hushed voice. Wispy, hanging gray moss blew ghostly shapes in the wind. The still water looked deep and treacherous, and hulking trees dotted as far out as one could see.

Ryan scanned the black water, and shrugged. "Naw, it's fine. Me and some guys run lines at out here at night because it's the best place for white perch. You should come with us."

"At night? With alligators?" Alyssa imagined the boat tipping over, and gators coming out of nowhere to stealthily pull them under. She shuddered and gave him an incredulous look. "You have lost your mind if you think I'm coming out here in the dark, just so we can catch some fish."

He chuckled. "It's not dark, we have lanterns."

"No thanks, I'll pass," she said with an emphatic shake of her head.

"And here I thought you liked coming fishing with me." He leaned against the railing casually. "Remember that time when we were fishing at the river and you caught that alligator gar? You thought it was a snake and screamed bloody murder. I still can't believe you threw your rod in the water."

Ryan shook his head as if her reaction had been utterly ridiculous. "I thought it would crawl up the line and bite me." She cocked her head defensively and plunked her hands on her hips.

"I was yelling for you to wait on me, but you just threw it anyway," he grumbled, and gave her a long suffering look.

"Well, I'm sorry, Ryan! I panicked! Goodness, I had no idea that that still bothered you so much."

He studied her amused, lovely face and arched an

eyebrow challengingly. "No, but I do wish you would listen to me more. Almost lost a perfectly good fishing pole that day." His voice turned low and serious as he pulled her to him. "Alyssa, I know you don't want me to leave, and I'm sorry that I am."

Her smile fell away and the spark in her luminous eyes dimmed.

"Listen to me. Listen." He gave her upper arms a light shake. "It's not going to be that bad. I don't have to leave till the middle of July, and I'm going to try my best to make it in for Christmas. And before you know it, I'll be home next summer. Alyssa, when I leave…I don't want it to be over between us."

"I don't either."

His heart swelled with love and relief.

"And I need you too, Ryan. To fill up this hole in my heart." Her voice broke as she whispered, "But I do wish you didn't have to go."

"We'll talk about it another time, okay?" Tenderness for her crowded his chest. She loved him and she didn't want him to leave her. How could he be angry at her for that? Gently enfolding her in his arms, he stroked heavy locks of hair back from her face, all the while murmuring sweet things in her ear. Alyssa leaned her soft body against him and he wished time could stand still. She was warm and familiar in his arms, and his chest tightened with the complex feelings crowding his heart and mind.

Long minutes later, she pulled back.

"What are you thinking?" It slipped out before he could help himself.

"I'm thinking that I'll wait on you forever," she vowed, sending shivers through him as her fingernails traced up and down his spine. "But... I'm terrified you'll forget about me."

He shook his head, staggered she could think that of him. "Forget about you? I don't believe in many things, but I believe in *you,* Alyssa Martin. I'll call you and write you so much, you'll be complaining because I'm getting on your nerves."

She matched his good natured smile. "I'd never complain about that." Alyssa gripped his hand hard as they walked across the shadowy boards. "There better not be any slithery reptiles pop out of that water," she muttered.

"I just hope the battery starts."

Her eyes flew to his as he lifted his broad shoulders in an easy shrug. "Ryan! Do you think it won't?" The idea of being stuck out here on the bayou at night was terrifying. No lights, and the truck dead, alligators....Alyssa didn't want to think about it.

Ryan's thoughts, on the other hand, had detoured on a darker, sensual route. Just him and her, all alone, no interruptions...

The truck started without a problem. "Well, thank God!" Alyssa exclaimed.

"You wouldn't want to spend the night out here with me?" He winked over at her and she felt her ears grow hot.

"Umm, Ryan... I don't know."

But her inner voice laughed in convulsive fits at her cowardice. There was nothing more she'd like better than to lie in his strong arms all night, feel his tall, muscled body against her naked one. She'd dreamed of it, hungered for him. But another part of her wanted to hold that last, ultimate, connection at length. Because when he left....she'd be lost to him forever, she feared. Her body and soul would belong to him, and he'd be gone, leaving her with just a shell of herself. She was afraid, deathly afraid. Even though her soul sang in joy at having him here beside her, she couldn't help but feel their precious time ticking away.

"It's okay, babe. I was just teasing you."

"Were you?"

"Well, no, not really." His eyes danced, and the crooked grin she adored broke across his handsome face.

"If things were different..." she began, and changed the subject when she saw his brows start to draw together in a scowl. "I really like your truck. It runs great."

"Yeah, I had to get something dependable that I could take to New York with me. The athletic department is going to find me a job."

Her heart dropped like an anchor to the pit of her belly. "Yes," she replied softly, "this is perfect for you."

He gave her a measuring look. "Alyssa, I'm not leaving forever. Cypress Bayou is my home."

"I know." But he'd be different, she knew that too. And he'd be back to visit, not to stay. Nothing would ever be the same.

They pulled up in her yard and she looped her arms around his neck. Their lips joined in a blazing kiss that had her tingling with need. She pulled away with a low moan as his passion clouded eyes snapped open

"What the hell..." he growled, and attempted to haul her back to him.

She resisted and whispered, "I've gotta go, Ryan."

"I'll pick you up in the morning."

"Okay. Can Fran ride too?"

He sighed, and grudgingly gave in. "I guess so." He'd really wanted it to just the two of them.

"Bye, Ryan."

Without even giving him a chance to say goodbye, she ran to the house. Ryan cursed under his breath when the screen door banged shut. Alyssa was made up of so many elusive layers that sometimes he only floundered around in an attempt to gain a slippery hold on her heart.

****

The next morning, Ryan drove through the gray, drizzling rain to Alyssa's house. She scooted in next to him and laid her hand on his thigh. "Good morning, beautiful," he said huskily in her ear.

"Morning," she smiled at him.

"Thanks, Ryan!" Fran said. "This sure beats riding the bus. I love your truck, it's really nice."

"You're welcome. And thanks."

They pulled onto the road and Alyssa settled closer against him. "When I get out of school, I'm going to go put in an application at Fantasia's. I saw an ad in the paper where they're hiring cashiers."

"I love that store, they have got the cutest clothes," Fran said.

"If I get hired, we'd get a discount, sis," Alyssa smiled.

Ryan squeezed Alyssa's knee. "I wish I could take you but I've got basketball practice, and then I have to work at the store till nine."

"Oh, it's okay. I'll just use the truck."

Fran giggled. "You look funny driving that big ole'

thing."

"So do you!" Alyssa said with a grin.

Ryan laughed, and pulled in the parking lot of the high school.

"Bye, y'all." Fran stepped out with a wave.

As soon as the door shut behind her, Ryan drew Alyssa's soft body against his. "Finally, I get you all to myself." He tipped her chin up to his and tasted her minty breath with a deep groan of satisfaction. Ryan grew lost in her charms, her sensuality... A chill shot down his spine despite the warmth of her pressed next to him. He wasn't even sure where he should be, so how could he be lost?

CHAPTER 9

"I got the job at Fantasia's!" Alyssa raced across her yard and threw her arms around Ryan's lean midsection. "They said I'll be working after school, and every other Saturday."

"That's great, babe. Come on, I'll buy you a strawberry shake to celebrate."

"Aw thanks, my favorite." Alyssa stood up on her tiptoes to give him a kiss.

"I'm glad I'm off today so I can spend a little time with my girl before she starts working." He winked at her, his eyes glowing in the dim winter afternoon light.

"Me too. Let's go to the river, and listen to some music. I'll get my jacket."

Between Ryan's hectic schedule and hers, they still managed to squeeze in time for each other. Alyssa cherished her time with him, she was the happiest she'd ever been in her life. The weeks flew by, and then it was Valentine's Day.

Fran paused in the doorway of their room. "Wow, you look amazing! Where's Ryan taking you?"

"I don't know, he won't tell me. It's a secret."

She grinned when Fran crossed her hands over her heart and sighed with a dramatic air.

"He is so sweet, Fran, you just wouldn't believe the nice things he does for me. You know how I love Mexican food, and he's always bringing me tacos and those yummy sour cream enchiladas from Pedro's on my lunch breaks."

Alyssa smiled, thinking of the day before. They had watched a horror movie at his house, curled up close on the sofa. And later on when he'd taken her home…their passionate kisses had wildly aroused the baser desires in her inexperienced body.

"He really cares about you, I can tell. I'm so glad y'all are back together."

"Oh, so am I. Are you and Jeremy going out?"

"No, we're going over to his house and he's grilling steaks. His parents will be gone on a date."

"Nice! Have fun, and happy Valentine's Day, sis." Alyssa heard the sound of Ryan's truck, and headed towards the living room door.

"Mama, I'm going now. I won't be out too late."

Mamas gaze never left the television. "That's fine."

When Alyssa opened the door, Ryan caught her hand in his, words failing him as he absorbed her exquisiteness. Golden hair floated down her back in a mass of thick waves, and her flawless skin glowed in the moonlight. Eyes like cut jewels gleamed at him beneath winged brows in her heart shaped face. The becoming black dress she wore was cut low, and allowed tantalizing glimpses of her breasts.

"Alyssa….you're so gorgeous."

"You're pretty cute yourself," she grinned. "Happy Valentine's Day, Ryan."

He cupped her bottom and hugged her close. "Happy Valentine's Day, sweetheart." Savoring her tempting scent, he brought her lips to his and devoured them in a heady, intense kiss. Despite the cool air, heated blood rushed through him and he broke away with a reluctant groan.

"Nana wants us to come by so she can take pictures." He leaned his forehead against hers, and stroked her arms.

"Well, we better go before you mess up my makeup," she giggled.

"Just your lipstick," he murmured in her ear.

He held the door open for her, and she slid in. "So where are you taking me, anyway?"

"You'll see."

"I bet I can get it out of you," she teased, and trailed nerve jangling kisses to his ear.

His hands tightened on the steering wheel. "Woman, are you trying to run us off the road?"

"No, I'm hungry," she whispered in his ear and blew in it mischievously.

"Is that all I am to you, a meal ticket?"

"Of course not, Ryan," she giggled. "You're also my ride."

He laughed and slanted a baleful glare her way. "It's bread and water for you tonight."

Alyssa reached for the door handle to get out, but he stilled her with a staying hand. "You know, I thought this necklace matched your eyes, but it doesn't do them justice." Her dimples emerged as she smiled and he rubbed the clefts gently with his thumbs. "I'm going to miss these when I'm gone."

Her smile fell and a sober expression crossed her pretty face. "And I'm going to miss you, Ryan, everything single thing about you," she whispered back, her eyes never leaving his. "I wish New York wasn't so far away."

The proverbial sands of time were running out

much, much too quickly. He smoothed her hair back with one hand. "I do too, honey."

She drew a deep, shaky breath, and he watched with an aching heart as the fragile bones of her neckline were revealed. "Well, we better go in. I just saw the front door open."

Ryan's grandmother greeted Alyssa with open arms. "Oh my goodness, don't y'all make a dashing couple! Just let me go get my camera." She patted Alyssa's arm as she passed. "You're as pretty as a princess, my dear."

"Thank you."

Ryan's warm fingers intertwined through hers and tugged her closer to his tall frame. He wore a blue dress shirt that stretched across his broad shoulders and he was so good looking, she couldn't help but stare in admiration.

Ms. Clare returned, chortling in excitement. "Now, you two lovebirds come over here by the mantel so I can get some pictures."

Alyssa laughed and pulled Ryan over to where his grandmother pointed. After taking the pictures, she gave Ms. Clare a fond goodbye hug.

"Y'all be careful out there, and have a good time," Ryan's grandmother called from the front porch.

"We will."

They waved goodbye to her, and headed out to celebrate Valentine's Day.

Ryan drove in silence while Alyssa stared out the dusky window. She glanced over at him, surprised to see a muscle jumping in his tight jaw. Alyssa frowned; his mood had turned dark for some reason. The miles passed, and then they pulled up to a ritzy restaurant in

Cadeyville that she had never been to.

"We're here." He shut off the engine but sat unmoving, seemingly lost in his thoughts.

"Ryan…" she said softly. His gaze met hers, bright blue eyes darkened by sad shadows lurking in them. Strange, she'd never really thought about his pain, only her own. How selfish of her. He'd be leaving everything, and everyone he'd ever known.

She scooted over to him and framed his face with her hands. "I didn't know it was possible, to love someone as much as I do you. And I know that I'll be spending a lot of time alone, just for that little time we'll have together. But that's okay, because I'd rather have some of you, Ryan, than not have you at all."

"Will it be enough?"

"Of course it will," she whispered fiercely.

He hung his head and dropped it heavily onto her shoulder, while she smoothed his thick, satiny hair, feeling like her heart was breaking. She kissed the side of his neck, and he shivered against her.

Ryan felt a wave of iciness flow over him, wretched decisions freezing his mind. He'd found out the other day his new job started the first of June, but he hadn't had the heart to tell her yet. Alyssa had become the axis his life revolved around. Once he left, all he'd have was sports again, and there was no comparison between the two.

He closed his eyes and concentrated on the delicious feel of her. Her generous breasts pressed seductively against him as the feminine curves of her body intoxicated him. He drew deep breaths, trying to get a hold of the erotic sensations swerving through him. Sometimes all he thought about was her luscious body, and how he'd love to worship it, all the way from her head to her toes. But he held himself in check, sensing her wariness at taking that next step. Was it because he was leaving? But he'd never know, would he? Deep rooted derision sunk his spirits to a new low.

Finally, he raised his head and met her worried gaze. "I'm better now." He stroked her soft cheek. "Are you ready to go eat?"

"Um, sure." They went into the fancy restaurant and proceeded to order. Although the food was delicious, they could have been eating sandwiches as far as Alyssa was concerned. Ryan remained broodingly silent throughout the meal while she picked at her food.

On the way home, he wrapped his free arm around her. She pushed away her apprehension and turned into his side.

"Alyssa, I'll be leaving as soon as school is out. They've found me a job, working at an athletic store not far from the college."

She froze and edged away from him. "That's not far away."

"No…no, it's not."

Alyssa twisted her hands in her lap. His words were a stab in the heart, *I'll be leaving...* She'd thought they would have most of the summer together, no school, just the two of them. Life without him seemed unbearable, she'd come to depend on him, love him more than words could say. Without him, she feared her life would be empty. After a long, tense ride, they arrived back at her house.

To his amazement, she jumped out before the truck had even come to a complete stop. "Alyssa! Wait!" His feet hit the ground after her. He sprinted to where she'd stopped and spun her towards him. "Don't start this! Why do you always run away? Don't you want me to be honest with you?"

"Don't start what?" she shouted, her voice shaking. "Ryan, I don't know what you want me to say when you tell me things like this. I can't help but be upset. Why don't you understand that?" She held her hands over her eyes and his gut clenched. "You can't have everything the way you want it, that's not the way the world works. I learned that a long time ago." Her voice grew lower, thick with tears.

"I don't want to make you cry, Alyssa," he said hoarsely, her sadness draining away his anger. "Can't we just talk to each other? Please?" he coaxed. She looked at him with pain- brightened eyes.

"Talk about what?"

His heart broke at her sad tone. "I'm sorry for yelling at you," he said, and took her small hand in his. She snatched it back and he stared at her in disbelief. "What in the hell is the matter with you?"

"You already have a job, Ryan, you could stay the summer here with me if you really wanted to!" she screamed, and pushed him away with all her strength.

Caught off guard, he staggered back for a second, and then grabbed her hands before she could take off again. "But they need someone when school lets out, and they're not going to hold it for me. I have to get an apartment, plus still pay for my truck and the insurance, and everything else too. You know how much it costs to live, come on, Alyssa, you're not stupid! And it's even higher up North."

She stared at him, her chest rising and falling in

rapid breaths. "You just want me to be here for you, happy and accommodating while you make plans behind my back. Well, that's not me. I won't be happy you're leaving, I can't! I can't pretend feelings I don't have!"

He studied her flushed face with a sinking heart. "They called me. I haven't made any plans behind-"

She tore herself from his grip. "Just leave me alone, Ryan," she whispered fiercely.

He watched her disappear in the house, no longer sure of anything.

CHAPTER 10

The next morning he stopped to pick them up, but Joyce informed him they'd already taken the bus. He missed Alyssa's soft body pressed up against him, her cheeky responses to his teasing, and the heated kiss they shared each morning.

They passed each other in the hallway, but she turned her face away. Ryan shook his head angrily at her hardheadedness, who was she trying to fool? The days passed, but there was still no communication between the two of them.

Fed up with her foolishness, he approached her a few days later in the hallway. "Alyssa, look at me."

She never turned her stubborn gaze from the inside of her locker.

Ryan's temples throbbed. "Alyssa..." he ground out.

Still, she refused.

Incensed, he slammed the rattling, metal door shut with the flat of his hand. Alyssa gasped and wide, startled eyes flew to meet his.

"Meet me at my truck after school," he bit out.

She met his unyielding stare with her eyebrows raised. "No."

"What the fuck is-"

Alyssa turned her back to him, and rushed away.

No? That's all she had to say to him? The word

pounded through his head. He slammed his fist against her locker, and bit back the urge to shout her name down the hallway. Nosy onlookers rushed to get out of his way as he stalked to his class, furious at her childish behavior.

But… if that's the way she wanted it. Ryan's pained heart hardened. *Then so be it.*

When he wasn't working, he pushed himself at the football field till he was drenched in sweat, and his muscles burned in agony from the punishment.

As for Alyssa, she threw herself into work and school, determined to keep her wandering thoughts away from Ryan. And it worked, sort of. Every night she fell into an exhausted, dreamless sleep, but when she awoke, she still felt tired and wore out.

Spring arrived and it lifted her spirits to see the green, hopeful buds peeping out. Alyssa worked whenever she wasn't at school, signing up for extra hours nobody else wanted. She had to save as much money as she could. The house had been sold, and they had thirty days to pack up everything. Mama was moving in with her cousin, Janice, and she and Fran were moving in with Casey.

"Can you believe we're finally getting out of this house?" Her sister spun in a circle with her arms outstretched.

Alyssa looked around at the small living room where they were boxing up old vinyl records. "Once I leave, I'll finally feel better. It won't be real until then." Fran nodded, only she knew the struggle it had been just to survive in their home.

"I'm sorry about you and Ryan," Fran said gently. "I really hoped it would work out this time."

Alyssa shook her head. She didn't want to talk about it, not even with Fran.

Mama came in from the hallway and gathered some boxes to take back to her room. "So much to do!"

Alyssa silently continued to pack. Even Mama was excited; she'd wondered how she would react when the time came to move.

The first weekend in May arrived; their allotted time was almost up. The sisters loaded the last of the boxes onto the truck and slammed the tailgate together, exchanging a happy grin.

Alyssa wiped off her damp brow and walked away from Fran to reflect upon the house they'd grown up in. She wished there were more happy remembrances to associate with this place, but they were few and far between. Daddy's horrid memories would last a lifetime, no matter where they were. She couldn't help but rub the raised scars on her lower back, it happened every time she thought of him. She hoped the people that were moving in would make it into a happy, loving home, the way it should be. Not one shadowed by fear and pain.

"Alyssa!" Fran called, "let's go!"

"I'm coming."

They were keeping the truck; Mama was going to buy her a car from the small proceeds of the house. Alyssa ran her hand over the weathered arm of the swing one last time, and walked back to her sister. Mama was already at Janice's; they'd dropped her off yesterday. As they pulled onto the road, she gazed tearfully in the direction where Ryan lived and wished she had the courage to tell him goodbye.

Ryan noticed the old blue truck wasn't in its usual

spot on his way home from work that evening. He tensed with trepidation and pulled into the silent, empty yard.

Alyssa was gone.

A sharp pang shot through his middle as he shook his head, disgusted. They'd thrown away precious time they could've had together, and now it was too late.

He sat down on the wooden swing and spied a few long hairs caught in the upper slats. With great care he worked out amber, silken strands, and held them in his grip while the wind fluttered them in the breeze. Bittersweet memories flashed through his mind; Alyssa riding beside him on her bike, flaxen hair streaming out from behind her just like a golden banner. How silky it had felt against his fingers when they'd glided through to cradle her skull, and bring her sweet lips to his hungry ones.

Ryan opened his hand and somberly watched as they floated away in the wind, the symbolism not lost on him. Life, with its many twists and turns, had set them on different paths. Could they ever meet in the middle, or was a compromise even possible?

Alyssa was so bull headed and she wouldn't listen to reason, no matter how he tried to reassure her. Not able to deal with the fact that he was leaving, she pushed him away. How much of it was from her upbringing, he couldn't tell. Who knew the emotional toll her childhood had inflicted upon her, the damage it had caused. What he did know was that she was a sweet, funny girl whom he loved with all his heart.

But he couldn't have her.

His throat grew tight, and Ryan swallowed the hard lump down as he recalled their passionate embraces.

Never had anyone aroused such feelings in him, she was a sorceress. She'd taken hold of his heart and body and now he had to move on without her. Rising quickly, he strode to his truck and didn't look back.

****

"Quit moving, Fran! If you don't be still…" Alyssa waved the curling iron in a threatening motion towards her sister's head.

Fran grinned at her as she talked with Jeremy on the phone. "I'll see you in a little while. Okay, I will. Love you too."

Alyssa's heart twisted at their casual exchange. No one had said those words to her in months.

"We're going to the levy tonight, there's going to be a huge party. Everybody is going to be there!" Fran's eyes shone with anticipation.

"Well, we're not even gonna make it to the graduation ceremony if you don't let me finish," Alyssa grumbled. She knew Fran expected her to go to the party but she had no intention to. She'd just make up an excuse that she didn't feel good if anyone asked because she was positive Ryan would be there. Time hadn't eased the pain, not the way she thought it would. Every time she saw him, a little piece of her died. It was too hard.

Since that scene at the locker, he looked at her as if he hated her. But she didn't hate him. In fact, the exact opposite. She loved him with all that she was. *A fat lot of good that does me. After tonight, I won't see him again till…when? A year from now?* By then, he'd be a college football star. The hopelessness of it washed over her and she longed to just stay home. But she couldn't miss Fran's graduation, what kind of sister would she be?

"Alright, I'm finally done. You're beautiful, sis, especially your hair," she said with a teasing grin.

Fran's light blue eyes shimmered. "Thanks, now you better get ready yourself."

"It won't take me long." Alyssa put on a flattering, sleeveless dark pink dress and topped it with a short, white cardigan. She touched up her lip gloss and peered at herself in the mirror. Her cheeks were flushed with nervousness and her eyes seemed huge in her face.

Fran jingled the keys at her as she grabbed her purse off the bed. "I'm ready, let's go. I'm so proud of you, Fran."

Her sister beamed. "Just think, this time next year, you'll be the one wearing this." Fran held up on side of the shapeless red gown that swallowed her petite form.

"Not a day soon enough for me."

****

Alyssa strained to see where Fran was sitting in the sea of red by the stage and tensed as her gaze unwittingly collided with Ryan's. Unspoken, bitter words seemed to fly in the air between them as he straightened to his full height and singled her out among the crowd. Finally, he turned brusquely towards the chairs, as if dismissing her and the whole tiresome connection between them. Her stomach churned, shaken by his animosity.

The ceremony soon began and Alyssa cheered as Fran walked the stage.

When it was Ryan's turn, the crowd went crazy. "And our very own Ryan Sutherby has received a full scholarship to attend New York State and play for them as quarterback!" the principal shouted over loud applause and whistles. Ryan accepted his diploma, and the crowded gym's rafters shook from roars of excitement.

You would think he discovered the cure for cancer or something. A proud smile broke across his handsome face and she bit her lip hard, ashamed for her mean thought. Cheers rang out all around her but Alyssa stayed motionless.

After the ceremony ended, she met her sister over by the crowded stage.

"Why don't you just ride with me and Jeremy to the party? We can come back later and get the truck."

"I'm not going; I've got a bad headache."

"Uh huh." Fran shook her blond head. "Alyssa, just come on-"

"No!" Heads jerked their way so she lowered her voice. "Fran, I'm going home."

Her sister scrutinized her for a long moment and then sighed. "Alright. Go home then."

Alyssa walked out the gym doors and drew in deep breaths of fresh air. "Where's the dang truck?" she muttered to herself, and turned in a circle in the crowded parking lot.

Suddenly, a large hand seized her arm and she shrieked. Adrenaline rushed through her veins as she spun around, ready to nail whoever it was with her purse. Ryan stood over her like a dark angel of the night, crystal blue eyes blazing. The frightened scream died in her throat.

"What are you trying to do, Ryan, scare me to death? Is that why you're sneaking up on me?" She jerked her arm free from his restraining hold.

"No, you looked like you were lost. By the way,

your truck's right there." With a sardonic crook of his brows, he pointed four vehicles away to the left.

"Then I wasn't very lost, because I was just about to find it," she informed him coolly. "Thanks anyway, though," she said over her shoulder.

"That's right, Alyssa, run away like you always do," he called after her.

She drew in a sharp breath and whirled back around to face him. "What did you say?"

"You heard me," he said in a clipped tone.

"I don't-," but he cut her off.

"Yes, you do. The going gets too tough; and bam!" Ryan smacked his hands together and leveled his piercing glare on her. "There goes Alyssa."

"That's not true!"

"Yeah, it is." He stalked towards her and grasped her by the shoulders. "I leave in two days, and we've wasted all this time. Why?"

"You're acting like this is all my fault, Ryan, and it's not! You're to blame, too."

"And how is that?" A look of impatience crossed the handsome angles of his shadowed face as he raked his hand wildly through his hair.

"You know why! I don't have to say it." She glared up at him; he just wanted her to grovel at his feet. "What are you doing out here anyways, I'm sure all your admirers are missing you," she said sarcastically and flung her arm towards the gym.

"I wanted to see you," he replied coldly. "Although now, I'm trying to remember why."

Her feelings stung, she retorted, "Well, you found me. Congratulations. But I'm leaving."

A humorless, grim smile touched Ryan's lips as he

shook his head slowly. "Look at that. You've just proven me right, babe."

Alyssa folded her arms across her chest, she wasn't about to leave now.

"I asked you a question, Alyssa. Answer it," he demanded.

Her heart quaked as she studied his angry countenance. Ryan was more powerfully built than ever, his broad shoulders and rippled chest strained at the white dress shirt he wore. Like a rakish pirate, his dark as night hair ruffled in the humid breeze. It should be a sin to be that good looking.

"I'm waiting."

"I'm…I'm not sure."

"That's bullshit! You're lying to me," he bit out.

Alyssa clenched her fists, righteous anger snapping her out of her reverie. "Fine! I'll tell you why. Because you're leaving, Ryan! You care more about some game than you do me! And once you get up there around all those college girls up North, you'll forget all about me. I'll just be some hick from Cypress Bayou, the town you couldn't wait to escape from." Her voice broke and tears filled her eyes. "Why would I want to grow even closer to you? So my heart will be even more broken in the end? I have to go on without you, just like you are without me," she whispered.

His set face softened imperceptibly and the tight grip on her shoulders eased.

People were starting to straggle towards them as headlights flashed from all directions. Ryan's sharp gaze flicked over her head and came back to rest on her face. "Come with me so we can talk." He took her by the arm, but she balked. "Dammit, Alyssa, I'm not asking you, I'm telling you."

Alyssa felt exhausted all of a sudden. She allowed him to lead her to his truck and got in when he opened the door for her.

A strained silence hovered as they traveled down the road. After a while, he pulled off onto the desolate boat launch at the bayou and cut the engine.

Ryan studied the misty, moon lit bayou for long seconds before turning to her. "Alyssa, you're not going to get anywhere in life if you can't learn to trust people."

Alyssa felt the color drain from her face as she shrunk a little inside from the compassion on his face. "I trust people," she said in a low voice.

His eyebrows shot up in an incredulous frown. "Who? Fran? Who else? Because you damn sure don't trust me. And I wanna know what you think I'm going to do when I get up there. Screw every girl I meet or something?"

"I don't know what you're going to do because I won't see you!"

Ryan's eyes flashed furiously at her as his voice grew even louder. "So it all comes back to this. I'm sick of this bullshit with you, Alyssa! There's no reasoning with you, you don't listen to a goddamn word I say!"

Alyssa slumped back against the seat and bit her lip, not sure how to respond.

His gaze narrowed on her mouth and before she could move; his lips trapped hers in a demanding kiss that collapsed her defensive walls. Ryan's hand settled on her back as he dragged her up against the hard length of him. She trembled from the fierceness of his arousal and he gentled, caressing his tongue against hers. Their joined mouths melded against the others in a passionate desertion of their mountain of odds. Alyssa moaned, transfixed by the exquisite pleasure. He leaned back as his fingers drifted over her sensitized lips.

"I don't know what to do with you," he whispered hoarsely. "You drive me crazy, Alyssa, and I can't stop thinking about you. Why do you torture me so?"

Alyssa stilled, her breath frozen in her chest. Why did he have to make this so hard for her, pushing her, demanding things from her all the time? And why did he have to make her feel like she was some kind of mental case, like she belonged in the nuthouse? He wanted her, yes, that was obvious, but it didn't change the facts. She'd been doing better, but now...

On the brink of a breakdown, she swallowed hard and forged on. "Ryan, will you take me back to the school?"

He jolted up so violently his head bumped the headliner of the truck. She glanced over at him and froze when she saw his white-knuckled hands vibrating with rage on the steering wheel.

"I'm done, Alyssa. I'm done." His voice came out low and shaky, but profound in its iron resolve.

Ryan's hard gaze flicked to the emerald necklace and back to her eyes. His jaw ticking, he started the engine. It seemed like it took forever to get back to the school as she stared out the window, breathing shallowly, her heart cut into a million pieces.

"Ryan, I-"

He shook his head roughly. "Save it, Alyssa." One hand gestured towards the window. "We're here. Right where you wanted."

She flinched from his coldness and stepped out

onto the dark, deserted parking lot. The squeal of his tires blew up the silence as soon as she shut the door behind her. She watched till his taillights faded away to nothing, and the emptiness inside her threatened to swallow her whole..

CHAPTER 11

Ryan put the last of his bags in the truck and went back inside to tell Nana goodbye. As he gazed around at the small house he'd spent the last fourteen years of his life, his eyes were inevitably drawn to the framed picture of him and Alyssa on the mantel.

He studied every nuance of her radiant smile while pain drove stakes deep into his soul. *Why, Alyssa?* Unable to look at their happy faces shining back at him any longer, he closed his eyes and tried to block the image from his mind.

"You can take it with you if you'd like, I have more," Nana said from behind him.

Ryan quickly placed the photo back. "No. I don't want it."

She ignored his rudeness and continued on. "I hope Alyssa still comes to visit with me, she's such a sweetheart, and so pretty." Nana looked up at his set face with a sympathetic look. "The course of true love never did run smooth." That's a quote from Shakespeare, one of my favorites."

Ryan shook his head. "Nana, I know what you're trying to say, but it's complicated. Alyssa just won't…" His eyes wandered back to the picture as he wished he could hold her in his arms one last time. Recalling how that night had ended, his heart grew frigid. "It's over between us. She ended it, not me."

"We all make mistakes, remember that." Nana gave him a hug, and he leaned down to kiss her cheek.

"I'm going to miss you, Nana."

"And I'm going to miss you, my sweet boy. I'm so proud of you. This house is going to be empty with just me rattling around here."

Ryan's throat grew tight and his grandmother patted his cheek. "Now, you better get going. Your Uncle James is expecting you before dark. I've packed you a lunch, and don't forget to give him the jars of sweet pickles I put up for him. He'll have a fit if you do," she chuckled.

"I'm going to miss your cooking, too. Probably gonna lose about twenty pounds," he joked.

"I doubt that, not with your appetite!"

She walked him out to the truck. "I love you, and you be careful driving. I'm going to miss saying that," she sniffed. "Call me when you get to your uncle's house."

"I will. I love you too, Nana."

Ryan hit the highway and a slow grin of amazement crossed his face. *I really did it; I'm actually leaving Cypress Bayou.* Wind blew freely in through the windows and the sky stretched out before him in an endless road of blue.

He turned the rock station up, and then back off as a new song began. He'd danced with Alyssa one night at the river to that song… Barefoot with only a sandbar as their stage, he'd dipped and twirled her till they'd fell to the ground in a breathless tangle. "Everywhere I turn, I see you," he whispered. He shook his head to clear it, and swallowed down the inner cries that threatened to escape. "It's good I'm leaving."

****

Alyssa awoke that Sunday morning with a heavy heart. She'd had a terrible, sleepless weekend; Ryan's shocked face had popped into her mind every time she'd closed her eyes.

And now he was truly gone.

Maybe he was right, maybe there really was something wrong with her. It was just too much to deal with. She went to take a shower and put it on cool so the water would soothe her swollen eyes.

Fran banged on the door. "Alyssa, are you in there?"

"Yeah, come on in."

Fran walked to the sink. "Don't use all the hot water, Jeremy wants to take a shower too."

"I'm almost finished."

Alyssa wrapped a towel around her and stepped out of the shower. "Uh, Fran, are y'all being careful?" she asked with a meaningful look at her sister.

Fran paused, mascara wand in hand. "Careful? Oh yeah, of course. I'm not stupid."

"I know you're not. I was just making sure."

"Well, don't worry. I'm not ready for a baby, and neither is Jeremy."

Alyssa let out a sigh of relief and Fran grinned mischievously at her. "Not ready to be Aunt Alyssa?"

"No!" she laughed.

"It's good to see you smile. You've been moping around here for weeks."

"I know. I'm trying, Fran, I really am."

"I could fix you up with one of Jeremy's friends. That'll snap you right out of your funk."

"Don't you dare!" she exclaimed, aghast at the

thought. "No, that's the last thing I want."

"Alyssa, Ryan's gone. And he's going to date other girls, I guarantee it," Fran said with a firm nod of her head.

"I know that, don't you think I know that!" Alyssa turned to the mirror and began to furiously brush her wet hair.

"I was just saying…"

Alyssa cut in irritably. "I'm sure you think that would help, but it won't. I just want to be left alone for right now."

Her sister threw her hands up in the air. "I give up!"

"Good!" Alyssa shot back irritably.

"You're about as stubborn as a mule," Fran muttered and left the bathroom.

Alyssa shook her head in disbelief, Fran was crazy! There was no way she was ready to go out on a date. Having to make small talk, and then he'd probably put a move on her… The thought made her shudder. No thank you, she fumed. She had to be at work at eleven so she dressed and did her hair and makeup.

All day long, it felt like she wore a mask. She smiled and greeted the customers like she was supposed to, but at the end of the day, she went home hollow and depressed.

It's going to get better, it's going to get better. Well, I can hardly wait for that day.

.

CHAPTER 12

The summer passed quickly for Alyssa. Her and Fran sold the old truck and split the money so they could each buy a car. A couple of weeks before school started, they were all sitting out on the sunny patio. She sat with her feet propped up on a stool and a magazine in her lap.

"Sis, I've got someone I want you to meet," Fran said cheerfully.

Alyssa groaned and slowly put the magazine down. She already knew what this was about; Fran thought the cure for every girl's blues was a man. She'd brought home several of her and Jeremy's friends home, each time hoping Alyssa would show an interest in one of them.

But none could hold a candle to Ryan. They'd stare at her slack jawed and then stammer out questions. One had even dared to try and kiss her goodbye; she'd had to fight her way free of his pawing hands. She'd been infuriated, the nerve of him! Besides, she didn't need a boyfriend, she was perfectly happy the way things were. Casey, Fran, and her got along wonderfully, and work kept her busy.

Noting Casey's amused face; she rolled her eyes and stood up. Casey was in her early twenties, cute and petite with long, dark brown hair. She found it hilarious Fran was so determined to find her sister a boyfriend.

"Alyssa, this is Gary," Fran beamed.

You would think she'd given birth to him or something. She felt Gary's brown eyes sweep over her.

"Nice to meet you," he said with a huge smile.

Alyssa grudgingly smiled back, and Fran prattled on. "Here, Gary, you can sit right here beside Alyssa. Gary is in training to be an assistant manager at Auto Parts Express. Alyssa, didn't you say you needed some new tires?"

She shot Fran a narrow eyed glare. "Uh, yeah, I did."

Gary sat down and Alyssa resumed her seat.

"We've got a great sale going on right now."

He was nice looking, Alyssa thought in a distant manner. Probably around nineteen or so, tall, with a nice build.

"Really?" she asked, wide eyed.

From the corner of her eye, she saw Casey bite her lip to hold the laughter back. Casey knew sarcasm when she saw it, Gary obviously did not.

"Oh yeah, and tires are 10% off," he said with an eager nod of his wavy, light brown head.

"Wow," she breathed.

Fran cut in with a glower her way, and gushed, "That's a really good deal, isn't it, Alyssa?"

Alyssa picked up her magazine. "Sure is."

Fran snatched it out of her hand. "You don't need that; we're just about to eat."

"Great, I'm starving. What are we having?" Gary asked Fran.

Alyssa turned to him in disbelief, and shot Casey a look. Casey turned away, her shoulders shaking with laughter.

"Steaks, with grilled potatoes, and Alyssa made baked beans. My sister is a great cook."

Now that was definitely stretching the truth, she was passable, not great.

Gary turned to her, a satisfied gleam in his eyes. "Well, I can't cook at all, so that's a plus for you. This is going to work out fine."

Alyssa's mouth dropped. "Huh?"

"Oh look, Jeremy's taking the steaks off now! Come on everybody, come fix a plate," Fran sang out.

After the evening was finally over, Alyssa turned on her sister. "Fran," she hissed, "what the hell is the matter with you, bringing Gary home? He's an obnoxious jerk!"

Fran waved her hand nonchalantly. "Oh, he's harmless, he was just nervous. Give him a chance; he's really a nice guy."

"Nervous? You could've fooled me! And if he's so great, you date him."

"Alyssa," Fran sighed. "Quit being so dramatic. He's coming swimming with us tomorrow, so wear that cute purple bathing suit."

"You invited him to go to the river with us? You should've asked me!"

"Gary is Jeremy's friend too." Fran crossed her arms over her chest defensively.

"Whatever! But don't expect me to pay any attention to him."

"One day I bet you'll thank me," Fran grinned.

Alyssa shook her head adamantly. "Don't hold your breath for that," she muttered.

Alyssa decided to go see Ryan's grandmother while she was over that way. Ms. Clare opened her front door with a squeal of delight. "Alyssa, dear, come in, come in. I just made some brownies."

"Yum, I love your brownies," she grinned.

"I remember. Just make yourself at home and I'll be right back."

Alyssa walked into the living room and her heart skipped a couple of beats when she came to the picture on the mantel. Through the cold glass, she traced a finger over Ryan's smiling face. *How handsome he is.* His crystalline blue eyes surrounded by thick black eyelashes and that chiseled, square cut jaw she'd caressed, captivated by him. His broad shoulders made hers seem tiny. "We look so happy," she whispered, her heart aching, and they had been.

She fingered the necklace at her throat. She refused to take it off, no matter the strange way Fran had looked at her when she'd informed her emphatically that it wasn't leaving her neck.

Ms. Clare came into the room, and she spun around.

"I just adore that picture of you and Ryan. I have more if you'd like one."

"I would. Thank you."

Ms. Clare placed a plate of brownies on the coffee table and patted the couch cushion beside her as she sat down. "You're welcome, sweetie. Now come over here and visit with me for a little while."

Sometime later, Alyssa left the house with the photo clutched in her hand. She studied it again in the car and tears filled her eyes. "Oh Ryan, I miss you so much. I'm so sorry, please come back home."

****

Ryan opened his eyes with a pained groan. He'd

gone with his two roommates to a sorority party and they hadn't gotten back till four in the morning. Plus he'd drank too much, something he didn't normally do, but they were out on Christmas break.

He rubbed his face wearily and thought about the twelve hour shift he had to work today. "I hope like hell it's slow today," he muttered. The phone rang on the nightstand beside him and he reached for it.

"Hi, Ryan! This is Jennifer! Remember we met last night?"

"Sure, I remember," he lied. There had been so many girls last night, they all ran together.

"Well, we're having a party at our sorority house tonight and we want you to come!"

Ryan winced and held the phone away from his ear; her high pitched voice was making his head throb harder. "I'll see, I don't know."

"Try to come, okay? We'd love it if you could!" She gave him the directions and he scrawled them on a receipt on his nightstand.

Ryan leaned back with a sigh. College was very different from how he thought it was going to be. The teachers were easy on him since he played football so he didn't have to devote much time to studying. Most nights he was off he went out, sometimes with his roommates, or on dates with different girls. Ryan thought about the weekend before and grinned. He'd gone out with Tamera, a certified party girl. They'd rented a hotel room and spent the whole weekend in bed.

He stretched his long body and lumbered to the shower.

"Dammit," he said under his breath as he reached

for the soap. He'd forgotten to put Nana's Christmas present in the mail yesterday and it probably wouldn't make it there in time now. He'd hoped to go home for break, but his work schedule made it impossible. He missed Cypress Bayou, he felt like he didn't belong here sometimes.

But they certainly made him feel welcome, he thought wryly. He was constantly invited to parties, and the girls chased him relentlessly. They were hot and heavy for the new quarterback, as his roommates liked to tease him. His face grew serious as he thought about Alyssa.

She'd been right.

He wondered how she was, if she was doing okay. Nana had mentioned her a few times; he knew Alyssa went to visit with her and took her places. He was grateful to her for that.

Did she have a boyfriend? Ryan ground his teeth together and closed his eyes as he shook his head. He couldn't bear to even think about it. Not that he had any room to talk. He'd been with several girls since he'd been here, but nothing lasting. And he'd certainly never cared about them, not the way he had Alyssa. It had just been sex. Nothing more.

Ryan suddenly wished he could see Alyssa again, talk with her. He missed her, beyond what he'd even thought possible. There was an aching hollowness within him only she could fill.

CHAPTER 13

"Woo hoo! I'm done with high school!" Alyssa threw her arms around her sister happily.

"Mama didn't waste any time leaving, did she?" Fran eyed the parking lot with a brooding expression.

Alyssa snorted in disgust and flung her hair over her shoulder with a shrug. "I'm surprised she even came. I mean, she hasn't called us in weeks. All she cares about is playing bingo. It just boggles my mind, it really does." She shook her head. Until Mama moved in with Janice, she'd never been to a bingo game in her life. Now she cleaned houses during the day and spent her evenings with Janice in the bingo hall.

"Mine too," Fran sighed. "Well, I'm fixing to go. Oh, and Jeremy is picking up the drinks." Fran wagged her eyebrows up and down and Alyssa laughed. "So don't worry about that. And then we're going to pick Gary up and meet you at the levy, okay?"

"Gary…" Alyssa groaned. "Just shoot me in the head now. Couldn't my graduation present been the gift of no Gary?" She cocked her head sideways at Fran, eyebrows raised in amusement.

"Alyssa, everybody is going! He was going to drive, but his truck is in the shop. He's nice, if you'd just give him a chance. *And* he really likes you," she added.

"Yeah, I know," she replied dryly.

"I don't know what's the matter with you. He's

really cute; plenty of other girls would love to go out with him."

"Exactly, *other girls,*" Alyssa stressed. "Not me."

"I'm leaving!" Fran threw her hands up and Alyssa grinned at her.

"I'll give you an A for effort, though."

"You better!" Fran laughed. "Bye, sis, see you in a little while."

Alyssa walked back inside and found Ms. Clare talking with some ladies from her church.

"Sweetie, I was just telling them about your scholarship. Won't she be a wonderful nurse?" Ms. Clare proudly declared.

Alyssa's heart warmed and filled with love for this kind lady. The circle of elderly women nodded in agreement, and poured forth their congratulations.

"Thanks, I'm really happy about it. I can't wait to start," she said, smiling at them.

"I'll see y'all Sunday, it's getting late," Ms. Clare told her friends, and after a chorus of goodbyes, the two of them walked to Alyssa's car. Ms. Clare didn't like to drive at night, only if necessary, she'd told Alyssa.

"That was a nice ceremony. It doesn't seem like it's been a year since I was at Ryan's, though."

Alyssa thought about the past year, and all the changes that had occurred in her life. "No, it doesn't."

At first it had been hard to hear Ryan's name, but she'd grown accustomed to it. Ms. Clare would casually mention him in conversation, giving tidbits from his calls and letters. Alyssa always pretended casual indifference, not wanting Ms. Clare to think she still carried a torch for her grandson.

"Ryan will be home soon. He's already called and

told me all of his favorite dishes he wants me to cook for him, "Ms. Clare chuckled.

Alyssa seethed inwardly, not a word to her in a year, and he was worried about *food*? "Well, you are the best cook around," she said brightly. "How's your garden?"

"Oh, it's coming along just fine. The squash and cucumbers have really grown in the last couple of weeks with all this sunshine we've had."

They chatted companionably till Alyssa pulled up to her house.

"Oh my goodness, look at Daisy!" The big dog they'd found together jumped up and laid her paws against Ms. Clare's door.

Alyssa laughed at the pitiful look Daisy gave them through the window. "That dog is crazy. No wonder someone just left her!"

"I love having her, I really do. She keeps me company, yes she does." Ms. Clare's voice went high pitched as she opened the door and petted an ecstatic Daisy. "Have fun, and be careful tonight, dear."

"Oh, I will." Alyssa walked Ms. Clare to the porch and gave her a hug goodbye.

****

"Do you think you got enough?" Alyssa stared in amazement at the large assortment of alcohol in the bed of Jeremy's truck.

"Well, I didn't buy it all for me," Jeremy grinned. "We all pitched in." Jeremy nodded at Gary who was walking up from the fire.

Alyssa shook her head. She rarely drank, and then only wine coolers or fruity mixed drinks. "You've got enough here to last for weeks."

"Ha! That'll be gone by tonight. I can tell you haven't been out here in a while." Jeremy laughed and tossed her a wine cooler.

"That obvious, huh," Alyssa said with a smile. "Where's Fran at?"

"Over there talking to Megan and some other people."

"Alrighty, thanks for this." She grinned and held the bottle up.

"No problem, you know where they're at if you want more."

Gary caught up with her and boomed, "Congratulations! How's it feel to be a graduate?"

Oh, lord, Alyssa groaned to herself. "Feels great."

Gary slung his arm around her shoulders. "Hold up, don't go anywhere yet. I wanna ask you something." he slurred.

Alyssa shrugged free of his heavy arm and snapped, "What?"

"How 'bout me and you go to the movies tomorrow?"

"Can't, I have to work."

"Now why is it every time I ask you to do something, you say you have to work? I'm beginning to think you don't like me," Gary said thickly.

You thought right. "Bills don't pay themselves," she said instead, and crossed her arms over her chest.

He fixed his bloodshot eyes on her. "You move in with me, and I'll take care of you. You won't have to worry your pretty little head about a thing." Gary leaned over to her and the reek of alcohol fumes hit her straight in the face.

"I suggest you go sober up, because you're talking

crazy, Gary! I'm going to see Fran." *Idiot*. Alyssa fumed the whole way over to her sister.

"Fran, you won't believe what Gary is over there saying, he said that he's going to "take care of me.""

She burst out laughing.

"He gets on my last nerve."

Her sister's laughter grew louder and Alyssa glowered at her. "This is all your fault, I still remember the day you brought him home. He was a pain in the ass then!

"Well, he is pretty wasted."

"Drunk or not, he's still irritating." Alyssa glared over at Gary.

Fran sighed. "Well, I didn't want you to be lonely, that's all." A delighted expression crossed her face. "Hey, there's this new guy that works with Jeremy-"

"Stop!" Alyssa laughed and held up her hand. "I'm sure I can find someone on my own."

Fran raised her eyebrows. "If you say so."

"I do. So quit playing matchmaker all the time. Who do think you are; Cupid or something?"

Fran grinned and pretended to shoot an arrow. "Gotcha!"

"You've lost your mind." Alyssa laughed and linked an arm through her sister's as they walked over to the fire to hang out with their friends.

****

Fran's screams of "No!" awoke her before dawn the next morning.

She ran to the kitchen to see her sister holding on to Casey, tears pouring down both of their faces. Alyssa looked over at Casey frantically. "What's happened? What's wrong?"

"Jeremy...Jeremy hit a tree on his way home, and he-he died. They're saying he was drunk," she choked out.

Alyssa's hand flew to her mouth. "Oh Fran, I'm so sorry. Oh my God, Casey."

"Jeremy!" Fran screamed shrilly.

Alyssa looked at her in shock; still trying to process Jeremy was gone. Snapping to, she wrapped her arms around Fran's shaking body. "Fran, Fran, shhhhh," she soothed her sobbing sister. The pain in the kitchen grew palpable, shocked sadness filling every corner.

Fran sank to the floor, keening and rocking with her hands over her face. "Not Jeremy," she cried.

****

Ryan sat at the back of the packed church with his former teammates, and observed the hushed sadness of the flower filled chapel. He'd driven home as fast as he'd dared when LaDarius had called and gave him the horrific news. Scanning the crowd again, he frowned in confusion. *Where was Alyssa?*

The preacher asked everyone to bow their heads in a moment of silence for Jeremy and Ryan closed his eyes with a sigh of disappointment.

The quaint cemetery had a range of fairly new tombstones to ones so old the etching could barely be made out. It was out on a rural road past the bayou, and the tall, deep green pine trees out past the fence formed an arresting backdrop against the clear, blue sky. Ryan made his way beside LaDarius just as the preacher started to pray. "Our Heavenly Father, we are gathered here to honor the memory of-"

"Jeremy!" a female voice screamed. Heads snapped up as a collective gasp rose from the crowd.

People began to murmur and strain their necks to see, but Ryan's height gave him an advantage.

"Who is that?" LaDarius asked. Ryan's heart sank when he saw it was Fran. She was on her knees beside the black coffin, crying.

Suddenly, someone broke through the crowd and Alyssa appeared beside her sister. She stroked Fran's back and whispered in her ear, but Fran only continued to sob. Ryan froze in place, observing the heartbreaking scene unfold in front of the stunned group. Her golden brown, sun streaked wavy hair was longer, almost touching her bottom, and the simple black column dress emphasized her curves as she knelt down. Ryan wished he could see her face, but her shimmering head was bent over Fran's lighter one in concern.

"Is that Fran?" LaDarius whispered beside him.

"Yeah."

"Aw man, poor girl."

Alyssa attempted to rise with her sister, but Fran remained slumped on the ground. She raised her head to look at someone in the front row and Ryan forgot to breathe as he caught his first glimpse of her in a year. She was even more beautiful than he remembered, more alluring than he'd dreamed of while he was in New York.

"Damn, this is sad," his friend muttered beside him, but Ryan barely heard. Glittering like emerald gems, Alyssa's eyes were huge in her stricken face, and he could see her chest rapidly rising and falling as she tried to comfort her sister.

Jeremy's mother rose and rocked Fran back and forth against her plump body until she quieted down.

Ryan's sharp gaze followed Alyssa as she went and

stood by the edge of the people lined in front, trembling hands pressed to her mouth. He swallowed hard, his chest filled with emotion from Fran's breakdown, and the effect Alyssa still had on him.

Fran walked back to her seat with Jeremy's mother's arm wrapped around her waist, and the preacher haltingly began the prayer once again.

Nana waved goodbye to him as she headed off to the church to help serve the repast that followed the service.

"I still can't believe Jeremy is gone, and Fran…to say she's not taking it well is an understatement," Ryan remarked in a low voice to LaDarius.

"Man, I was there that night. We'd all been drinking, but I didn't think he'd …" LaDarius stayed quiet for a long moment. "It's messed up, you know? Jeremy was too young to die, man, too young."

Ryan sighed heavily and shook his head. "Yeah, he was."

They walked through the gate of the cemetery and he pulled up short.

"Who in the hell is that guy?" Ryan jerked his thumb towards Alyssa and a tall, brown haired man. They were standing by a white, late model car, and engaged in what seemed to be an intense conversation. Her golden eyebrows were drawn together in a worried frown, and he saw her bite her lip in an agitated gesture. The man appeared to be about their age, and it was apparent from his build he hit the gym regularly.

"I don't know his name, but he works up at the auto store." LaDarius looked over at him with a slight smile. "Why? You still got the hots for Alyssa?"

Ryan examined the pair of them and didn't answer.

There wasn't any physical contact going on, just simple talking. A rush of relief flooded through his body, he must not be her boyfriend.

But then the man put his arm around Alyssa's shoulders and hugged her lithe body close to him. Dread filled Ryan's chest as his hands fisted at his sides. *It seems Alyssa just might have a boyfriend, after all.* Striding towards them, he decided it was high time to see her again, and while he was at it, meet this new fellow.

****

"Jeremy was going to take me home, but I rode with Kenneth instead since he lived closer." Gary stared dismally off in the distance. "I feel so guilty."

"You couldn't have known, nobody did." She'd said those same exact words to Fran a few hours ago. Her brows drew together as her mind drifted to her sister, gazing unseeingly at Gary as he spoke. Fran was.... she was....*oh my God.* They hadn't even been able to go the service at the church; Fran had been such a wreck.

Alyssa gulped convulsively and tried to make sense of Gary's words. "...and we've got to stick together, lean on each other," he was saying, then suddenly grabbed her and squeezed tight with sweaty hands.

"Uh, sure," she said, eyeing him a little suspiciously now as she stepped back.

"Who is that?" he asked in a loud tone and stared over her shoulder.

Alyssa turned her head, and then her heart leapt crazily in her chest.

Ryan.

Her mouth went dry at the sight of his well-defined

muscles shifting smoothly as he approached them. A sense of deja vu washed over her, remembering the sleek black panther they'd encountered while deep in the woods as children. Nobody had believed them; the large felines were so elusive in Louisiana some considered them to be a myth. But that beautiful, majestic creature had been just as real as the incarnation of the man before her.

"Hello, Alyssa," he said in his deep, timbered, familiar voice. The sun glinted off his rich, ebony locks of hair and softened the handsome angles of his face.

Alyssa wet her lips nervously and Ryan's penetrating gaze shot to her mouth, making her even more self-conscious. "Hi, Ryan. Um, this is Gary."

"Nice to meet you." Gary stuck out his hand and the two men shook.

"We grew up together. Ryan, Jeremy, Fran, and me," she explained softly.

"I know. Even though I didn't go to school here, I've heard all about you. Ryan Sutherby, home town hero," Gary drawled sarcastically. Jeremy had also filled him in on Alyssa and Ryan's past. He'd known there had to be a reason why she refused to go out with him and here he was now, in the livid, living flesh.

"Well, I better head to the church. I'll see you there, Alyssa." Gary patted her on the shoulder as he passed, and returned Ryan's threatening glare with one of his own.

That son of a bitch doesn't know who he's messing with, Ryan thought irritably.

"When did you get in?" Alyssa asked, and his gaze shifted to her smooth, tanned visage. Silken locks of hair framed her high cheekbones, and a bolt of desire shot through him at the sight of her rosy, slightly parted lips.

"This morning." He paused at the sight of the emerald nestled above her tempting cleavage.

"Who was that?" he asked suddenly.

"Gary, like I said. A friend of Jeremy's."

"And that's all?"

"That's all."

Alyssa studied him with a level look in her arresting green eyes, almost as if she could see into the past. *That wouldn't be good.*

"Will you ride with me to the church?"

She glanced away and shiny hair spilled over her shoulder in golden waves. He wished he could run his hand over the softness of it, hell, he wished he even had that privilege.

"Thanks, but I've got my car. See?" She gestured towards the car she was standing next to.

"I like it."

"Me too," she replied simply, and rolled the window down as she got in. "Bye, Ryan."

"Wait! Just... wait a minute." Ryan hunched down till he was level with her startled face, not quite sure what he wanted to say, but not wanting her to leave either. Unable to stop himself, he reached his hand inside the window frame and cupped her soft cheek with his big, calloused hand. She nuzzled against him like a trusting kitten as joy exploded in his chest.

"I've missed you, Alyssa. So damn much," he whispered huskily.

She gulped and closed her eyes, a vulnerable expression crossing her winsome face. His hand slid to the flaxen mane of hair at her nape and tightened as a wave of emotion washed over him.

"I've missed you too," she said in a shaky voice. Heedless to whoever was around, Ryan drew her to him in a kiss that shattered the very air around them. He felt like a starved man as he feasted on her luscious lips. Moaning with rapture, his hands cupped each side of her head and he leaned his forehead against hers. Their breath-stealing kiss slowly came to an end, only a prelude of what lie ahead.

"You're not getting away this time, Alyssa. I hope you know that."

"I don't want to."

The dimples he'd dreamed of emerged as she grinned infectiously at him and he smiled back, the void within him filled.

CHAPTER 14

"Fran, eat a piece of chicken at least."

"Would you quit trying to shove food down my throat? You're driving me crazy!"

"Well, you have to eat something!" Alyssa was worried sick about her sister. She'd found her passed out on the patio with a near empty bottle of wine beside her last night. And that was the second night in a row. Alyssa rubbed Fran's back, and felt her small body trembling beneath her hand.

"I'm ready to leave."

Alyssa examined the dark circles under her sister's eyes. "Okay, let's go. We've got tons of food at the house."

"I told you I'm not hungry."

Alyssa sighed. "You can just ride with me home."

"No, I don't want to leave my car here. I'll drive myself."

"Alright, but don't stop by the liquor store, Fran."

Her sister shot her a glare of pure loathing. "Last time I checked, I was grown. So don't think for a minute you can tell me what to do." She snatched up her purse and slammed out of the church kitchen where they'd been alone.

Alyssa started to take off after her but stopped, remembering Ryan. She found him in the dining area talking with some friends. He smiled as she walked up to him and hugged her close to his side.

"Where've you been?"

"Talking with Fran."

Ryan examined her for a moment, and then tugged her by the hand over to the window.

"How are you doing?"

"Me? I'm fine." She paused to gather her courage. "I'm leaving, but will you come by tonight? Here's the address."

He tucked the piece of paper in his pocket. "I'll be over after dropping by my house."

"Okay." Ryan's thumb rubbed across the top of her hand and she almost trembled from that slight gesture. She jerked her eyes from their joined hands to his, and her worries faded away for a moment as she grew lost in their depths as true as the summer sky.

****

After he'd eaten supper with Nana, Ryan pulled up to the large, brick house with dark green shutters and parked behind Alyssa's car.

She answered the door and his mouth went bone dry. She looked irresistible in a yellow tank top paired with white shorts that emphasized her long, tanned legs and bare feet.

"Hi, come on in. Remember, this was Casey's grandmother's house," she laughed. "But it's really comfy. We call it vintage."

The inside was painted beige, with wall to wall green shag carpeting, and old fashioned orange printed wagon wheel furniture.

She grinned up at him and he snagged her around the waist. "Well, tell me what you call that mongrel at my house. Is that supposed to be a dog or a small

147

horse?"

She furrowed her eyebrows in mock concentration. "Are you referring to Daisy?"

"Yeah, *Daisy,*" he drawled. "She almost knocked me over when I got out of my truck, and then tried to lick me to death. And let me tell you, she doesn't smell like a flower."

Alyssa laughed out loud. "Well, she can get a little excited. Your grandmother has probably told her all about you, and she thought y'all were already friends."

"You know, Nana mentioned she got a dog, but I thought she meant a poodle or something, not that flea bitten hound."

Alyssa's mouth dropped. "Ryan! She does not have fleas! I gave her a bath myself. And the vet said she has some lab and German Shepherd in her, so she's not a *hound.*"

"German Shepherd's are good watchdogs, so she must have just a drop of that breed," he countered in amusement.

"She does bark at people, she just knew you were nice. Dogs can sense those things, you know."

She nodded at him while he eyed her skeptically. "Hmmm, we'll see."

"She was about to get ran over at the flea market, we just couldn't leave her there. And your grandmother loves her."

"Okay, okay. She is kind of cute, in an overgrown, shaggy, smelly, kind of way."

Alyssa glowered at him playfully, and he leaned over and kissed her on the soft bow of her mouth. "But not nearly as cute as you," he whispered against her lips.

Alyssa's face broke into a slow, dazzling smile. Desire raged through his veins and he groaned, unable to believe his body's reaction to just a simple kiss. Alyssa ran her fingers up the nape of his neck and pressed her soft body against his.

"Alyssa..." he breathed, his voice unsteady.

A nuzzling kiss swept across his neck and he dropped his head against hers, feeling as if he'd landed in a sweet kind of hell. The sound of a glass door sliding open penetrated through the erotic fog in his brain and Alyssa backed away from him a few feet.

Damn. Ryan gazed into her wide set, vivid eyes, swirling with a wary fervor. It was as if they'd never been parted, the same powerful force that drew them together also chained them to the other. He watched as she gulped unsteadily and drew a deep, fortifying breath himself, determined to lay Alyssa's fears to rest this time around. Clasping her hand in his, he squeezed comfortingly.

"How about taking me on the grand tour?"

She led him to the large kitchen where sliding glass doors let out onto the dark brick patio. A small figure sat huddled sideways in a chair, wine glass in hand.

"Is that Fran?"

"Yes. She's been drinking and smoking cigarettes like crazy since Jeremy passed away, and will barely eat anything. I've tried talking to her, but... she's really depressed."

He looked back at Fran staring out at nothing and his heart squeezed in sympathy for her. His gaze flicked to her distraught sister. "She has to have time to grieve. Be patient and she'll come around."

Alyssa nodded and pressed her lips together. "I

149

know."

"Where's your room?" he asked quietly, and surprised eyes flew to meet his.

"Um, down the hallway, I'll show you."

He followed, admiring the lush curve of her bottom and sway of her hips.

A heavy wooden four poster bed sat against the opposite wall of the spacious room, draped in a deep purple and crimson red satin coverlet. *Of course I'd notice the bed first.* Ryan shook his head in derision.

"My very first own room." Alyssa spun in a circle on the thick beige carpet and closed the door behind her. "At first, it was kind of scary. I'd always been with Fran." She glanced away and shrugged. "But as time went by, I got used to it."

Ryan felt a chill go through him, and wondered if he'd been dismissed in the same manner. A jolt of surprise shot through him as he saw the photo of him and Alyssa from Valentine's Day on her dresser. He picked it up, and circled his arms around her waist.

"Beauty and the beast," he murmured over her shoulder. She laughed low and he growled against the creamy skin of her neck. "I've often thought about devouring you, my pretty."

She shivered and grasped his arms hard. He felt an urgency rising in her, the sensations webbed over to him. Ryan decided to just flow with it, go wherever it took them on this river of rapture. Alyssa turned in his embrace to face him and he set the picture back down with a forgotten thud.

"Oh Ryan" she whispered, and ran her fingers up under his shirt to caress his bare skin. He shuddered from the feel of her soft, cool hands on his overheated skin.

"Alyssa," he groaned raggedly.

She stood on her tiptoes and pulled him down for a hot, wet kiss. Her tongue danced seductively against his and he deepened the kiss, swallowing her gasp with his mouth. *It's been so long, too long*, and dragged her closer to him. It felt as if lightning danced through his veins, instead of mere blood.

Ryan's hands grasped her curvy waist, and his breaths quickened as his shaking hands neared her breasts. Ripe and deliciously heavy in his hands, he rubbed his thumbs against the stiffening peaks.

Alyssa panted damply into his neck. "Ryan, oh Ryan, that feels so good."

"I know, baby," he whispered back, so turned on a red haze had clouded his brain.

Drawing her shirt up, he unfastened her lacy bra and pulled it out of the front of the tank top with quick, hasty motions. Her head fell back and he dropped heated kisses down the column of her neck.

"You taste so damn good," he rasped.

She dug her fingernails into his back and leaned into him.

"Christ," he hissed when her breasts pressed against his head. Unable to help himself, he caught a rosy nipple in his mouth, suckling gently while she writhed against him and moaned his name. The roaring in his brain grew louder, driven on by her soft sounds of pleasure. "Come over here," he murmured. His hands slid down her back and froze when he felt the welts that crossed her lower back and disappeared into the band of her shorts.

"Stop!" she said in a low, warning voice, and he

started in confusion when Alyssa shoved him away. She jerked her shirt back down as desire drained away from her face, only to be replaced by a blanched dread.

"What is going on?" he demanded.

"Nothing! Just slow down, okay?" She crossed her hands behind her back, almost in an embarrassed gesture.

"Alyssa, you were fine until I touched those marks. What in the hell happened to you?"

Her lovely face grew even paler, and she shook her head silently at him. "I don't want to talk about it. It's fine," she said after a long moment.

Ryan had a strong suspicion where the scars had come from and he fought to keep his voice calm. "Who did this to you? Tell me," he coaxed, and gathered her resisting body in his muscular arms. She slowly relaxed and lay pliant against him. His hands finally drifted cautiously lower when she twisted against him

"No, just stop! I don't want you to touch me there!" Distrustful eyes flashed with resentment. "And who do you think did it?" she asked bitterly.

Ryan's head felt ready to explode from the fury pounding through him. "Let me see." he ordered roughly. He spun her protesting form around and raised her shirt. And then he could only stare in horrified disbelief at the thin, white scars that crisscrossed her lower back, and dipped into her nude bikini panties.

"Goddammit," he ground out. "Why didn't you tell me? Why, Alyssa?" he demanded frantically, unable to believe this had went on right under his nose. Without pausing for her to answer, he raged on. "I'd kill him right now if he wasn't already dead! That son of a bitch died just like the coward he was! Fuck!" Ryan kicked the bedpost hard while he wished it was Billy Martin's teeth he'd just knocked down his throat. "I'd break his evil hands before I killed him, though," he swore in a low voice, his eyes fastened on her back.

She began to sob and tenderness welled up in him. Ryan leaned down and kissed her marred skin with gentle care.

"Stop… please stop, Ryan," she whimpered, and his heart broke again for her.

He continued raining kisses all over the slender column of her back. "I wish I could take away the pain, all of it." Alyssa's heart raced against his arm, her muscles tense, poised for an unknown danger.

How dare that bastard. The scars on her back looked like somebody had whipped her. *No, not somebody. Her own damn father.*

His hands stilled their soothing motions and he closed his eyes, the night of their first kiss playing in his mind. Heaven, followed by pure hell. Her swollen cheek and eye had turned almost purplish black by the fourth day, and he remembered how long it had taken to heal. Much, much too long. A primeval, protective rage had charged through him every time he'd looked at her.

He turned her around in his arms, but she turned her face away. "I wonder what else you haven't told me," he rasped, shaken to his core from the evidence of violence that had been inflicted upon her.

Alyssa shook her head side to side, seemingly lost in her thoughts, till he finally raised her chin to meet his eyes. She stared at him, her breath coming in fast pants as tears streaked down her flushed skin.

"Hey, I've seen the bruises on you, remember? You can't pretend it didn't happen."

Alyssa wondered wildly if his penetrating stare could pull the vivid memories from her mind. "I don't want to talk about the past because it will destroy me. I just want to live in the present and think about the future." She drew an unsteady gulp of air and bit her lip. "That's it."

Ryan's dark brows drew together. "I'm no psychiatrist, but I'm pretty sure talking about is good."

Alyssa regarded him silently, taking in his frustrated scowl and smiled softly. "I know you want to help, but…" She laid her head against him. The steady rhythm of his heart thudded against her jaw, and peace overtook the uneasy, fearful churnings of her belly. His masculine scent overwhelmed her with its familiarity and relieved tears sprung to her eyes, so grateful he hadn't changed.

"This helps." She said patted his hard chest. "More than anything else. When I'm with you, I feel safe." Only rarely did she visit the buried places in her mind where her childhood lurked, and she wished it could somehow be forgotten.

He hugged her to him and rested his head on top of hers. Alyssa felt his strength melting into her, infusing her mind and body. "You'll always be safe and sound when you're with me. I love you, honey, I never stopped," he whispered into her ear.

She stiffened in disbelief. "You haven't called or anything, and the way you looked at me that last time…you hated me."

"I was angry, yes. But I couldn't hate you even if I tried, Alyssa. Hey, look at me," he urged in a low voice.

Although her eyes were puffy and red, she was still unparalleled in her beauty. *And mine.* He kissed her lips in gentle assurance. "I thought about you a lot, wondered how you were. I even called Nana more just to hear her say your name." His fingers threaded through the soft tendrils of hair by her ear. "I couldn't wait till the summer just so I could see you again."

Alyssa's hand came up between them and she laid it over his heart in a gesture that found its way to the deepest depths of his soul. "I love you too, Ryan. I never stopped either."

And therein lay the difference between them; he believed her. Stark and powerful, there was no doubting the sincerity on her guileless, heart shaped face.

She swallowed audibly hard when he stroked her naked back, and golden locks of hair fell forward as he tickled feather-light caresses over her scarred flesh.

Ryan studied the troubled expression on her face with one of his, hardly able to draw a breath in his tight chest. Her eyes held so much pain, but she possessed the spirit of a fighter. "My lionhearted girl," he whispered. Love for her pumped like adrenaline through his veins, and he swore fiercely no harm would come to her again as he swept her slight weight up in his arms.

She shrieked in surprise and clung to his neck. "You still weigh the same as you did when you were thirteen."

"I don't remember that. You must be thinking about some other girl." She slanted him a playful glance from under long lashes.

"Nope. I can't believe you've forgot that. I'm about to throw you on the bed, I swear I am." He swung her in that direction as she tightened her hold on him.

"I'm thinking, Ryan! Wait, are you talking about

that time my flip flops got stuck in the mud?" She scrunched her nose at him. "That hardly counts; you gave me a *piggyback ride.*"

He grunted and deposited her in the middle of the bed. "Yeah, and you're still heavy."

Alyssa slapped him on the arm as he stretched out beside her. "Whatever! "

"Ow!" He cradled his forearm and she rolled her eyes.

"You deserve way worse than that, calling me fat," she grumbled.

"Aw now, I never called you fat." He ran his gaze over her luscious, curvy form. "You're perfect, baby. Perfect," he whispered huskily, and nestled her closer to him. Weariness took over as he murmured into her fragrant hair, "Now where's your nightgown?"

Alyssa laughed low and pulled back to look at him. "Why?"

"Because I'm exhausted. I drove nonstop yesterday and last night to get here in time for the funeral."

Shivers of anticipation sparked through her at the thought of him in her bed. She ran her fingers through his silky black hair and nodded, noting his heavy lids. "You do look wore out. I'm going to check on Fran before we go to sleep." They exchanged a glance, and Ryan sat up on the bed to pull off his shoes. "I'll be back in a few minutes. There's extra toothbrushes in the top drawer of the bathroom cabinet."

"I take it I'm not the first guy to stay over," he joked.

"Well, no," she replied slowly.

Ryan turned incredulous eyes to her and Alyssa burst out laughing. "But you're the first guy *I've* had stay the night, though."

"Better be," he muttered.

She smiled at the dark frown that crossed his face. "You are so adorable."

He gave her a pained look. "Please don't let anybody hear you say that. I'm a football player, remember?"

"As if I could forget," she retorted grumpily, and he blew out an exasperated breath.

"You know, most girls would be thrilled to be dating a quarterback, but, oh no, not you," he said dryly.

"Yeah, but not if it means you have to move halfway across the country. I am proud of you, it's just…I don't know, it's hard to explain." She didn't want to tell him she absolutely hated the fact that he played football, and it wasn't just the distance. She was positive those college girls were making a fool of themselves over their new, handsome quarterback. Alyssa cringed inwardly; it was beyond humiliating to discover she was this insecure.

He regarded her evenly and cupped her cheek with one big hand. "I'm here now. We'll always find our way back to each other. Don't you know that, Alyssa?"

"Yes, always," she whispered back.

****

Alyssa watched her sister take another drink of wine and slid open the glass door. "I hope you have bug spray on."

Fran picked up a bottle off the ground and waved it at her. "Yes, *Mother*, I do," she replied sarcastically.

"When are you coming in?" Alyssa asked, determined to have a civil conversation.

"When I feel like it," Fran returned coolly, head cocked to the side.

"Fran...I know you're sad, and you have every right to be. But do you think drinking is really helping?"

She drained the rest of her glass, and lit a cigarette with shaking hands. "It helps me sleep, so yeah, I'd say it was helping."

"You can't use alcohol-"

Her sister cut her off. "I'm not."

"Did you eat that sandwich I fixed for you?" She remembered suddenly Fran had refused to eat it earlier.

"*Yes.*"

Alyssa sighed in irritation. "I guess I'm going back in. And if you need to talk, I'm right here. Anytime."

Fran nodded and crossed her arms over her chest.

"Okay...well, good night."

"Night," Fran snapped.

Unable to help herself, Alyssa nagged her sister again when she got to the door. "Fran, you don't need to stay up too late, and don't be drinking all night, either."

Fran stood up and faced her. "And *you* don't start telling me what to do with my life!"

"I'm not trying to, but I don't like seeing you drink! And this is the third night in a row!"

Fran groaned dramatically and threw up her arms. "Well, go sign me up for AA, why don't you? Alyssa, just go to bed and get off my back."

Alyssa studied her sister's pale face with a sinking heart. "I'll see you in the morning."

"They gave me the week off, so don't wake me up."

"I won't," she replied, her mind already on the man waiting in her bedroom.

Ryan was lying with his arms crossed under his head when Alyssa walked in. She'd changed into a short, pink nightgown that emphasized every bare curve beneath, and her hair flowed down her back in a shiny, silken mass. She was so tempting that despite his bone deep exhaustion, Ryan felt his body stir in response.

He jerked the covers back and patted the space beside him. "Come here, beautiful," he said huskily.

She scooted in beside him. Ryan turned and engulfed her in his embrace, his senses filled with her unique honey scent. He swallowed against the tightness in his throat and smoothed her hair gently back with both hands, savoring the feel of the soft strands against his tough hands.

"I can't believe you're here, Ryan. It seems like you've been gone forever," she said in a quiet voice.

He tucked her against him and rested his head on hers. "It does to me too. I wanted to come home for Christmas, but I couldn't get off work. I thought about home all the time, it's just so different in New York. Everybody knows I'm from the South as soon as I start talking." He grinned ruefully and she laughed.

"I guess we've got that southern drawl."

"I guess so."

She sighed happily and snuggled into his embrace. "I hoped when you came home for the summer you'd be here with me, just like this."

"Me too, baby. I've dreamed of this for months." He stroked her back, and felt her shapely limbs grow lax. Overwhelming feelings of deep contentment and gratitude for this woman rushed through him and he kissed her forehead, her lips. "I love you."

"Love you, too," she mumbled back.

Ryan settled on his back and brought her with him so her head was cradled against his shoulder. She was surely worn out from all that had happened in the past few days. He pulled the covers over them and closed his eyes, the whisper of her breath soft on his skin.

****

Alyssa's eyes flew open in surprise at the feel of a hand stroking her breast and then drifting off to her shoulder. A half smile crossed Ryan's sensuous mouth when she rubbed her face against the crisp hairs on his bare, powerful chest and kissed the side of his neck.

"Good morning, sweetheart," his sleep-roughened voice rumbled against her ear. She shivered as he drew his hand up her nape and tangled his fingers through her hair.

"Mornin', did you sleep good?"

She had, she'd slept like a log. The last thing she remembered before closing her eyes was feeling safe and toasty warm in his sinewy arms.

"Well..." he drawled.

Alyssa leaned back. "Well, what?"

"Let's just say I wasn't aware you snored." He tipped his face down to hers, eyes bright with amusement in his dark face.

"I do not snore!" Alyssa gasped, horrified at the thought.

"Surely Fran told you." Ryan shrugged easily as she stared at him.

Actually, Fran had mentioned it a couple of times before when she'd been sick with a cold... "Did I really?"

Ryan laughed. "No, you didn't. Still gullible as ever, I see."

She thumped his shoulder and giggled. "Sometimes I can't stand you, did you know that?"

"You sure have funny ways of showing it." He nuzzled her neck and she sighed in mock despair.

"I know; I've got to work on that."

She kissed the hollow of his throat as his laugh vibrated against her lips. His long fingers caressed her back and then wandered to her bottom in a leisurely fashion.

"Who knew we'd be here, lying together like this," she wondered out loud.

Ryan's hand stilled. "I knew," he said in a low voice, and she twisted away from him to look in his face. A shadow of a beard sharpened his fiercely masculine features, and the arresting appeal in his sapphire eyes made her realize his seriousness.

"I get off at 4:30. Come over after then," she dared to whisper while at the same time whispering to her inner protesting self, *quit being so damn paranoid.*

"I will." He hugged her to him and kissed the top of her head. "I'm eating lunch with Nana today; you won't believe how much I've missed her cooking."

"Oh, yes I would," she said in a dry tone, and couldn't help but laugh at his quizzical frown.

****

Ryan took a bite of country fried steak smothered in pepper gravy and groaned in satisfaction. "This is the best meal I've had in a year, Nana. I promise you it is."

His grandmother smiled. "I'm so glad you're home, it's no fun cooking just for me."

"Well, I intend to take full advantage of your

Dara Morris

culinary skills," he assured her with a firm nod of his head.

"Oh, and I've made your favorite for dessert, coconut meringue pie."

"Just when I thought it couldn't get any better," he declared.

Nana chuckled. "Why, one would think you starved up there!"

"I ate burgers and pizza mostly."

He grinned as Nana made a disgusted sound. "That garbage isn't good for you. I'm just gonna have to teach you to cook, that's all there is to it."

"That's not a bad idea, actually." Ryan took a drink of sweet tea. He didn't think he could survive the next three years on fast food. "Teach me to cook *this.*" He gestured around at the feast on the table.

Nana waved her hand dismissively. "None of this is hard to make. And then you can have a good, home cooked meal, instead of eating that mess. I'll have you cooking in no time, don't you worry."

"I'm ready." He took a bite of fresh corn on the cob.

"I showed Alyssa how to make apple fritters. She helped me make them for my Sunday school class, and they were delicious."

At the sound of her name, he sat up straighter in the seat. "Speaking of Alyssa, I'd like to have her over for supper one day this week."

"She's welcome here anytime. Why, I don't know what I'd do without her, she's sweet as pie. We have such fun together, I just adore her."

"I do too."

Nana gave him a small, wise smile and wagged her

finger at him. "Ever since I first saw you two together, I knew there was something special there. And she's such a lovely girl, with those unusual green eyes."

"Yes, she is," Ryan agreed quietly.

He stood up to help Nana clear the table. "Hey now! What are you doing with that steak?"

"Steak is one of her favorites. Isn't it, girl?" Nana crooned as she tore off pieces to feed a blissful Daisy.

The mutt didn't even chew before gulping it down. "It's one of my favorites, too," he grumbled.

"I'll make more before you leave; my goodness."

Nana's blue eyes sparkled with merriment, and she didn't seem like she'd aged in the past year, Ryan noted with relief. Even though she always sounded cheerful and upbeat when they spoke, he still worried about her.

"Good." He grinned at his grandmother when she rolled her eyes heavenward in mock exasperation.

"I never thought I'd live to see the day when you were jealous of a dog."

"Well, when you start feeding it steak, yeah, I get a little jealous. I'm not afraid to admit it," he joked.

Chuckling still, she shook her head. "I see I had better get started quickly on those cooking lessons."

Ryan gave his grandmother a hug. "There's no one who can cook like you."

"Thank you, honey. I sure have missed you."

"I've missed you too." He looked down at the woman who had raised him, and felt a rush of love as he gazed upon her plump cheeks and colorful housedress. "Is that a new dress?"

"Yes sir; just finished it last weekend."

"It's nice, next you'll have to teach me to sew," he joked.

"I thought you were only going to be in six weeks! I can't work miracles, you know."

"Just teaching me to cook will be a miracle itself." Ryan raised his eyebrows doubtfully and added, "But if I do learn, my roommates will be calling you with their undying gratitude."

His grandmother beamed. "Now, I wouldn't mind that a bit."

"I'm going to stay the night with LaDarius again, so I'll be over around eleven in the morning to help you." He hated to lie to his grandmother, but with her strict values, knew she'd never approve of him staying the night with Alyssa.

"Alright, sweetie, I'll see you then."

They hugged goodbye and Ryan left. He figured he'd kill some time by going over to LaDarius's house until Alyssa got off work.

CHAPTER 15

"What do you think?" Alyssa twirled around so Casey could see her spaghetti strap white sundress.

"It looks really good on you. And I can definitely see how Ryan spoiled you for other men, he is gorgeous!"

Alyssa laughed. "He is, isn't he? But it's not just that. He's a good person, the best kind of person," she said wistfully, remembering the gentle way he'd held her last night.

"Well, he sure has you in a tizzy! I've never seen you fuss over what you're wearing like you are now."

"This is the first time we've gone out in over a year, it's hard to believe he's really back." She put in silver dangly earrings and met Casey's eyes in the mirror. "Fran is drinking again tonight." She shook her head. "I wish they hadn't given her the whole week off work now. All she's doing is getting drunk! And then she has the nerve to get an attitude when I try and talk to her!"

"I know it. I tried talking to her too and she told me to shut up."

"She didn't! Maybe she was just kidding," she offered.

"No, she was serious. But its fine, I understand. I miss Jeremy too."

"We all do." The doorbell rang, and Alyssa's pulse

jumped with excitement. "I'll go answer it, it's probably Ryan."

"You two have fun. And don't worry about Fran; I won't let her drive off or anything."

"Well, gee thanks, I hadn't even thought about that." She rolled her eyes as Casey laughed.

Ryan caught her hand as they walked to his truck and opened the door for her.

"So where are we going?"

"I figured we'd just ride around like we used to. I've missed driving my truck down these ole' country roads," he drawled.

"Talk about a cheap date," she teased, and gestured down to her dress.

His gaze flicked from the road to her and an appreciative grin split his rugged features. "Hey, I think you're beautiful, babe. I wouldn't change not one thing."

Alyssa's heart warmed to the brink of overfilling and she scooted closer over to him. "You sweet talker, you," she murmured, and he brought his arm around her.

"I saw Mr. Mack today, and he told me about this pretty little sandbar way out on River Road. We're going to eat there; I've packed blankets and everything."

"That sounds fun. It'll be like old times." She laid her head on his broad chest.

"Yes, but even better," he replied softly, and lifted her hand to kiss her fingers.

They looped the long way around the horseshoe shaped bayou and took the old highway out to River Road. An occasional truck passed, but only the most dedicated fishermen ventured out this far.

"Ryan, I start school at Central Louisiana University this fall. I got a scholarship."

"Nana told me. I'm proud of you, babe, you're going to be a great nurse. But then you've always done anything you've ever set your mind to, so I wasn't surprised at all." He cupped the back of her head. "Look at us, Alyssa, we did pretty good for ourselves, didn't we?"

"Yes, we have." She paused for a moment. "How long are you going to be in?"

Ryan glanced down at her golden crown of hair. "Six weeks, I go back the second week in July."

"That's more than I thought."

Encouraged by her mild response, he continued. "I requested to be off since training camp doesn't start until the end of July. I was surprised myself when my boss approved it. But he said to not expect any time off for the rest of the year, so I won't be able to come in for Christmas."

She wrapped her arm around to his side and squeezed. "Well, then I'll just have to come see you. I'll save up my money and fly up there."

"That's a great idea, baby. And I'll help you pay for it." He caressed her arm, thinking of all the places he could show her. "I sure don't want you driving; I'd have a heart attack."

"I've never even been out of Louisiana."

"Yeah, I know. That's why I said that," he said in a dry tone.

"Hey, you drove all the way up there not long after you got your truck! What's the difference?"

"There's a big difference. Alyssa, what's the

furthest you've drove?"

She straightened up, flinging her long hair over her shoulder. "I don't see how that matters. Everybody has to start somewhere, Ryan. And I think it'd be fun, seeing all the different states."

"It is," he conceded. "The mountains in Tennessee are beautiful."

"Mountains? I bet that was amazing."

"Yeah, it really is. But it's nice here too, just in a different way."

"I know, I love it here. I just wish you did too."

Ryan sighed, how to explain it to her, when it was something he didn't understand himself; this clawing desire to leave Cypress Bayou.

"Alyssa, I…"

"It's okay," she interrupted.

His heart clenched at the withdrawn expression that settled on her face. They drove in silence down the gravel road till he reached the first big curve. "This is it," he announced, and pulled beside a grove of stately oak trees.

She glanced over at him and he reached out a hand to caress the smooth line of her jaw. "This time that we spend together will be the only thing that keeps me going in the cold nights when I'm missing you, babe. Let's not have this same argument we had a year ago."

"We won't," she said quietly.

He leaned over to capture her sweet lips in a kiss. "You're not getting out of here till I see a smile."

"There," she whispered back and grinned.

He kissed a dimple, and watched as her eyes glowed even brighter. "Now that's better. Let's go."

They walked from the truck, and entered a circle of

tall trees that held a small clearing within. Like an emerald carpet, thick grass graced the circumference and hanging branches intertwined like a group hug. Songbirds filled the space with their music, light and airy as a flute. She gasped and squeezed his hand. "Oh, it's beautiful, Ryan."

"It is," he agreed. He'd been astounded by the gorgeous, green lushness when he'd came out here earlier.

"And Mr. Mack told you about this?" The sun's rays struck gold off her flawless face as she shook her head in awe. "I can't believe we've never heard of this place. It's so pretty."

"He said he used to take his wife out here and that it was a very special spot. His exact words."

"It is very special," she said softly. Her eyebrows dipped in a serious line. "Poor Mr. Mack. After all these years, he still misses her."

Ryan pulled her body close to his. "He said she was his true love and there's nobody who can replace her in his heart."

A smile curved her rosy lips. "Yes, I've heard him say that. Look, there's the path to the river." She pointed over his shoulder.

"Let's go see it." He stepped in front to lead her down and she held tight to his hand. "Be careful, it's steep." The Red River flowed before them, gray-green and sparkling in the bright sunshine.

"You should've told me to bring a bathing suit." She kicked off her sandals to walk barefoot in the white, powdery sand.

"Hey, you don't need a bathing suit to swim. Fish don't wear them," he teased.

"I bet you told me not to bring one on purpose," she said suspiciously, and laughed when he grinned at her.

"All part of my ulterior plan, my dear." Alyssa's hair whipped out like a silk flag in the warm breeze and tickled across his cheek. "I need to get the fire going. You wanna help me gather up some wood?"

"Sure."

Before long there was a fire blazing, and Ryan went to get the ice chest out of the truck. Drinks in hand, he walked back to Alyssa. She'd spread a blanket out on the ground and sat staring pensively into the flames, looking adorably out of place in her bright dress.

"Here, I got you some wine."

"Wine?" Her surprised face tipped up to his.

"Well, I didn't think you'd want beer," he lazily replied. "It's strawberry."

She took it from his outstretched hand and peered into the Styrofoam cup as if there were snakes swimming in it.

"It's not going to bite you."

"I've had wine before." As if to prove a point, she took a long swallow. "I was ten when I first tried it, actually. Fran dared me and of course I couldn't back down."

"No, of course not," he said with a grin, and twisted the top off his beer. "So how'd you like it?"

"Well, this tastes a lot better than that crap Mama used to buy," she laughed.

He sat on the blanket behind her and pulled her soft body to his bare chest.

A delicious warmth spread through her as she took

a drink of her third cup of wine, half listening to Ryan as he talked about the football program at New York State. "... and next season I'll be playing more because the starting quarterback graduated. I hope we get to a bowl game this year."

"Then I'd see you playing on TV," she smiled. "Oh my gosh, your grandmother would throw a party. That house would be packed. Actually, the whole town would be watching it, come to think of it."

He shrugged. "We've got a lot of talent and as long as our key players stay healthy, I think we've got a good shot. But enough talk about football, are you ready to go swimming?"

"Seriously?"

"Yep." He rose to his feet and clasped her hand in his to pull her up beside him. "It's only around seven; we've still got plenty of time to swim."

"But I don't have a bathing suit, remember?"

"I remember." His bold gaze skimmed over her. "Just swim naked," he said in a deep, suggestive voice that sent quivers down her. Ryan's muscles rippled with strength as he turned to throw more logs on the fire. "I will if you will."

She giggled and drained the rest of her wine. "Okay, but if somebody comes out here, you're dead meat."

"Nobody will, I promise. Look around, we're out in the middle of nowhere." He laced their fingers together.

"Well, that's true. I wonder how Mr. Mack even found it."

"I don't know, but I'm glad he told me about it. I got the feeling he hasn't told many people."

She raised her eyebrows is a thoughtful slant. "Hmm, probably not. If he has, they've kept it a secret too." She stumbled on the steep path down as her foot caught on a protruding root.

"Steady, now," he said, and grasped her hand securely in his. .

Alyssa gazed out at the unbroken waters of the wide river once they reached the sandbar.

"Do you realize it's been two years since we've went swimming together?" Ryan rested his head on her shoulder as his bare skin burned against hers in a growing storm.

Closing her eyes, they snapped back open when a dizzy wave washed over her. She sagged against him for a moment and he whispered in her ear, "off with the dress, Alyssa."

She pulled the hem up and then hesitated. "I cannot believe you want to go skinny dipping. I've never even swam in a two piece."

"Why not?"

"Because…because of the scars," she said in a tentative voice.

His dark brows lifted. "Ah. Well, it's just me and you, babe."

"I know, but still… I'm keeping my bra and panties on."

"Hey, I can compromise." He held his hands up and winked.

She smiled and in a swift movement, lifted her dress over her head to reveal a satin pink polka dotted bra and panty set. Desire flared in his eyes as he curved his big hand around her waist. "Damn," he said in a low, husky voice. "I love what you've got on."

Alyssa resisted the urge to shield herself from his smoldering stare. "Um, thanks."

She snuck a quick peep at his black boxer briefs when he dropped his rolled-up jeans.

"Let's go in together. One, two, three!" She tugged his hand and they both plunged in the warm river. "Oh, it's cold right here," she exclaimed as they swam further out to a cool pocket of water.

Ryan tugged her close and she wrapped her legs around his lean waist. The intense light in his gaze caused her nerves to tingle and dance along her spine.

"You're beautiful," she said softly, caressing the strong line of his jaw and line of his straight, dark brows. He had the look of a noble warrior from another time she thought dreamily, and glided her hands down his slick, powerful chest.

"Beautiful?" he asked with a sardonic twist of his well-formed lips.

"Yes, beautiful." She fondled the dark strands of hair at his nape as she brought her hands around his neck. "Don't tell me I'm the only one who's noticed those baby blues of yours."

To her surprise, an uncomfortable expression crossed his face. Her eyes narrowed suspiciously and she remarked with an innocent air, "So tell me, how *was* it in New York? I mean, besides football."

"It was fine."

"You were there a whole year and all you have to say is, "it was fine?"

His strong countenance hardened in an irritated scowl. "Well, let's see, Alyssa, I went to school, played football, and worked. That's about it."

She huffed in annoyance and splashed water on his

face.

"Hey, that's cold!"

"What's your point?" she laughed.

"Oh, you're in for it now," he warned, and she shrieked as he tossed her away from him.

She emerged sputtering and plunked her hands on her hips. "You don't play fair, Ryan. You just throw me around!"

He laughed and swam up to her, drawing their wet bodies flush against each other. "I'm sorry," he murmured.

Alyssa melted inside as she met his contrite gaze. "It's okay, I was just kidding."

His lips curved in a smile full of sensual promise and then she felt the thrill of his kiss once more.

"You are so sexy," he whispered. Her bra had been rendered transparent by the water, causing her nipples to jut out impudently. The sight nearly did him in and he grasped her bottom almost desperately. Their lips shared a savage exchange of passion, full of pent up cravings. He needed every part, every bit of her, and had for so long now.

His grip eased on her and slid under the front of her panties. "Oh my God, Ryan," she panted against his mouth and practically tried to crawl into his skin. Dying to feel her, he pulled the skimpy material to the side and caressed her most intimate parts.

She shuddered against him, and he imitated in her mouth what he was doing with his fingers. Slowly easing one long finger in, he marveled at the tightness of her and brought it back out, stroking her bud of ecstasy. Her lips danced over his neck as he ground his hard arousal against her, her moans of pleasure urging him to a mindless frenzy.

"Alyssa," he groaned, on fire for her despite the cool water lapping at their bodies. Slowly sliding a second finger in, he watched her with heavy-lidded eyes. Her long lashes flew open at the intrusion, and he whispered thickly, "It's okay, baby. Just relax." Hot-blooded lust surged madly through him, and he leaned down to taste her delicious pink-tipped breast. Alyssa's fingernails dug deep into his back, and he held fast against the erotic sensations wracking his body. Lavishing the same treatment on her other nipple, he suckled wildly as her lips worked magic on the sensitive area by his ear.

His thumb rubbed against the engorged nub and she pulled his head to hers, kissing him frantically as she gasped his name. "Just let it happen, baby," he whispered, barely able to speak.

"Ryan!" she cried out, her body quaking, and moisture flooded against his fingers. He hugged her to him and buried his face against wet locks of hair, absorbing every quiver of her shaking body. Never had he experienced such soul shattering honesty and wild abandonment.

"Oh, Ryan," she said in a choked voice near his ear and he tightened his hold on her, desire and tenderness coursing a potent path.

Alyssa was shaken to the depths of her core by what had just happened. The sensual magic she'd been under had been addictive, and she wasn't the only one caught up in its web. Even now, she could feel him jutting rigidly against her.

"Let's go back to the fire," he said in a low, strained voice.

Dara Morris

"Okay," she whispered, and swam back to the shore.

Alyssa slipped her dress on and turned back to look at the man who'd just given her a level of sensuality she'd only heard of. "Come on." She grabbed his hand and they ran up to the path, breathless with laughter and anticipation.

A strange sensation assailed her as she stepped back onto the springy grass and smelt the honeysuckle aroma blended with wood smoke.

"What's wrong?" Ryan looked at her in concern when she stopped in her tracks.

"I don't know, I just…I got this weird feeling for a minute." She shook her head to clear it. "Probably just the wine."

He smiled and kissed her lips. "Maybe it was that third cup. You sit tight and I'll get this fire going again. And then we'll grill some hotdogs and s'mores."

"Yum, I haven't had s'mores in forever."

"Neither have I." He patted her bottom as he turned away towards the truck.

Ryan came back with his jeans on and pointed to a log by the fire. "Why don't you take off your wet clothes, and lay them over there with my boxers to dry."

"Okay. My bra is getting my dress all wet."

"I'll help you take it off." One corner of his mouth lifted in a slow smile, and his fingers slid around to unfasten it in a smooth motion. She sucked her breath in as he drifted lower and hooked his thumbs over the sides of her panties, trailing them down her thighs.

Ryan's head swam with heady sensations as he fought the urge to lean forward and taste her. "Here,

176

babe," he said hoarsely, and handed her the sodden scrap as he stood back up.

"It's so peaceful out here, I love it. It's like we're in our little world out here." Alyssa gestured to the ring of trees that surrounded them. He took an unsteady gulp of his beer when she walked back towards him, bare breasts swaying deliciously under the thin cotton. Their gazes met and simmered, hot as the fire that burned before them.

She sat down and patted the spot beside her. "And it's nice and soft with all these blankets."

"I robbed Nana's linen closet. I told her I was staying at LaDarius's house, so stick with the story if she says anything." He lowered himself to sit beside her and stretched his bare feet towards the hot flames.

"Mmm, I'd wondered what you told her."

"Certainly not the truth," he stated wryly.

"No," she agreed, sipping on her wine.

"I'm going to see if we can get a signal on the radio." Moments later, a song from Aerosmith filled the circle of trees.

"Good choice," she remarked as he walked back towards her.

He hunkered down by the fire and stirred up the coals. It was now pitch dark and she leaned back on her hands, feeling warm and tingly all over. "Hey, will you pour me some more wine?"

"Sure, I was about to get me another beer."

She leaned her head against Ryan's shoulder when he sat beside her. Singing along to songs on the radio, she laughed when he raised his eyebrows skeptically.

"Let's see if you can do better then," she challenged.

"Hey, I didn't do choir for a reason. I can't sing."

Alyssa felt her head spinning as she gazed at his sinfully handsome face smiling at her, not able to tell if it was from all the alcohol she'd consumed, or just the sheer effect he had on her. She giggled. Definitely the latter.

Ryan took another pull of his beer and set it on the ground beside them. Magical waves of destiny shimmered before her eyes as he took the drink from her hand and set it beside his. The mood transformed, fiery red purple and alive with a raw, primitive awareness of the other. His piercing sapphire gaze raked over her, burning with a light she'd never witnessed.

"Do you know how much I want you?"

"I'm guessing as much as I want you," she whispered back.

Wide eyes met his and he paused, struck by the glimmer of fear in their brilliant depths. Truth be told, he was nervous himself, he'd never been with a virgin before. And this was Alyssa, the girl he'd fell in love with an eternity ago. He'd waited for this day for so long, a lifetime it seemed. But he'd rather cut off his own arm than hurt her.

She tasted as sweet as berries, and he moaned against her lips when she returned his seeking kiss urgently.

"Take this off," he rasped, and she slipped her dress over her head with slender arms. The necklace gleamed against the naked wonder of her as he ran his hand down her feminine curves. In the light of the full moon, her body shone gold and smooth...perfect. Exhaling deeply, his voice vibrated with desire.

"You're gorgeous, Alyssa."

He stilled, startled by the tear that fell on his arm. "What's wrong?"

"You're too nice," she sniffed.

"Listen to me," he coaxed, and cupped the smooth line of her jaw. "Tonight you'll know, Lyssa."

Her brows knitted in confusion. "Know what?"

"You'll know the love of a man." He clasped her hands in his and held them up. Admiring eyes swept over her and his erection throbbed harder at the sight of her creamy, full breasts. "But not just any man, Alyssa. Only me." He spoke determinedly, capturing her gaze.

She smiled, her face aglow with its own powerful light, and twined her arms around his neck. "Who do you think I've been waiting for, silly?"

His pulse skyrocketed. Her ripe breasts thrust proudly out, and blood roared through him as he leaned down to taste a rosy nipple. It hardened even more in his mouth and he suckled, drinking in the taste of her. Cupping her other breast in his hand, he rubbed his finger lightly over the little bud.

She gasped and dug her fingers into his thick hair, needing something to hold on as she felt an ache unfurl deep within that begged to be fulfilled. "Please, Ryan," she panted.

"Oh, I'm going to make love to you. Baby, you don't know how long I've fantasized about this," he murmured, and devoured her lips in a fierce, plundering kiss.

She was barely aware of him laying her on the blankets, and then his magical lips covered hers again. His hot tongue swept into her mouth, overwhelming her senses with slow, deliberate strokes. Ryan groaned her name and she arched in love- blinding need against him.

"Christ," he rasped, and released her lips in a slow, sucking motion. His head moved lowed to her round, firm breasts. She writhed against him as he teased her taut nipple, and his hand drifted down lower. He slid past her hips and stopped, feeling her brace herself. Tensing with what, he wondered. Surely not fear of him? The unknown?

"Please, Alyssa," he whispered hoarsely.

He'd never felt so out of control, he felt he'd surely go insane if he couldn't possess her completely. He looked into her passion darkened eyes, and raging need pulsated through him. Her legs parted sweetly and he closed his eyes against her neck, feeling how hot and wet she already was. His fingers slid over her slippery wetness and played with the swollen axis of her pleasure. Her whimpers and gasps drove him over the edge of no return.

"That's it, honey," he murmured, hardly even aware of what he was saying. She rubbed herself against his hand and turned on to her side toward him, unknowingly giving him even better access.

"Oh, God," he muttered, so hard and aching with need he grabbed her hand. "Feel me," he demanded, and groaned from the feel of her tight grip on his powerful arousal. He'd never been so desperate for anything in his life. Her hand didn't even wrap around him completely but he thrust himself against her, catching her lips in a swirling, exhilarating mating of all senses as they ground themselves against each other till he gasped, shaking from the force of his desire.

"I can't wait any longer, Alyssa," he ground out.

"I don't want you to," she cried out.

He poised himself at her soft, quivering folds of flesh and stopped. "Look at me, Lyssa." Taking her lips in his, he gently pushed deep into her body and swallowed her startled cry when he felt the gates of her innocence give way. "You feel so good, baby" he whispered, beads of sweat popping out on his brow. His muscles screamed for him to move in the exquisiteness of her tight sheath, to revel in his fortune. "I'm sorry, honey. But it won't hurt anymore after this, okay?"

She nodded and he kissed her gently, the kiss quickly turning heated. Her naked body moved beneath his in restless hunger and he felt himself swelling even harder in her. 'Tell me if it hurts."

"Okay." The courageous love shining from her eyes wrapped satin ribbons around his heart, claiming it forever as hers.

He covered his big body over hers and slowly began to move within the tight confines of her. A ragged groan escaped from deep inside of him, he couldn't believe his dreams were now this hot-blooded reality.

"Ryan!" she cried out, and he almost lost it then.

"Does it feel better?" he asked breathlessly.

"Oh, yes!" she answered choppily, her breath coming in short pants.

He buried his face against her neck, feeling her tighten even more and she shuddered, screaming, "Oh my God, oh my God!"

Ryan rose up on his arms, pushing into her with a savage obsession. His tendons stood out on his arms and sweat dripped from him onto her, creating a sliding friction that promised to end in a volcanic conclusion

Dara Morris

unlike anything he'd ever known before.

Alyssa clenched around him, her hips jerking wildly as an uncontrollable ache built deep within her. "I can't...oooh!" She felt another climax tear through her body and met his thrusts instinctively, both lost in a sexual haze. They were the only two in the world and this was all that mattered. Desire conquered every sensation she possessed, she relished the feel of his hard body moving over hers.

The coarse hair on his chest rubbed against her sensitive breasts and she leaned upward, kissing and sucking on his small, hard nipples. He tasted salty and delicious, and his masculine smell intoxicated her. An agonized groan vibrated in his massive chest as his hands gripped her hips to his.

"Alyssa," he panted over and over, driving deep into her with jerky thrusts.

She wailed his name as spasms of pleasure overtook her.

"Jesus," he hissed, and her world shattered in a million pieces as he buried himself to the hilt and rocked against her, his muscles taut and corded in his upper body. With a strangled groan, he exploded deep within her, his powerful body shuddering from the force. "Oh, Ryan," she choked out. She wrapped her legs around him, never wanting him to let go.

Ryan absorbed her quivering body close, and rolled them over on their sides so he wouldn't crush her. His chest grew tight with tenderness as he smoothed her tangled hair from her face. "Are you alright?" She nodded against him and thoroughly sated, he closed his eyes.

Their hearts pounded together, her silken limbs

wrapped around him. The poignancy of their naked embrace stirred emotion deep within him and he swallowed hard, pressing his lips to her hair.

"Ryan?"

"Hmmm," he murmured, drugged by their lovemaking.

"That was amazing," she whispered, and to his shock, he leapt to life within her warm, slick flesh.

"Alyssa," he ground out. "I'm sorry, babe, but I can't control myself around you." "Good, because neither can I." She kissed him in a fiery, long exchange that charged every nerve. Potent need overtook him and clasping her tight, he set a fast, demanding pace that had them filling the charmed realm they lay in with the sounds of their vibrant passion.

Ryan stroked her sweat dampened, panting body and collapsed on his back, assured she was fine. Exhilarating emotions surged within his drained body as he took deep breaths to regain his strength. Finally, he turned on his side towards her, and laid a hand on her naked hip.

"Hey," he said quietly.

Alyssa's eyes were closed, her lips parted as if in sleep. Thick, black lashes fluttered open in a dreamy smile. "Hey."

"I'm going to get this fire built up, I'll be right back."

She stretched in delicious exhaustion when the heat reached her. She felt wonderful, her soul sang with love and fulfillment.

Ryan crouched beside her and her eyes widened. "Just lie still," he instructed, and stroked a warm, wet cloth over her sensitive skin. Lightly finishing, he tossed the cloth to the side.

Twinges of pain shot through her when she sat up and slipped her dress over her head. Ryan's strong arm braced her as he took long drinks of his beer.

"Are you sure you're alright?" Ryan shifted his sharp gaze to her.

Alyssa jumped, she'd been mesmerized by his somber, masculine profile. "I'm positive," she vowed, and patted his thigh. "I just felt dizzy because of all the wine and we haven't eaten yet."

"I'm about to fix that problem." He strode to the ice chest.

Before long, she had a fresh cup of wine and a hot dog. "Why does food always taste better when it's cooked outside," she mused between bites.

"I don't know but you're right, it does. Are you ready for those s'mores?"

"No, not yet. I just want to sit and watch the fire."

He leaned over and gave her a soft kiss on the temple. "Come here, I want to show you something."

"Right now? But I don't want to move."

"You'll like this, I promise." Coaxing midnight blue eyes met hers and she accepted his offered hand. He led them past the truck and shone his flashlight straight ahead. To her surprise, the largest in the ring of towering oak trees had been carved with their initials.

Tears filled her eyes. "When did you do this?" She ran her hands over his back, reveling in the feel of smooth skin over firm muscle. "Oh Ryan, I love it. It's the sweetest thing anyone has ever done for me." She gave him an accusing look. "You had this all planned, didn't you?"

"Guilty," he grinned, and shrugged his shoulders.

"Hey, I had to come out here and check the water out. I know how you are about snakes and alligators. Act like a durn city girl."

"I do not! I'm staying the night out here with you, aren't I?"

She walked up to the tree and traced the letters. They were straight and true, etched deep into the tree, RS + AM.

"Yeah you are, and I can't tell you how happy that makes me." He smoothed her hair back, and she relaxed against him as they admired the carving together. "It's our tree. We'll come out here and do it every now and then," he said in a teasing voice near her ear.

Alyssa shook her head in amusement. "Such a romantic way of putting it. How can I say no?"

"That was the plan," he grinned. "I forgot one thing. Here, hold the flashlight."

He opened up a knife and the sharp edge glistened in the moonlight. The image of a heart began to emerge around their initials as Alyssa's own melted.

"Dammit!" Ryan grabbed his hand and the blade fell to the ground, streaked with blood.

Alyssa gasped; her heart in her throat. "What happened?"

"I accidentally hit the release with my pinky and it snapped shut across my hand. Grab me a rag out of my glove box."

She ran back with it, horrified to see blood dripping down his fingers. "We have to go to the hospital! Right now!"

"No."

Let me see, Ryan," she urged. He released the pressure and blood welled up at the cut on top of his hand. "You need stitches! Please, let's go to the emergency room."

"Just wrap it up tight," he instructed, his teeth gritted.

"Okay," she said quietly, and folded the clean rag into a bandage. She finished by tying it in a snug knot around his hand and looked up at his shadowed face. "I wish you hadn't got hurt."

"Hey, it was worth it. I'll finish the heart in the morning." He felt like her luminous eyes scraped his soul as they searched his face endearingly.

"Thank you," she whispered, and gave him a sweet kiss on the lips. Overcome with love, he closed his eyes and hugged her, thanking the twinkling stars above for this girl.

****

The unfamiliar sight of smoldering embers was the first thing Alyssa saw when she sleepily opened her eyes in the dawn light. Ryan lay pressed warmly against her body, his heavy arm thrown across her. Contentment washed over her as she cuddled under his sheltering side. She and Ryan were now truly together in every sense of the word, and she adored every inch of him.

"Oh no," she whispered, round-eyed, frozen by a new memory. They hadn't used any protection. How utterly stupid. She twisted towards him. "Ryan!"

He was gloriously naked and her eyes drifted downward. Even relaxed in sleep, he was big. He seemed to stir while she watched and grow even larger. Her eyes flew to his now- awake, grinning face.

"You're naughty," he chuckled, blue eyes twinkling. She flushed guiltily. "Spying on a sleeping, helpless man. Hmmm, what should be your punishment?"

He was so arrogant sometimes, it was infuriating. "I wasn't spying on you; I wanted to ask you something."

"What's that?" His eyebrows cocked upward.

"Um, we didn't use any protection, did we?"

Ryan groaned and rubbed his forehead. "No, I left them in the truck. Drank too damn much."

Her jaw dropped, aghast at the thought that he kept condoms in his truck, and the fact that they hadn't used them.

"I just bought them yesterday, Alyssa."

Somewhat mollified, she snapped her mouth shut. "Oh. Well, surely just one night wouldn't..." Her voice trailed off, brain wildly spinning towards all the implications a pregnancy would have.

Ryan's firm voice pulled her back to the present. "We'll be careful from now on. Now come on, let's go swimming."

"It's perfect," she declared, and hugged him tight. Alyssa's fingers curled deep into his damp hair and she kissed his bristly jaw, thinking how divinely handsome he was. He smiled at her and the early morning sunlight seemed to grow brighter. "I love you, Ryan."

"I love you too, babe, but I don't know about perfect. It's kind of crooked, don't you think?" He looked back at the tree with a skeptical frown.

"No, but I do think we should to go back to my house. That cut on your hand looks bad; I wish you would go to the doctor. The river water is full of germs and it could get infected."

He shook his head. "As long as you have peroxide

and some bandages, I'll be fine."

Exasperated, she blew out her breath and crossed her arms. "You are unbelievably stubborn, Ryan Matthew Sutherby."

"Ha! Look who's talking." His cobalt blue eyes were alight with humor. "I can't stay long at your house though. I'm going to help Nana cook."

"You know how to cook?"

"Not yet, but I will. Hopefully." He grinned at her. "A man can only live off of fast food for so long."

"I know what you mean. I eat out way too much, it's just easier. But sometimes easy isn't always what's best for you." She drew a deep breath. "I get off at eight. Will you stay with me tonight?"

"Of course I will," he murmured, and bent down to take her lips in a dark, heart-stealing kiss that tingled all the way down to her bare toes.

CHAPTER 16

Ryan whistled a tune as he fried up a big batch of catfish fillets and French fries. Alyssa sat on the patio with Fran, reading a magazine. His gaze drifted back to her long, tanned legs and relived how they'd felt clasped tight against his hips last night. She'd rode him to a mind shattering orgasm, one so intense he'd sighed with relief when he saw the condom was still intact.

"That smells good. Nana's cooking lessons sure are paying off!"

Ryan spun around guiltily, as if Casey could read his thoughts. "Yeah, aren't you glad?"

"My stomach is," she replied good-naturedly, and poured a glass of tea. "Holy cow, and homemade tartar sauce? Alyssa had better hang on to you."

"Make sure you tell her that. This will be ready in about ten minutes or so."

"Can't wait." Casey disappeared down the hallway off the kitchen.

He gripped the counter hard and fought his gnawing anxiety as he stared at Alyssa through the glass door. *Two weeks, that's all we have left.*

Alyssa turned on her side towards him and yawned. "I'm just gonna close my eyes for a minute; I'm not going to sleep."

"Yeah, okay," he drawled.

"It was all that good food you cooked. I'm full as a

tick," she mumbled drowsily and scooted closer. He cradled her in his arms as she dozed off moments later. Cool air blew across the bed, and he drew the blanket over Alyssa's chilled, bare shoulder. One gentle finger traced her delicate eyelids then traveled slowly down to the soft contours of her lips. Ryan regarded her peaceful form in the moonlit room, his chest tight.

The last four weeks had been the best of his life; he couldn't wait for her to get off work so they could be together. Simple times, just revolving around each other, and more valuable to him than anything he'd ever known before. They'd laughed and played like kids again, while all the time making sacred, soul consuming love. The thought of leaving seemed like a cruel joke, they'd grown inseparable.

He kissed her forehead and laid his head on top of hers. She smelled like the sweet smelling oil she bathed in and unable to resist, pulled her warm, slumbering curves closer to him. Alone with his thoughts, he wondered how he'd lived without her before, and how he would now.

"Wake up, sleepyhead," a voice cooed next to his ear the next morning.

Ryan grunted and wrapped a strong arm around Alyssa's waist. "What time is it?" He rubbed his bleary eyes with his other hand.

"Seven."

He stopped, taking in her appearance. She'd braided her hair in a long rope down her back and her lovely face was scrubbed free of makeup. "You look like you're about sixteen, I swear."

"Well, I'm not." She sat back on her heels and arched her eyebrows.

"Oh, I know you're not," he assured her with a wink. "I thought you were off today. Why are you up so early?"

"I am, but I couldn't go back to sleep so I made you breakfast. See, you cook for me, and I'll cook for you. Doesn't that sound fair?" She gave him a sunny smile.

"Very fair. It smells good, whatever it is."

"Blueberry muffins and coffee, made just the way you like it." She reached over and handed him a steaming cup of coffee.

"Thanks, babe."

He took bracing sips and studied the beauty of her profile as she nibbled on a muffin. Alyssa sat cross legged beside him on the bed, dressed in a tee shirt and pajama shorts. His hand traveled up her back to capture her long, golden rope of hair in his hand. "I know what I want for dessert."

She slanted him a mischievous grin. "I've never heard of dessert for breakfast, I didn't make any."

He unraveled the braid, allowing her glorious hair to spill over her shoulders. Smoky emerald eyes gazed back at him, and he whispered huskily, "Come here, babe."

Ryan fell back asleep as she caressed his muscular shoulders and arms. He spent his afternoons with LaDarius, working out in the weight room and on the field at the high school. There wasn't an ounce of fat on him, she marveled. She'd come to know his athletic body as well as her own, where he was most sensitive, and what him groan with need.

His hand lay across her naked breast and she kissed the jagged scar the knife had left. Alyssa's heart wept in misery. *Don't go. Don't leave me.* Familiar, heavy feelings of betrayal swept through her, but she pushed them aside. *It'll be Christmas before I know it, and then I'll be in New York with Ryan.*

Her eyes softened; Ryan was boyishly handsome in sleep, his strong features relaxed. She threaded her fingers idly through his dark, satiny hair and prayed fervently the months between summer and winter would fly by.

****

"Fran, just ride with us. There's no sense in taking two separate cars." Alyssa tapped her foot impatiently against the floor of her sister's room.

"I don't want to ride with you because when I'm ready to leave, that's what I'm going to do."

"When you get ready to leave, we'll leave. Ryan can catch a ride with somebody, or I'll go back and get him. Alright?"

Fran rolled her eyes. "I don't see what the big deal is, but whatever. If you'll leave me alone, I guess I'll ride with you."

"Well, this is the first time we've been out to the levy since…" Alyssa cleared her throat and finished softly, "Jeremy passed away. I just think it'd be better if we rode together."

A dark shadow crossed her sister's pretty face as she sat down on her bed.

"Fran, we don't have to go. The only person that has to is Ryan, it's his goodbye party. To tell you the truth, I don't really want to go anyway."

Fran gave her a small, sympathetic smile. "Ryan would be upset if you didn't."

"I know, he would, wouldn't he?" Alyssa shook

192

her head and gazed out the window. It was Friday night, and he left Sunday morning. *Two days, and then my world leaves.* Long summer days had passed like the shortest of winters'.

"Hey, why the long faces?" Both jumped at the sound of Ryan's deep voice.

"No reason," Alyssa shrugged. She exchanged a glance with Fran and walked to the doorway. "It won't take me long to get ready."

Ryan closed the bedroom door behind them. She pulled a shirt out of the closet and fought the tears gathering in her chest. Her emotions seemed so perilously close to the surface these days.

"I don't want to leave, Alyssa," he said in a low, deep voice from behind her.

Startled, she dropped the shirt and watched as he leaned down to pick it up for her. His kindness snapped the fragile thread of her control and she started to cry; great, gulping sobs that scared even her with their ferocity. Alyssa held shaking hands to her eyes as she felt herself being drawn into his arms.

He let out an agonized groan against her stiff form. "Please, baby. Stop."

Ryan's hands roamed over her back and then she was in his arms. He set her down on the bed and held her close, cursing softly when she couldn't stop crying. Then he said nothing, just rubbed her back till she calmed down.

"I'm sorry; I don't know what came over me." She drew a deep, shuddering breath, and leaned back to look into eyes darkened with concern.

Ryan smoothed her hair back from her damp face. "It's okay." .

But it wasn't. No matter how she pretended, she wasn't okay.

****

Ryan's gaze flicked over to Alyssa where she sat beside Fran and Megan, chatting about their upcoming classes. Her eyes were still swollen and pink, he noted with a pang. He sighed and stretched his legs out towards the fire, looking up at the half moon. Alyssa had been so brave, cheerfully talking about how she couldn't wait to come see him for Christmas. Now he didn't know what to think, not after her breakdown earlier.

LaDarius nudged him hard in the ribs. "Man, sit up. It's that guy again."

"What the hell?" Ryan sprang to his feet as he observed Gary standing undeservedly close to Alyssa.

Gary's face flamed red when Ryan slipped a possessive arm around Alyssa's waist and he drew up to his full height. "I bet those girls up north sure are missing their Cajun quarterback. And when you're gone, Alyssa-"

Fury exploded inside Ryan and he leapt on the sneering Gary, tackling him to the ground in an instant. "Her name doesn't cross your lips, you son of a bitch. Don't mess with what's mine, or it'll be your last day on earth."

"She deserves better! Why has she been crying? Tell me that!" Gary panted, and struggled to escape. He craned his neck towards Alyssa. "Get your head out of the clouds! Don't be a fool; he's not going to be faithful to you!"

Alyssa sucked in a loud breath and glared at the pair of them on the ground. "Gary, this is none of your business! Ryan, let go of him!"

Ryan shoved Gary hard on the shoulders before he let him loose. "Get the fuck out of here," he snarled.

Gary stood up, brushing the dirt off his clothes while he stalked away.

Ryan turned to see Alyssa's eyes on him, and his jaw tightened as he saw an uncertain expression cross her pretty features.

"Did you have a girlfriend in New York?"

Ryan groaned inwardly, he should've known this was coming. "No."

Alyssa's fine boned hands fiddled with the sheets. "So how many girls did you sleep with?"

He felt speared by her green, direct gaze and sat up in a quick, fluid motion, her body lying across his lap.

She rose and glared at him. "What's the problem, Ryan? Either you can't remember, or you don't want to say."

She was right about that, there was no way he was going to tell her. Hell, he'd have to go back and think, and the number floating around in his head sounded horribly steep, even to him. "It doesn't matter. Because now there's only you." He tucked a flaxen strand of hair behind her ears and coaxed her reluctant lips to meld with his in a gentle kiss. Her sweet response caused a pang deep within as he lay his forehead against hers. "I'm in love with you, Alyssa. I love you. I don't know how else to say it."

Soft hands clasped his face. "I love you, too. And you're the only man I want." She arched her eyebrows as she gazed up at him. "Just like always. But I guess some people are more loyal than others." He frowned and started to respond, but Alyssa held her finger over his lips. "You don't have to say anything, I was just teasing you." She dropped her eyes, but not before he saw a flicker of distress in their vivid depths.

His jaw tight with suspicion, he raised her chin and forced her to look at him. "Listen to me. I don't want you worrying that I'm off in New York having this grand old time without you. I'm not. The only reason why I'm there is to get a degree, and that's it. Trust me, Alyssa...I need you to trust me."

"I do," she whispered.

As he studied her lovely, solemn face, Ryan wished wholeheartedly he knew what thoughts lay within.

****

Alyssa walked slowly out to the truck and placed a thermos of hot coffee on the seat.

"I had to put a quart of oil in it." Ryan dropped the hood with a loud slam. "Everything else was fine."

He came and stood in front of her. "Please be careful," she whispered, and laid her hand on his hard chest.

An intense light filled the sapphire blue of his eyes. "I will."

He wrapped his arms around her and she relaxed in his strong, welcoming embrace, afraid to say anything for fear she'd burst into tears again. He'd looked so alarmed the other night.

Dewy winds blew around them in the early morning light and still they stayed, heart to heart. He smelled so good, they'd taken a long shower together, and she'd caressed him from head to toe with the soap. And then he'd washed her...Alyssa gulped, remembering the tender touch of his hands.

"I love you, Ryan," she whispered.

"And I love you. More than anything, baby."

His voice shook and then she felt a warm wetness on her forehead. Overpowering sadness gathered in her and she wept, heartbroken tears mingling with his.

CHAPTER 17

OCTOBER 1995

"Where am I? This is the stupidest idea I've ever had." Alyssa threw the map over on the seat. Fran and Casey had tried to talk her out of coming to see Ryan, but she'd refused to hear a word of their protests.

"Sir," she called out to the guy at the gas pump.

"Yeah?"

"How far am I from East Stansbury and how do I get there?"

"About two hours. Just stay on I-86 east and you'll be there in no time."

"Thanks."

Almost there. Her heart raced in excitement as she sat straighter on the seat. Figuring she might as well go to the bathroom while she was here, Alyssa pulled up to the bright lights of the station. It was cold outside, so she gathered her new long coat around her as she hurried into the store.

She was ready to see Ryan, needed to see him.

****

Ryan dropped his shoes on the closet floor and walked to the window. He flicked open the blinds and closed them back, barely able to see anything through the rain-splattered glass.

There was a quick rap on the door. Jason, one of

his roommates, stuck his shaggy, blonde head in. "Uh, there's a girl here to see you."

Who could that be? He walked to the living room, and then his heart stopped in his chest.

"Alyssa! What are you doing here? How…? Why didn't you call me?" He couldn't believe what he was seeing. Alyssa, here? In his apartment?

"Well, I…she trailed off, and he clasped her hand in his.

"Let's go to my room."

Ryan closed the door behind him and watched as she paced by the bed. Alyssa was soaked, but clutched her black trench coat close. Wet locks of dark golden hair streamed past her shoulders, and her emerald eyes shined excitedly in her pale face. "Ryan, I didn't think I was ever going to get here! Remember how I told you we only had classes for half this week?"

"Yeah, I remember," he said slowly, and stared at her in confounded amazement.

"Well, I borrowed Casey's car so I could come see you."

"When did you leave?"

"After class let out at noon yesterday. I stopped at a motel around eleven last night, and then I got back on the road when it was light this morning. And now I'm here." She smiled proudly at him and he felt the warmth fill the room.

"But it's almost midnight, what took you so long? And why didn't you call me, Alyssa? What if something had happened?" The thought struck fear deep into him, and he shook his head hard. "I don't understand why you didn't tell me you were coming."

Alyssa licked her lips nervously and wrung her

hands in front of her. "Well, I wanted to surprise you." She'd thought of nothing else but him for the last two days and sat down on the bed, so relieved to finally be there. Alyssa flinched as she thought about what she'd came to tell him. That night under the stars had yielded far more than they'd bargained for... she was pregnant.

"I'm definitely surprised," he said in a deep, incredulous voice. "And so pissed off I could bend you over my knee." Glittering blue eyes pierced her with their intensity and she stiffened in indignation.

"What? Why are you mad?"

A dark frown creased his forehead. "Are you fucking kidding me, Alyssa? You drive all the way up here with what, a map and a flashlight? And you don't even bother to tell me you were coming? What if I hadn't been here?"

"Where else would you be at this time of night?" she demanded.

"Nowhere! I'm just making a point!"

She threw her hands up in the air. "Okay, so I should've called! But then it wouldn't have been a surprise."

He stayed quiet for a long moment as the furious scowl on his handsome face cleared a tiny bit. "I'm sorry, babe, but you've threw me for a loop. I'm glad you're here, though."

He sat down and reached for her. She snuggled close to the soothing presence of him and felt his strength meld into her. She'd been so scared, felt so alone. His sensuous lips touched hers, and she drew in a ragged breath. Their kiss gradually gained momentum and warmed her cold blood until she moaned helplessly against his mouth. She shivered, raw sexual desire pooling deep within.

"Take this wet coat off," Ryan said, his voice rough with need. Alyssa was here, in his arms. He'd dreamed of this every night, their being together. Lonely nights and days had stretched into a long monotone, broken only by her sweet voice on their weekly phone calls. His grip loosened and he leaned down to look at her.

"I can't believe you're here, Lyssa." He stroked her cool, smooth cheek.

"I know," she responded simply.

He admired her pure beauty and swallowed down the lump in his throat. "You're tired, aren't you?" Smudged shadows lay under her overly bright eyes and except for the flush on her cheeks, her delicate face was colorless.

"A little bit."

She shivered uncontrollably and he frowned. "You're going to get sick, this coat has to go." She yanked it from his hands as he stared at her in shock and stood up. "What the hell are you doing, Alyssa? Take that coat off."

"Ryan…" she said hesitantly.

"What is it?" *What was wrong with her*? She was staring at the floor, her arms wrapped around her waist.

"Um…I'm-I'm going to have a baby."

"What?" He felt dazed, as if he'd been hit in the head with a wayward football.

She looked up at him, luminous eyes huge. "That's why I came. Because I wanted to tell you in person, I didn't want to tell you on the phone. And I couldn't wait until Christmas."

Alyssa shivered again and he sprang into action,

pulling the coat gently from her. "Lay down," he urged hoarsely, and quickly pulled the covers back. She slipped off her shoes and scooted under the blankets. "That's my girl." He settled beside her on his side and ran his hand down to the small mound of Alyssa's tummy. "Our baby," he whispered.

She placed her cold hands over his. "From that night, remember? When you carved the heart in the tree?"

Of course our child was created that beautiful night. A rush of pride flooded through Ryan and his throat grew tighter. He rubbed gently, awed by how taut her belly was. Under his hand there was a flutter and his eyes met her soulful ones. "Is that the baby?"

Alyssa nodded and bit her lip. "Yeah, he's been moving around a lot lately."

"He?"

"Well, I just say "he". I haven't had an ultrasound yet."

Lost in thought, he smiled when a resounding kick landed against his fingers. "Have you been to the doctor?"

"When I found out. I thought I had the flu, but…I had a baby."

His hand stilled as she shrugged helplessly.

"That was when you called Casey and told her to take me to the doctor."

"That was three weeks ago and you said that you had a virus." He frowned and she scrunched her nose at him playfully.

"Yeah, well, it's the nine month kind," she teased.

She was already five months pregnant, in fact, she'd been almost two months gone when he left

Louisiana. The realization stunned him as he stared first at her, and then at her belly. "You were here all the time, weren't you? And nobody even knew." Ryan laid his head against her stomach and kissed where their child grew. Her fingers gently ran through his hair as he felt the hot sting of tears hit the back of his eyelids. *Our baby. And Alyssa was the mother.*

The wonder of it struck him hard and he pulled up to lie beside her on the pillow. She let out a long sigh. "You're exhausted." The idea infuriated him, but it was all too clear in Alyssa's weary features.

"I am. I would've got here a lot earlier, but I kept having to stop to go to the bathroom. But I read that happens when you're pregnant because the baby is putting pressure on your bladder."

A muscle in his jaw ticked spasmodically as he imagined her stopping at strange gas stations all over the country, but he didn't want to upset her. Not now. "Did you leave your bag out in the car?"

Alyssa nodded with her eyes closed and Ryan felt his heart turn over. "I'll go out there later and get it. You can just sleep in one of my tee shirts."

"That sounds perfect." She sat up and yawned before wriggling out of her clothes and handing them to him.

"Here, babe." A jolt of desire shafted through him as the oversized shirt slid over her ripe breasts.

"Thanks. Come lay down with me, Ryan."

"I am."

She smiled when he stretched out beside her.

"Now go to sleep. I know you're tired." He smoothed her damp hair back till her breaths came deep and regular. "Dear God," he whispered, and laid a hand on her swollen tummy, a million thoughts swirling through his brain.

****

"Are you sure she's pregnant?" Jason stared at him in horror.

"Yes, I'm sure. And she's going to be here till Saturday."

Ryan had stopped by the dining room they'd turned into a makeshift den, not surprised to see his roommates still up playing video games even though it was well after midnight.

Vince shook his dark head from side to side in slow motions. "Damn, what are you going to do?"

"We haven't had a chance to talk yet. She's worn out."

"I'm sure, that's one helluva drive. Especially for a pregnant lady."

Ryan nodded grimly. Vince came from a huge Italian family, so Ryan was sure if anybody knew, he did.

"She's a knockout," Jason threw in, and Ryan's eyebrows snapped together.

Vince glared over at Jason. "Man, shut up. Ryan, ignore this fool."

"I usually do." He punched Jason in the shoulder with a grin.

They were all good friends and teammates, and like Ryan, neither was from New York. They'd explored the city of East Stansbury together, discovering the best places to eat and play.

But Ryan hadn't been to a party since he'd came back during the summer, had no desire to, and they had learned to stop asking. It was a struggle being so far away from Alyssa; he'd had no idea a long distance relationship would be so difficult. Every time he hung the phone up, he questioned whether or not he was doing the right thing.

Especially lately.

She sounded different, tense and vibrating with a nervous energy. Ryan's mouth twisted with derision as he considered the irony of it.

He'd hoped it wasn't his fault, but as it turned out, it was.

****

Alyssa lay on her side with her back to him, and her familiar scent soothed the turmoil in his mind as he drew her supple curves up against him. His hand moved gently down, registering the changes in her deliciously female body. Her soft breasts were larger, and her usually flat belly was now rounded.

Would it be a boy or girl?

He didn't mind either way, although the thought of having a son made him glow with a quiet satisfaction. He'd be the kind of father he'd never had. He'd play ball with his son and take him fishing, teach him everything he knew. But a little girl would be wonderful too, picturing a miniature Alyssa with her bright hair and striking green eyes.

Their baby rolled and kicked beneath his hand while he marveled she could sleep through the feisty movements. It felt surreal, having Alyssa here, pregnant with his baby. He kissed her neck and his arm tightened protectively around her. She stirred, turning into his embrace.

"Ryan?"

"What, sweetheart?"

"I have to go to the bathroom."

"There's one in here, I've got my own."

She sat up, rubbing her eyes. "That's handy."

"Pure luck, babe. We flipped a coin for it." He reached over to turn the lamp on.

Alyssa laughed. "Oh, good, you brought my bag in. I need to brush my teeth."

"Ugh, I feel so grubby," she muttered. And cold, she couldn't get warmed up. She looked around curiously at the black throw rugs and sleek chrome accessories. A shower would make her feel better, she felt chilled and achy to her bones.

Stepping under the hot water, Alyssa rubbed soap over her body and paused on her tummy. "My little baby," she murmured lovingly, awe filling her. He'd just started kicking recently, and was at it with a vengeance the past couple of days.

She'd been terrified to find out she was pregnant, in fact, the doctor had scrambled to grab some smelling salts when she'd swayed dizzily in the chair. Although now, Alyssa didn't see how she had missed the signs, despite the spotting she'd experienced early on in her pregnancy. Ryan had took the news unexpectedly well, Alyssa mused gratefully. It had been burning a hole in her, the desire to tell him.

"Whore! Slut!"

Her father's voice had jumped out of nowhere every time she'd attempted, paralyzing the words in her throat. It had seemed like a sign from above when the college had announced their half week closure, and she'd begged Casey to use her car. There was no way she'd trust her old car, it probably wouldn't even make it past Arkansas.

And the harrowing, mind-numbing long journey had been worth it because once again, they were together.

****

The soft yellow glow from the lamp illuminated Ryan's magnificent, sculpted physique as if he were a museum piece. Alyssa had to resist the urge to pinch herself; it was like a dream walking into his room. She, who had never even been out of the state, was actually here in New York.

He lay with one sinewy arm over his eyes, and the other wrapped around her securely when she soundlessly curled up next to him. "I feel a thousand times better." She rubbed his bare, muscular torso. "I was freezing."

"What was the temperature when you left Louisiana?" He moved his arm and looked over at her.

"Eighty."

Ryan's lips quirked upward. "It's thirty degrees here," he said wryly.

"And it's raining. It's a good thing I'm here to keep you warm," she said with an inviting smile.

"Alyssa, let's not even get into what possessed you to drive up here," he growled roughly, and brought his other arm around to encircle her in his embrace. "When I think of what could've happened…Christ, don't you know I can't live without you?"

If his words hadn't convinced her, the intensity of his tortured tone did. She laid a hand on his chest. "I'm sorry, but I wanted to see you. And I don't regret it not one bit." Ryan's dark expression cleared a tiny bit. "Please don't be angry at me," she whispered. She kissed him, coaxing his sensuous lips to part with distracting little nips.

The hunger that had been building since they'd first touched burst in a wet intermingling of their needy tongues. Heat washed over her in endless waves while his harsh breathing in her ear only inflamed the burning ache within. Ryan's restraint break with a guttural groan that seemed torn from his chest, and the desperation in his shaking arms that clasped her to him almost brought tears to her eyes, it struck her so poignantly.

It wasn't fair, that cruel clock that always ticked faster when they were together. He drew his lips from hers and she opened her eyes to look into blazing blue orbs of sexual energy.

"I want to feel your skin against mine, babe, sit up."

"Okay," she breathed, and he pulled the tee-shirt over her head.

His smoldering gaze swept over her full, thrusting breasts, and she heard him suck in a deep breath. "Are they sensitive?" His big hands caressed her bare, blue-veined breasts as chills of anticipation shot down her spine.

"Yes," she moaned. He leaned forward, his lips tracing kisses to the swollen mounds. Alyssa jerked when his mouth covered her throbbing nipple, crying out mindlessly. She couldn't breathe; the pleasure drove her crazy. He gently pushed her to her back and followed, his lips suckling its twin.

"Ryan," she pleaded, craving him deep inside her, longing for them to be one. Alyssa slid her hands down the smooth expanse of his rippled chest and traveled lower to capture the long, thick length of him. He felt like satin over steel as she stroked him seductively from tip to end, erotic shivers filling her feminine core by the familiar, hard reality of him. Her heart thudded in her chest, and she hardly heard Ryan's ragged groans as he thrust himself against her hand.

The roaring in Ryan's head was growing louder by the minute. Alyssa tasted like sweet southern strawberries, and he captured her lips again in a tumult of heady desire. She was going to make him explode any minute now; her sure, knowing movements were sending insane shudders screaming through every muscle.

"Oh God," he groaned, wanting her so badly he didn't know if he could endure the sweet ecstasy much longer. He reached between her smooth thighs and caressed her warm, slippery moistness. Alyssa arched her back in that timeless show of feminine hunger as he slid one long finger in. Her warm muscles rippled against him, a sensation so hot he had to gasp for air.

"Please, Ryan!" She grabbed his hips to pull him closer but he resisted, resting his weight on his elbows.

"I don't want to hurt you, honey."

"You won't, I promise," Alyssa assured him quickly in a breathless voice, and he felt devoured by her passionate, green gaze. Wrapping his arms around her, they kissed, their tongues twining hungrily together. Alyssa's writhing, delectable body beneath his drove away all thoughts of taking it slow and easy. He lowered himself, taking care not to put pressure on her stomach and with a surge, was inside her snug depths. She shrieked against his mouth, moaning his name.

"I've needed you so bad, Alyssa" he ground out, shaking from the feel of her velvet soft walls pulsating around him. Her hips met his rocking thrusts and she locked her long legs behind him, pulling him deeper.

Ryan was fighting for breath now, for control.

"Jesus," he groaned, knowing he couldn't last much longer. Alyssa's fingers dug into his back, bringing him even closer to the brink.

"Ryan!" He caught her lips in his to hush her screams.

His hips met hers in one last thrust, and he exploded deep within her sweet flesh. Electric shock waves wracked through his body holding him to her, until finally, he collapsed beside her panting body.

After his racing heartbeat had ebbed to a steady drum, Ryan reached out an unsteady hand to push the silken mass of hair off her cheek.

"Alyssa...look at me."

"I can't move," she mumbled.

He laughed; a deep rumble in his winded lungs. "You can open your eyelids surely."

Alyssa wasn't too sure of that. She felt sapped of energy, delicious waves of pleasure had bolted through her body, leaving her limp. A hard kick in her belly revived her and her hand flew down to her stomach, horrified she'd forgotten about the baby while in the grips of sensual escape.

"What's wrong?" Ryan's voice was urgent, all humor gone.

She rubbed her tummy, all seemed well. "Nothing, he's fine. I just wanted to make sure." Her heart melted at the relieved smile that crossed his handsome face and she scooted over to kiss him on the lips. "You're going to be such a good daddy."

A worried line furrowed between his clear blue

eyes. "I hope so," he said slowly. "You know I don't remember mine hardly, but I think I can be a good father."

The uncertain expression on his face whispered to Alyssa's kindred soul. She laid her head against his hard chest, and crossed one leg over his hair roughened one. "We're both going to have to learn, aren't we? I'll never be the kind of mother mine is. Don't worry," she said fiercely. Her eyes narrowed as she thought about Joyce. They hadn't talked in months; you would think they lived hours away from each other, instead of only thirty minutes.

He placed a hand on the curve of her belly. "We've got ourselves in one hell of a mess. It was hard before, but now…"

He didn't have to tell her, she already knew. Swallowing hard, she closed her eyes. She didn't want to think about it anymore, that's all she'd done for the past three weeks. Simply walking away from her scholarship was unimaginable, and Ryan had worked so hard for his…

Except it wasn't just the two of them anymore either. There was three, and their baby needed both of his parents.

But how?

She felt herself drifting, sated beyond belief. Tired, she was so tired. The combination of Ryan's warm body and woodsy scent swathed her, lulling her into a sound, dreamless sleep.

****

Ryan turned off the alarm clock, and rolled back over on his side towards Alyssa. "What time is it?" she mumbled.

"Seven."

"Mmmm." She stretched and sat up, golden hair tumbling in waves down to the white sheets. "I'll be back."

He admired her lush, rounded bottom and killer curves as she walked to the bathroom naked and let out a low whistle. *Damn.* Pregnancy hadn't diminished her feminine sensuality not one bit, only added to it.

He gave her a few minutes and followed to see Alyssa brushing her teeth. His hands massaged her trim backside, his mood turning pensive as he traced the scars that crossed her smooth skin. She was strong, but foolishly brave, too. Who else would've drove twenty-two hours for something that could've been said over the phone?

Ryan linked his fingers around her swollen belly and kissed the nape of her neck where her long hair fell over her shoulders. "I get out of class at noon, and after that I'm not going to work. I'll think of something to tell them."

She patted her mouth with the towel and smiled at him in the mirror. "Really? Will you show me around? I'd love to see the city and bring some souvenirs back for everybody."

With a fond pat to her bottom, Ryan picked up his toothbrush. "Sure, we'll go eat lunch first. Mario's has got the best New York style pizza around, you'll love it." He tossed the towel in the hamper and hugged her close. Alyssa's face brightened as the dimples he adored so much shone at him.

"Yum. Ryan, you have no idea how glad I am to be here. You're not still mad, are you?"

Leaning against him with the hard mound of her

stomach pressed into him, there was a slight thump, as if the baby was reminding them of his presence. Ryan nodded his head in the affirmative, eyebrows raised. "Yes, actually I am. I don't like the idea of you driving back home. If I didn't have a game tomorrow, I'd follow you. Every time you stop, I want you to call me. And if you get tired, stop at a motel. I'll give you some money in case you need to stay another night." He sighed raggedly and shook his head. "I'm going to be a nervous wreck until you get back home."

Alyssa's heart squeezed in adoration, Ryan was so handsome and strong standing there splendidly naked. Nobody had ever cared for her the way he did, cherished her. Standing up on her tiptoes, she wrapped her arms around his neck and whispered emotionally against his lips, "I love you."

They kissed; a gentle kiss full of hope and pure joy. Her fingers clenched in his silky hair, and then she laid her head against his shoulder while his strong arms tightened around her for long moments. He squeezed her bare bottom and spoke in a husky whisper near her ear. "I love you too, honey. Now, I want you to get back in that bed and stay till I get back."

She yawned and nodded her head. "I am. I'm still sleepy anyways." She put her nightgown back on and burrowed back under the covers, chilled again.

Ryan hurriedly dressed in a charcoal gray pullover and low-slung faded blue jeans. "I'll be back around 12:30. The kitchen's right off of the living room if you get hungry." He gave her a meaningful look, eyebrows raised. "And Alyssa, we're going to have a long talk this afternoon." He laid his hand on her tummy and leaned down to give her a kiss.

"We'll be waiting," she said cheerfully.

He smiled as he slung his backpack over his shoulder. "Bye, babe."

"Bye, Ryan."

The door shut behind him and Alyssa blinked dreamily upward, savoring his masculine scent surrounding her. Minutes later, she was sound asleep.

****

"I can't believe I forgot my blow dryer," Alyssa muttered. And she already knew without searching Ryan didn't own one. Deciding to see his roommates might have one, she followed the aroma of coffee to the kitchen

The same tall, blond haired man who'd answered the door last night stood at the counter with a steaming cup in his hand. "Good morning. I'm Jason, by the way." He gestured towards the top of the refrigerator with an apologetic shrug. "Are you hungry? We've got cereal."

"Good morning. That'll work, thanks." She fixed herself a bowl and sat down at the table to eat. "By any chance, do you have a blow dryer I can borrow? I forgot mine."

"No," he grinned. "There's not any blow dryers in this apartment."

"Dang. Well, I guess I'll go to the store then. I remember passing one a few blocks up. This isn't Louisiana for sure," she laughed. "It's too cold to have wet hair." *And there's no way I'm going out with Ryan with a wet ponytail hanging down my back.*

"You're right about that. I'm from Texas, and I still haven't gotten used to the weather up here."

She studied the kitchen that led out to the living

room. A large green rug covered the floor, and it was homey with the hardwood floors shining beyond to the living room. The simply decorated living room looked barely used. Alyssa finished her bowl of cereal and drank a glass of juice. "I'm about to head to the store, but I'll be right back."

Jason paused, toast in hand. "It's still raining pretty hard. I can give you a ride, it's no problem."

"Oh, I'll be fine," she assured him. "After all, I just drove thirteen hundred miles," she said with a grin.

She braided her hair and then headed out with an umbrella she'd found in Ryan's closet.

"It's freezing out here, brrrr." She shivered and turned the heat up to high. Rain beat against the windshield in sheets as she drove and Alyssa peered out the dimness, recalling the drugstore was on the corner of an intersection.

"It was right over here, somewhere…"

She unbuckled her seat belt and leaned forward to get a better look out of the foggy windshield. In the next second, a force struck her car with an ear-splitting boom. It felt like she was falling into a swirling world of kaleidoscope lights and the horrific sounds of crunching metal. Panicked, her arm shot out to brace herself, but bright pain exploded in Alyssa's brain as she cracked her forehead against the dashboard. Fearful screams filled the small car until blackness overtook her, and then she knew no more.

CHAPTER 18

Ryan sped home, his thoughts of Alyssa. He'd barely been able to concentrate on his tests and had already decided they weren't going straight to lunch. First, he planned on joining her in bed and enjoying her delectable body. He doubted she'd put up much of a fuss, and one corner of his mouth lifted in an anticipatory grin. She was every bit as fascinated with his body as he was with hers. And her being pregnant had its definite advantages. No condoms, foremost. How warm and tight she was, the rippled muscles squeezing him mercilessly. And her breasts…they were as ripe as melons.

He pulled his truck in the apartment parking lot, and his eyebrows lowered in confusion. Casey's car was gone.

Where in the hell was Alyssa?

He strode up the stairwell and ran into a frantic Jason. "Ryan, you have to go to St. Joseph's Hospital! They just called and said Alyssa's been in a car wreck!"

"A wreck?" The stunned question sounded hollow, as if he were standing in a tunnel.

His friend's voice lowered. "They wouldn't give me any details, but I think you'd better get up there quick. Do you want me to take you?"

"No, I'll drive." Ryan turned on his heel, and raced back to his truck.

****

"*Please be okay, please be okay, please be okay.*" He came to a screeching halt in the parking lot of the hospital and ran straight for the boldly lettered emergency room.

A heavy-set woman slid the glass window open as he rushed in. "Can I help you?"

"Alyssa Martin? She was in a car wreck. I need to see her." His words spilled out in a frantic plea.

She pushed a button and the doors swung open. "Come right back."

Fluorescent lights and beeping noises filled the room beyond as he approached the busy desk on unsteady legs. "Ma'am?"

"Yes?" asked a kind faced nurse with eyeglasses perched on the end of her nose.

"Alyssa…" His voice dropped off and he cleared his tight throat. "Alyssa Martin, please, I need to see her."

The nurse nodded. "Oh yes, we went through her purse that the ambulance brought in with her, and yours was the only local number in there. What relation are you to her?"

"My name is Ryan Sutherby, and I'm her boyfriend. She's here visiting me. Is she okay? Can I see her?" The questions were spoken in rapid succession. He whirled around, listening and looking for any trace of her.

"Let me get her doctor for you, Mr. Sutherby." The nurse hurried down the hallway beside the desk.

Ryan waited in nervous terror, his heart pounding against his chest. Why did they have to go through her purse? What was wrong, why didn't she just tell them

217

his number? He was no stranger to emergency rooms, but never had he experienced the terror he was feeling now.

Alyssa and their baby…

The nurse returned, along with a middle-aged man of Asian descent in a long white coat. Ryan felt the blood start to rush to his head at the solemn look on both of their faces.

"I'm Dr. Lee, and I've been taking care of Miss Martin since the ambulance brought her in at 11:00 o' clock. During that time-"

"How is she?" Ryan rasped, unable to stand it any longer. He broke out in a cold sweat as he fought the rage rising in him. This was torturous, why the hell weren't they telling him anything? "Is the baby okay?"

The doctor's face gentled and he laid a hand on Ryan's shoulder. "Mr. Sutherby, from what I understand, your girlfriend's car was struck by a motorist that ran a red light. The impact from that pushed her into another car. She didn't have her seat belt on, so she was basically thrown around like a rag doll."

Ryan froze, his heart plunging. *This cannot be happening.* He raked his fingers through his hair, breathing harshly. "What are you saying?"

"I'm very sorry, Mr. Sutherby, but there has been some bleeding due to the placenta detaching from her uterus. Miss Martin also has a concussion and a fractured wrist, and she has not regained consciousness since she arrived. We're monitoring her and the baby's condition very closely with fetal monitors and in the last thirty minutes, they have started to detect regular contractions. Her condition has steadily deteriorated so we've had no choice but to call in Dr. Jackson to perform an emergency C-section. Again, I'm very sorry."

The words were spoken in concise, accented English, but Ryan barely heard, only saw the doctor's mouth moving while his brain processed the horrible words. "I want to see her," he said hoarsely, desperate to lay his eyes on her.

Dr. Lee nodded. "I understand. Follow me."

He led him to the first room off the hallway and Ryan's pulse stuttered in shock. Except for the large purple knot on her forehead, Alyssa's lovely face was as pale as the sheets she lay on. Long black lashes rested against her white cheeks, and he smoothed her satiny hair back as he dropped weak-kneed beside the bed.

"Alyssa, oh my sweet girl," he whispered. "I'm here, honey." This was far worse than he'd even dared to imagine.

Picking up her small, clammy hand he held it within his, his whole body shaking with fear. Her bottom lip was split badly, bright red blood still oozing from the deep gash. She looked so young and defenseless, her chest rising and falling in rapid, short pants. An oxygen mask covered the lower portion of her face, and he could detect the lumps of the monitors on her stomach through a pile of blankets on top of her.

At the thought of what was about to happen, he tucked his head down against her side. Pained tears ran down his cheeks and he tried to swallow past the constriction in his throat as he gently rubbed her tummy through the wires. Even now, he could feel their baby moving. The beep of the fetal monitor drummed an insane tempo in his ears and he couldn't breathe, black dots danced before his eyes as he gulped for air in his tight throat.

"Mr. Sutherby…?"

He slowly drew up to face a room full of medical staff. "Is there any chance…?"

Dr. Lee pursed his lips sadly and sighed. "I'm afraid not. At this stage, the lungs are not developed fully enough. The baby may live for a little while, but he will eventually stop breathing. You may hold him after delivery. Your baby is a boy, did you know that?"

Ryan shook his head grimly; his jaw so tight he thought it might crack.

"Yes. We did an ultrasound to determine fetal age."

The nurses clicked the bed rails up, and Ryan stepped back with slow movements.

"Dr. Jackson is waiting in labor and delivery. I know this is moving very fast, but she is in shock and still losing blood. I'm very concerned, this condition is life-threatening. She must deliver now, Mr. Sutherby."

Ryan looked away and shook his head, not trusting himself to speak as hostile emotions swamped him. He wished he could scream, *Stop!* and somehow all the madness would.

"We have to save the life of the mother-"

Ryan angrily interrupted. "And that's exactly what I want you to do! Alyssa means everything to me…she always has. We've known each other since we were children."

"Mr. Sutherby, we will do everything in our power to help her." Dr. Lee nodded, his lips set in a straight, serious line.

Impotent frustration washed over him, and he felt like breaking down as he stared at the doctor.

The dark haired nurse near him gently touched his arm. "Mr. Sutherby? Would you like to follow us? Labor and delivery is on the second floor."

"Yes." Reaching over, he pulled the blankets gently up to Alyssa's shoulders, his hands shaking with rage at her vulnerability. "I want to know who did this," he demanded, and spun around to face the doctor.

Dr. Lee sighed. "The man that struck her is eighty-seven years old, and has severe injuries himself. Several broken bones and lacerations. He claims he never saw the red light through the rain."

Ryan cursed, wishing he could punch something. That blind son of a bitch had killed his baby, plain and simple. And the damage to Alyssa…the enormity of that was yet to be measured.

"Then he shouldn't have been driving if he couldn't see!" he snarled furiously.

"You're absolutely right, Mr. Sutherby."

The doctor studied Alyssa with a furrowed brow, and motioned for the nurses to go. "She's in good hands. Dr. Jackson is an excellent doctor."

As they passed through the doorway, a sympathetic pat landed on Ryan's shoulder but he barely noticed. This was a nightmare, a nightmare he wished he could wake up from and never remember. That warm, fuzzy, happy glow was gone as if it had never existed.

They passed under the large labor and delivery sign, and horror dropped his stomach to the pit.

"Mr. Sutherby?"

Ryan shifted his steadfast gaze from Alyssa to a nurse who stood across the bed.

221

"There's a waiting room here to your right, and we'll come get you as soon as it's time for you to come in."

"Alright." He kissed Alyssa's limp hand and wished history could be rewritten, if only for a few hours.

"Sir? We have to go now."

It took every bit of willpower within him to step away. "Please… take care of her."

"We will," the nurse assured him with a sympathetic nod, and then they disappeared through the electronic doors.

Ryan paced the length of the small waiting room. How would Alyssa react when she woke up? Although she'd been scared, he could tell she was excited about having a baby. And where had she been going anyway? With no seat belt? He shook his head as fury threatened to engulf him.

He should've stayed home with her, instead of going to take his tests. He could've made them up on Monday… Why hadn't he done that? Right now, they would be eating lunch at Mario's. "Fuck!" he swore under his breath. Everything had spun wildly out of control, threatening to swirl into a vortex of irreversible despair. Ryan took in deep breaths, his soul bleak. Their baby boy…he didn't even have a chance.

A woman's voice broke through his seething red haze of self- recrimination. "Sir? Sir, once you change into these scrubs, I'll take you back. There's a bathroom in the hallway to the right. Wash your hands after dressing, please."

He followed her to the operating room and his eyes fastened on Alyssa, a blue sheet hung over her midsection on the table.

"There's a chair for you right there by her head," a nurse instructed.

He caressed Alyssa's bright hair back from her pale face. "You're going to be just fine, honey," he crooned in a low voice.

"We've given her a spinal block, so she won't feel anything if she wakes up," said a voice from above him.

He nodded stoically and leaned to kiss Alyssa's hand, feeling her pounding pulse under his fingers. Her breathing terrified him, so fast and shallow. Was the oxygen even helping? "It's okay, baby. Just calm down," he begged her, wondering if Alyssa was locked in some private hell.

There was a united somberness among the staff in the room; it was obvious this was no happy birth. "I'm sorry, Alyssa, so sorry," he whispered against her ear. She'd never wanted him to move, and in this heartbreaking moment, he wished with all his being he'd listened to her.

It seemed they had brought him in at the very end because within the next instant, there was a flurry of activity behind the curtain and then a tiny baby was brought to the warming bed. Ryan watched with his heart in his throat as a doctor held a stethoscope to his premature son's chest.

"Hello, Mr. Sutherby. I'm Dr. Jackson."

A tall, thin older man stood with a grave expression in front of him, breaking his line of vision.

"Your girlfriend is doing very well, considering. She's lost a fair amount of blood, so she will be receiving a transfusion very shortly." He shook his balding head sadly. "I want you to know how sorry I am for your son. He may live for two minutes or two hours… we don't know, but you can hold him. In fact, we encourage it."

"Of course I want to hold him. It's not like Alyssa can," he choked out, the doctor's plain spoken words sending excruciating loss through him. What did they think? He didn't want his son to die all alone, to never know he was loved.

Dr. Jackson pursed his lips regretfully. "She'll wake up soon. Your girlfriend had quite a blow to the head, and then the loss of blood only worsened matters. But once she gets the transfusion, she'll feel much better. Sometimes in cases of placental abruption a hysterectomy has to be done to stop the bleeding, but thankfully, not this time. She'll be able to have more children one day. She's young and healthy, she'll recover nicely."

Ryan nodded and smoothed the strap of the oxygen mask flat across Alyssa's cheek.

"Are you ready to hold him?"

A nurse stood next to him with a blanket-wrapped bundle in her arms. He paused for a moment, longing for and dreading this all at the same time.

"Yes, I'm ready."

She placed the baby in his arms, and a fierce tenderness washed over him as he saw the sweet face of his son. Tiny brows were scrunched together over a little button nose and Ryan pulled back the blanket to hold his hand. One miniature finger tried to wrap around his pinky, and he watched in rapt fascination as he moved his other arm. He was so little, but perfect in every way. Pressing his lips to the dark wisps of hair that lightly covered his head, he cradled his son's warm body close. "Hey, little guy," he whispered, feeling the tiny chest rise and fall rapidly against his hand.

"Here's your Mama," he whispered. Tears scalded his eyes and ran unchecked down his face; he didn't think he could bear the pain. The broken collarbone he'd had in ninth grade was nothing compared to this, his chest was an aching, fiery cavity of misery as he held their son against an unaware Alyssa.

Leaning closer to them, he wrapped his other arm around her protectively and melded their warmth together. He kissed them both and closed his eyes to the harsh lights, powerful emotions surging through him. They lay sweetly together, oblivious to the blur of motion around them.

Minutes, hours, later he realized with a devastating certainty the baby's breaths were slowing down. Ryan held his son against his chest, and reached to gently place Alyssa's hand over their baby's back. "We love you," he whispered, and kissed the soft, delicate skin of his son's forehead. "We'll never forget you," he promised, wanting to scream with the injustice of it all. Time seemed irrelevant in the rapidly moving room, he felt detached, like he was an observer watching a foreign scene. What happened from here? The baby that was so robust and almost frightening in its life-changing presence only this morning was now fragile, almost diminished.

Ryan rocked his son gently back and forth, praying for a miracle. Under his hand and against his chest, he felt his baby's breathing slow …slower… slower…and then… to nothing. "Please, no," he rasped. Rough, shuddering sobs tore through him in the hushed sadness of the room as unimaginable pain spread through his reeling heart.

"Mr. Sutherby…? Mr. Sutherby?" Ryan raised his head to look at the tear-streaked face of a nurse. "I'll take him now. I'm so sorry for the loss of your son. He is a beautiful baby," she said in a choked voice.

Ryan inhaled a shaky breath and kissed his son's dark, downy hair one last time. He returned Alyssa's limp hand to her side and silently placed the warm weight of their baby in the nurse's arms. A chilling hollowness filled him as she walked away, and he dropped his face in his hands, fighting for composure.

His son was gone. In little less than a day, he'd dropped in and out of his father's life, changing it irrevocably.

CHAPTER 19

"What the hell were you thinking, letting Alyssa use your car to drive up here? She's never even been out of Louisiana, Casey! Hell, she's barely been out of Cypress Bayou! You should've called me, dammit!" Ryan shouted, his voice shaking uncontrollably.

"I'm sorry, but she begged me and I couldn't say no. I never thought this would happen, my God!"

Casey's crying grew louder, and Ryan made a herculean effort to rein in his raging temper. "Either you or Fran should've called me," he insisted, his voice dropping an octave lower as his eyes fell on Alyssa's small form under the covers. "I could have talked to her; she didn't have to do this!"

"She wanted to surprise you, Ryan."

He almost growled; he was so angry at that ridiculous statement coming from Casey too. "Did anyone consider the danger she was putting herself in? She didn't even get here until almost midnight last night, did you know that?" he demanded.

Casey spoke in a trembling, gasping voice. "I know; she called us collect from a payphone when she got to East Stansbury."

Ryan gripped the phone tightly, wanting so badly to slam it down with all his might. "Jesus. A pay phone?" he spat bitterly. "Late at night and in a strange city, but this struck nobody as the slightest bit strange?

Alyssa couldn't have been thinking straight!"

"Of course she wasn't! She was scared to death about being pregnant, and all she wanted was to see you, Ryan!"

He set his jaw rigidly against pangs of guilt that throbbed against his temples. "And so you and her sister let her go anyway, without even picking up the fucking phone?" he gritted out.

"I tried and tried to talk her out of it, we both did. You know how stubborn she is! She was bound and determined to go and if she hadn't borrowed my car, she would've borrowed someone else's. I'm sorry. I love her too, you know. And I'm so sorry about the baby. I felt him kick right before she left, it was the sweetest thing. She was so excited when he first moved… "

Casey was crying so hard he could barely understand her and he shook his head, helplessness over the whole situation making him mute with fury.

"Tell Fran what happened," he bit out.

"I will, as soon as she gets home."

"Alright. I'll keep you updated."

He hung the phone up and sighed heavily. Alyssa appeared to be resting quietly, her color was better since the transfusion. But she was still unconscious, and nearly eight hours had passed since the accident.

"Alyssa? Wake up, honey." He caressed her arm and winced at the scrapes covering it. Was there any part of her unscathed? He'd seen the terrible bruises that marred her legs and back when her gown had been changed, startling in their vividness.

"Please, sweetheart, open your eyes. I want to see those pretty green eyes," he whispered. And it was true.

Even though what he had to tell her was going to be inconceivably hard, he wanted her to wake up. A hideous fear had gripped him to his bones and wouldn't relent till she was conscious.

He couldn't lose them both.

****

Alyssa felt woozy, almost as if she was drunk. She turned her head and a bolt of pain shafted through her neck. Blinking through heavy eyelids, she tried to focus on what she thought she was seeing. *What was Ryan doing?* He was asleep in a chair beside her and she was…

Alyssa froze, blurrily seeing the IV in her arm, and on her other arm, *was that a cast*…? "Ryan!" she shrieked. The loud sound lit up like an aura around her hammering head.

He lurched awake and she drew back, taken off guard by the haggard intensity of his light blue stare. Ryan looked different, older somehow, and she didn't think the dim light of the room had nothing to do with it.

"What's happened? Why am I here?" She tried to sit up but drew in a sharp gasp, startled by the strange, burning hurt in her stomach.

"Don't move!" He shoved his chair back with a loud scrape and moved to stand beside her.

"Why not?" she asked tremulously, scared witless by the haunted light in his bloodshot eyes. Her left hand inched down to her stomach, but Ryan caught it between both of his and kissed it. She waited, heart racing while he bowed his head, broad shoulders hunched forward.

"Alyssa, you were in a really bad car wreck. This

eighty -seven year old man ran a red light, hitting you…and the baby…" He shook his head, and looked away, a tortured expression on his weary face. "He didn't make it because he was too little. The placenta separated from your uterus, and they had to do a C-section to stop the bleeding."

She began shaking her head, whispering, "No."

His voice grew louder over her monosyllable chant. "To save your life, you could've died."

He reached up to stroke her hair, but she jerked back. "No! Nobody even asked me," she gasped, agonized denial in her uneven voice. "You can't just do that! That's not right! You have to have their permission! That's against the law, Ryan!" She was pretty sure she was rambling, making no sense, but couldn't stop herself. A car wreck? The last thing she remembered was looking for the store. But it was dark outside through the half opened blinds, and it'd been before noon when she left the apartment…

Ignoring the pain, she snatched her hand free of his grasp to pat her belly. Her face crumpled in tears when she felt her strangely deflated stomach. "I want my baby, Ryan, I want my baby," she sobbed.

He sat beside her on the bed, a dark, desolate look on his face. "Alyssa, shhhh," and lay down, holding her close to the heat and hardness of his body. "His lungs weren't developed enough," he said hoarsely. "But he was beautiful, honey, he had black hair, and he was perfect in every way."

Her precious baby boy. She'd imagined a sturdy dark haired little boy with morning sky blue eyes; she'd wanted their son to look just like Ryan. She cried in raw, harsh sobs till her head felt like it was going to explode. He stroked her back soothingly and smoothed her hair down her back, but she hardly noticed. It was impossible to draw a deep breath as she gulped for air, her whole body trembling.

"I-I want my baby," she said faintly, teeth chattering. Even that sounded too loud in her sore head and she whimpered in panicked confusion from rolling waves of pain.

He leaned back and studied her for a long moment, cursing softly, but it was nearly impossible to focus on his distorted features.

"Alyssa, I'm sorry, but…he's gone."

Ryan's voice vibrated through her and the finality registered true. She couldn't muster the strength to even pick up her head and lay weakly against him, shivering and panting. The emptiness in her womb dashed all of her dreams of her and Ryan becoming a family, she was alone once again. Alyssa couldn't bear the idea that her innocent baby had been so cruelly snatched from the warmth and security he'd ever known, sheltered within her loving body. Sickened, she began gagging and felt Ryan jump up.

"Here," he said quickly, and held a plastic basin to her chin. She threw up what little was in her stomach while he braced her forward. Her tormented body shook in deep quivers, and she barely comprehended when he laid her gently back. Relentless nausea churned in her fiery stomach as she squeezed her eyes shut. "I hurt so bad. Make it stop," she panted, not able to catch her breath.

"I need a nurse in here," she heard Ryan say frantically. Her head, her back, her stomach, her heart…every part of her throbbed in a terrible crescendo. Daddy's beatings paled in comparison.

"How long has she been awake?" A female voice swirled above her, and then a cold stethoscope was pressed to her chest.

"She woke up about thirty minutes ago, but she doesn't remember the car accident. She just threw up, and she said she's in pain."

"Poor thing. Let's get her covered up, and put the oxygen back on. I don't like her vitals. I'll call the doctor and let him know she's awake because he'll want to see her. She's due for some meds, too."

The nurse and Ryan spread blankets over her contracted, huddled body, and Alyssa groaned from the painful weight, adrift on a cloud of floating, icy agony.

****

"I'll be back this afternoon. As soon as the game is over, I'll be here." Ryan watched as the new morning nurse checked Alyssa's vitals.

The tall, middle-aged nurse smiled at him. "We'll take good care of her. You just go out there and get us a win!"

He said nothing, was this some sort of sick joke? His eyes narrowed at the red-haired woman and after an awkward stretch, she turned to dab ointment on Alyssa's cut lip.

He caressed Alyssa's silky head and looked at the time. Nine in the morning. He had to go, as bad as he hated to leave her, and found himself looking forward to the twelve o' clock game without his usual appreciation.

"Here's the numbers where I'll be at."

The nurse nodded and placed the piece of paper on her clipboard. "We'll let you know if there are any changes.

Ryan leaned down and gave Alyssa a kiss on the soft curve of her cheek. "Bye sweetheart, I'll be back soon," he whispered, and studied her thick lashes. Was she asleep? Or unconscious? He couldn't tell.

Last night had been a heart wrenching ordeal. His comforting measures had proved futile, and her pitiful moans had shredded his emotions, not able to help her. After tucking the covers securely around her and placing the call button within reach, he reluctantly left the hospital.

****

The roar of the crowd in the packed stadium did nothing to improve Ryan's spirits and he focused single mindedly on moving the ball down the field, throw after determined throw. Doggedly pursuing an open wide receiver as he scrambled to the right, he got the ball off just as he was blindsided by a two hundred-fifty pound defensive end. The force slammed him to the turf and sent his helmet flying. He jumped up, fury erasing the pain.

A red haze erupted before his eyes and he charged the opposing player ruthlessly, just as he was rising. The other guy stumbled back for a moment and then regained his balance. He threw his helmet to the ground and shouted, "Come on!"

"No, Ryan! Don't!" he heard Vince dimly calling, but he was past reason. Rage had sharpened itself to a fine point, spearing his soul, and was searching for a way to unload that hurt on someone.

"You son of a bitch," Ryan growled, hitting the beefy defensive end in the face and before he could duck, was slammed in the mouth with a hard-knuckled fist. The two grappled on the ground for supremacy in front of thousands of transfixed fans, throwing punches with a vicious purpose. They were finally pulled apart by a least a dozen players and coaches, and Ryan wiped away the blood trickling from one corner of his mouth as he stood on the field.

"You're ejected!" a referee screamed.

Ryan picked up his helmet and turned to the sideline.

"What was that, Sutherby!" Coach Thomas shouted, his face mottled red with anger. "Get your ass in the locker room. We'll discuss this when I'm done here!"

****

"You're probably going to get suspended for a couple of games." Jason shook his head and stared at the floor.

"I realize that," Ryan said icily.

Vince patted him on the shoulder as he passed. "Coach is headed this way."

About damn time. Ryan blew out a loud breath. He didn't have time for this right now; he should already be back at the hospital. The fact that he'd never been in trouble before would help, but in no way would excuse the spectacle he'd caused in front of a packed home crowd. Ryan fully expected to be suspended for at least two games and the fact that he'd let down his team disgusted him. Thankfully they'd won this game; the four touchdowns he'd scored had put them well in the lead.

Ryan rubbed his face, he hadn't slept but maybe an hour or so last night, and worry had long past turned into bone-deep anxiety. He'd been gone all day. He prayed the nurses had taken good care of Alyssa and stood up, spotting Coach Thomas coming his way.

"Sutherby, let's go talk." Coach Thomas closed the door behind him and flung his cap on his desk. "You could've blown the whole game with that little stunt! You're suspended for two games, and I don't ever want to see that crap on my field again. You got it?" he demanded.

"Yes, Coach, I got it."

"Alright. I'll see you at practice Monday. Close the door on your way out," he grumbled.

****

Ryan approached the hospital bed with a sinking sensation in his guts. Alyssa's lips were crimson red in her flushed face. He placed his hand on her forehead, appalled to find her skin as hot as fire. "Oh my God," he whispered in horror.

He whirled around and stalked to the nearby nurse's station. "I need a nurse in room 228 immediately. She's burning up with a fever."

The nurse cowed at the menacing expression on his bruised face, and stuttered, "Yes, I'll page Rebecca now."

Ryan got a couple of wet washcloths and laid one over her forehead, and another on her chest. He moved the emerald out of the way and stared at her chest, alarmed by her shallow pants for air.

"Alyssa, please get better. All I've ever wanted to do is love you. That's all," he whispered. "I can't stand seeing you like this, it's tearing me apart." He kissed her palm as her too warm skin seared his lips, and his soul.

He smoothed her hair back and watched the clock

impatiently. With a curse, he jabbed the call button.

"Can I help you?"

"What the hell is wrong with this hospital? My girlfriend is running a fever and she just had surgery yesterday. I asked for help ten goddamn minutes ago!"

"Sir, there's no need to curse-"

"Then send some help, dammit!" Alyssa hadn't even moved, he noted with a heavy sigh.

Minutes later, a nurse hurried in with her hands full. "We've just received her medicine from the pharmacy. The doctor came around earlier and ordered some antibiotics for the infection that's causing her to run a fever. I'm hanging it now, along with some more fluids," she hastened to explain.

"What infection?" he snapped.

"Her white blood cell count is elevated, but we're not sure where the infection is at yet. The doctor ordered other tests that are still pending, so we'll know more soon."

"How long has she been running a fever?"

"Since around noon, but we gave her Tylenol and now she's due for another dose."

Ryan shook his head as he watched the nurse hang bags of medicines on the IV pole. "Has she been awake at all?"

The nurse's tone took on a sympathetic note. "Not that I'm aware of. But when she does, please let me know. My name is Rebecca. Now, I'm about to give her a suppository of Tylenol since she's not able to swallow a pill."

"Good," he said in relief, not caring how the fever was broken, just as long as it was.

Ryan helped the nurse change Alyssa's gown and

put fresh linens on the bed. After securing the IV with fresh strips of tape, Rebecca headed towards the door.

"Just push the button if you need us, and I'll be back soon to check on her." She pulled the door shut behind her, and he went to the bathroom to grab a wet washcloth.

Alyssa's fever was beginning to break, her hair was damp at her temples, and she thrashed around restlessly. "Shhh," he murmured, and smoothed the cool cloth over her flushed face. "It's okay, honey. You're going to be just fine." Ryan watched as her temperature slowly dropped, not sure if his shattered heart could take much more.

A long while later, he sat down and held her hand in his, alone with his regrets.

****

The sound of her whimpering broke his light sleep and he jolted up, his eyes flying to the clock. One in the morning.

"Baby, wake up."

"Ryan, I'm thirsty," she rasped. His heart leapt in joy when she said his name.

"I'll get you some water."

She drank long sips and then lay back against the pillows. Dark shadows lurked in her expressive eyes, vivid against her pale cheeks.

"How do you feel?"

"Horrible. I hurt all over. I think I would feel better if I could walk around, though. My shoulder feels like it's on fire, I've got to get out of this bed."

"Uh, I don't know. Let's ask the nurse." He pressed the call button. Backup needed, asap. He wanted her to rest, at least for a couple more days.

"I need to brush my teeth at least."

"You're not getting out of that bed. Just sit tight, I'll get everything."

Alyssa watched him rummage through her bag. "What day is it?"

He met her eyes and paused before walking into the bathroom. "Early Sunday morning."

So she'd been asleep since...Friday night? Her belly felt odd, empty, and Alyssa gulped down the aching lump in her throat. She missed her baby, the little rolls and kicks she'd grown used to. She was scared to touch her stomach, wary of what she'd find. She'd never had surgery in her life. The squeak of rolling wheels penetrated her thoughts and she jumped as he positioned the tray over her.

"You're all set now."

Alyssa smiled softly at him, he was so sweet. There was nothing she wouldn't do for this man, she loved him so much. "Ryan, what happened to your face?" She laid her hand against the swollen outline of his bristly jaw.

"Rough game yesterday," he said abruptly, and moved away from her.

"Oh." Something told her it was much more and the chilly expression that settled on his face confirmed it.

"Are you going to be able to manage?"

"I think so."

He handed her the toothbrush with toothpaste already on it and she began to brush her teeth. The IV made it difficult and her split lip burned, but she felt better when she finished. She lay back against the pillows and smiled weakly at Ryan. Her right arm throbbed, sending surges of pain shooting down to her hand.

"Is my arm broken?"

"No, your wrist is," he said in a low voice, jaw tight in his unreadable features.

Light from the hallway flooded the room and a heavy set nurse with a bouncing ponytail entered. "I'm so glad to see you're awake. How are you feeling?"

"I hurt, but I want to get up. I think that would help." From beside her, she heard Ryan blow out an aggravated breath.

"Well, your doctor has you on bed rest, but I'm sure once you talk to him, he'll let you get up and move around a little bit."

"When will the doctor be here?"

"Around seven or so. They make their rounds early on Sunday's." The nurse stuck a thermometer in her mouth and shook her head at the results. "Still running fever, I'll go get you some Tylenol." After the nurse finished checking her out, she left the room.

"Ryan?"

"Hmmm?" He was settled in the recliner chair, long legs stretched out in front of him.

"Will you lie down beside me?"

She saw him glance over to the IV pole and sensed his hesitation. "Please?" She felt so lonely and he seemed so far away, even though he was right beside her. He'd hardly spoke to her, and she felt an acute pain ripple through her at his aloofness.

Ryan frowned and shook his head. "I don't think that's a good idea. The nurse said the doctor will be around early, and I don't want to bump you accidentally."

"Okay," she replied softly, wounded to the quick.

He fell asleep almost immediately, but she was not so lucky. As she studied his bruised jaw, she feared that this was only the dawn of a terrible course change she wanted no part of.

****

"They said I'll probably get out Thursday or Friday. I'll go home with antibiotics, and follow up with my doctor at home."

"Is Ryan going to bring you home?"

"I don't know, Fran. Did you call my work?"

"Yes, I talked to one of the assistant managers, and told her you won't be in this week. Everything is fine, don't worry. And I'm going to call the college tomorrow since today is Sunday"

"Thanks."

"I love you sis, and I'll call you in the morning."

"Love you too." Alyssa hung up the phone, missing her sister.

She picked up the paper with her son's footprints on it, and pressed quivering lips together as she traced them with a shaking hand. Tiny little feet with ten perfect toes. How she would have loved to kiss them and put little sneakers on them, just like his Daddy.

At the thought of Ryan, her troubled expression deepened. A nurse had come around earlier, and they'd had to decide upon a name and the funeral arrangements. They'd named their son after Ryan's father, Matthew. The next decision had been unbearably harder, but with the kind woman's help had finally decided upon cremation, since neither of them lived in New York.

Ryan had become even more withdrawn after the

nurse had left, and his dark silences had nipped away at her fragile emotional state. She'd been almost relieved when he'd left for work so she could be alone. Every time he looked at her, she quelled inside from the censure in his haunted gaze.

"I'm so sorry, baby Matthew," she cried to the emptiness, despising herself.

****

"Why are up walking around?" Ryan snapped as he walked into the room.

Alyssa turned to give him a look of disbelief. "What are you talking about? The doctor said that I could. You were right there," she pointed out.

"You shouldn't unless someone is in here with you. You just had surgery five days ago!"

"I'm never going to get better if I just lay in bed. And besides, I've hardly seen you the last couple of days, Ryan! Am I supposed to wait until when you finally make it here?"

"I've had school and work. I'm sorry, but I can't take off."

His quick, flippant response implied that he was anything but apologetic, and Alyssa had an awful feeling he was avoiding her.

It was hard to even stand upright; she had to hunch over when she walked. She eased down on the bed as agony surged through her at the change in position. Her stomach burned with a fiery, needlelike pain and she pressed her palm against the incision before speaking. "I wish I never came here," she admitted softly, and swallowed when a fierce scowl crossed his handsome face.

"Oh, you say that now, don't you," he mocked. He

shook his head grimly at her, his jaw tight. "It's too damn bad you didn't call me first because I would've told you the same exact thing, Alyssa!"

Glacial blue eyes pierced her with their resentment; they reminded her of her father's. She shivered with pain, her heart running a close second to the agony in her belly. "Why are you acting like this? I didn't do anything wrong, Ryan! Go blame the man who hit me!"

He growled low in his throat, his fists drawn at his sides. "I do! If he wasn't practically already in a coma, I'd put him in one. I swear I would." Ryan sat on the chair and rubbed his face with both hands before focusing on her. "Where were you going anyway?"

Alyssa stayed quiet for a long moment. Her answer was so inane, so stupidly selfish, she almost lied. "To the store to get a blow dryer. I'd forgotten mine," she whispered.

"Jesus," he muttered, and jolted back up. "Are you serious, Alyssa? A blow dryer?" he scoffed in an incredulous voice.

"Yes, I'm serious!" she shouted and began sobbing when he stalked to the bed. "Just leave me alone," she cried out.

She flinched when he bent down to her, his face a contorted mask of rage. "Let me tell you something, Alyssa," he said in a low, dangerous voice. "I held him, held our baby until he took his last breath. He died in my arms, and then the nurse came and took my son away from me. Do you have any idea how that felt?"

"Yes!" She picked up the phone beside her and threw it at him with all her might. "How can you ask me that? And you don't blame him, you blame me! Just say it, Ryan! That's what you think so just say it!"

Tears poured down her face and the quaking in her belly turned into deep shudders that wracked her body.

The phone slammed against his chest and clattered to the floor with a bang. "Calm down, Alyssa!"

"Let me go! I don't want your hands on me!" she screamed hysterically.

The door crashed open and a stern-faced nurse came in, along with two others. "Sir, you have to leave. Right now. She needs her rest."

"No, we're trying to talk here. Just give us a minute," Ryan demanded, his furious face inches from hers.

Alyssa struggled against his bruising grasp, struck down to her marrow. "Stop, you're hurting me," she choked out.

"Call Security!" the nurse shouted behind her.

Ryan released his hold and held his hands outstretched above her long moments before he tore his icy, mesmerizing stare from hers. Without looking back, he strode powerfully from the room.

Alyssa held shaking fingers over her face to hold the tears back. Intense, unbearable pain filled her, she'd lost their baby, and now she'd lost Ryan. The hate she'd seen in his eyes, the portals to his soul…there was no mistaking it.

****

Ryan tossed and turned all night, guilt gnawing at him. How could he treat Alyssa that way? Hadn't she been through enough?

He stopped by the store after work and bought a colorful bunch of flowers, relieved beyond measure when nobody stopped him from entering her room. "What in the hell," he breathed. The room was empty, not a trace of her remained. Had they moved her because of him? "Fuck!" He stepped back out in the hallway and spied Rebecca.

"Where's Alyssa at?"

She glanced down at the flowers, and shook her head sadly. "She was discharged around six. She left something for you, though."

Ryan stared at the nurse for heart-stopping seconds before he could form the words to speak. "What? Where'd she go?"

"Home. Her sister came and got her."

Ah. Of course. Ryan's eyes narrowed off into the distance, and then swung back to the nurse. "How did she get discharged? She was in no way ready to leave the hospital!" He felt like he was going to explode from the anger pounding through every muscle.

"She begged the doctor and he's a sucker for pretty faces," Rebecca chuckled, while he longed to throttle this incompetent doctor. Rebecca walked behind the nurse's station, and handed him a small wad of paper towel.

Ryan strode out of the hospital and didn't open his fist till he got to his truck. He felt a painful catch in his throat when the emerald was revealed and winked at him merrily in the golden sunshine.

She'd left

Purposely. And heartlessly. Without even a word to him, she was gone. His heart and soul froze over with icy bitterness. *Damn her.*

****

His roommates looked up in surprise from their video game as he stalked past them. Vince pressed pause and asked curiously, "What are you doing here? I thought you were staying the night with Alyssa."

"Don't ever mention that bitch's name to me again," he snarled, and slammed the door to his room with a resonant thud.

CHAPTER 20

AUGUST 2005

"I'm sorry, sis," Fran said sheepishly. "I should've met you at the stop sign in Lucas's truck."

Alyssa sighed and bit her lip to stop the trembling. "It's okay," she whispered. Seeing where her precious baby had been created and thinking about Ryan...she felt miserable.

Fran's expression grew sympathetic. "Oh Alyssa, it was hard, wasn't it? Seeing the tree?"

She took a long drink of her sweet tea. "Yeah, it was really hard." All of the feelings and memories she'd tamped down seemed closer, almost within reach, as though it hadn't been so long ago.

"I don't guess Ryan will ever come back home, will he?" Fran stopped mashing potatoes and looked at her intently across the counter.

She'd wondered the same question herself countless times. "No, I don't think so," she answered finally, and swallowed the lump down in her throat. All of the memories came back, but Ryan... he never did.

"What does his grandmother say about all of it? I mean, it's a little weird he hasn't been home, not since that summer..."

"Ms. Clare doesn't say anything, not anymore. At first she complained, but she goes up there and sees him sometimes, so she's happy, I guess." Alyssa swirled the ice cubes in her glass absently.

"Hmm." Fran shook her head and sighed. "Well, I love her new house. I stopped by there a while back, and she told me Ryan bought it for her because he didn't like her living way out there on Sutton Road."

Alyssa glared at her sister. *Oh, check out Mr. Perfect.* "Can we change the subject? He is the very last person on Earth I want to talk about!" She jumped up from the stool to walk out onto the large wooden deck which overlooked a beautiful portion of the Red River. Lucas stood on the lower deck grilling, and her stomach growled at the delicious aroma.

"Okay, so we won't talk about Ryan. How's it going at work?" Fran changed the subject good-naturedly, and Alyssa relaxed.

"Pretty good, but we've been crazy busy. I worked sixteen hours yesterday because we were short -handed. And then I had to hike to your house today so I could eat lunch." She flashed a grin at her sister.

Fran laughed. "Then let's hope Lucas doesn't burn the meat on his new grill. It took him forever to put that thing together." She turned the volume of the rock station up on the radio. "Listen, it's his new single!" The sound of Lucas's deep, husky voice singing a soulful ballad filled the room.

Alyssa smiled at the joy on her sister's face. "Fran, I still can't believe you're engaged to Luke Winters, it's just crazy. But he's just a regular guy, so down to earth." The people closest to him called him Lucas, Luke was his stage name.

Fran's eyes softened. "He's so good to me. I've never felt this way about anyone."

247

Alyssa walked over to her, and squeezed her sister's arm to her side affectionately. "I can't wait to be your maid of honor. But you better not try and fix me up with Chris again just because he's the best man," she warned jokingly.

Fran tilted her head and waved the potato covered spoon at her. "He's very talented. Lucas said he's the best drummer he's ever played with."

"Yeah, and he also thinks he's God's gift to women. You should've seen his face when I turned him down after their concert in New Orleans." Alyssa raised her eyebrows. "No. Not my type at all." She grinned at her sister. "Too bad though because he is really hot."

Fran laughed. "Well, I just hope we make it to the wedding. Lucas keeps threatening to fly us to Vegas for one of those quickie ceremonies. He's so impatient," she said with a fond smile out the opened glass doors.

"Fran, it's in two weeks. Lucas is just gonna have to hold his horses," Alyssa retorted. "It's not every day my only sibling gets married, you know. I swear I'll strangle both of you if I miss it." She glanced at her sister. "What did Mama say?"

Fran twisted her long hair over her shoulder. "She said yes, but you know how that goes…"

Alyssa shook her head in disgust and sat back on the stool. "Yep. Expect a phone call Friday night telling you she's not going to be able to make it."

Fran pressed her lips together and shook her head. "I'm not going to let her get under my skin."

Alyssa studied Fran's troubled expression with a sinking heart. Her older sister had always been so hurt by their mother's actions, no matter what other words she spoke. "Good, I'm glad. It's her loss, not yours."

Lucas entered the kitchen with a platter of grilled chicken, and Fran smiled as he leaned down to kiss her on the lips softly. "As long as this stud is at the wedding, that's all that matters."

Lucas's hazel eyes crinkled endearingly at his fiancée. "I'll be there. You couldn't keep me away," he murmured, and Fran sighed happily as he pulled her against his lean, sinewy body. He set the plate on the counter behind Fran and looked her way.

"Hey, Alyssa, where'd you park at? I didn't see your car."

"Oh, about two miles down the road," she said dryly.

Lucas shook his dark head, straight hair swinging down to his neck. A rock star he was, adored by millions. But he adored only one. Fran. It was apparent in how he held her close, a natural blending of love. Ryan had looked at her that same way once… Alyssa pulled herself together as she heard Lucas curse.

"Dammit. Sorry about that. With all the trucks coming in and out during the construction of the house, this road has gotten really bad."

Fran stirred the baked beans and placed it beside the potato salad and chicken. "But thankfully, we're next on the parish's schedule to be paved."

"After we eat, I'll go pull you out," Lucas said from over his shoulder as he fixed a plateful.

"Thanks. Hey, we heard your song on the radio just before you came in, it's so good! Everybody I work with wants your autograph by the way." She and Fran burst out laughing when he frowned uncomfortably. "Poor Luke, being a celebrity isn't all what it's cracked up to be?" she teased.

Dara Morris

"Well, it does have its advantages. Like hearing the song I wrote for my favorite girl playing on the radio."

Fran stood up on her tip-toes to kiss him on the lips. "And I love it. Every time I hear it, I just stop what I'm doing and listen."

"I bet that doesn't go over too well in the middle of a haircut," he joked.

They laughed and sat down at the kitchen table. Between bites of food, she helped her sister make wedding plans. Hours later, the ghostly moon hung low over the river and Alyssa waved goodbye to them as she got in her car they'd left at the turnoff.

****

"No, get back," she scolded. Her two dogs crowded the front door, toenails clicking on the tile floor as they greeted her. "Stop, Dixie. You know better." Dixie, her cocker spaniel, jumped up on her legs and Alyssa gently pushed her back down. "Hey, pretty girl," she crooned, and patted Sammy's soft reddish, gold head. Sammy was a Labrador mix and had a sweet, gentle disposition.

Alyssa walked into her bedroom and changed into her pajamas. "Come on guy's; let's go outside so I can brush you." She laughed as Dixie ran in front and leaped through the doggy door. "You just have to show off don't you, you crazy thing?" She dragged the brush down Dixie's silky back. "Come on, Sammy, you're next."

She finished and sat down on the wooden steps of the small deck. "Hi, sweet boy," she whispered, and gazed up at the star scattered sky. "Mama thinks about you every day, but today...today I especially did. I saw where me and your Daddy made you, and I-I miss you so much."

Matthew would be nine years old if he had lived, and in her mind she pictured a dark haired little boy with clear blue eyes. Right now, she'd probably be tucking him in bed. Tears slipped down her cheeks and she drew in a deep, shaky breath. She'd come back home broken, spirit and body, after losing him. And Ryan had never called, never tried to contact her in any way. She'd thought she would die from the pain of it. Even now, the betrayal she felt from him turned her blood to ice. She hated him for that…Ryan had become someone she'd never thought he would be. Someone who didn't care.

Looking back now, Alyssa marveled she'd survived it. The infection had raged out of control and kept her in the hospital for nine days. Delirious with fever and pain, she'd called for him over and over till her voice was gone, and Fran and Casey had begged the nurses to give her something so she would stop. Alyssa wasn't sure what she had thought. Did she really think he'd come back home for that silly, love-struck girl she'd been?

A cold, wet nose nudged her, and she jumped when Sammy snuffed loudly in her ear. "Hey, girl," she whispered, and hooked an arm around the big dog's neck.

That had been the darkest time of her life, when all she coveted most was wiped away in a disastrous tsunami, leaving her with nothing but a shattered soul. Slowly she'd put herself back together, the bits and pieces coming together like the jagged pieces of a complex puzzle. There was only one person who was capable of tearing her apart like that again…only one.

"But he never will," Alyssa vowed, fierce resolve rippling through to her bones.

****

"Good morning, Ryan." Janice, one of the office assistants, spoke over her shoulder from the filing cabinet.

"Morning." He whooped aloud while reading his email, and buzzed over to Jason's office. "Man, what time is Vince's flight getting in from Boston? That joker picked us up four new clients in one day." Ryan smiled broadly and leaned back in his leather chair, muscular arms crossed behind his head.

"He said around six when I talked to him earlier." Jason laughed excitedly. "Dude, I can't believe it. Four in one day? We're going to be swamped."

"That's why I've got a guy coming in at ten. His name is Jeff, and he's a network designer, comes highly recommended. He'll be installing new servers that will process orders quicker so the website doesn't crash because of the extra traffic."

"Good deal. Let's meet up at Sal's and celebrate around eight thirty."

"Alright, I'll give Vince a call when he lands."

Ryan studied the report in satisfaction. They had over two hundred clients now, and business was growing every day. He'd majored in computer science, knowing the odds of making it into the NFL were slim. After graduation, he'd worked in the IT department of a large pharmaceutical company in San Francisco for a couple of years, while on the side developing a program for an online payment processing service with Vince and Jason.

And EzPay had taken off; in a few short years

they'd grown from a small suite in a strip mall to a large, glass-fronted building in downtown San Francisco. The three of them worked long hours, along with two office assistants they'd hired to help with the increasing demand for their services. Department stores and online businesses made up the bulk up their clients; they processed payments for everything from perfume to tools.

He loved it, thrived on the challenge of depending solely on him and what he could accomplish. Playing sports since he was a young boy, there was always somebody urging him on, screaming at him to do better, move faster. Now it was just him and his two old friends, at first eking out a pitiful living. But it had expanded, flourished beyond their wildest dreams. The internet had taken over. Everybody shopped online now, addicted by the ease of shopping with the click of a button.

Janice's voice came over the intercom. "Ryan, Jeff Dawson is here."

"I'm on my way." Taking one last glance at the report with their four new clients listed, he closed out his email. It was time to get back to work.

****

"I'm impressed. Great job, Vince."

"Man, it was like selling candy to a baby. They were begging for us, Ryan. I didn't even have to get into the whole spill how it would expand their business and all."

Ryan grinned in satisfaction and took a long swallow of beer. "Pretty soon, they'll be knocking on our doors. By the way, we've got a meeting with Northwinds lawyers tomorrow to sign all the

Dara Morris

documents at ten. Our office. I'll send Janice or Terry for pastries."

Jason arrived with his fiancée, Pamela, and a stunningly statuesque woman.

"Vince, my man!" Jason boomed. "You set a new record. We've got to ship you off more often," he joked.

Pamela tossed her platinum blonde hair over her shoulder and cut in. "Hey, guys. Ryan, this is Jodie, my friend I was telling you about."

Very nice. Ryan admired her long legs emerging from the short, red dress she wore. "Hello, Pamela. Good to meet you, Jodie." He stood up and pulled the chair out for her.

"And you," she replied with a seductive smile. "I've heard so much about you from Pamela and Jason. In fact, Ryan, I feel like I already know you," she purred, and raked long, dark red nails down his arm. "It's crazy that all of you are so young, but run such a successful business. You must be really smart," she cooed.

Ah. Ever since EzPay had become a household name, women were constantly coming on to them, turned on by their money.

He shrugged a shoulder and smirked over at his friend. "Smarter than most."

Vince let out a loud snort.

Ryan took the last bite of his steak and threw his napkin on the table.

"Don't rush off just yet," Pamela begged as she shot a glance to a pouting Jodie. Jodie's claw-like hand slid up his leg under the table and squeezed his thigh.

He jerked up from his chair. "See you in the

morning, Jason, Vince. Goodnight, ladies."

Ryan saw Jodie's eyes turn to Vince with a speculative gleam and he laughed inwardly. *Yeah, good luck with that.* Vince was as cynical as Ryan, having been burned once too many by a conniving woman.

Ryan walked out to the parking lot and got in his truck to head home. A year ago he'd bought a house in the North Bay area of San Francisco, an affluent region that was accessible only by bridge.

He pulled up in the driveway and tossed his keys on a marble side table in the foyer. The glimmer of the Golden Gate Bridge beckoned, drew him out on the deck. It was a beautiful scene but Ryan scarcely noticed the view, instead focusing his attention on the mighty Pacific below. An eerie green glow bounced from the misty rays and caused a pang to strike deep within his heart. Its unusual color brought up hauntingly familiar feelings he longed to move on from. It'd been months, years, since he'd last seen her…why did she still cross his mind?

"Alyssa." He closed his eyes against the rush of portent emotions that name evoked. He missed her, his soul and body yearned for that bond they'd once shared. He'd never met a woman more beautiful since, her fresh, unspoiled loveliness was incomparable. The ease of their relationship, that natural feeling of mutual companionship…it had never been experienced with another.

Her youthful, all-consuming love had cemented him; he had been powerless against Alyssa's siren-like magic. "Christ," he groaned, despising his weakness. That was why he could never go back to Cypress Bayou. Because once he did…

He didn't trust himself, plain and simple. The pain she'd caused time and time again stabbed like a double edged sword, and he drew in a ragged breath. But good memories crowded out the bad, and he suddenly desired more than anything else to hold her soft curves against him, have her sweet honey scent envelope all his senses. She'd given him so much to remember. Theirs was a road strewn with doubts, goodbyes... Ryan gripped the railing hard. *And absolute happiness.*

He stared somberly out at the foggy bay and imagined himself back in Cypress Bayou. Things hardly changed in the slow moving South, he knew Alyssa and all their old friends still went swimming at the Red River during the hot summer days, and grilled at each other's houses on the weekends. He missed everybody from back home; he'd seen LaDarius only twice in ten years. Nana would mention how Alyssa took her here and there, but gave no insights into her personal life, and he never asked.

Would it always be like this? Would he always gaze up at the starry sky they shared and relive that enchanting night from so long ago? He'd believed with all his soul their love would last an eternity.

Nana fussed at him that it was time to settle down, start a family. Maybe she was right. But he felt guilty just thinking about it, as if he were somehow betraying Alyssa and Matthew.

He walked across the rich, teak floors of his living room and stepped into the large master bedroom. The urn that held Matthew's ashes sat on a high shelf in the corner. It was a simple, silver design he'd picked out himself; Alyssa was already gone when the funeral home had called.

Amidst the thick silence rent the muffled ring of his cell phone. "Shit," he muttered beneath his breath as the urn nearly slipped through his grasp.

He drew his phone out of his pocket and sighed when he saw who it was. "Hi, Nana."

"Hello, honey. How are you doing?"

"Good, just working. Been busy."

"You're always busy," she scolded. "When are you going to take a break and come home for a visit?"

"Soon, Nana, soon," he said, giving her the same answer he always did, and listened to her huff out an aggravated breath.

"Hmph." She paused moodily and Ryan stayed silent, hoping she'd drop it.

"Well, I wanted to tell you what Dr. Sims said today at my appointment. They can't do nothing else for this arthritis in my knee but surgery so I went ahead and scheduled it. I'm having it done on the fifteenth at eight in the morning. That's on a Monday." she concluded brightly.

Ryan frowned. "Whoa, Nana, you can't just go rushing off to surgery. Have you had a second opinion?"

His grandmother's voice grew firmer. "I don't need a second opinion. This is the same knee that's been bothering me for years now, and it's only getting worse. Gladys had her knee replaced last year and she said she wishes she'd gotten it done earlier, it feels so much better. I can hardly even do my gardening anymore because it's so painful. Why, if it wasn't for Alyssa and people coming over from church to help me, I don't know what I'd do."

Guilt washed over Ryan. "I told you I'd hire

someone to help you."

"No, I don't want you spending anymore of your money. You've done enough."

Ryan raked his fingers irritably through his hair and opened the sliding glass doors in his bedroom. "Nana, that's the craziest thing I've ever heard you say. What does it matter, how much I spend? It's not like I can't afford it. I want to help you," he emphasized.

"I'm managing just fine, and besides, I don't want strangers poking around in my stuff," she stubbornly retorted. "Now, I'll be in the hospital for about three days and after I get out, I'll have to do rehab for a couple of months. The ladies from my Bible study group are going to take me back and forth. I've got it all worked out, dear," she said in a satisfied voice.

Ryan walked out on his deck and studied the blurred stars through the artificially illuminated nightline. "And I'll be there to help too. I'll come home, Nana." Raw emotions battled against ingrained duty in his heart and mind.

His grandmother gasped, and he felt like the lowest bastard on earth as he heard shock fill her voice.

"You will?"

"Yes. I'll be there before your surgery."

"Now you can see my new house! Oh, Ryan, you're going to love it!"

He smiled; her joy radiated through the phone and warmed him. Going home…after ten long years away, he was finally going back to Cypress Bayou.

CHAPTER 21

"Casey, toss me that bottle of suntan oil, mine's melted away. Damn, it's hot out here. I'm about to go jump in with the kids." Alyssa piled her hair up in a messy bun and spread the coconut-scented oil onto her shoulders.

"No argument here. Although..." Casey raised her leg and pointed her toe downward, admiring her bronzed skin. "I have one helluva tan. You do, too."

"Thanks."

"Too bad Fran couldn't make it. We haven't all hung out since the crawfish boil at Megan's house."

"I guess she's too busy for us little people now," Alyssa joked. They laughed and leaned back on the sun chairs they'd set in the sand so they could keep a watchful eye on the kids.

Country music played in the background as the aroma of grilled hot dogs and burgers drifted across the large sandbar that was a popular place for swimming at the Red River. Savannah and Hunter, Casey's seven year old twins, splashed in the shallow water with the other kids, giggling and playing.

"What time is Ms. Clare's surgery tomorrow?"

Alyssa took a long sip of water and adjusted her sunglasses. "Eight in the morning, but she's checking in today. I'm going to go see her tonight. Do you want to come with me?"

"I wish I could but the twins are having a recital at church tonight. I'll go up there tomorrow around noon. Will she be back in her room by then?"

"Yeah, she should be."

"Do you think Ryan will come in since she's having surgery? I mean, has Ms. Clare said?" Casey asked in a hesitant voice.

Alyssa shrugged her shoulders jerkily. "I have no idea if he is or not."

"Oh, well, then he must not be coming because she'd be telling everybody," Casey remarked casually.

Alyssa yanked off her sunglasses and glared at her friend. "I don't understand why everybody keeps asking me Ryan's whereabouts! You'd be better off asking that tree over there!" She gestured furiously off in the distance.

"I'm sorry, Alyssa! I just thought Ms. Clare might have mentioned it."

"Well, she hasn't." Silence fell, and Alyssa sighed helplessly. "Sometimes I feel like it's my fault Ryan has stayed away. If I hadn't gone up there-"

Casey cut her off sharply. "Ryan not coming home has nothing to do with you, Alyssa! What happened was an accident, a horrible accident." She gave her a sympathetic pat on the arm.

"Yes, it was," Alyssa agreed quietly.

"And Ryan should feel bad, not you! I mean, I know he was mad at you for leaving but he should've at least called and checked on you, something! I called his apartment practically every day when you were in the hospital to tell him, but no one ever answered." Casey shook her head in a peeved motion.

That's it, Casey, just rub it in. Alyssa sighed, her

heart heavy and hurting. Most of her friends were married now, had kids.

But not her.

She'd dated some, once even having a relationship last over a year. He'd started to push marriage and Alyssa had shied away at the idea, until finally breaking it off with him. She'd actually been relieved when it was over.

"Mama, we're thirsty!" Savannah belted out, and Alyssa smiled at the sight of her little tanned legs flying across the sand towards them.

"We've got juice or water," Casey offered, and Savannah grabbed two juices out of the ice chest.

"They are so cute." Settling back to resume tanning, she tried to banish Ryan from her thoughts with little success. *Would he come back?*

****

Alyssa dragged the cellophane wrapped basket she'd made for Ms. Clare off the backseat of her car, and bumped the door shut with her hip. Unfortunately, the crossword magazines she'd arranged to stand up so prettily obstructed her vision. "Real smart," she muttered, and clutched the heavy basket against her chest. It was a short walk from the parking garage to the lobby of Cadeyville's hospital but she was still out of breath by the time she reached it. The electronic doors swung open, and she rushed to the rapidly closing elevator.

"Four, please," she said to the tall form that'd gone in front of her. Glancing over to make sure the correct floor was pressed; she froze. That long, uneven scar that stretched across his agile, big hand... She'd recognize it half blind; she'd caressed it so often.

Ryan.

She didn't even have to see his face to know, that scar from so long ago was like a brand that had been forced upon him to forever remind them of that night. Her eyes slowly traveled up his lean torso and broad shoulders till finally, she raised her head. Their gazes collided as she registered the grim surprise in his clear, blue penetrating stare. His devastatingly good looks had matured into a rugged handsomeness that literally took her breath away, she felt light-headed as she studied his set expression, her heart pounding madly in her chest. Gone was the rakish black hair she'd glided her fingers gently through as he'd slept. Now his soft, dark as night waves were cropped close to his head and emphasized the masculine planes of his lean face. Confidence radiated from all six foot plus of him, clad in jeans and a light blue button down shirt.

Alyssa breathed a sigh of relief when the elevator doors opened. To her absolute mortification, the basket slipped clumsily through her hands. She sucked in a sharp gasp as it crashed to the floor of the empty hallway.

"I'll get it." Ryan bent down at the same time and she saw stars for a moment when his forehead smacked against hers midair.

She shot him a furious glare and cradled her throbbing forehead.

"Damn. You're still hard headed, I see," he muttered. "I'm sorry; I was trying to help you."

"*I'll* get it! I don't need your help with anything, I promise you that!"

A short, cynical laugh escaped from his tight chest as he savored the delicious, tropical scent emanating from her. Time seemed to have stood still for Alyssa. With her blond streaked hair and rosy cheeks, she was the very essence of innocent, glowing youth.

"Then it's all yours, sweetheart," he drawled sarcastically, and gestured towards the big basket.

"Don't call me sweetheart, you fucking jerk!" she hissed, and flung long locks of shiny hair over her shoulder as she swooped down.

So much for the innocent part. Ryan shook his head when she struggled upward with it and raised his eyebrows sardonically. "Tsk tsk, we're in a hospital, remember Alyssa? No cursing."

"If you only knew what I really wanted to say…" Her luminous eyes blazed a dark, vivid green as he squashed the urge to duck, sure she was about to hurl the basket at him.

"Oh, I can guess," he answered dryly. "Sure you don't need any help?"

"I'm positive," she gritted out between clenched teeth.

Ryan turned down the hallway. "Have it your way."

Muttered curse words reached his ears from behind him, and he would have thought the situation comical if it wasn't for the anguish ripping through his mind as memory upon memory piled upon one another.

"Hi, Nana, I brought you some magazines."

"Hello, dear."

He leaned down to give her a hug as Alyssa walked in behind him.

"Hi, Ms. Clare, I made this for you," she said cheerfully, and pointedly ignored him.

"Oh my, what is this? Goodness gracious, there's

all kinds of stuff in here!" Alyssa helped his grandmother unwrap the basket with Nana exclaiming excitedly the whole while. "Thank you, honey. These fuzzy socks will keep my cold feet warm."

"You're welcome. It was fun picking everything out for you." Alyssa gave her a kiss on the cheek and Ryan's pulse picked up speed, remembering how her soft lips had felt.

"I'm so glad we're all three together again." A wide smile broke across Nana's face as she held their hands.

An awkward cloud bloomed in the air when neither responded. Ryan's gaze flicked over to Alyssa's lovely profile on the opposite side of the bed and a reluctant tenderness touched him. "Yeah, it's been a long time, hasn't it, Nana?" His eyes never wavered from Alyssa, wishing she would look at him. And for the space of a heartbeat she did, and it felt as if he'd been drop-kicked in the stomach at the tangible emotion he saw in her wide, candid eyes.

"Yes, it has. Way too long," Nana replied. She squeezed their hands and let go. "Now, Ryan, make sure you take good care of Daisy while I'm in here. I've boiled plenty of chicken to last the whole week, all you have to do is mix it in with her dog food."

"No wonder she's so fat, I swear she's gained fifty pounds since I saw her last," he joked.

"Oh, she has not!" Nana laughed. "But the vet did say she needs to lose some weight. That's why I give her chicken now, instead of red meat." Nana continued to give him instructions while he watched Alyssa from the corner of his eye.

"Nana, I'll be fine," he interrupted. "I can cook,

you know. Those lessons you gave me haven't gone to waste."

She beamed. "You were a quick learner, honey. Oh, that was the most wonderful summer, wasn't it?"

Ryan nodded and Alyssa's brilliant eyes snapped to his, long hair framing her smooth cheeks sweetly. "Indeed it was," he agreed, his voice sounding harsh, even to his own ears. "The best I've ever had." A summer of light and love, where nothing else had mattered, except being with her. Alyssa looked away from him and their bond was broken, slamming his heart like a sledge hammer. He'd gained wealth and power but what he desired most was here, in this very room.

Nana's perceptive gaze lingered on them and Ryan cleared his throat. "You don't have to worry about a thing. I just want you to concentrate on getting better after your surgery."

Alyssa jumped up suddenly. "Ms. Clare, I'm going to head home but I'll be back in the morning. And if you need anything, just call me."

"Alright, sweetie. Thanks again for my gift; that was very thoughtful of you."

"I'm glad you like it," she said quickly.

Ryan admired her rounded bottom as she left without a word to him, and his brows drew together in a pensive frown. He wanted her, already. All that he'd believed in, he was ready to throw it out the window. He was a fool.

Nana spoke up and cut off his inward reflections. "What happened between the two of you, honey? I asked Alyssa about it one time, but... well, she got so upset, I never had the heart to ask again. It was when you were in your second year of college, right before Thanksgiving. I hadn't heard from her in weeks, so I decided to take her one of my pecan pies. And Ryan, I could've fell through the floor when I first saw her. It was plum pitiful! Nothing but skin and bones!"

Agonized pain blasted like a bomb within his heart and he looked away, sudden tears pricking his eyes at the image the words wrought. What had happened to her?

"Why didn't you tell me that, Nana?"

"I tried to. I called your apartment I don't know how many times, and never could get an answer. And after that happened with Alyssa, I just left it alone."

Ryan shook his head in slow measures. It was true, the living room phone at their old apartment had hardly ever gotten answered unless he'd picked up, and he recalled staying solely in his room for months after that horrible October.

"I can't deal with this," he muttered wearily, and rubbed his face with his hands. "And I don't want to talk about it, either." The thought of Alyssa suffering because of him…his fists drew together as his chest heaved with raw, exposed nerves. He had to leave, get out in the open air. "Nana, I'm sorry, but I'm about to go. I think I've still got jet lag."

Nana gestured with her hands in an appealing motion. "I wasn't trying to upset you, honey."

"I know," he said vaguely, and hugged her goodbye.

Breathing in deep gulps of air outside, he got in the new black Ford F-150 he'd rented from the airport and headed back to Cypress Bayou. Much had changed in the decade since he'd been gone. Stores and strip malls now dotted both sides of the long stretch of highway, and there was more traffic than he recalled.

Even Cypress Bayou had grown. The same boutiques and restaurants surrounded the square around the courthouse, but further out were fast food places and shiny, well lit stores he'd never seen. But he'd missed it, more than he realized. A startling sense of homecoming had washed over him when he'd stepped off the plane and felt the humid, muggy heat warming his skin.

Nana's grey brick house with white wooden shutters was set in a quiet neighborhood just past the grocery store. He patted Daisy when she greeted him at the door, tail wagging with excitement. Warring emotions churned through him and he stopped in the hallway before he opened Nana's door, sure it was in there.

"Just like I thought," he murmured, and picked up the picture of him and Alyssa off of the dresser. He felt like he was transported back in time as he absorbed every detail of the photo. The way she'd fitted against him, her silky hair when it had brushed against his arm.... Her love had touched a part of him nothing else ever had.

Torturous sensations flitted through him and he set the picture back down with a thud. She'd left him, dammit. So why in the hell did he feel so guilty?

****

Alyssa inspected her navy and cream striped sundress in the mirror, chewing on her lip with indecision.

Ryan...

Just knowing he was back in town set her nerves

on edge, she'd tossed and turned all night. How she longed to feel his arms around her, he'd made her feel so feminine and desirable when they were together. Even while he'd slept, he'd always had at least one powerful hand on her, piercing her with the evidence of his caring. No man had ever made her feel the way he did, he'd always been there in her heart.

She'd only had two intimate relationships since her and Ryan had split up, and the comparison was…well, there was none.

I bet you he's had way more than that.

She knew it with an innate certainty, sexual prowess exuded from every magnificent foot of him. How it hurt, knowing his familiar arms had been around scores of other women. Well, what did she expect? Him to be a monk, swearing off all others if he couldn't have her? Yeah, right. *Dream on.*

The sun shone bright in the clear blue sky as Alyssa drove the thirty minute trip to the hospital.

She stood motionless in the hallway, riveted by the man who was separated by only a wall. Not hundreds of miles. *Just go in.* With a deep, indrawn breath, she gathered her long hair nervously over one shoulder and pushed the door open.

Ms. Clare was on the phone, hand waving as she carried on an animated conversation. Ryan stood by the window and a jolt of electricity sizzled along her spine as his sharp gaze skimmed over her from head to toe. He walked over till he stood in front of her.

"Um, hello Ryan," she said softly.

"Good morning," he murmured deeply, and shivers danced through to her core. He was dressed in a black vintage tee-shirt that accentuated muscled biceps and faded jeans. She gulped when he lightly caressed her arm.

"I'm sorry about yesterday; I didn't mean to be a fucking jerk." His eyes crinkled with amusement as she grudgingly smiled back at the big, handsome man.

"I guess you can't help it," she replied archly.

He raised his dark brows in a speculative frown. "We need to talk. Alone. You and I both know there's a lot of unfinished business between us."

A light of possessiveness gleamed in his eyes and she gasped in furious indignation as his hand tightened on her arm. "There's nothing between us, Ryan! Not anymore!"

Her cheeks heated when he leaned closer to drawl in her ear. "Alyssa darlin', there's always been something between us, no matter how you try to fight it. You know it as well as I do."

She stared up at him, her breath coming in shallow, fast pants and saw the promise of victory in his stance, the way his thumbs soothed the underside of her trembling arms. It was hard to believe this was the same man who had so coldly turned his back on his hometown, on everyone who had loved and believed in him, not once coming home in ten years.

"Ryan..." She licked her dry lips and pressed on determinedly. "Ryan, was it because of me? Is that why you never came home?"

His hands dropped as he backed up a step, steely arrogance evident in the defensive frown that replaced the spellbinding haze which had reeled her in against her will. "Yes," he ground out in a hard tone.

"But...why?" she asked shakily. Had he wanted to forget her that much, hated her that much? His lips twisted in derision, but she didn't get the answer she was terrified for, yet had to hear.

Two nurses came in the room and Ms. Clare hung up the phone. Alyssa looked over at her. She was like a mother to her, much more than Joyce would ever be. Even though she knew the chances of anything going wrong were small, she couldn't help but worry. "I'll be here when they bring you back." She leaned down to give her a hug.

Ms. Clare patted her back. "Thank you, sweetie."

Alyssa watched as Ryan gave her a hug, and wished she had a camera to capture the poignant scene. His midnight black head dropped close to her gray one as he embraced her against his broad chest in the hospital bed, and then he stepped back so they could raise the rails.

Ms. Clare spoke up in the sudden silence. "I'm going to be just fine so the both of you can stop worrying. Now honey, why don't you walk Alyssa down to the cafeteria and get something to eat while y'all wait for me to get back?"

Ryan's hooded, speculative gaze flicked over to her. "Alright. Alyssa, do you want to?"

"I guess so," she said slowly, her emotions churning.

With a satisfied smile, Ms. Clare blew them a kiss and was wheeled away.

The door swung back to close on its own and a sense of victory, however misplaced, charged through Ryan. *They were alone*. He drank in the proud tilt of Alyssa's profile, his heart pounding.

"I hope everything goes okay," she said, dark golden eyebrows creased as she turned his way.

"It will. Dr. Anders is one of the best surgeons in the state. I made sure of it."

"Yes, he is. I checked him out too."

The hospital room seemed cavernous without the bed in it, silent and sterile white. He moved closer to her, but stopped in surprise when her eyes narrowed warily at him. "What's the matter with you?"

"I thought we were going down to the cafeteria."

"We are."

Her shiny, long hair parted down the middle and he reached to stroke a soft strand back. She glowered at him reproachfully, making him feel like a first grader who couldn't keep his hands to himself.

"Well, I'm ready to go *now*."

"Are you really that hungry?"

"No, but I'd rather be down there than here, alone with you!"

"Why is that?" he asked tightly.

She shook her head as a glimmer of tears appeared on her long lashes. "I'm shocked you even want to be around me, considering I've kept you away for ten years," she whispered bitterly.

The pulse in her neck beat a frantic tempo and remorse filled him, maybe he shouldn't have come back. But it was too late now. He was here, as was she. Her shadow had haunted him in his bed; there was something about her he'd never gotten over.

"Alyssa..." He groaned her name with agonizing emotion, her distress tore him apart. It always had. "I made a mistake. A huge mistake. Look at me," he coaxed, and cupped her face between his hands.

She gave him a mutinous, disbelieving look. "It's not that easy, Ryan! You're not just going to waltz back into my life after all this time and think I'm going to collapse at your feet, praising God!"

"I wish," he answered dryly.

"Yeah, you just keep on wishing. I want you to leave me alone! All you've ever done is bring me misery," she practically shouted at him, and scrambled out of his grasp.

She bit her trembling bottom lip, and like a knife digging deep, his chest ached at her resentful glare.

"That's not true. We used to be friends, remember? Really good friends." Bittersweet images of them flipped through his mind like pages from a photo album.

Her eyes shut for a moment before speaking. "Of course I remember. You were my best friend, Ryan. Why do you think I never wanted you to leave?" Her voice broke at the end.

With a ragged moan, he pulled her slender, shaking body close to him. Tenderness exploded deep within as she drew in a shuddering breath and curled her hands around to his nape. "I'm going to kiss you, so be still this time," he ordered huskily, and smiled at the warm light that filled her eyes. He felt unable to stop even if an army had commanded it. His arms tightened around her, their lips meeting in a hungry, needy rush as old fires were rekindled in an explosion of brilliant white fireworks.

Alyssa's head spun in an exhilarating, wild dance. Ryan was really here and so close, his heady, masculine smell intoxicated her. She nestled close to his hard chest, needing the anchor of him to steady herself against the crashing waves of desire she rode on. Their tongues interlaced in a long, devouring kiss, their mouths melding together feverishly while heat consumed her. How long she had she dreamed of this, imagined herself in this man's arms?

An intercom buzzed overhead and Ryan groaned deep in his chest. He slowly drew his lips from hers, trailing a line of seductive kisses to her neck.

"Alyssa…" Her nipples hardened, tingled, at the desperate, lusty tone of his hoarse voice. He rubbed her back with shaky hands, gradually dulling her passion-fired senses as they both fought for breath.

She tightened her arms around his lean waist and wished they could stay like this forever. But they were too many unsaid words, too many hurdles to cross. He didn't even live here. She gulped before dropping her arms, feeling like it was one of the hardest things she'd had to do yet in her life.

"Um, we should go to the cafeteria now." She winced at the tremor in her voice.

Ryan shook his head; eyes narrowed into slits. "Why? Oh, that's right; you don't want to be alone with me." His strong arms held her tighter and she stiffened. "Aren't you forgetting something, Alyssa?"

Pulse racing, she just knew she was going to faint if he didn't let go of her soon. "What?" she gasped, gazing hugely into scorching, blue depths.

"You're the one who left. Without a fucking word, nothing. The only thing you left was that goddamn necklace. That, and the baby's ashes," he stated furiously. Rage filled him, suppressed hurt rising from long ago demons he'd masqueraded, determined to make it without her.

His heart turned over as Alyssa struggled for breath, her face as white as the walls around them.

Horrified, he loosened his iron tight grasp and she dropped to the floor to her knees. Deep cries edged with hysteria wracked her small body and he squeezed his eyes shut for a moment before he stooped down.

"Honey, oh God. Please stop." He stroked soft strands of golden hair away from her downturned face. Was this what they invariably did to each other, this tumultuous roller coaster of euphoric highs and tragic lows?

"Don't touch me," she whispered pitifully.

Shame coursed through him. "I can't help it. Alyssa. That's why I never came back. I couldn't, because I didn't trust myself around you."

Her head snapped up, eyes aglow with a savage light. "That's not why you didn't come back," she choked out bitterly. "You never came back because you didn't care! You wouldn't be here now, Ryan, not if it wasn't for your grandmother!"

Ah, how the truth stung. He said nothing but lifted his hands from her shoulders, slowly, almost symbolically. The fortress around her heart resurrected itself and she drew her knees to her chest, sobbing quietly.

The baby's ashes... My Matthew, my little angel. "I thought I was being fair, I had the footprints, and you-you had...him," she struggled to say, needing him to understand.

He towered over her in a swift motion. "What the hell did you ever do that was *fair?* Drive up there without even telling me you were coming? Going to the store in a goddamn thunderstorm without a seat belt when you said you'd stay until I got back? The way you left me... you call that *fair,* Alyssa?"

Each snarled word was like a razor striping across her soul, hadn't she paid the price for her blinding love for him? Her head felt like it was going to explode from the fury coursing through her and she stood up, meeting his hostile, glinting eyes.

"I hate you, you sorry, fucking bastard," she said in a deadly, calm voice, colored with vehemence. "It wasn't my fault he ran the red light! And I don't know how my seat belt came off; I put it on before I left your apartment. All I remember is driving down the road. I don't remember him hitting me, nothing. And I had to leave, Ryan! You blamed me then, just like you still do!"

A strange, haunted expression crossed his handsome face as he tilted his head down. "What happened after you got back here, Alyssa? What happened to you?"

His question threw her off balance even more. "I don't know what you're talking about."

"That's bullshit," he gritted out, his a muscle in his jaw ticking ominously. "You know exactly what I'm talking about."

"What in the hell do you care, Ryan! You never even called me!" she cried out, and shoved him as hard as she could out of her way.

Why was he asking now, after all this time? It made no sense to her. Alyssa took off down the hallway and ducked into the women's restroom.

"Oh my goodness, I look horrible." She wiped off her smudged mascara and studied her flushed face. Never would she tell Ryan how she'd cried for him, needed him. "Why did he have to come back?" she whispered to the mirror.

And a total knee replacement, that took months to fully recover from. But he had his work in San Francisco, and besides, he hated it here in Cypress Bayou. He'd be leaving just as soon as he could; she'd stake a hundred bucks on it.

****

Ryan stayed where Alyssa had shoved him for a few minutes, feeling like he'd been hit by a train. One taste of her…and he realized how starved he was. If that page hadn't gone off, he believed he'd have pushed her into the bathroom, damn the regrets later. And he didn't think he would've had much trouble persuading her either, judging from her passionate response. Nothing had changed between them, raw desire burned as true as it had since they were teenagers.

He didn't want to argue with Alyssa. The truth was, he'd come to terms with the fact that it wasn't her fault a long time ago. But now, thanks to his stupidity, he'd spoken irrational, angry words he wished he could take back. Ryan rubbed his face and looked at the clock. Nine thirty; it would be around noon before they brought Nana back.

He searched the cafeteria and outside, but there was no sign of Alyssa. "Why in the hell am I surprised," he muttered with a sardonic twist of his lips. She'd disappeared. *As usual.* Ryan slammed the door to the newspaper machine shut and walked back up to the room.

He'd just finished a business call when his phone rang again. "Hey, Vince."

"Hey, man. How's your grandmother doing?"

"She's still in surgery, but she'll be back in about an hour."

"That's one sweet lady. Tell her we're thinking of her, and hope she gets well soon."

"I will."

Vince and Jason loved his grandmother. When she came and visited, they always had supper at his house at least once, with Nana cooking a huge feast for them and whoever else they invited. How long would it be before Nana would be able to come out to visit? Knee replacement surgery...that was major. It'd be months before Nana was back to her old self.

"How did the meeting with Grant's lawyers go? Everything ready to go for next Monday?"

"Ryan, like I've told you a million times before, you take care of Ms. Clare and we'll take care of this. Capiche?"

"Yeah, yeah, I hear ya," he joked.

The door opened and he looked up, hoping it was Alyssa. Nope, Casey. And she definitely didn't look happy to see him.

"Hey, man, give me a call when we get confirmation from Silver Star."

"Will do, man."

Casey's voice rose above the din of the sports channel. "Well, I must say I'm shocked to see you using a phone," she sneered rudely.

Ryan flipped his phone shut and turned the TV off. "What the hell is that supposed to mean?"

Casey pinched her lips together, her eyes narrowed. "Never mind. When will your grandmother be back from surgery?"

"In about an hour." Ryan regarded her steadily. "So that gives you plenty of time to explain why you're so shocked to see I can work a phone." He clenched his jaw. "I know something happened after she got back here. Tell me, Casey. I asked Alyssa but she won't."

Casey's expression softened slightly. "Well…okay." She drew a deep breath, and an awful sense of foreboding sent chills down his spine.

"The insurance company had got me a rental car after the accident and Alyssa called, crying so hard I could barely even understand a word of what she was saying. She wanted us to come get her, so we did; me and Fran. We took turns driving."

Her eyes dropped to the floor and she shook her head, lost in thought. "She started throwing up, running fever on the way back. I was so scared, me and Fran both. I remember we weren't home but a few hours and she was just getting even sicker, so we took her to the emergency room. She could barely even walk, she was hurting so bad. It was some kind of infection, I don't remember the name of it now, but it was bad…really bad. She stayed in the hospital for over a week."

Ryan's heart sunk lower with every word, as if a hammer was pounding a stake deep down, and a cold sweat popped out on his brow.

"I tried calling you to tell you they'd admitted her, but… She shrugged her shoulders helplessly. "You never did answer. And then she started calling for you, over and over and over again. She was delirious, from the fever, from the pain, or maybe from the medicines, I don't know. The nurses had to give her sedatives to make her stop."

She hugged her arms around her middle, and studied the floor in the ensuing, heavy silence. "I wish that I never told her I'd tried to call you. It just made it worse, because then she thought you were coming to see her."

Agony so great in strength exploded within him, crashing mercilessly against his hurting heart. Pain Alyssa must have felt when he never came. His poor girl...her life had been fraught with undeserved betrayals, and the very worst of it had come from him. For she'd truly loved him, loved him fiercely enough to take risks, just to be with him. And he'd let her down, when she had needed him more than ever before.

What kind of friend was he?

How she must hate him, now wholly understanding the wounded darkness he'd glimpsed in her beautiful eyes. The newspaper fell wordlessly from Ryan's hands as he stood up and stalked from the room, despising himself and the selfish choices he'd made.

****

Alyssa took a sip of the strawberry shake she'd gotten at the drive through, and glanced at the clock. 11:30. Thirty more minutes till they brought Ms. Clare back. There was no way she would sit alone in the room alone with Ryan and feel his accusing eyes on her. How stupid she was, to fall right back in his arms. One touch...and she trembled with desire. Ryan didn't play fair, but then he never had.

Alyssa's eyes widened in alarm and she slunk down in her seat. "This cannot be happening," she muttered and turned the radio down. The very man she'd been cursing to hell and back was walking slowly across the parking lot, broad shoulders hunched forward. He seemed distracted, sad almost...

Alyssa jumped out of her car and ran up to Ryan breathlessly. "What's wrong with your grandmother?"

A look of shock crossed his face at her sudden

Dara Morris

appearance, and she tugged his arm impatiently when he didn't answer. Ryan looked ten years older with his bright eyes dimmed by a terrible, nameless emotion.

Alyssa bit the inside of her cheek. "Ryan…what is it?"

His face cleared slightly as he stared at her. "Nothing's wrong. She'll be back soon; I just had to get some air. Casey is up there now."

"Oh. You scared me, that look you had on your face… I thought something had happened."

She jumped when his hand covered hers, and his deep, husky voice when he spoke turned her insides to jelly. "Alyssa… Casey told me what happened after you got back here."

"Casey and her big mouth." She shook her head and looked away, positive Casey had told him every humiliating detail. He rubbed her shoulders with his big, warm hands, and a crack rippled across her armored heart.

"I never heard the phone, and Jason and Vince were always playing video games back then, they sure weren't going to answer it. I was so depressed after you left…I just stayed in my room, for months. When Matthew passed away, something died in me too, and I…I fucked up everything." He shook his head as his fingers trailed down her cheek in a gentle motion. "I'd have taken the first plane out of there if I'd have known you were in the hospital. I swear I would've, honey." He nudged her chin upward. "Nothing would have kept me away. Say you believe me, Alyssa."

"I believe you," she whispered. His words were like a miracle salve to a searing wound that had never quite healed, and the honest appeal in his tortured gaze tugged at her heartstrings.

He hugged her close, despite the heat of the early morning sun. She closed her eyes and a pang struck deep within when he brushed his lips against her forehead, chokingly whispering her name.

"Alyssa… Lyssa, I'm so sorry."

"It's okay," she said in a low voice, and he shook his head in harsh denial.

"No. No, it's not. I'll never forgive myself for not being there."

She was too good for him; he'd done nothing in his life to deserve this beautiful woman who trusted what he said without reservations, and brought peace to his severed soul. The heartbreaking image of her calling for him, sick after having his baby, was one he'd carry with him to his grave.

He smoothed his hand down her long hair, the feel of it like satin sheets. "Will you eat supper with me tonight? My treat."

She clasped his face and for the first time, smiled genuinely. He felt a catch in his throat at the charming dimples he'd missed so much.

"Free food? I'm there," she teased.

"I feel like I just ran in the winning touchdown at the Super Bowl," he murmured in her ear.

She laughed, her eyes glowing with a joy he knew was mirrored in his. "That good, huh?"

"Yep, that good," he whispered, and they kissed, a curing touch of their lips as hopeful as a butterfly's wings unfurling.

He drew back and caught her hand in his. "Come on; let's go see if Nana is back yet."

"Alright."

Ryan glanced over at her as they rode up the elevator and shook his head in amazement.

"What are you staring at?" She arched her eyebrows in a playful gesture.

"You. You're the prettiest thing I've ever seen in my life. Even with your red nose," he said and grinned. The wall she'd hid behind was gone.

"Thanks, I think," she laughed, and scrunched her nose at him playfully.

Nana was there when they got back, and Ryan watched Casey's face turn suspicious when she saw Alyssa's red-rimmed eyes. But it soon relaxed when he placed his hand on Alyssa's shoulder, and the sweet smile she gave him caused his stomach to dip from emotion.

"I was wondering where the two of you were," Casey remarked.

Alyssa shot her friend a glare. "Uh huh, mouth of the south, I bet you were." She took Nana's hand in hers from across of the bed. "How do you feel?"

"I'm sleepy," Nana drowsily responded. "Think I'll take a nap," she muttered.

"Is that normal?" Ryan looked over at Alyssa as his grandmother dozed off.

"Yes, the anesthesia hasn't wore off all the way yet. But I'm going to warn you, the first few days are going to be rough. The physical therapist will have her sitting in the chair tomorrow and using a walker to go to the bathroom. She's going to be hurting, even with the pain meds."

Ryan nodded. "Yeah, I did some reading up on it. I know it's not going to be easy on her."

"Medicare will cover some home health and I'll be

there to help, too."

"I've hired someone, actually. Her name is Patricia Mills, and she has a lot of experience with patients recovering from surgery. Nana liked her."

Alyssa raised her eyebrows, and gave him a surprised look. "You've been busy."

"She works for a home health agency, Caring Hearts. I called them after Nana told me she was going to have surgery."

Alyssa smiled at him and Ryan felt like even more of the asshole he really was. She had to be silently comparing this to how he'd treated her when she was in that shitty hospital in East Stansbury.

"That was thoughtful." She twisted her hair in a long rope over her shoulder and sat down beside Casey.

"Yes, it was," Casey agreed.

Ryan shifted uneasily, vastly relieved to see some of Nana's friends coming in the room.

"Hello, Alyssa and Casey, and is that…? Well, I'll be! Ryan, we were beginning to wonder if you'd forgotten all about us!"

Ms. Edith gave him a hug, and he felt a touch of nostalgia as he smelled the strong scent of her rose perfume he remembered since he was a little boy.

"Hi, Ms. Edith. How've you been?"

"Oh, just fine. Now, don't you do that to us again, Ryan," she admonished him, and patted his cheek. "Your grandmother missed you and so did we. Didn't we, girls?"

The "girls" all nodded their gray heads enthusiastically, and chimed in their sentiments.

He held up his hands in defeat to the ladies who'd hugged him at church, and cheered him on at football games. How he'd missed this town and the people who lived here… "I won't, I promise. I plan on coming home a lot more."

"Thank the Lord!" beamed Ms. Edith. "Now tell me, how is your grandmother doing?"

"She said she wasn't hurting, she was just tired."

"Bless her heart. I remember when I had my knee done…

CHAPTER 22

"I'm pretty sure at least half the town stopped by." Ryan rubbed his forehead and then dropped his hand to look over at Alyssa.

"And you were the star attraction. Poor Ms. Clare," she teased. "You know you loved every bit of it."

"I don't know about that. But it was good seeing everybody. I've missed them."

"Have you?" Alyssa asked seriously, her eyes wide and quizzical.

"Yes, I grew up with everybody here. I don't have that kind of connection with anybody in San Francisco."

Alyssa nodded as his guts twisted at the wistful expression on her face. "What's wrong?"

"Nothing."

"Hmmm," he replied suspiciously, their gazes locking and sizzling like static. They were at her house; he'd come over with pizza and wine after letting Daisy out.

They'd finished eating and sat together on the couch, soft rock music playing in the background. Alyssa had a nice home, stylishly but comfortably furnished with brown leather furniture, and earthy, muted tones of greens and reds. Metallic accents and lit candles were casually placed, giving it a homey, relaxing feel.

She sat cross legged and bare foot, her knee touching his thigh. Even that slight contact sent his imagination running amok. He cleared his tight throat and made himself look away from the tempting sight of her cleavage.

She'd changed into a white tank top and short blue athletic shorts, an outfit that was driving him crazier than any revealing dress ever had on the myriad of women he'd been out with. Her tan skin glowed against the white, and golden waves of hair tumbled almost to her waist. He felt like he was transported back to that idyllic summer, when everything was right in his world.

Crossing his hands in front of him, he turned to her. Luminous, long lashed eyes rose upwards to his, and he suddenly realized how much he longed for things to be the way they once were.

"Alyssa, I thought about you a lot over the years. Every year on your birthday, I'd pick up the phone to call you, but..." His eyes narrowed, he shook his head in regret. "I wish that I had."

She plunked her wine glass down with a slosh on the coffee table and jumped off the couch. "You don't have to say things that aren't true just to make me feel better, because it doesn't," she said in a low voice, her face blazing with distrust.

Ryan stalked after her and grasped her by the shoulders. "Dammit, I'm not lying. I thought we'd be together forever, Alyssa. Didn't you?" He spoke softly, baring his soul.

The mood changed instantly, charged with an intensity that promised to suck them both down in a whirlpool of powerful, endless currents they were unable to break away from.

Alyssa stared at him, her visual senses stimulated, filled, by the man who held her tightly in his arms, throbbing need reverberating from him.

"I wanted to, but… I was afraid to hope too much," she replied honestly.

His mouth twisted in an ironic frown as he shook his head. "We were never on the same accord, it seems." He tucked her hair gently behind her ears. Quaking tenderness filled her and she forgot to breathe when his hands slid around to her back, pulling her flush against his muscled, tall body.

"Except for on one thing," he said beside her ear.

His hands roamed restlessly over her body as hot kisses landed everywhere, upon her cheek, her temple, her lips… She was putty in his hands, literally.

"What's that?" she asked, passion clouded senses barely coherent, and leaned against the strength of him.

"We loved each other. We still do," he murmured huskily, the latter sentence spoken with a fierce power.

"Yes, we do," she whispered, and cupped his face between her hands. She remembered the handsome boy she loved when she was a little girl, so gallant, her knight in shining armor. And now he was a man, dark and handsome, the opposite of her light, and she was trapped…devoured by the alluring promise of him. "I've missed you, Ryan."

"I've missed you, honey. Not a day went by that I didn't think about you." He slid a strong arm under her thighs and in one quick motion, cradled her against him.

"Mmmm, you taste so good," she whispered in his ear, feeling him shudder when she pressed open mouthed, hot kisses to his neck. He smelled delicious, a mixture of his own masculine aroma and the woodsy cologne he used. "At the end of the hallway."

He sat her down on the bed and followed, his big body covering hers as they lay down as one. Primal desire radiated from him, matching hers as they stared heatedly at each other. His breath quickened to an uneven, rough pant and he clasped her bottom hard against his raging erection, startling her with its hugeness. Sexual tension charged the air, so fast it astounded her. "Alyssa... I want you so much. I still need you."

She nuzzled closer to him, reveling in the feel of firm muscles over smooth skin. "And I need you too, Ryan."

They'd spoke those very same words so long ago and they still held fast, unbreakable bonds that had stood the test of time. She swallowed hard, her heart soaring and hurting all at the same time.

His hands roamed under her shirt, eager to feel her silky skin next to his. As each piece of her clothing was shed he moaned; rapturous passion barely contained as her assets were revealed. His hand curled around her naked ribcage, caressing appreciatively from her smooth shoulders down to her shapely thighs in the softly illuminated room. Candles, tall and small, burned on the dresser, bathing Alyssa's curvy form in the mysterious shadows of the dark room. "You're beautiful, love," he murmured.

Her full breasts were as perfect as he remembered, and she gasped when he teased one hard nipple with his mouth. He trailed kisses to her other breast, but she leaned down and pulled him to her in a hungry explosion of sensual wanting. They came back together in a rush, their tongue mimicking what was yet to come in a deep, wet kiss, and his low groans of pleasure filled the room.

"You're mine, Alyssa," he said against her lips, and rubbed her trembling body with soothing, possessive hands.

"Always," she moaned, her soft breasts pressing into him.

"Am I dreaming?" he whispered in the hushed dimness.

She smiled slowly at him, bewitching him with her beauty. "Not this time. It's really me."

"Thank the lord," he muttered fervently. "There's no going back now, Lyssa." He pulled her soft curves closer. Her hands drifted downward and his nostrils flared as her fingers wrapped around him, stroking his pulsating length.

"There's sure not," she answered, and sucked his lower lip into her hot, alluring mouth.

"Jesus Christ," he rasped, shaking from the unbelievable power of her cool hand on him. Her thighs fell open at his urging and he caressed her, drawn to her slick folds. Gliding two long fingers in her as he rubbed her swollen nub, she clutched him harder in her hand and her hips shot off the bed.

"Ryan!" she cried out, moaning restlessly. She was so tight, clenched around his fingers. He began to sweat, imagining his painfully hard shaft deep within her sweet flesh.

"Right now, I want you right now," she panted.

"Protection," he bit out. It took all his resolve to roll to the side of the bed and reach for his pants. She licked and kissed his sensitive nipples when he came back to her. "Alyssa, babe, I can't even think when you do that." Her soft lips drove him to the edge of erotic madness and he fumbled with the condom for insanely long seconds. It was habit; he'd never forgotten to wear one since that last disastrous time. But never before had he possessed the urge to throw caution to the wind like he did now. He wanted to feel her again after all this time, free from boundaries, and surrender to the tight walls contracting around him as he let go deep with within her.

The condom finally in place, he posed above her and gritted his teeth. "Alyssa…"

Sultry emerald eyes met his, burning with a voracious, sensual glow.

"You're tight, really tight." He spoke in a low rasp, beads of sweat gathering on his forehead. Jesus, she was killing him. He couldn't be still any longer. "I'm gonna go slow. I won't hurt you, honey."

She tensed as he penetrated, he was large and rock hard.

"Shhhh, easy, baby," he said in a gravelly voice, and watched the engorged head disappear into her hot, wet channel. It was like coming home, he groaned raggedly with a shudder. Where he belonged. "You feel so good," he murmured thickly, consumed by erotic bliss. He reached between their flushed bodies and caressed the most sensitive part of her. She groaned, thrashing her head side to side. Unable to wait a second longer, he thrust deep and took full possession.

"Oh my God," she cried out, the sensations piled over her demanded, took, and all she could do was surrender to the raw, sexual overtaking. He filled her, stretched her tender walls, one in heart and body.

Grabbing her hips in a tight hold, he set a slow, rocking rhythm. It was torture, the most exquisite, mind-bending torment she had ever experienced. Beads of sweat glistened off of his lean physique, every hard muscle and tendon standing out in stark rigidness.

"Faster, Ryan, please!" she gasped, needing all of him, everything he was capable of giving her. It was like unleashing a caged tiger. With a deep groan, he locked her mouth to his and wrapped his arm around her.

"Hold on, baby," he grunted hoarsely and kissed her, tongues tangling together breathlessly. Passion stoked higher, the candle lit room filled with the sounds of their whispers and groans of bliss. Steady strokes ignited into a frenzy of feverish thrusts as wicked hot tremors overtook her. By the fifth stroke she climaxed, screaming his name and holding on to him with a near desperation.

"Baby, you make me so fucking crazy," he muttered huskily, and drove into her with a cadence that had her sensitive flesh quivering. He groaned, bracing his head on her shoulder, and she wrapped her arms around him as he grew bigger and longer by the second in her.

"Oh, God," she gasped, sucking, kissing on his neck, his ear, anywhere her mouth could touch. And then they kissed again, a devouring kiss that stole every thought out of her brain.

Except for Ryan.

He was everything; no man had ever felt like this but him. All of a sudden, another orgasm ripped through her and she went over the edge, lights exploding behind her shut eyes.

He groaned deeply against her lips and stiffened, his big body shaking. Tears burned her eyes as his warm weight covered her and she felt their hearts pounding together.

"You okay?" He kissed her neck and she tightened her grip around him, not ever wanting this moment to end.

"Oh yes, better than okay," she smiled. She felt free, rid of all the inhibitions and fears she'd carried around for a decade. He smoothed her hair out of her face and rolled over on his side.

"I love you," he whispered tenderly in the romantic glow.

"I love you too." The air shimmered, golden bright, magical rays of the most cherished, most powerful, human emotion enveloping every shrouded corner.

After a few minutes, Ryan sat up with a reluctant grimace. "I'll be right back babe; I've got to get rid of this condom."

He rolled away from her and she leaned up, kissing him on his back. "Let's go take a shower. We've worked up a sweat somehow."

She giggled as he turned to nuzzle her neck. "Mmmm, I know how." He smiled at her and she shivered from the primal glow in his clear eyes. "That was only the beginning, Alyssa. And that's a promise."

Ryan playfully pinched her naked, lush bottom as she walked to the bathroom. She flipped on the light and he frowned. The scars had faded to thin white lines that crisscrossed her back and all these years later, it still infuriated him to see them. He splayed his hand over her, a temporary shield to the trauma she had suffered. He would never understand why anybody would want to harm Alyssa, much less her own father. She was a gentle, rare beauty, inside and out. He rubbed his hand up and down the slim column of her back while she adjusted the temperature of the water.

"That is a very serious face you have there, Mr. Sutherby. Let me wash away all your troubles." She pulled him into the shower with a playful tug.

"Oh, please do," he lazily replied, lips quirked upward in amusement.

She lathered shower gel on a sponge and he shook his head. "I'm going to smell like a girl."

"Yep sorry," she quipped with a shrug, her lips curved in a smile.

"Hmm, you don't sound too sorry." She laughed, her face aglow, and his hands reached out to draw her sleek form next to his. Water streamed in rivulets down her shapely body and his eyes lustfully followed.

From out of the blue, she stilled with a jerk. "Can you see it?"

Yes, of course he could, noticing the moment she asked. Her scar from the C-section. His gaze flicked to Alyssa's face, surprised by the angry glare she threw at him. He took the soapy sponge from her hand and began to smooth it over her skin. Her chest heaved in fast breaths, and her pulse leapt frantically in her throat as he neared the thin, bikini cut line.

"Alyssa, I can barely even see it. Why are you getting upset? Of course you're going to have a scar, you had surgery."

She looked away and shook her head.

With a deep sigh, he hugged her close to his body and washed her back. Tense muscles relaxed and he swallowed the lump in his throat when she kissed his chest, warm water beating down on both of them.

"Sometimes I hate looking in the mirror. These scars… They're all bad memories. And I don't like for other people to see them either," she said in a small, wobbly voice.

Empathy exploded inside his soul; there were too many ghosts lurking in her vulnerable eyes. "Alyssa, you're a strong person and those scars show you overcame something that was really hard." He held up his right hand and laid it against her stomach. The almost matching horizontal scars brought him to a standstill and Alyssa stared downward, until finally raising solemn eyes to his. Her pupils were dilated, so huge her eyes were almost black, fringed by a circle of emerald.

"We all have our scars, sweetheart, they mean you're a survivor." His voice lowered to a whisper as he smoothed water droplets across her brow with his thumb. "I think you're really brave, I always have." A small smile broke across her features as relief leaped and bounded through him. "Nobody else is going to see you, not unless it's a doctor or something. From now on it's just me, baby, and every bit of you is incredibly gorgeous." He laced his fingers through hers and kissed her knuckles.

"I love you, Ryan. I'm so sorry…" her voice broke, and then forged on, her nails digging into his hand. "I'm sorry for everything that happened." Regret and guilt flooded the transparent depths of her eyes and he grasped her slumped shoulders firmly, giving her a slight shake.

"You don't have anything to be sorry for, nothing. None of it was your fault. Not your parents, not what happened with the baby, not any of it," he commanded. He felt totally undone by the despair that emanated from her, only silence greeted his statement.

She reached past him to turn off the water and hopped out in a flash to wrap a fluffy, white towel around her.

He studied her drained expression under the bathroom light. "Come on, honey, let's go back to bed."

She grasped his hand like it was a lifeline. He blew the candles out, and kissed the nape of her neck as he lay down. She turned in the circle of his arms and he held her tight, thanking the heavens above he'd been given another chance.

"Go to sleep, I'm not going anywhere."

Her supple, naked body melted against his as she drifted off. His heart swelled with love, even while his brain screamed warnings at him. Their relationship would never be stable until one of them made some life changing decisions.

But which one would it be? How could he leave San Francisco? Vince and Jason could handle it for a short while, but in no way could he be gone for extended periods of time.

But Alyssa…she was a nurse. She could work anywhere, not that she had to. He tried to imagine her living in San Francisco. Would she be happy away from her sister, her friends, and the small town she'd lived her entire life in?

He tucked wayward strands of hair back from her smooth cheek, while shame, stronger than ever, rolled through him. It was his fault, these past ten years, and he'd lost so damn much. As a grown man, it was hard to believe he'd never even called to check on her. He was terrified; terrified his idiocy would conquer and topple the love that blazed from her. Only comfort and warmth greeted him when she snuggled closer, and Ryan closed his eyes wearily, dark misgivings briefly forgotten.

CHAPTER 23

"They must be barking at a squirrel." Alyssa blinked open sleepy eyes, and saw a tiny shadow of morning light peeping around the blinds. "Shut up, dogs," she mumbled.

"Mmmm." The sound vibrated from the chest of the man who lay behind her. Ryan had kept her deliciously close all night, even now, his hand imperceptibly tightened on her hip as she twisted to peer at her cell phone. She wrapped her arms around him and kissed his muscled chest.

Ryan tipped his head down and opened his eyes. "What are you grinning like a possum for?"

Alyssa laughed out loud at his silly question. "Still a country boy at heart, I see. And it's because you smell like flowers." She giggled when he scowled irritably. "But I like it. In fact, I think it kind of suits you," she teased.

She ran her fingers through his hair, still laughing when he rolled her beneath him and propped himself above her with his palms flat.

"Oh really?" he taunted. Ripped muscles strained taut in his shoulders as she stared in fascination at the huge, powerful man that she loved. His rigid erection jutted against her thighs while desire flamed hotly within.

"Well, maybe not. You definitely deserve

something more manly," she said in a breathless voice. He drew her sensitive nipples in his seductive mouth, and liquid heat boiled in her most intimate parts. She gasped, pulling him closer to her.

"One sec, babe." He slipped a condom on and then reached for her again. He kissed her neck, her shoulders, making her shiver when the rough stubble on his face rasped across her skin.

Their lips met in a wildly, erotic dance, and he thrust deeply inside the same moment his tongue plundered her mouth, taking away her breath all at once. She wrapped her legs tightly around him as his hot spear spread a blaze that would consume her. She screamed, moaned into his mouth, and dug her nails deep into his back as she held in for the ride of her life.

Wrenching her lips from his, she strained against him in a haze of need. He rolled his hips, deliberately rubbing in an upward motion before driving forward, right against her throbbing, swollen axis of rapture. Suckling an aching, thrusting nipple in his mouth languidly, she felt herself jerking against him, and heard his animalistic groans as he lunged deeper and more rapidly.

"Ryan!" she shrieked, before succumbing to the aftermath of catastrophic climax that racked her quivering body.

At that final scream, he buried his head against her neck and gathered her limp body close, pounding so deeply within she felt another orgasm building. His groans of satisfaction turned her on anew, and tiny muscles within her tightened around him like a vice. He gasped her name as her eyes fluttered open to see his head thrust back, an expression of intense pleasure on his face. Ryan shuddered and groaned desperately, his hot shaft filling every empty part of her. And for that moment in time, they were truly one. One in heart, mind and body. Ryan collapsed on top of her, both trembling from the aftershocks of their fiery, addictive climaxes.

He raised himself to kiss her, his lips a hot pant of breathless victory. "Alyssa... Nothing is ever going to keep us apart again, you hear me?"

"No, nothing," she agreed unsteadily, shaken to the very depths of her. He'd taken her heart and replaced it with a treasure chest of love that only he could unlock.

****

Alyssa awoke a little while later and stretched, the aroma of coffee filling her nostrils. Ryan stood beside the bed, a relaxed smile on his handsome face.

"Mornin', sunshine. This'll wake you up."

"Good morning," she smiled back, and sat up in bed. "Mmm, this is yummy."

He sat beside her and took a drink from his cup. "I'm surprised you didn't wake up earlier. Dixie was going crazy out there. As soon as she saw me, she started running back and forth from the kitchen to the living room, sliding each way. It was pretty funny, actually."

Alyssa shook her head in amusement. "She can get a little excited. She's not used to having men over here."

He glanced her way, hand paused mid- air. "Ever?"

Ryan's intense stare held hers as she gazed somberly back, knowing what he was asking. If she answered...well, she'd wondered the same question of him.

"Only two," she said softly.

His straight, dark eyebrows shot up and then lowered.

"One time was when I was in college, a stupid one night stand. I'd gone to a party, and got really drunk." She shook her head wryly. "I never did that again. And then a couple of years ago, I met this guy named Zack and we started dating."

She shrugged her shoulders and picked up her cell phone to see what time it was. They had to get to the hospital soon. Good, only a little after eight. "We dated for about a year, and then he wanted to get married. But I couldn't marry him, so we split up."

"Why not?"

"I didn't love him enough, not the way I should. I knew what true love was, and it just wasn't there." She paused for a second and raised her eyebrows. "What about you, Ryan?" she asked in a challenging voice.

Ryan, who had been thoroughly touched, froze like a deer caught in headlights. "Well, more than two," he said in a forced light tone, and watched her set the cup down with an ominous thump.

"Yeah, I bet it was."

He drew a deep breath, and took her hands in his. "We weren't together, Alyssa. I was single, you were single... things happened. You can't be angry at me for what happened in the past. My God, it's been ten years!"

Outrage filled her lovely face as she pushed him away with a hard shove. "I'm not angry! If you want to hop from bed to bed, then that's your business, Ryan!"

She started to leave, but he grabbed her wrist in a steely grip. Furious green eyes flicked to his. "It wasn't like that," he ground out. "And you don't have anything to worry about, I always wear a condom."

She recoiled as if he'd struck her, her jaw dropping in disbelief in the deafening silence that followed.

"No, not always," she whispered and shook her head.

His eyes closed for a brief moment. "Alyssa, wait-"

She rushed to the master bathroom, and latched the door with a resounding scrape.

"Dammit," he swore under his breath. The sound of running water interrupted his thoughts, and he contemplated the locked door a long moment before heading to the other bathroom to take a shower.

****

Insensitive prick. Plus, he'd basically just added to her to the long line of women he'd slept with over the years. Alyssa blew out an annoyed huff.

She dialed the number to the hospital, and watched Ryan's long legs stride into the house to let Daisy out.

"Good morning, Ms. Patricia, how's Ms. Clare doing? Did she have any problems through the night?"

"No, she slept just fine. She's sitting up in the chair now."

"That's great. Does she need anything?"

"No, her grandson has got her all stocked up. She doesn't need a thing."

"Okay. Well, I'm leaving now, so I'll be there in about thirty minutes or so."

Alyssa glanced over at Ryan as he got back in the driver's seat of the truck.

"I'll tell her. She'll be glad to hear it."

After saying goodbye, Alyssa turned the volume up on the rock station and settled back in her seat as Ryan turned the truck onto the main road.

A couple of songs later, the radio went quiet.

"Why'd you do that?" she snapped.

"Because I want to talk."

"That's too damn bad, I don't feel like talking. I just want to get to the hospital."

Ryan sighed heavily, as if he was dealing with a cranky two year old she thought in irritation. After driving for a few more minutes, he pulled onto a deserted gravel road and parked on the grass past the shoulder.

Alyssa looked around at the forest of pine trees, and then glared at him. "What is it?"

He pulled off his aviator sunglasses with a dark frown. "What I said earlier…that came out wrong. We were so young back then, and I didn't think…" He shook his head, a tormented light in the indigo blue depths. "I never thought you would get pregnant, Alyssa."

Anger vanished, replaced by a deep sense of sadness. "I know you didn't. Neither did I." Her gaze drifted over to his scarred hand resting on his knee and she went still. "But at least you got to hold him," she said softly, uttering wretched words she'd never given voice to. "I wish that I could have. I never even saw him." Stifling grief welled up from repressed memories, and she jerked the door open to flee.

Ryan stayed behind for a lengthy moment, her admission stealing his breath, his thoughts. He found her near the tree line; small shoulders hunched pitifully. It was true, whether deliberate or not, he'd inflicted tremendous pain on the person he'd least intended to. The last words she'd said to him in the hospital had haunted him for a decade. *You're hurting me,* while tears of bewilderment had rolled down her pale cheeks. He eased her body into the circle of his arms, and breathed in the clean scent of her hair. "I wish you could have too, I wanted you to wake up so bad, Alyssa," he whispered hoarsely.

"It wasn't fair…none of it was fair." She cried silently, inconsolable, and his heart broke at the testimony of her sadness.

He kissed her tear-streaked face, and wished he could swallow her sadness. "No, it wasn't fair, you're right. But…we have to move on. This is going to tear us apart, just like it did before. And God knows I don't want that." He nudged her face upwards towards him. "Matthew is our baby in heaven. We'll never forget him; he lives on right here, in our hearts." Taking her hand in his, he clasped them against his chest. "I talk to him sometimes," he added quietly.

Grave liquid eyes flicked up to his, startling against the flushed smoothness of her tanned complexion.

Ryan swallowed the construction in his throat. "I want to make you happy, and I want us to be together. You're my heart, my everything. I've been in love with you since I was seventeen years old." He bent down till he was eye level with her and smiled. "Actually, way before then."

Alyssa's rosy lips parted and he took them in a needy onslaught. She tasted so good, like peaches, and he was hungry for her. Again. After a decade of wanting, he didn't think he could get enough.

Ryan tasted and nipped as she moaned, and sucked in a breath. He loved that he could make her breathless so quickly. His big hands cupped her shapely bottom and he panted, heated with desire. Great, now he was the one who couldn't catch his breath. Holding his face against her neck, he groaned inwardly, fighting for control. The raging hard on he was sporting begged to plant itself in her sweet body.

But not here and not now. It was already almost ten; they had to get to the hospital.

"I love you, Lyssa" he said in a tight voice. The aromatic pine trees around him reminded him of another time, when two teenagers had shared a starry night never to be forgotten. He rubbed his hands up and down her back. "Are you alright?"

Alyssa's eyes glittered brightly still and he linked his fingers through hers, thinking she was the most gorgeous woman on the planet.

"Yes, I'm better, I really am." She stood up on her toes and kissed his lips. "I love you too. Now come on, I know your grandmother is probably wondering what's taking us so long."

Alyssa gazed upon his strong profile as he drove, and smiled at him when he glanced over. He kissed her fingers and laced them through his.

"I feel like I'm seventeen again, riding around in your old truck."

A ghost of a smile touched his lips. "You don't look much older than that," he said wryly.

She laughed and squeezed his hand. "You haven't changed much, either. Your hair is shorter, that's about it."

"Yeah, I had to cut it after college. I went to work at a pharmaceutical company in the IT department, and it was strictly business. Button-down shirts, dress pants, the works. But it's more relaxed at our office. Unless we're meeting with a client, we wear jeans."

"I get to dress casual, too. Scrubs and sneakers," she said with a grin. "You'll see tomorrow."

Ryan winked suggestively at her, and her heart did a flip. "Mmm, I can't wait. But I like you best in nothing at all."

Alyssa laughed and scrunched her nose at him playfully. "I know you do." He made her feel perfect, whole and unblemished.

****

"Well, it's about time! What took y'all so long?" Ms. Clare chortled mischievously to her audience of Patricia and Fran.

Alyssa flashed a peek over at Ryan. To all of the women's amusement, a ruddy blush was creeping over his grimaced face. "Uh, we stopped and ate breakfast on the way."

It was all too clear he was decidedly uncomfortable with his grandmother's barely concealed insinuation, and Alyssa glared at her little sister when she giggled even louder.

"Hey sis, I thought you'd be here earlier," she said, mock confused innocence on her pretty face "Don't forget we're meeting with the wedding planner at 1:30."

"How can I forget? You sent me four texts," Alyssa retorted in annoyance.

Fran raised her eyebrows. "So why didn't you answer?" Her gaze slid over to Ryan. "Well, hello, stranger. My, I was blown away when your grandmother told me you were in."

Alyssa felt Ryan tense beside her. "Good to see you too, Fran," he replied, his voice casual.

Alyssa ignored her sister's wildly questioning eyes towards them. She gave Ms. Clare a kiss on the cheek. "How are you feeling? You look a lot better than you did yesterday."

"As long as I don't get up, the pain isn't bad. But when I walk to the bathroom, it hurts like the very devil."

"Aw, I hate for you to be hurting. Did you tell your doctor? Maybe they need to change your medicine." Alyssa squeezed in the recliner beside Fran, and Ryan sat on the other side of the bed.

"I told him and he said I would still have some pain, even with it. That medicine makes me so durn woozy. But don't fret; I'm coming to that wedding next weekend even if I have to go in a wheelchair!" Ms. Clare declared, and the sisters laughed.

"You most definitely are," Fran agreed. "Ryan, you have to come too! It's going to be a lot of fun, and everybody from high school is going to be there. They'll be so happy to see you."

Ryan gave Alyssa a curious look, and she knew he was wondering why she hadn't told him. Truth be told, she'd had other things on her mind.

She smiled at him softly and he smiled back, like they were the only two in the room. Magical, and of the most potent form, was the love in her heart for him.

"I'd love to come, thanks. Who's the lucky guy?"

"Lucas Winters. You might have heard of him, he's a musician. But his stage name is Luke Winters."

Ryan raised his eyebrows, clearly impressed. "Sure, I've heard of him. He's great. A master on the guitar."

"He is," Fran agreed wholeheartedly. "I can't wait

for you to meet him. You and Alyssa will have to come out for supper one night. We just built a new house over on…uh… River Road."

Fran glanced over at Alyssa, who purposely gave no indication she heard her. Remembrances lie everywhere they turned, threatening to set fire to their fragile truce.

"River Road?"

"Yep. We can go fishing; it's right on the water."

"Thanks, but I'll have to take you up on that later," he said in a low, deep voice.

Alyssa's gaze flicked across the bed to him, struck by the profound reflection in the grave set of his strong profile. She longed to comfort him, to lay her head in his lap. After all this time she knew they both, finally, were just beginning to let go of the burden of bitterness they'd nurtured for so long.

Ryan wheeled the hospital tray from over the bed. "Nana, do you want the rest of your tea?"

"Yes." She leaned up and took a drink through the straw.

"You should take a nap," he urged when she lay heavily back on the pillows.

"I think I will, honey." She closed her eyes, and fell asleep minutes later.

Ryan sighed, hoping her weariness was only from the pain medications and the long day. The room was filled with flowers friends of Nana had dropped off and he shook his head, recalling the steady stream. Hell, all the people had worn him out. Even LaDarius had stopped by, making Nana laugh when he'd brought up the enormous amounts of food she'd cooked for them as teenagers.

Through the hospital window, he contemplated the descending ball of golden amber in the gray sky. He stepped out in the hallway to call Alyssa, his own sunshine in the bleakness.

"Hey," she softly greeted him.

"Hey, babe. Did I wake you up?"

She yawned and his blood heated, imagining her silken limbs stretching in her bed. "Yes, I was so sleepy. You kept me up way past my bedtime last night," she said with a smile in her voice.

"Me?" he said, laughing.

"Yes, you," she insisted playfully. "And then Fran drug me all over town today. Until this, I had no idea a wedding was so much work. That's all we've done for the last month, I'm not kidding you."

"Well, as soon as Ms. Patricia gets here, I'll head that way and grab something to eat. How does cheeseburgers from the diner sound?"

"Sounds yummy."

Ryan rolled to his side and wrapped his arm around Alyssa's warm body. "Uncle James will be here tomorrow. Aunt Barbara, too."

"What about your cousins?"

"Stacy will be here Sunday, and Neil sometime next week. I'm going to have to come over here and hide from them."

Alyssa smiled and then her eyes narrowed. "I haven't liked your cousin Neil since I was ten and he pushed me on that swing, higher and higher until I just knew I was gonna fly off and break my neck. Remember, in the camp we built in the woods? Jeremy's dad hung that swing up, way up on that huge tree."

"I remember. I could hear you yelling from the stream." Ryan gave a wry shake of his head.

Alyssa slipped her arms around his neck as her flawless face glowed with an inner light that made his chest clench. "So you came and rescued me. Pushed him down, even though he was fourteen, and you were only eleven. You were my hero." She smacked her lips to his affectionately. "Of course, you were way bigger than he was, even then."

"I still am."

Ryan pulled her close as he buried his face in her fragrant hair, recalling that hot summer day. Her cheeks had been red, streaked with tears, and long hair streamed down both sides of her frightened face. Despite being small for her age, he remembered the blazing anger in her bunched fists when he'd brought the swing to a halt.

Alyssa laughed. "I blame Neil for my fear of heights, just so you know. But I can't wait to see Stacy. She hasn't been here since last Christmas."

"I haven't seen them in a while, either."

She leaned back and raked her nails lightly against his shoulder. "Ryan, do you like being back home?"

He watched her as she settled on the pillow. Damn, it was better each time they made love. She was heaven. No. Paradise, actually. All the corny words and phrases he'd ever heard wouldn't do justice to the passion he felt for her.

"Yeah, I do," he answered slowly, and locked his gaze to hers. "It's been hell not having you. There was always a part of me that wanted you, no matter where I was." She kissed his neck and he took her in his embrace, where she fit perfectly. "And in some ways, it's like I never left. But then I look around and so much has changed. Take Nana. Even before the surgery, I could tell she wasn't as strong as she used to be. She could barely get of her chair when I first got here."

"She's seventy, Ryan. And this surgery will help her mobility a lot, you'll see."

"I hope so." He paused, thinking with a heartfelt pang how fast Nana had aged in just the last year. He knew he wasn't imagining it.

"LaDarius came by the hospital today after you left. He's married now, with two boys."

"And they look just like him, believe you me," Alyssa smiled.

"Poor kids." She laughed as he drew long, silken strands through his fingers, wondering what to do far past when she fell into the escape of dreams.

CHAPTER 24

Alyssa took a bite of her salad and studied the telemetry monitors in the nurse's station. "I don't know; we haven't really talked about it." She contemplated a made-up problem with a patient, Fran's steady line of questions about her and Ryan was getting to be downright annoying.

"Why not?"

"Well, I've worked twelve hour shifts for the last two days, and then Ryan doesn't get to my house till late." Alyssa blew out an exasperated breath. "I thought you called for something about the wedding."

"Actually, I did call you about your dress. They want to do a final fitting tomorrow."

Tomorrow was Saturday, the last day of her work shift, and then she'd be on vacation for the next week.

"I can't, Fran. I don't get off till seven."

"Damn."

"I'll go up there next week. Goodness, I'm still the same size. I was just there not even a month ago."

"That's true. Okay, I'll tell them." Fran paused for a moment. "Well, I hope you and Ryan can work it out."

"We will, sis. Quit worrying."

Ryan had only made vague references to their future, no foundation had been laid. She could only pine for what she desired. Her appetite gone, she threw her lunch in the trash and concentrated on caring for her patients.

****

Dixie's big brown eyes gazed up at Ryan adoringly as he scratched her between the ears. Alyssa leaned her hands back on the wooden deck of her porch and watched in amusement. "You just charm all the girls, don't you?"

"What can I say, it's a gift." He shot her an inquiring glance. "How was your day?"

"It was good, what about yours?"

"Nana was happy to be at home. Especially since Uncle James and Aunt Barbara are there." He looked over at her, eyebrows raised. "By the way, she knows I've been staying over here. That old story about being at LaDarius's house isn't going to work anymore. But I'm pretty sure she didn't fall for it the first time, either."

Alyssa laughed and dropped her head on her knees. They were sitting outside on her deck, Ryan with his legs stretched out before him, and hers pulled up tight to her chest.

"We're going straight to hell," she quipped.

He smiled, and then rubbed his face with his hands wearily.

"What's wrong?" she asked softly, and electric bolts flashed through her when crystalline blue eyes snapped to hers.

"Alyssa…I have to go back to San Francisco."

"Why?" she asked in a hesitant voice.

"We picked up three more clients, and Vince and Jason are drowning in work."

"Will you be back for the wedding?"

His sculpted mouth twisted as a frown shadowed his square jaw. "I don't know. I want to. But it depends on how it's going there."

Alyssa said nothing; crushing waves of destruction were swarming through her, chilling her to the bone in their thoroughness.

"I know what you're thinking, but this time is going to be different," he said, relieved to see her devastated expression replaced by one of guarded interest.

"How?" She flinched away when he reached out to touch her arm.

"I want you to come back with me to San Francisco." It had been the first thing that had sprung into his mind after getting off the phone with Vince earlier.

Alyssa's mouth dropped open. "What? I can't leave right now, Ryan. I have to help my sister with the wedding."

"Just for a couple of days at least. We'll leave early Sunday morning and then you can come back Wednesday. That's still plenty of time to help her before the wedding."

Alyssa made an exasperated sound. "You don't know what's left to do, you're just saying that."

"I know that she has a wedding planner. Isn't that their damn job? And besides, your sister would want you to come with me." He cupped her face in his hands. "It hasn't even been a week yet, I don't want to be away from you, sweetheart."

Her soft lips closed and the frown vanished. "Alright," she agreed quietly. "I'll go."

He leaned his forehead against hers and hugged her

close, wishing so many miles didn't separate their homes and their lives.

****

The roar of an engine drew them over to the expansive windows that looked out onto the runway of Cadeyville Regional Airport. "What is that?" Alyssa pointed outside. "I know we're not fixing to get on that itty bitty plane out there." She stared at him in incredulous horror.

"Babe, it's fine," he stated patiently.

She looked at the runway again and shook her head in apparent disbelief.

"I've rode planes like that a hundred times before. They're perfectly safe. And when we get to Dallas, we'll transfer to a bigger plane if that makes you feel better."

She crinkled her eyebrows skeptically.

"First class," he added with a playful wink.

Alyssa stood up on her tiptoes and gave him a soft kiss. "Well, that's good, I guess. That one there looks like a baby plane," she muttered darkly.

Ryan's lips twisted with humor as he linked her hand through his.

Alyssa's eyes narrowed on him. "I see that look you have on your face. I'm scared to fly. After all, I never thought I'd be jetting off to San Francisco this weekend."

"I know what you mean. I was surprised myself," he teased.

Alyssa smiled; a secret, sensual curve of her lips he adored.

He squeezed her hand in his and led her towards the gift shop. "Do you want a snack before we get on?

It's almost time."

"Sure."

Alyssa leaned her head on Ryan's broad shoulder and surveyed the spacious first class cabin. "I like this plane a lot better."

"Me too. I'm not too fond of those puddle jumpers myself, but I would've said anything to make sure you came with me."

Alyssa shook her head in wry amusement and slid her arm across his lean middle. "You're not going to be working the whole time, are you? I leave Wednesday morning so that only gives us two days together."

"No, I'll be home by six at the latest tomorrow. And I'll leave the office early Tuesday so we can go do something."

"Yay." Alyssa smiled up at him, admiring the fine line of his straight nose. "Let's go to the beach."

"The beach?" He tipped his head down to look at her. "I thought you'd want to go see San Francisco."

"I can't go to California and not swim in the ocean. When I go to the Gulf, I never want to leave because it's so pretty."

"This is too, but the water isn't warm like the Gulf. Especially when the wind starts blowing hard, it can get downright cold, even in the summer."

"That's okay, it'll still be fun. It's been so long since we've been swimming together."

He kissed her forehead and murmured, "The beach it is then."

"I have to get some sunscreen so I don't burn. I'd hate to be a peeling mess at the wedding, Fran would kill me." Alyssa giggled, imagining her sister's reaction. "I hope you're able to come. You'll like

Lucas, he's great."

"I'm going to do my best, babe."

She traced the scar on his hand with one finger and nodded.

Ryan rested his head against hers. "You never told me how they met."

"They met at Mack's, actually." She leaned back and smiled at him. "Crazy, huh? Lucas was on break from tour, and he rented a cabin out on the bayou to get some rest and privacy. He's from down south, not far from New Orleans." She shook her head, lost in thought.

"What's the matter?" He nuzzled her neck and she shivered as his sexy, scruffy jaw brushed against her.

"I worried about Fran for a long time…I'm just glad she's doing better."

"What was wrong with her?"

Alyssa bit down on the inside of her cheek. She'd been so scared for her sister. "Well, she was popping pills. And then drinking too…" She glanced over to gauge his reaction.

Ryan sat up and frowned. "Damn. I can't believe Fran got mixed up with all that. I remember how depressed she was when Jeremy passed away, but I thought she'd snap out of it after a few months."

"We all did." Pausing, she added softly, the words slow coming forth. "But it wasn't just that, though." Achingly compassionate sapphire blue eyes flicked to hers, and she fought her rising panic down forcibly. Ryan knew her better than anyone, and if she couldn't let him close, then who could she?

"No. Of course it wasn't, Alyssa," he quietly agreed.

Deep pain faded out her joy. But the pure love she knew was in this man's soul for her was so glorious, it took her higher, floating above than the earth ridden abuse she'd endured as a child. Taking a deep breath, she linked her hand through his warm, strong one. "Luke said he fell head over heels in love with Fran when he first saw her."

A beam of sunlight shone through the window and spotlighted Alyssa's golden loveliness, lustrous hair framing the sweet oval of her face. Like dew sparkling on blades of new green grass, her eyes were heavy with unshed tears.

Ryan cupped the delicate curve of her jaw and caressed soft skin with his thumb. "I know exactly how he feels. There's something about you Martin sisters a man can't live without," he whispered half -jokingly. "Thank you for coming back with me, sweetheart."

She laid her head back on his shoulder cozily. "As if I could tell you no."

"Let's see how true that is…" he said in a low voice, grateful for the private setting.

She tilted her head up. "What does that mean?"

"Don't you want to be a member of the mile high club?" She promptly burst out laughing and he frowned, one amused brow lifted. "That wasn't that funny."

"Yeah, it was," she nodded. "Have you seen those bathrooms? How would that even work with how big you are?"

"You like it," he said in a voice tinged with love and humor.

"Oh, you are so bad, Ryan Matthew Sutherby," she giggled, and he pulled her close for a warm hug.

****

"Your house is incredible, Ryan. And huge! You didn't tell me you were a gazillionaire." She was astounded, actually, by his obvious wealth. His modern, glass-fronted house sat on a rocky cliff that overlooked the deep blue waters of the Pacific.

"I'm not a gazillionaire," he laughed, and caught her hand in his to lead her across the shiny wood floors to a steel deck outside.

"Oh, wow," she breathed in awe at the gorgeous view. Huge white capped waves crashed against the rocks below, and the Golden Gate Bridge was visible in the orange-tinged distance. "This is amazing."

Ryan's hand curved around her waist and she looked up to see him regarding her with a small smile, blue eyes as true as the churning water below. She turned to bury her face against the comfort of his chest. Ripped muscular arms enfolded around her, and she squeezed him back tight.

"I hate myself for all the time we've wasted. Ten long years without the love of my life," he said in a low voice, his head bent close to hers.

"We were so stupid, Ryan," she whispered, and leaned back to look him in the face.

"Yeah, we were." With a tender hand, he tucked windblown strands of hair behind her ear. "But we're older and wiser now, right?" He raised his eyebrows and waited for an answer.

She nodded. "Definitely."

Alyssa tossed the bottle of mustard across the granite kitchen island. "Hey, think fast." She whistled when Ryan snatched it out of the air.

He grinned. "I've still got all my moves, babe.

They didn't call me white lightning in high school for nothing."

She laughed and smacked his well-formed backside on the way to the refrigerator. "Oh lord, I'd forgotten all about that. I see you haven't though."

"Nope," he agreed good- naturedly, and taking the last bite of his sandwich, reached past her to grab a beer.

"Come on, I wanna show you something."

"Okay, let me get something to drink."

"Do you want a beer? That's all there is, we should've stopped at the store."

With a shrug, Alyssa took the opened beer from his outstretched hand and took a long drink. "This is fine."

She ran her hand over the soft Italian leather furniture as she followed him across the living area, her eyes appreciatively traveling the length of the room. It was a simple, masculine design, understated elegance that set one at ease. Large tropical plants blended perfectly with billowing white linen curtains of the open glass doors. A glorious setting sun afforded the only light as peachy- purple shadows danced against the textured walls.

But the man who held her hand in his captivated her even more. He'd given her a tour of his home earlier, but had left this room out inexplicably.

"I'm going to show you why I bought this house."

They crossed the enormous master bedroom and he opened glass doors that led onto another deck, this one laid with redwood planks. Alyssa gasped when she saw the lighted hot tub with the wild turquoise Pacific as its backdrop.

"This is unbelievable." She walked to the railing

and gazed out at the white, foamy sea. The scene was so powerfully majestic and thought provoking, it brought a lump of dread to her throat.

What was going to happen between her and Ryan? How would their lives align? Together, peacefully? He came up behind her and wrapped his long body around her.

"Are you ready to get in the hot tub?" His voice was a velvet purr as he kissed her neck seductively and she nodded, shivers of excitement dancing down her spine.

"The only rule is no clothes on." Ryan could barely form a rational thought, he only knew he wanted her naked, willing, and screaming his name.

"I don't see that posted anywhere," she smiled.

"It's a new rule." He winked suggestively as she giggled. With impatient fingers, they helped each other undress. He looked down at her earnest face and his eyes traveled lower, admiring her delectable body. His breath grew harsh and needy as he pulled her naked body to his; she was soft and rounded in all the right places.

"You're so warm," she whispered.

"You set me on fire," he rasped, and nearly exploded at her first caress on his painfully hard shaft. "Oh God," he groaned. "Come here."

Alyssa squealed with excitement, and he kept his hand on the small of her back as they got in, guiding her towards him. She straddled him and he hissed, grinding his teeth together to keep from thrusting upward into her sweet folds.

Alyssa stared at him in a daze of need; the intensity of his desire for her palpable. "Make love to me, Ryan," she pleaded. The answers to her questions be damned, she wanted him.

"I'm going to love you all night long, darling."

He coaxed her lips to meld with his in a kiss so heartfelt; it brought tears to her eyes. And then the kiss turned heated, tongues and hands roaming freely over each other's body.

He whispered her name, desperately needing her clenched tight around him. "I want you to take me deep inside of you. All of me."

He lifted her up, taut with anticipation as she slowly lowered herself onto him. Her eyes were closed and he leaned forward, tasting and teasing her nipples into hard buds.

"Oh, God…" she moaned, taking him inch by inch into her tight depths.

"This is sheer torture," he rasped, and grasped her waist.

Blazing desire erupted in his loins and he guided the pace, feeling her small body adjust to fit him. Driving up into her harder and deeper, she cried out at each penetration until he was shaking with an erotic hunger only she could slake.

"Dammit, baby," he panted, "you feel incredible."

His grip tightened when she threw her head back, bare breasts bouncing sexily. At the sight of her provocative pose, something snapped in him and he pulled her down to him so he could take one of her round breasts in his mouth. Suckling mindlessly, his hands gripped the firm curve of her bottom with a desperate groan.

"Oh, yes," she whimpered when he took complete control, and dug her nails deep in his back. He held her hips steady as he thrust upward in a race he never wanted to finish. Steamy sweat poured off both of them, and he didn't know where heaven and hell met in this sizzling bond of paradise. With a swiftness that enthralled him, her curvy, luscious body quivered and arched in the ecstatic throes of climax. "Ryan!" she screamed, and that was all it took.

A mind-blowing orgasm roared through his body and with a sharp sense of loss, he withdrew from her. He held her tight against him as his seed pulsed forth between their hot embrace. Alyssa hugged him when he collapsed in a slump, and stroked his back.

He lifted his head up to study her. "You okay?"

"What do you think?" she said with a low laugh.

"I'd say you're thinking you've died and gone to heaven." He smoothed her hair back from her flushed face and she nestled closer in his arms, laughing.

"You're right, I am." Her chest heaved against his as they both tried to catch their breath while bubbling jets of water swirled around them.

Ryan kissed her neck, and suckled on her delicious skin. "You taste so good."

"Mmm," she breathed.

"My feet are turning into prunes," she muttered after a few minutes.

"I guess that's my cue." His lips quirked upward and he heaved himself out of the hot tub.

She stepped onto the windy patio as his eyes feasted on her steaming, curvy body. "Here, babe."

"Thanks." She caught the towel he tossed her and raced inside.

Alyssa stopped mid-step, her wondering perusal of his room forgotten. Standing on her tiptoes, she retrieved the silver urn off of the shelf and gasped when the engraving confirmed her instincts. She ran her fingers over her baby's name etched in the shiny surface, Matthew Chase Sutherby. Icy regret chilled every part of her body as she vaguely registered Ryan's footsteps behind her.

"I was going to show you that," he stated quietly.

"It's really pretty; you picked out a nice design." Her voice came from a distance, like it belonged to someone else. She felt numb inside, blurred by the intensity of the night. She kissed where Matthew's name was engraved, and wished it was his beloved, warm face, instead of mere cold metal.

Ryan's hands slid around her waist, not stopping till they rested on top of hers.

"I love you, Alyssa, I love you," he said next to her ear, and like a physical caress, his soothing words repaired her broken soul.

"And I love you. So much, Ryan," she whispered back.

He placed the urn down and swept her up in his powerful hold. She wrapped her arms around his hard, muscular shoulders, thinking how much she adored him. This was true love; blood-red and pumping so hard she ached from its fierceness.

He sat on the bed with her on his lap, and his deep voice rumbled against her head when he spoke. "I want you to have something back."

She looked up and his striking eyes glinted in the dark shadows of his lightly bearded face, giving him a dangerous, sexy appeal. "What?" she asked, curious now.

He reached over to his nightstand and drew out a

small box. Alyssa's heart thumped faster.

"I gave this to you when you turned seventeen, and you promised to never take it off. But I didn't keep my promises, either." He shook his head gravely.

Her breath caught in her throat, carefully watching him as he draped the beloved emerald necklace around her neck. Her world was now complete; he'd slayed all the monsters that had daunted her countless times.

"Thank you. I've missed this."

"It never should've left your pretty neck."

She clenched the gem in her hand. "Do you remember what else I told you that night?"

"Yes." His narrowed eyes touched her with their gravity, and she knew he recalled her reverent vow to him.

"I did wait for you, Ryan," she whispered. "For a long, long time." The old familiar hurt swept through her chest and she swallowed hard.

Ryan was at a loss of what to say for a moment. She wasn't angry, but her quiet reflection pierced him with the force of it. He hugged her close and murmured in her ear, "I know you did, honey. But we're together now, thank God."

"Until Wednesday morning," she replied simply, remarkable green eyes solemn.

He raked his hand through his hair and gritted his teeth, not able to think how she left in only two days. *Always apart-*

"So we'll just have to make the most of it," she whispered, and cupped his face.

Her hands cooled his overheated skin and Ryan sighed heavily, grateful she'd taken pity on his obvious frustration. "Yeah, we will." Alyssa yawned, curling into him as they lay down and he kissed the top of her head with a slight smile.

She stroked his back and breathed silky words that flowed over him, soothed him. *"Good night, my love."*

Alyssa sat up in bed with her knees pulled up to her chest, and watched Ryan as he buttoned up his white dress shirt. They'd taken a shower together, and her aroused nerves quivered still from the masculine aroma of his soap that clung to her skin.

"Alyssa…" He cleared his throat, and her attention shifted from rock hard abs. "Did you want to take me to work-"

"No!" A relieved expression eased the tense set of his face. "I mean, I'll just stay here. It's like being on vacation," she said, and tried to interject some semblance of gaiety to her voice.

"Alright, I'll be back this evening." Ryan gave her a lingering kiss on the lips, and playfully nipped her ear. She laughed and reached under his black sports coat to tickle his ribs. He fell with one knee on the bed, and twisted to avoid her quick hands.

"Oh, that's how you want to play it, huh?" he taunted with a grin, and flipped her over to tickle the back of her thighs.

"Stop, Ryan!" she squealed, and giggled till she was out of breath. He finally let her loose and she rolled back over, weak now from laughter.

"That'll teach you to mess with the master," he said with a satisfied grin.

"You make me sick," she grumbled, and smiled when he leaned down to cover her back up with the blanket.

"I love you too." And after a quick kiss on the lips,

he was gone.

****

Alyssa gasped in pure pleasure as she saw the picturesque beach below. "Come on, Ryan!"

She ran down the steep, sandy path and waited impatiently for him at the bottom, flip flops in hand. She loved the water; it filled her with a centering peace like no other earthly destination. Powdery sand stretched out to the sparkling, white capped waves of the moderately populated shore line, and she closed her eyes for a moment, inhaling the sharp, salty air.

"We're lucky the sun is out. It's usually foggy as hell." Ryan linked her hand through his as they walked to the water's edge.

"Do you come out here a lot?"

"No, not really. This is my first time out here this year."

"What? Why?" She stared at him, frankly amazed.

"I work all the time, Alyssa. I usually don't get home till nine, ten o clock." He raised his eyebrows wryly. "Too late for swimming in the ocean."

"True, that *is* when the sharks come out," she teased. "Although, I wouldn't dare go swimming in the river at night, the alligators might get me."

He tucked her flying hair behind her ears. "You've always been part fish."

"You used to say I was a minnow when I was younger," she smiled.

"Well, you've been upgraded to a mermaid since we're at the beach. And a very sexy one at that." He whistled loudly as she pulled off her yellow sundress, and heads swiveled their way.

"Ryan! I'm gonna dunk you when we get in that

water, you just wait," she threatened sternly in answer to his smug grin.

"Ha! Not on your best day, woman," he lazily replied. He hooked an arm around her shoulders and dragged her close to his lean, hard body. Her heart drummed a primitive love song, so glad she hadn't given up all hope.

"Come on, you big bully," she said with a grin, and caught his hand in hers to step into the lapping sea.

"It's cold!" Alyssa's surprised eyes swung to his.

Ryan laughed deeply and shook his head. "I tried to tell you." Strong currents whirled against their calves as he tightened his grip on her hand.

They walked further out, and she let go to dive under the blue-green waves. He followed, and they surfaced together. His hot stare devoured every outlined curve of her as she wrapped her tanned legs around his waist, and looped her arms around his neck.

"See, it's not so bad when you get used to it."

"I'll stick with the hot tub. But the cold water does have its perks, no pun intended." He rubbed his thumbs over her hard nipples.

She swatted his arm, dimples shining in her flawless face. Her green eyes glowed brighter than he'd ever seen.

"You take my breath away," he whispered.

She blinked, sobering instantly.

"I don't want you to leave, baby. Move here with me, after the wedding." Her jaw dropped, almost theatrically. A grim weight settled in his chest.

"Ryan," she breathed. "I like being here with you, but this…this isn't home," she stammered.

"I know this isn't home, but I'm here, Alyssa.

Doesn't that count for a goddamn thing?"

Alyssa drew back, stunned by the force of his sudden, fierce anger. The corded muscles in his arms rippled and grew taut as he pulled her closer.

"Be more than something I remember, sweetheart, it's not enough. We've come too far to go back, and a long distance relationship isn't the answer. My life without you is empty, pointless."

"Ryan, I love you, but-"

"But what? You love a town more?"

"No! Of course not. But my sister is there, Ms. Clare, my friends… And I've- I've never lived anywhere else."

His tone grew gentler. "You can go visit whenever you want, and if I'm not busy at the office, I'll go with you."

"How would I do that, Ryan? I don't want to stop working, I love being a nurse. And even if I lived here, I would still barely see you! You were three hours late yesterday!"

"That's so I could leave early today," he said through his teeth.

She dropped away from him and swam under the cool waves, her heart and mind battling against the other. Her heart claimed victory effortlessly.

Iron hard hands grabbed her leg, and she popped to the surface in alarm. Ryan stood above her with a dark scowl on his face. "There's rip currents out here. People drown at this same beach every summer; you can't go just swimming away, Alyssa!"

"I'm fine! I just wanted to clear my mind for a minute," she added quietly, and his smoky blue eyes cleared a tiny bit. She shivered jerkily; the water really was freezing, even with the sunrays beating down on her wet hair.

"It's time to go," he announced abruptly, and grasped her hand tight in his.

Her mind racing like a runaway horse, she couldn't help but admire his muscled back as they left the water.

****

Ryan glanced at her sideways through his sunglasses as he drove. "I'm going to stop and pick up some Mexican food. I don't know about you, but I'm starving. And you'll love this, this is the real deal. "

"Now you're really trying to butter me up."

He reached over to caress her open hand lying on her knee, and she bit her lip. "I'll move here with you, but I have to give the hospital two weeks' notice at least. And then…I'll sell my house or maybe I can rent it… I don't know, but I'll figure it out."

A huge smile broke across Ryan's face. He turned into the nearest gas station and parked his truck with a jolt as they both unbuckled their seat belts at the same time.

His hands tangled through her hair and he brought her face to his in a quick motion. "You won't regret it, baby. I swear you won't."

"I'll be with you. How could I? If I only saw you for one minute a day, Ryan, it would be worth it," she whispered back.

Their lips met in a rush, so genuine she thought she would weep from the raw sentiments that were evoked. She moaned helplessly as his tongue stroked against hers with a savage appetite. An ache unfurled deep down and she panted hotly as he tore his mouth from hers to press damp kisses to her eyelids, her cheek.

"Ohh," she murmured, every nerve ending strung tight.

"There's food in the refrigerator, we don't have to stop anywhere." She grasped his hard length through his suddenly too tight shorts.

"We'll order a pizza," he muttered huskily, and only the loud blare of a truck horn stopped him from pulling her atop him. They both jumped and she giggled; a girlish trill he adored.

"Let's go home, honey."

Her hand moved up to his chest. "I'll go anywhere with you, just as long as we're together."

"I'll never let you go, Alyssa," he whispered against her mouth. "Never." Their lips joined in a possessive, sensual drug of a kiss, and love for her gripped his soul. Busy sounds faded to a dull blur, he was conscious of only her in his arms, the one who made him happier than any other.

He reluctantly broke their passionate bond, and leaned his forehead again hers. When he was finally able to open his eyes, he was transported back to a summer day long past when he was thirteen years old. The bright afternoon sunlight glowed, glowed so bright he had to squint to see her, but she outshone it.

This little light of mine, I'm gonna let it shine, let it shine, let it shine, let it shine... They'd shared a secret smile that day in church, and he had stopped singing until he was poked in the side by Nana's sharp elbow.

He'd loved her even then.

She whispered his name, and his voice cracked with emotion when he spoke. "Only you, Alyssa, it's always been you."

CHAPTER 25

Alyssa patted her dogs and laughed at their excitement. "I missed y'all, too." She crouched down to smooth their ears back. "Awww, look at you, Dixie, such a pretty girl! Was she good, Fran?"

"Um, kind of. She wouldn't let me put a bow in her hair, though." She frowned at the wiggling spaniel. "She's like a little Tasmanian devil."

Alyssa shook her head in amusement and unsnapped the dog's leashes. "Hey, you should open up a salon where you can bring your dog in, too. It'd be one of a kind."

"No, I prefer to groom humans. At least they kind of listen."

They laughed and walked into the kitchen.

"Do you have any crackers?"

Alyssa shrugged her shoulders. "I think so." She watched as her sister opened the pantry, and took a deep, fortifying breath before speaking. "Fran...I'm going to move in with Ryan."

The door slammed shut, and Alyssa watched in dismay as her sister's eyes filled with tears. "What?" Fran gasped. "You're moving to San Francisco? When?"

"Within a few weeks." Alyssa fought her own tears as Fran's spilled down her cheeks.

"But...I'm pregnant, I was just about to tell you,"

her sister sniffed, light blue eyes wide in her beautiful face.

Alyssa inhaled a shocked breath, and her hand flew to her mouth as she stared across the kitchen. "A baby? Fran! How far along are you?"

Fran laughed shakily. "Um, about three months."

Alyssa hugged her, both laughing and crying with pure happiness, all at the same time. "Congratulations! How have you been feeling?"

"Ugh, I've been so sick. I had to stop and puke on my way over here," she grumbled.

Alyssa smiled affectionately, and smoothed her sister's long, light blonde hair out of her flushed face. "The worst will be over soon. And then you'll feel a lot better."

"I can't wait." Fran gripped her hand hard. "I wish Ryan didn't live in San Francisco."

"I wish he didn't, either. But I'll be back to visit, and you can come see me too." Alyssa took a deep breath, and tried her best to hold it together. Fran looked ready to burst into tears again. "It's going to be okay," she soothed. "I'll still be here for you, you'll see."

Her sister nodded slowly, and Alyssa's heart sank with unforeseen guilt.

****

Ryan got up from his office chair, a long sigh escaping his tight chest as he gazed out at the congested street below. The door opened and he turned to see Vince waving his arms in excitement.

"Come over to Jason's office and jump on this call. Didn't you hear me when I paged you?"

"No, apparently not," he answered dryly. It was

difficult to concentrate, his mind drifted to Alyssa invariably, even though only two days had passed since she left. She was his favorite thought. And he wouldn't be satisfied till she was next to him every morning. Sharing his life, his bed…he wasn't sure he could stand the wait.

"Cameron wants to talk to us about an offer for the company."

"What in the hell…" Ryan stared at Vince in astonishment and strode past him to hear Cameron's voice on the speakerphone in Jason's office. Cameron was their lawyer, and a damned good one. He and his team had negotiated dozens of contracts for them over the years.

"Hey Cameron, this is Ryan." He took a seat across from Jason.

"Hello, Ryan. Is everyone there now?"

"Yes, we're all here." He glanced over at Jason behind the desk, and Vince leaning against the wall.

"I received an interesting call today, and to make a long story short, a very generous offer has been made for EzPay."

The words swirled around in Ryan's head as the three men stared at each other in amazement. "How generous?" he asked finally, eyes narrowed at the phone.

"Forty-seven million."

"Forty-seven million," Ryan repeated slowly, and looked across at Jason's face. His eyes were bulging almost comically out of his flushed face, and Vince's jaw had dropped even further. "Let us talk about it, and we'll get back to you."

"I understand completely, but I do need to know

something by Monday."

"We'll be in touch. Thanks, Cameron." Ryan leaned back in the chair, and looked up at the ceiling fan. If they sold the company, he could move home. Home was Cypress Bayou, where Alyssa was, and Nana, and LaDarius, and so many more…

He had to clear his throat twice before he could speak in the stunned silence. "I think we should take it." A wide, relieved smile broke over his face as Jason and Vince grinned.

"I'm going to be a goddamn millionaire," Jason said in a hushed, awed voice, and clasped him and Vince both in a bear hug. "We're celebrating at Sal's tonight. I can't believe this shit…"

Ryan awoke with an agonized groan, and fumbled around in his pockets till he found his phone. "Great, just fucking great," he muttered. It was dead.

His head pounded viciously against his temples, and the early morning light spilling through the bay windows only multiplied it. He walked to the shower and braced against the marble walls with trembling, muscled arms. He'd drunk too damned much last night, taking shot after celebratory shot with Jason and Vince. Eyes closed, he hung his head low and let the water wash over him.

It was Saturday; the wedding was at six. And there was no way in hell he was missing it.

****

Alyssa tied a purple satin bow in Savannah's long, dark brown hair, and gave her a kiss on the cheek. "You're the prettiest flower girl I've ever seen in my whole life." She turned the little girl towards the bathroom mirror and smiled. "Look how beautiful you are."

"Thank you Aunt Alyssa," Savannah said in her clear, sweet voice.

"You're very welcome."

Fran called out from the bedroom. "Alyssa, come help me when you get done, will you?"

"Sure. I'll be there in a sec."

Fran was having a dreamy, romantic wedding and after all these weeks of preparation, Alyssa was determined to enjoy it, despite her smoldering fury at Ryan. She hadn't talked to him since yesterday morning, when he'd called her before going to the gym. His husky good morning had made her heart throb.

Fran shot her a curious glance. "What's your problem?"

"I tried calling Ryan three times last night! Just wait till he does answer, he's getting an earful." She glared out the window. "I don't even know if he's coming."

"Oh, I hope he does. I want him and Lucas to meet."

"Well, it's already four o clock and I haven't heard from him, so…" She shook her head and sighed. "I'm pretty sure he's not." She took in Fran, shimmering in her white, satiny wedding dress. "Uh, sis," Alyssa said in a low voice, alarmed by the expanse of bosom spilling out of the bodice. She started to laugh helplessly.

Fran began to giggle. "Stop laughing at my big boobs."

Alyssa only grew louder. "Did you go to your final fitting? That's who you should've been worried about, instead of me."

"What kind of maid of honor are you anyway?" Fran laughed. "You're supposed to help me! Where's Casey? She'll know what to do."

"She's probably in the kitchen. Savannah, run and go get your mom." Alyssa held her hands over her mouth to hold the laughter in.

"My God, this is a nightmare." Fran moaned, and tugged at the neckline of her dress.

Alyssa watched nervously. "Don't yank it! It might rip!"

Her sister's hands dropped instantly.

Casey came in the room with the wedding planner, Mary, in tow. Mary's eyes dropped to Fran's voluptuous breasts, and nodded her head decisively. "I'll put a gusset in it. Take it off and we'll have it ready by show time. Don't you fret, sweetie."

"Thank you," Fran gushed gratefully.

Alyssa walked over to her phone and tried Ryan's number. Straight to voice mail. Again. She shut her phone with a snap and stuffed it in her purse.

****

Ryan called Alyssa from his rental car, and twisted his lips in disappointment when there was no answer. He strode in through the living room at Nana's as she smiled from her recliner.

"You made it just in time. I was beginning to worry."

"How are you feeling?"

"I've been better," she said ruefully, and frowned at her propped-up legs. "I'll be a lot better when I don't have to use that walker over there."

Ryan shook his head at his cranky grandmother.

"You're just mad because you can't rip and run like you usually do."

A wry smile touched the corners of Nana's rouged cheeks. "You're not too old to take over my knee anymore, young man," she warned.

They were both laughing when Stacy walked in. "My favorite cousin!" She gave him a big hug and pushed him towards the hallway. "It's after five, now go get ready! The iron is already plugged in," she called after him as he strode towards the bathroom, bags in hand.

CHAPTER 26

Alyssa's gaze stopped in exhilarating disbelief on Ryan's dark head. The audience hushed upon seeing her, but she had eyes for none other than him. Her hand clutched Chris's arm involuntarily, and she didn't miss the flash of anger that crossed Ryan's handsome face when he turned to face her, sapphire blue eyes piercing through her like a laser. She stared spellbound, his fierce strength and confidence holding her hostage, oblivious to the growing murmur around her.

"Alyssa!" Chris whispered, but her satin shoes were glued to the pedal-strewn makeshift aisle, waiting. Waiting for a sign, a sign from the man she loved unconditionally, the man she'd waited her whole life for.

The surreal background of ivory roses and lavender permeated the air with their beauty, while gilded torches cast waves of candlelight over the transformed expanse of land that lay before the ageless river.

One corner of Ryan's sensuous mouth lifted in a sign of reassurance meant only for her, and she basked in the warm glow. She smiled back and the wedding guests let out a wistful, romantic sigh.

Ryan's rapid pulse slowed with relief when she began to glide down the makeshift aisle again.

"Oh my, isn't she pretty," Nana said from beside him.

"Yes, she is," he said in a low voice, blatantly studying Alyssa's graceful curves in the dusky purple satin gown she wore.

A band of lavender and ivory miniature roses adorned Alyssa's shiny, loose waves, and she was so soft and feminine he wanted nothing more than to sweep her away like the fairy princess she resembled.

Harmony encased his soul when he closed his hand over the engagement ring he'd bought for her in his pocket. Music swelled over the murmurs, and the elegant, simple ceremony began.

****

"May I have this dance?" said a deep voice behind her, and Alyssa turned around with a loud gasp.

"Ryan!"

He enfolded her in his strong arms for long minutes, soothing unfounded fears. "I tried calling you," she said against his firm chest, the sound muffled.

"What?"

She looked up and smiled softly. "I said I tried to call you."

"I tried calling you too, ever since I got off the airplane"

"Oh. My phone's in my purse, it's been a crazy day."

"Yes, it has." Ryan raked his fingers through his hair.

She stared, struck by how utterly good looking he was, dressed in a tailored gray suit that fit his tall frame perfectly. "You clean up pretty nice." She curved her hand around his clean shaven jaw. "You look great."

Ryan laid a hand over hers and kissed her palm. "Thanks, babe, considering I had about three hours of sleep, and have spent my whole day jumping from one plane to the next to get here in time."

She dropped her hand from his. "What's going on? Why didn't you answer my calls last night?"

"I'm going to tell you all about it, just as soon as we're alone."

She gazed at him for a long moment, and then nodded. "Okay."

"You're beautiful, love" he said in a low voice, and caressed her full bottom lip with his thumb. "But then you always are."

"Thank you," she murmured.

His hand slid under the honey mass of her silky hair. "What took you so long to get here?"

"Well…Fran is sick, so I was upstairs with her. She's pregnant, Ryan. Can you believe it? I'm going to be an aunt. I told Fran I'm going to spoil that baby rotten," she grinned.

"I don't doubt that a bit," he agreed good naturedly and steered her towards the dance floor, where they ran into LaDarius.

LaDarius clapped him soundly on the back. "Some things never change, do they," he asked, eyebrows raised as he smiled knowingly at the pair of them.

"No, they sure don't." Ryan drew Alyssa's soft warmth to his side, and smiled back at his old friend.

"Hey LaDarius, where's Vanessa?" Alyssa asked.

He pointed towards the bar at his wife and joked, "I'll probably be carrying her out of here."

"Hey, it is free. Might as well drink up." Alyssa grinned and tugged at both of his hands. "Come on, Ryan. What happened to our dance?"

"Sorry, man," Ryan called over his shoulder.

"Isn't this pretty?" Alyssa gestured towards the dance floor, decorated by overhead strung lights and a band in the corner playing a variety of music.

"It's very nice," he agreed, and took her in his arms at the start of a slow rock song.

"Mmm," she sighed.

He cupped the back of her head and inhaled the sweet aroma of roses. "I was just about to come looking for you when I saw you walk in."

"I was saying goodbye to my mother, too. That's why I was gone for so long."

Ryan drew back in surprise. "I never saw her."

"She was sitting in the back because she doesn't like seeing everybody from around here." Alyssa shrugged her bare, smooth shoulders. "Don't ask me why."

His jaw tightened, and he shook his head angrily as he stroked the curve of her cheek. "She's probably ashamed. She knows she should've left that monster she married, and a long time before he passed away."

A shadow crossed her expressive, fine features. "Maybe," she muttered doubtfully.

"I don't know what she thinks, we hardly even talk."

She'd walked her mother out to her car, and they'd exchanged a few words about Fran's pregnancy. Nothing had changed; she and her mother would never be close, as painful as that undeniable truth was.

The opening bars of a slow, love song began and Alyssa moved closer into the powerful circle of his arms. She closed her eyes, transcended to a dark, swaying world of Ryan's delicious scent and his steady hold as they moved as one.

Ryan held her small, satin clad body close to his, the woman who would be his wife.

His wife.

He was weary, tired of fighting the world without her. She was his soul mate, only she had mended his broken heart. Several songs later, his hand slid up and down her back. "Let's walk over to the bar and get a drink."

"I want some champagne. Let's see if your grandmother wants any."

"Oh, she's had plenty. The waiters have kept her well supplied all night," he said dryly.

Alyssa laughed, and he reached over to push her hair back gently from her radiant face.

"She can't take a pain pill if she's been drinking."

"She knows. Aunt Barbara told her but she said it doesn't matter because she'll be drunk."

"Oh, that's funny." She linked her fingers through his. "Look, there's Mr. Mack. Did you talk to him?"

Ryan nodded, a half-smile playing on his sensuous lips. "While I was waiting for you. Hell, I've seen people I forgot I even knew. My back hurts from all the pats."

Alyssa laughed and squeezed his hand. "They're glad to see you. Just like I am."

She surveyed the beautiful scene; there were at least a hundred people in the festive tent, and more outside. Everybody had a drink in their hand, and lively voices blended in with the band playing a popular rock song. Fran must still be upstairs with Lucas, she mused, not seeing a sign of her. Alyssa's heart wrung in sympathy for her sister. Whether from pregnancy or just nerves, Fran was exhausted and drained from her constant nausea.

Casey came up to them as they walked off the dance floor; blue-green eyes alight with humor. "Alyssa, I thought for a minute I was going to have to run over there and give you a shove down the aisle. Poor Chris didn't know what to do."

Alyssa shot her a dirty look. "Don't remind me. I was surprised to see Ryan, that's all."

Casey snickered. "Yeah, we all figured that out."

"Hey, you leave her alone," Ryan said with a playful glower.

Alyssa exchanged a smile with Casey.

"Fine, fine, I'll leave her alone. I wasn't shocked," Casey said with an easy grin. "Not like everybody else was. I already know there's never a dull moment with you two."

"I guess that's one way of putting it," Ryan said with a shake of his head.

Savannah came running up to them and grabbed Casey's hand. "Mama, Hunter lost his shoes! And Daddy said he needs you right now."

"Of course he does." Casey laughed, and gave them each a quick hug goodbye. "Well, I'll see y'all later."

A waiter came by, and Ryan snagged two glasses of champagne off the tray.

"Thanks, I'm about to die of thirst." Alyssa took a gulp of the fruity, bubbly liquid. She took another swallow, and felt an instant head rush. She hadn't eaten since a quick bowl of cereal this morning. Busy with the wedding, they'd run around like chickens with their heads cut off all day. Alyssa smiled and drained her glass.

Ryan plucked it out of her hand and set it on a nearby table. "Let's go outside," he leaned over to whisper. Banked fires flamed out of control when his tongue dipped into her ear.

"Um, how about inside so I can change into something comfortable," she said in a breathless voice.

He touched his lips to hers, and desire coiled tightly within. "I like the way you think, lady."

She followed as he led her to the house, their hands joined.

"Unzip me, will you please?"

"Gladly." Ryan turned to lock the door of the upstairs bedroom first. "Hold your hair up." Ryan shuddered from the force of his desire when the almost weightless dress slid down her body. He caressed the round globes of her bottom flaunted by a transparent pair of lacy, white thongs.

"Damn, baby," he groaned raggedly, and twirled her around to face him.

"I thought you'd like them." Her lips curved wickedly.

"Indeed I do." Alyssa let out a small sigh as he spoke into her ear. "Stay up here with me."

"I don't know if I can…I told Fran I'd play hostess since she's sick."

"Oh, but this is way more fun." His lips moved down the side of her neck and licked the hollow spot at the base of her throat. "Isn't it?"

"Mmm-hmm," she murmured.

"Your body drives me insane, Alyssa. The way your skin feels next to mine…I can't let you leave, angel. Not this time," he said huskily.

Like the polar opposites of a magnet, he was lured

to her. He didn't think he'd ever wanted, needed anything more, the black and silver moonlight shining in through the curtains glistened against her curvy, delectable body.

He cupped her bottom hard in his hands, and nipped at her bottom lip. "Mmm, you're delicious," he whispered against her mouth. She whimpered; a sound of raw, naked surrender as the alpha beast in him howled. Again and again he tasted of her sweet nectar, till her kiss-swollen lips moaned his name. He lost his mind in their dark, desperate connection.

Alyssa pressed herself against his as he hardened to painful proportions in his constricting pants. His big hands cupped her full breasts, and then his lips followed. "So perfect," he whispered.

"Ryan!" she shrieked, and trembled with desire. Kisses blazed down her sensitized flesh, his mouth nipped and sucked at her erect nipples. Alyssa's world melted into him, she was barely aware when he laid her down on the bed. Ryan pulled her thongs down as the sensual promise in his eyes thrilled her.

"I want to taste every bit of you." He dragged his lips down her inner thigh, and dropped kisses to her smooth womanhood.

"Ohhh," she moaned. Ryan's tongue licked, twirled at her throbbing hard nub of nerves, the very center of her carnal being. His slow, teasing licks became more demanding as she writhed in blind need. "Ryan," she panted, "please... Her head spun with erotic pleasure. "Oh, God."

Her scent intoxicated him, drove him to want even more of her. Ryan twined one big hand around both of hers and held her immobile, spread open for his viewing and tasting pleasure. Thankfully, Alyssa's passionate, unrestrained cries blended in with the loud rock music from outside. His thumb rubbed the engorged nub as he continued to lap at her, and gazed at her rapturous face. "Do you like that?"

"Yes!" she cried out, and he drank in dewy drops of liquid from her. Alyssa's breath grew shallower, and he knew her orgasm was near. He suckled with gentle pressure and let her hands go to slide two fingers in her slick warmth. "Ryan!" she yelped, as her velvety walls clamped down hard on his fingers. Her body shook and thrashed on the bed. "Oh my God, oh my God," she said over and over, gripping his hair hard.

"Shhh, baby." He cupped one hand tight against her quivering flesh, and lay beside her on the pillow. Their flavors melded in an explosive kiss, and Ryan almost came when she grasped his hard length tightly.

"Give me a minute." He stilled her hand with his. Alyssa's palpable need had him teetering on the edge, a ticking bomb, and her very touch the detonator. He drew in deep breaths and dredged up thoughts of football to take himself out of the moment before it was over way too soon. After a few minutes, he laid a hand on the curve of her hip. They kissed with gentle strokes and sucking nips, savoring the other, craving what was to come.

Alyssa spread her hands over his solid torso. "Although you are sinfully handsome in this suit, sir, it must go."

"Then take it off," he drawled, a deep, sexy rasp that smoldered with nirvana promise. Her curiousness in his news was forgotten, and she unbuttoned his shirt in swift motions. "And these pants *definitely* have to go." She returned Ryan's lazy grin, her heart still hammering against her chest. Shock waves of pleasure still vibrated within her, and her limbs felt blissfully weightless. She needed his hot shaft inside her. Now.

Quicksilver hands ran down his lean hips, and the sensual fog in Ryan's brain jarred to awareness as he remembered the ring in his pocket. "Alyssa. Hold on." He strived for an ounce of control, and caught her hands firmly in his before they could dip lower.

"Why?"

He had to avert his gaze away from her full red lips before he could safely continue. "I want us to go to our tree. Tonight."

A range of emotions crossed her face. Desire, replaced by a wary hope. "Tonight? Um…okay, I guess so." A profound tenderness touched him. She was courageous, strong….all in her own way.

He brought their linked hands to his lips and kissed her fingers. "I stopped by there on my way here and gathered up some firewood. Plus I've got blankets in my car, and we'll snag a bottle of champagne on our way out." He cupped her smooth cheek and added in a soft tone, "Our tree still looks the same, just bigger."

"I know; I was out there not that long ago." His chest clenched at her shadowed eyes, and he forced her to look at him.

"Alyssa…let's go back to where it all began, and make things right."

"They already are," she said in a soft voice.

"No, they're not yet, but…they will be." Ryan gathered her small body up to his with a heavy sigh, and closed his eyes over her head. For so long now, that night, that special little clearing, had haunted his

347

thoughts and dreams. They must go back.

They were actually going back? She couldn't help but notice the change, the seriousness now on his face. She gulped down the hard knot in her throat, and reached for her bag on the bed.

Ryan eyed her while she slipped on a silky peasant top with a pair of jeans and sandals. "Are those the only shoes you brought? The grass is going to be wet."

"Yes. And Fran's feet are smaller than mine." She cast him a playful sideways glance. "I guess you'll have to carry me."

"It would be an honor to carry you, milady." Ryan bowed before her.

"Thank you, kind sir," she grinned. "You silly man," she whispered, and stood on her tiptoes to pull his mouth to hers for a seeking, powerful kiss. He squeezed her bottom with both hands. Ryan, fierce, protective... he was so masculine, and he was hers for the rest of her life. Never again would she be foolish enough to let him go. Kissing him, tasting him, she shivered from his intense, heady response. "I can't wait to leave. Go see how many people are out there," she urged breathlessly.

"Hopefully nobody," he growled against her lips. His long strides ate up the distance to the window, and she smiled helplessly when he frowned.

"Dammit. Everybody's going inside the tent. Something must be about to happen."

Alyssa drew in a sharp breath. "I can't believe I forgot! Lucas is going to sing a song for Fran. Come on, we have to hurry!"

They got to the huge, brightly lit tent just in time. The newly wedded couple stood at the front of the dance floor, and as they stepped to the edge of the enthused crowd, the song began.

"Look at Fran," Alyssa whispered, and tightened her hand around Ryan's.

Lucas's skilled, nimble fingers played an achingly soulful tune on the guitar while his deep, husky voice sent shivers through every female in the room. But his warm, amber eyes were aimed only on his wife. Fran's face glowed with a serene loveliness, an unspoken duet of warm, entwining strength

Walkin' through the maze of my life
With nightmares chasin' my every step
And all those screams I heard were just a temporary loan
From the haze of a soulless theft

My journey I thought I knew
I stopped to hold your hand
You held onto mine too
Until we found promised land

Dreams, oh dreams, they used to be so lonely
I had the devil in my head
Dreams, oh dreams, now they're so lovely
'Cause there's an angel sharing my bed

I've lived it all, seen it all
And I was convinced love was all a trick
I was proven wrong, my love, and how right it is

Dreams, oh dreams, they used to be so lonely
I had the devil in my head

Dreams, oh dreams, now they're so lovely
'Cause there's an angel sharing my bed
Dreams, oh dreams, and to this woman I wed

The last notes of the guitar faded away, and Ryan glanced over at Alyssa. The song had cast a web over him too, raw pain and healing expressed in not only the words, but in Lucas's deliverance.

"Honey, don't cry." He brought his arm around her.

"You have no idea how thankful I am for Lucas. Fran... He saved her, he really did." An ancient, haunted light crossed her delicate features as she gazed up at him. "I couldn't do it. I tried, God knows I did."

A waiter came by, and he handed her a glass of champagne. "She's better now, honey, that's what's important. And I know she couldn't have pulled through it without your help too, you've always been her rock."

Alyssa lifted one shoulder. "She's my sister," she said simply.

She began to pull away and his hand tightened around her wrist. "Where are you going?"

Alyssa gestured to the exiting crowd. "Everybody's leaving. I want to tell Fran goodbye. Come with me so you can meet Lucas."

He tilted her chin up to his determinedly. "Alright, but let's make this quick. You've got a date with me, darlin'."

"This will be the fastest hi and bye in history." Ryan watched in amusement as she took a long drink of champagne.

"Damn right it will be." He took the glass from her

and finished it off. "Now, let's do this." He winked, and her smile put the sparkling lights around them to shame.

CHAPTER 27

The passenger door opened and Alyssa jumped. She'd been caught up in her thoughts, the past and present intertwining.

"I've got a fire going. Grab the champagne, babe."

Alyssa laid her hand against Ryan's hard chest and felt for his beating heart.

"What's wrong?"

"This doesn't seem real. I-I didn't even know you were coming, and now we're here... I don't think this is a good idea."

"Alyssa." His deep voice seeped through the weighty upheaval of her emotions. The aroma in the air was the same, a brew of elemental, powerful, forces. The water, the fire, Ryan...

He studied her pale, shuttered face, and leaned down to kiss her gently. "Don't say anything... just come with me."

She nodded, luminous eyes flicking to his, and only faith shone in their expressive depths. His soul triumphed with the most ultimate of victories...her trust. He held out his hand, and the jagged scar flashed in the moonlight. He waited, teeth gritted, for sharp pains to stab his gut as he stared at it, but there was nothing. *It was only a scar.* An empowered freedom swept through him as swung her down from the truck. "Your hands are freezing, honey, come stand by the fire."

"I guess it's not so bad out here. Not when you're here with me." She gazed out at the dark river and crossed her arms around her waist.

He threaded his fingers through her long, flame brightened hair, inherently interpreting how she felt about this place. "We're not here to recreate anything, but to start anew. Be my wife, sweetheart. Marry me and let's spend the rest of our lives together. I want to wake up every single morning with you beside me… that's the only way I'll ever be happy." He framed her face between his hands. "Will you marry me, Alyssa?"

"Are you kidding me? Of course I will," she smiled through her tears.

"Yes!" He whirled her around in a circle, joy exploding through him.

"Ryan!" she shrieked happily, and he set her back down to take the princess-cut diamond ring out of his pocket.

"It's beautiful," she gasped when he slid it on her finger, and flung her arms around his neck. "This night is a new beginning with a happy ever after ending," she whispered in his ear.

Peace stole over him. Alyssa would be his forever, and he'd never relinquish her. "I don't want to wait any more. We can go to Arkansas or Las Vegas, but tomorrow, Alyssa, you will be my wife."

She drew back, and her dimples captivated him. "And you'll be my husband. *My husband,*" she repeated in awe.

"Yeah, it's a win -win, isn't it?" he asked, humor lacing his voice.

"Yes. Especially for me," she whispered, meaning

every word.

He bent down till he was eye level with her. "For both of us, honey. We've been apart far too long. But no more."

"I don't want to be alone anymore, Ryan."

"And you won't. I'll always be here for you. Always." His intent, blue flame gaze validated his deep spoken words and she sighed in contentment when Ryan pulled her close against his muscled chest. "I'm coming back home, Lyssa. We're selling EzPay to a larger company that does the same thing."

Her jaw dropped in amazement. "What! You're moving back here? To Cypress Bayou?"

He nodded, and his sexy, rumbled laugh warmed her more than the fire.

"I didn't even know you were trying to sell it."

"We weren't, the offer just came out of the blue yesterday. Forty-seven million dollars, Alyssa. There's some debts we have to pay off and it'll be split three ways, but it's safe to say we won't have to worry about money for a long time. It's insane... I'm still trying to process it all in." He shook his head in a slow motion.

"Hey, it's a great thing. I've always wanted to go to Australia, you know," she grinned.

"Oh, yeah?" he drawled. "Well, come see this first."

He led her toward the shrouded realm where their tree was, and pointed the flashlight straight ahead. "Look at what I did earlier."

"Oh Ryan..." she breathed.

"This time it will be forever, baby, I promise. Till we're old and gray, and sitting on the porch in our rocking chairs."

He'd etched 4 Ever under their initials, and the fresh, exposed wood shone in the lone beam.

"That's right. Forever and ever." She wrapped her arms around his middle and pulled him down for a soft kiss. "We'll never give up on our love again. I won't let us."

He almost dropped the flashlight as he instinctively reached to pull her closer. His body craved only her, and the salvation she brought. "Neither of us will. Let's go back to the fire," he said huskily.

They ran like children over the carpet of dewy grass, and landed breathlessly on the pile of blankets he'd laid down. His fingers swiftly moved to take off his shirt, but she brushed them away with a seductive smile.

"I never did finish earlier."

"Well, while you do that…"

He unfastened her jeans, and grinned when she kicked them off. Driven by an out of control hunger, they impatiently helped the other undress.

"Lay down," he said in a tight voice as his eyes drank in the nude goddess before him. Her skin was the color of molten gold in the flickering flames, and he ran his hand reverently over her full breasts, his thumb caressing her rosy nipples. "You're all I want and need, sweetheart. Every day of my life," he murmured.

He studied the emerald necklace, her only adornment, for a long moment before he spoke. "I didn't bring any protection, Alyssa."

Her rich green gaze seemed to probe his innermost soul. "I'm glad you didn't," she said finally, and her slender arms came up to circle his neck.

Ryan closed his eyes as a rush of tenderness hit

him. The gift of her love, his dreams...all had been restored. He was the luckiest of men.

Alyssa scanned the circle of trees they lay in, and back to him. Ryan's naked masculine form brought forth euphoric visions that swam low in her subconscious, experienced only in this otherworldly place.

She moaned when their lips met. His tongue swept against hers like a hot, velvet feather as he brought her flush against his lean, hard body.

"Are you sure?" he said against her mouth.

"Yes, I'm positive."

"I hope this night is as lucky as the last we spent here," he whispered, and sucked on her sensitized bottom lip.

"I think it will be... don't you just feel the magic around us, Ryan?"

With a growl, he cupped the back of her head and she whimpered in wild, wanton excitement. Their mouths melded as he dragged her closer, and consumed her with his kiss. She was so turned on; his erotic touch upon her skin was like lava dripping from his fingers as they glided down to where she burned deep for him.

"Oh God," she gasped against his lips, arching closer to him.

His lips gentled as he caressed silky heat to rub against her nub nestled in a wet fever. Astride on a cloud of decadence, she almost bit his lip when he slid one long finger in.

"Alyssa, honey."

Ryan's voice was a hoarse grunt and she opened her eyes to see him looking down at her with such an expression of wonder, she cried out. Her spiraling world erupted in an earth-shattering release as he crushed her quaking body to his broad chest. She felt his heart pound against hers and kissed his chest. "All you have to do is touch me, look at me, and I'm at your mercy. It's kind of humiliating."

He laughed deeply, one corner of his sensual mouth lifted in an arrogant grin. "It doesn't bother me, and baby, this thing between us, it only gets better," he promised.

She shivered and grasped his generous length in her hand, stroking him as he groaned deep. Ryan's head dropped against her breast with a sharp, indrawn breath. The fires of her need surged even higher as he leaned down to capture her aching nipple in his mouth. She bucked against him, and he thrust against her tight grip forcefully. He suckled with the softest of pressure, gradually growing stronger, and she moaned, wriggling beneath him.

His shaft grew even larger, rock hard, slick with needy excitement. She gasped when he worshiped her nipple's twin with the same loving attention, and pressed herself against him.

"Alyssa." Harsh breaths came fast against her rapidly rising and falling breasts.

"Now, Ryan, please!" she pleaded, her nails digging into his back. "Love me as I love you."

"Oh, I do, love. Don't you ever doubt that."

Here in this mystical ring of towering trees, her mesmerizing eyes glowed even brighter with passion. He rose above her, and whispered her name as he slid into her satiny embrace. Both gasped against each other's mouths, awash in hot, electric pleasure. He thrust in deeper and deeper till their hips met, melding them into one.

She felt so damn good, her silken, tight walls squeezing him with every push, he had to grit his teeth to keep from exploding into her snug, wet folds. "Damn, baby," he breathed, and broke out in a sweat when she wrapped her long legs around him. "You were made for me, I think."

"I was, Ryan. I'm yours, and you're mine."

He moved faster with hungry strokes and she clenched even tighter around him. "That's it, don't stop, babe," he said against her lips as she lifted her hips up to meet his every thrust.

"God, yes," he muttered, and felt his own release start to mount with each feel of her soft, pulsing warmth. He slowed and savored this moment, wanting it to last as long as possible for both of them.

Everything else faded away but her gasps of pleasure, her sweet flesh slippery with need, only those vital energies mattered in this other world. Sexual, erotic energy had him throbbing harder and faster within her. The two rocked as one and gave each other all they had, their moans growing louder in the moon-washed summer night. They pledged their love with their bodies, a pact never to be broken.

A torrent of lightning pleasure swept over him and Ryan opened clenched eyes to look down at her, she who owned his heart's joy.

"Ryan!" His name burst from her lips, and waves of bliss washed over Alyssa.

Powerful and magnificent, his biceps flexed and bunched beneath her hands as sweat dripped from him onto her, the sounds of their fated lovemaking echoing through the aware, waiting shadows. Gathering her body close to his, he pumped one final thrust and she soared… Away onto an exquisite ray of rapture, so high she had to hold on to Ryan to ground her. Spasms racked her and he cupped the back of her head close, lodged in so deep she never wanted it to end.

With a shout he stiffened above her, and copious waves of pleasure drenched her. Just as nature intended, his warmth spread to her womb in a dizzying rush of ecstasy. He collapsed on top of her for a minute and then drew them to their side. Their searching, panting lips found each other in a kiss full of hope, their bodies still joined as one.

At that moment, a shooting star lit up the sapphire night, and hovered brightly above them before it rocketed across the wide river. Its brilliance left a trail of shimmering stardust in its wake that rained down like tears of joy upon the dark water.

Alyssa exchanged a stunned glance with Ryan while his arms tightened fast around her. "What just happened?"

He leaned up on an elbow and looked out at the river, an odd expression on his face. "Mr. Mack asked me if I remembered this special place, just tonight. I wondered why… Alyssa, he sent us here for a reason, I just know it." Their gazes joined in an intense lock. "Do you believe in… magic?"

She remembered the strange sensations that had gripped her each time they'd been here, and the absolute perfection of the secluded circle. Could it be possible…? "I believe in the magic of true love. And that's what we have, Ryan."

A smile crossed his darkly handsome face, his midnight blue eyes alight. "We share a love that can never be found again, a love that is just as special as this place here. Come here, sweetheart."

He held out his arms and she laid her head on his strong chest, her soul bright with joy. "My life is changing, Ryan, and I couldn't be any happier."

"Neither could I," he murmured, and she cuddled closer to the man she loved with all her heart.

EPILOGUE

MAY 2006

Alyssa's eyes snapped open as she held a hand to her swollen stomach, frightened by the vicious cramp deep in her back. "Ouch," she whispered, and peered at the alarm clock glowing in the darkness. 2:50 in the morning. *Probably just Braxton Hick's contractions.* She scooted closer over to Ryan's warm body. He lay on his side turned towards her, with only a sheet covering his naked, powerful physique.

Deep and slow, breathe deep and slow. After another wrenching ache, Alyssa threw back the covers with an aggravated huff. "Okay, this isn't working." Halfway across their large bedroom, she felt liquid trickle down her thighs and stopped with a gasp of surprise. *Did I really just pee on myself?*

Ryan jerked awake when he heard his name whispered in a tone he'd never heard from his wife. He reached out for her, but there was only an empty space beside him.

"Alyssa?"

"I'm over here."

He fumbled around in the dark to switch on a lamp. She stood in the middle of the room, her gaze fastened on the floor. Ryan's eyebrows snapped together in confusion. "What's wrong?"

361

"Um, I think my water just broke," she said in a stricken voice, eyes huge in her pale face.

His heart slowed to time-warped thuds in his ears as he stared at his very pregnant wife. With a shake of his head to clear it, he jumped out of bed and splayed his hand across her rounded belly. "But the C-section isn't scheduled for another two weeks."

"I know that," she answered shakily. "But I'm pretty sure the baby doesn't." She squeezed his hand hard and sucked in a sharp breath. "I'm having contractions, too."

Ryan turned to snatch his jeans off of the chair. "Get dressed, babe, we're going to the hospital." He wrapped an arm around her waist. "Be careful, don't slip. We'll call the doctor once we get in the truck. Here, you sit right here and I'll-"

She shrugged free and headed towards the bathroom. "I have to brush my teeth first."

He stared after in disbelief till she reached the doorway. "Alyssa! "

She turned around with a startled expression, one hand pressed to her tummy. Ryan sprinted to her with his heart in his throat. She was ungainly in these last weeks, her natural grace gone.

"I'm sorry, honey, I didn't mean to scare you. But what the hell are you poking around for? You're about to have a baby!"

"Not this very second I'm not. Good grief," she muttered, and gave him a look as if he'd lost his mind. "Men."

He spoke through gritted teeth. "Just hurry up. Please."

"I will."

She smiled up at him, and his arms tightened around her soft body dressed in a long, white nightgown. Alyssa glowed in her pregnancy, like a surreal Madonna from another time. "You're so very beautiful, my wife." He felt their baby move under his hand, and rubbed her tummy gently.

"I can't wait to see our baby, Ryan," she whispered.

"Neither can I, and whether it's a boy or girl, it doesn't matter. I just want you and the baby to be healthy."

Her emerald eyes shone as he smoothed a strand of golden hair back from her cheek. "Me and the baby will be just fine. And then we'll be a family."

"Yes, we'll be a family, sweetheart." His throat grew tight, and he closed his eyes for a long minute over her head before he could let go.

"Are you okay?"

Ryan's worried face swam above her, and Alyssa shook her head. "No. I'm about to throw up." Her stomach rolled relentlessly through dizzy waves.

A voice sounded above her head. "That's fine; I've got suction right here. That's just the anesthesia making you sick."

Ryan wiped off her face and mouth with a wet towel. "See, you didn't have to brush your teeth after all," he teased.

"Very funny." Alyssa smiled as the bright lights of the operating room faded away to a dazed blur.

Bold, tugging sensations at her belly broke through the fog, and the next words she heard were Ryan's whispered near her ear. "Look, we have a boy, sweetheart. Six pounds and one ounce, and eighteen inches long. Alyssa, look at him."

Alyssa stared into eyes as blue as the sea. "He has your eyes." She stroked their son's full cheeks and dark, downy hair in absolute awe. "And your hair. Oh, Ryan, I can't believe we did this. He's so beautiful."

He leaned down to kiss her forehead. "Thank you for our son."

"Thank you," she whispered back, and they smiled at each other through their tears.

Late that night, Alyssa winced as the baby suckled hungrily at her breast. "He has your appetite too, Ryan. He acting like he's starving even though he just nursed an hour ago."

Her husband lay beside her on the hospital bed, long legs dangling off. One hand was propped under his head as he watched them avidly, and the other rested on their son's back. "I can't say as I hardly blame him," he murmured as an appreciative grin split his rugged features.

"You bad, bad man," she smiled, and settled down more comfortably in the bed with their baby nestled snug against her. "Hey, I think we're getting the hang of this breastfeeding thing."

Ryan's muscled arm circled around her. "That's my girl. So what are we going to name him?"

Alyssa cupped the back of her baby's round, perfect head, so full of happiness she couldn't speak for a moment. "Michael," she said softly.

"Michael…" Ryan patted the diapered rump of their baby in his light blue sleeper for a moment. His eyes darkened in the moonlit tranquility of the room, and he leaned down to kiss her lips. "That's perfect. I love you," he whispered against her mouth.

"And I love you." She studied her son's round cheeks as he drank of her nourishment, his little brows drawn together in fierce concentration. "Dreams do come true. Look at him, Ryan, isn't he precious?"

A fierce light shone in his crystalline eyes, and his big hand cupped her cheek. "Yes, he is. I'm so proud of you, honey." He shook his head slowly, his eyes on their baby. "A year ago how different my life was…and how lonely."

"And now we've come full circle, right here at this very hospital."

"We should call and tell Nana thank you." Ryan winked at her.

She laughed and leaned against his broad shoulder. A serene fatigue crashed over her and she drifted off, his warmth touching every part of her.

Ryan watched as Alyssa's eyes fluttered shut, and her rosy lips parted in sleep. Michael dozed off minutes later, his head nestled against his mother's naked, full breast, milk pooled in the corner of his lax mouth. Ryan held them both in his protective embrace, felt their beating hearts, and the rise and fall of their chests. No sounds came from the world outside of theirs as he drunk in the sight of his sweet love holding their baby boy.

He drew a ragged breath in his tight lungs. "C'mon little fella, let's get you burped." With gentle motions he picked him off of Alyssa's chest, and then covered her back up.

"We'll go sit in the rocking chair so we don't wake your Mama. She's had a big day, having you and all," he whispered. Michael yawned, his little nose scrunched up adorably. "Just like your Mama," Ryan smiled. "Already a charmer," he whispered, joy humming in his soul. His hand patted Michael's small back as he cuddled against his chest, lulled by the sway.

Light beckoned clear through the cracked blinds and Ryan stood to raise them, much to the displeasure of his son. "Shhh," he crooned, and Michael quieted down, his wide blue eyes blinking sleepily. He kissed his baby's head and pointed to the brightest of the stars in the dark sky. "See that one? That's your big brother, Matthew." Ryan swallowed an aching lump of tears down in his throat. "Matthew...I-I wish you were here with us, buddy. We love you, son." He stared out the window as deep seated pangs of guilt haunted his subconscious. That night of first's...

And history had been repeated, for Michael had been conceived on that magical, summer night of the shooting star, right where his parent's initials were forever carved in the mightiest tree. A sigh in his arms drew Ryan's attention downward. Michael smiled in his sleep as his dreamy dimples captivated his father. "I love you," he murmured, and laid him down in his bassinet beside the bed. "Thank you, Lord, for my many blessings. I never thought I'd have a family with Alyssa, never even dared to dream it..." Tears fell down his cheeks as he bowed his head and fervently gave thanks to the Almighty above.

His eyes fell on Alyssa's slight form under the stark whiteness of the sheets. How humbled he felt to be her husband, the father of her child. A primal, possessive surge of emotion rushed through him, and he edged carefully down beside her.

"Is the baby asleep?" she mumbled.

Ryan smoothed her cheek with his thumb, relieved

to find her silken skin cool. "He's snoring as we speak. How are you feeling, love?"

"Pretty good," she whispered with a drowsy smile.

Their fingers twined and he kissed their joined hands. "My sweet Lyssa." Ryan watched as her eyelids closed and with the soft sounds of his slumbering family around him, fell into a content, peaceful sleep.

A word about the author…

I have always loved to read since I was a little girl. I would lose myself in the pages of another world, one that always seemed more interesting and fun than mine! I excelled in writing in school but it wasn't until last year that I decided to write a book. And once I did…I became hooked. I can't imagine not writing now. It's like breathing to me, a must. I love to write romance and in the magic of true love.

I live in West Monroe, Louisiana with my three beautiful children, two teenagers and a seven year old. I also work full time so I stay pretty busy. Once I get home and everything is settled, I pop my earbuds in and it's just me, music, and my book. Writing brings so much happiness to my life and I hope my readers feel it too!

Thank you for purchasing
this publication of The Wild Rose Press, Inc.

For questions or more information
contact us at
info@thewildrosepress.com.

The Wild Rose Press, Inc.
www.thewildrosepress.com